SURVIVORS

THE EMPTY CITY
✦AND✦
A HIDDEN ENEMY

SURVIVORS

Also by ERIN HUNTER

WARRIORS

NOVELLAS

SEEKERS

RETURN TO THE WILD

MANGA

SURVIVORS

THE EMPTY CITY
◆AND◆
A HIDDEN ENEMY

ERIN
HUNTER

HARPER

An Imprint of HarperCollinsPublishers

Special thanks to Gillian Philip

Library of Congress catalog card number: 2014933028
ISBN 978-0-06-232146-6

Typography based on a design by Hilary Zarycky
14 15 16 17 18 OPM 10 9 8 7 6 5 4 3 2 1
❖
First Edition

For Lucy Philip and Jamie Philip

·CONTENTS·

SURVIVORS

THE EMPTY CITY

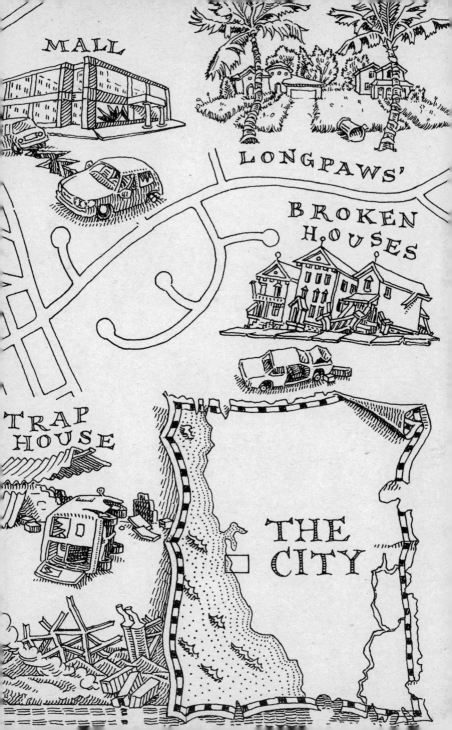

PROLOGUE

Yap wriggled, yawning, and gave a small, excited whimper. His litter-mates were a jumble of warmth against him, all paws and muzzles and small, fast heartbeats. Clambering over him, Squeak stuck a paw in his eye; Yap shook his head and rolled over, making her fall off. She squeaked with indignation as always, so he licked her nose to show there were no hard feelings.

The Mother-Dog stood over them, nuzzling the pups into order and licking their faces clean, treading her ritual circle before curling around them, ready for sleep.

"Wake up, Yap! Mother's going to tell us a story." That was Squeak again, bossy and demanding as ever. Their Mother-Dog washed her affectionately with her tongue, muffling her yelps.

"Would you like to hear about the Storm of Dogs?"

A thrill of excitement ran down Yap's spine, and he whimpered eagerly. "Yes!"

"Again?" whined Squeak.

But the others tumbled over her, drowning her protests. "Yes, Mother! The Storm of Dogs!"

The Mother-Dog settled around their small bodies, her tail thumping. Her voice grew low and solemn. "This is the story of Lightning, the swiftest of the dog warriors. The Sky-Dogs watched over him, and protected him. . . . But the Earth-Dog was jealous of Lightning. She thought Lightning had lived too long, and that it was time for him to die so that she could take his life force. But Lightning's speed was so great that he could outrun the Earth-Dog's terrible Growls—he could outrun death itself!"

"I want to be like Lightning," murmured Yowl sleepily. "I could run that fast; I bet I could."

"Shush!" said Squeak, squashing his nose with a golden-furred paw. In spite of her protest, Yap knew that she was caught up in the story like the rest of them.

"Then came the first great battle," the Mother-Dog went on, her voice hushed. "The terrible Storm of Dogs, when all the dogs of the world fought to see who would rule over the territories of the world. Many stories are told of those dreadful days, and many heroes were made and lost in the battle.

"At last, the Earth-Dog thought, Lightning's life force would

6

be freed and she would take his body, as was her right. But Lightning was cunning, and he was sure that with his speed he could dodge his death once more, so the Earth-Dog laid a trap for him."

Yip's ears flattened against her head. "That's so mean!"

Their mother nuzzled her. "No, it isn't, Yip. Earth-Dog was right to claim Lightning. That's the way things should be. When your Sire-Dog died, his body fed the earth, too."

Suddenly solemn, all of the pups listened in silence.

"Lightning tried to escape the Storm of Dogs with his speed. He ran so fast between the warring dogs that none of them could see him to tear his body apart with their teeth and claws. He was almost clear, almost free, when the Earth-Dog sent a Big Growl to open the ground in front of him."

Even though he'd heard the story so many times, Yap held his breath and huddled close to his littermates, imagining that this time Lightning would fall and be eaten by the terrible rip in the earth. . . .

"Lightning saw the ground open up to swallow him, but he was speeding so fast that he couldn't stop. He feared that the Earth-Dog had him at last. But the Sky-Dogs loved Lightning.

"Just as Lightning started to plummet to his death, the Sky-Dogs sent a great wind that spun so fast and so strong, it caught Lightning as he fell, lifted him up, and whirled him into the sky. And there he remains, with the Sky-Dogs, to this very day."

The pups snuggled more tightly against the Mother-Dog's side, gazing up at her.

"Will he always be there?" asked Yowl.

"Always. When you see fire flashing in the sky, when the Sky-Dogs howl, that's Lightning running down to the earth, teasing Earth-Dog, knowing that she will never catch him." She licked Yap's sleepy face. He could barely keep his eyes open. "I've heard dogs say that one day, there will be another great battle, when a dog displeases the Earth-Dog. Then, dog will fight against dog, and great heroes will rise and fall."

Yowl gave a great yawn, floppy with tiredness. "But not for a long time, right?"

"Ah, we don't know. It might come soon; it might not. We must always watch out for the signs. They say that when the world is turned upside down and broken open, the Storm of Dogs will come again and we'll have to fight to survive once more."

Yap let his eyelids droop. He loved to fall asleep to his mother's stories. This was how it would always be, he knew: her voice, fading as sleep overwhelmed him and his littermates. The

Mother-Dog curled protectively around him, the end of the story the last thing he heard. It ended the same way each time. . . .

"Watch out, little ones. Watch out for the Storm of Dogs. . . ."

CHAPTER ONE

Lucky startled awake, fear prickling in his bones and fur. He leaped to his feet, growling.

For an instant he'd thought he was tiny once more, safe in his Pup Pack and protected, but the comforting dream had already vanished. The air shivered with menace, tingling Lucky's skin. If only he could see what was coming, he could face it down—but the monster was invisible, scentless. He whined in terror. This was no sleep-time story: This fear was *real*.

The urge to run was almost unbearable; but he could only scrabble, snarl, and scratch in panic. There was nowhere to go: The wire of his cage hemmed him in on every side. His muzzle hurt when he tried to shove it through the gaps; when he backed away, snarling, the same wire bit into his haunches.

Others were close . . . familiar bodies, familiar scents. Those dogs were enclosed in this terrible place just as he was. Lucky raised his head and barked, over and over, high and desperate, but it was clear no dog could help him. His voice was drowned out by the chorus of frantic calls.

They were all *trapped*.

Dark panic overwhelmed him. His claws scrabbled at the earth floor, even though he knew it was hopeless.

He could smell the female swift-dog in the next cage, a friendly, comforting scent, overlaid now with the bitter tang of danger and fear. Yipping, he pressed closer to her, feeling the shivers in her muscles—but the wire still separated them.

"Sweet? Sweet, something's on its way. Something bad!"

"Yes, I feel it! What's happening?"

The longpaws—where were they? The longpaws held them captive in this Trap House but they had always seemed to care about the dogs. They brought food and water, they laid bedding, cleared the mess . . .

Surely the longpaws would come for them now.

The others barked and howled as one, and Lucky raised his voice with theirs.

Longpaws! Longpaws, it's COMING. . . .

Something shifted beneath him, making his cage tremble. In a sudden, terrible silence, Lucky crouched, frozen with horror.

Then, around and above him, chaos erupted.

The unseen monster was here . . . and its paws were right on the Trap House.

Lucky was flung back against the wire as the world heaved and tilted. For agonizing moments he didn't know which way was up or down. The monster tumbled him around, deafening him with the racket of falling rock and shattering clear-stone. His vision went dark as clouds of filth blinded him. The screaming, yelping howls of terrified dogs seemed to fill his skull. A great chunk of wall crashed off the wire in front of his nose, and Lucky leaped back. Was it the Earth-Dog, trying to take him?

Then, just as suddenly as the monster had come, it disappeared. One more wall crashed down in a cloud of choking dust. Torn wire screeched as a high cage toppled, then plummeted to the earth.

There was only silence and a dank metal scent.

Blood! thought Lucky. *Death . . .*

Panic stirred inside his belly again. He was lying on his side, the wire cage crumpled against him, and he thrashed his strong legs, trying to right himself. The cage rattled and rocked, but he couldn't get up. *No!* he thought. *I'm trapped!*

"Lucky! Lucky, are you all right?"

"Sweet? Where are you?"

Her long face pushed at his through the mangled wire. "My cage door—it broke when it fell! I thought I was dead. Lucky, I'm free—but you—"

"Help me, Sweet!"

The other faint whimpers had stopped. Did that mean the other dogs were . . . ? No. Lucky could not let himself think about that. He howled just to break the silence.

"I think I can pull the cage out a bit," said Sweet. "Your door's loose, too. We might be able to get it open." Seizing the wire with her teeth, she tugged.

Lucky fought to keep himself calm. All he wanted to do was fling himself against the cage until it broke. His hind legs kicked out wildly and he craned his head around, snapping at the wire. Sweet was gradually pulling the cage forward, stopping occasionally to scrabble at fallen stones with her paws.

"There. It's looser now. Wait while I—"

But Lucky could wait no longer. The cage door was torn at the upper corner, and he twisted until he could bite and claw at it. He worked his paw into the gap and pulled, hard.

The wire gave with a screech, just as Lucky felt a piercing

stab in his paw pad—but the door now hung at an awkward angle. Wriggling and squirming, he pulled himself free and stood upright at last.

His tail was tight between his legs as tremors bolted through his skin and muscles. He and Sweet stared at the carnage and chaos around them. There were broken cages—and broken bodies. A small, smooth-coated dog lay on the ground nearby, lifeless, eyes dull. Beneath the last wall that had fallen, nothing stirred, but a limp paw poked out from between stones. The scent of death was already spreading through the Trap House air.

Sweet began to whimper with grief. "What was that? What *happened?*"

"I think—" Lucky's voice shook, and he tried again. "It was a Growl. I used to—my Mother-Dog used to tell me stories about the Earth-Dog, and the Growls she sent. I think the monster was a Big Growl. . . ."

"We have to get away from here!" There was terror in Sweet's whine.

"Yes." Lucky backed slowly away, shaking his head to dispel the death-smell. But it followed him, clinging to his nostrils.

He glanced around, desperate. Where the wall had tumbled onto the other dog cages, the broken blocks had collapsed into a pile, and light shone bright through the haze of dust and smoke.

"There, Sweet, where the stones have crumbled in. Come on!"

She needed no more urging, leaping up over the rubble. Aware of his wounded paw, Lucky picked his way more carefully, nervously glancing around for longpaws. Surely they'd come when they saw the destruction?

He shuddered and quickened his pace, but even when he sprang down onto the street outside, following Sweet's lead, there was no sign of any longpaws.

Bewildered, he paused, and sniffed the air. It smelled so strange. . . .

"Let's get away from the Trap House," he told Sweet in a low voice. "I don't know what's happened, but we should go far away in case the longpaws come back."

Sweet gave a sharp whine as her head drooped. "Lucky, I don't think there are any longpaws left."

Their journey was slow and silent except for the distant wail of broken loudcages. A sense of threat grew in Lucky's belly; so many of the roads and alleys he knew were blocked. Still he persevered, nosing his way around the broken buildings through tangled, snaking coils torn from the ground. Despite what Sweet thought, Lucky was sure that the longpaws would return soon. He wanted to be far away from the destroyed Trap House when they did.

The sky was darkening by the time he felt it was safe to rest; Lucky sensed anyway that Sweet couldn't go much farther. Maybe swift-dogs weren't as good at long journeys as they were at quick dashes. He gazed back the way they'd come, shadows lengthening across the ground, hiding spaces emerging in dark corners. Lucky shivered—which other animals might be out there, scared and hungry?

But they were both exhausted from escaping the Big Growl. Sweet barely managed to tread her ritual sleep-circle before she slumped to the ground, laid her head on her forepaws, and closed her troubled eyes. Lucky pressed himself close against her flank for warmth and comfort. *I'll stay awake for a while,* he thought, *Keep watch . . . yes . . .*

He woke with a start, shivering, his heart racing.

He'd slept no-sun away. His dreams were full of the distant rumbling of the Big Growl and an endless line of longpaws running away from him and loudcages whining and beeping. There was no sign of others here now. The city seemed abandoned.

Beneath the thorny scrub, Sweet slept on, the flanks of her sleek body gently rising and falling with each breath. Something about Sweet's deep sleep was comforting, but suddenly he needed more than the scented warmth of her sleeping body; he needed her awake and alert. He nuzzled Sweet's long face, licking her ears until she responded with a happy murmuring growl. She got to her feet, sniffing and licking him in return.

"How's that paw, Lucky?"

Her words instantly brought the sting back. Remembering the wound, he sniffed at his paw pad. An angry red mark scored the flesh, pulsing with pain. He licked it gently. It was closed, but only just, and he didn't want to make it bleed again.

"It's better, I think," he said, more hopefully than he felt; then, as they both slunk out from beneath the dense branches, his spirits slumped.

The road before them was broken, wildly tilted, and cracked. Water sprayed into the sky from a long tube exposed by crumbling earth, making rainbows in the air. And it wasn't just here; in the sloping city streets, as far as Lucky could see, the light of the rising Sun-Dog glinted on tangled metal. A slick of water lay where he remembered that there had once been gardens, and the longpaw homes that used to seem tall and indestructible were now crumpled as if pummeled by a giant longpaw fist.

"The Big Growl," murmured Sweet, awestruck and afraid.

"Look what it's done."

Lucky shivered. "You were right about the longpaws. There were packs and packs of them. Now I don't see a single one." He cocked his ears and tasted the air with his tongue: dust and an under-earth stink. No fresh scents. "Even the loudcages aren't moving."

Lucky tilted his head toward one of them, tipped onto its side, its snout half-buried in a collapsed wall. Light gleamed from its metal flanks but there was no roar and grumble; it seemed dead.

Sweet looked startled. "I always wondered what those were for. What did you call it?"

Lucky gave her a doubtful look. She didn't know what a loud-cage was?

"Loudcages. You know—longpaws use them to get around. They can't run as fast as we can."

He couldn't believe she didn't know this most basic detail about the longpaws. It gave him a bad feeling about setting out with her. Sweet's naïveté wouldn't be much help when they were trying to survive.

Lucky sniffed the air again. The city's new smell made him uneasy. There was a rottenness, a lingering whiff of death and danger. *It doesn't smell like a home for dogs anymore*, he thought.

He padded over to where water sprayed from a wound in the earth. In the sunken hole was an oily lake, its surface shimmering with rainbow colors. It gave off an odd smell that Lucky didn't like, but he was too thirsty to care and lapped the water greedily, doing his best to ignore the foul taste. Beside him he saw Sweet's reflection as she also drank.

She was the first to lift her dripping muzzle, licking her pointed chops. "It's too quiet," she murmured. "We need to get out of this longpaw town." Sweet's fur lifted. "We should go to the hills. Find a wild place."

"We're as safe here as anywhere else," said Lucky. "We can use the old longpaw houses—maybe find food. And there are plenty of hiding places, believe me."

"Plenty of places for *other* things to hide," she retorted, bristling. "I don't like it."

"What do you have to be scared of?" Her legs looked long enough to race through high grasses and her frame was slender and light. "I bet you can run faster than anything!"

"Not around corners, I can't." She glanced nervously to left and right. "And a city has lots of corners. I need space to run. That's where I can pick up speed."

Lucky scanned the area, too. She was right—the buildings

19

crowded in on them. Maybe she had good reason to be edgy. "Let's at least keep moving. Some of those longpaws might still be close by, whether we can see them or not. I don't want to go back to the Trap House."

"Me neither," Sweet agreed, her lip curling to show her strong white teeth. "We should start looking for more dogs. We need a good, strong Pack!"

Lucky's muzzle wrinkled in doubt. He was not a Pack Dog. He had never understood what there was to like about living with a big mob of dogs, all dependent on one another, and having to submit to an Alpha. He didn't need anyone's help, and the last thing he wanted was someone who needed his. Just the thought of relying on other dogs made his skin prickle.

Obviously that isn't how Sweet feels, he thought. She was enthusiastic now, rattling off stories. "You would have loved my Pack! We ran together, and hunted together, catching rabbits and chasing rats. . . ." She became more subdued, and looked longingly toward the outskirts of the wrecked town. "Then the longpaws came and spoiled everything."

Lucky couldn't help responding to the sadness in her voice. "What happened?"

Sweet shook herself. "They rounded us up. So many of them,

and all in the same brown fur! Staying together, that's what got us trapped, but"—her growl grew fierce—"we wouldn't leave a single dog behind. That's Pack law. We stuck together, in good times and . . . bad." Sweet paused, her dark eyes distant, unable to repress an unhappy whimper.

"Your Pack was with you in the Trap House," murmured Lucky sympathetically.

"Yes." She came to an abrupt halt. "Wait, Lucky, we have to go back!"

He darted in front of her as she spun around, blocking her way. "No, Sweet!"

"We *have* to!" Lucky scrambled sideways to stop her from slipping past him. "They're my Packmates. I can't leave until I find what's happened to them! If any of them are still—"

"No, Sweet!" Lucky barked. "You saw how it was in that place!"

"But we might have missed—"

"Sweet." He tried a gentler tone, tentatively licking her unhappy face. "Back there, it's ruined. They're all dead, gone to the Earth-Dog. And we can't hang around here—the longpaws might come back. . . ."

That seemed to convince her. Sweet glanced over her shoulder

21

once more, then turned away again. With a deep sigh she began to walk on.

Lucky tried not to show his relief. He walked close beside her, their flanks brushing with every second step.

"Did you have friends in the Trap House, too?" Sweet asked.

"Me?" said Lucky lightly, trying to cheer her up. "No thanks. I'm a Lone Dog."

Sweet gave him an odd glance. "There's no such thing. Every dog needs a Pack!"

"Not me. I *like* being on my own. I mean, I'm sure a Pack's best for some dogs," he added hurriedly to spare her feelings, "but I've walked alone since I left my Pup Pack." He couldn't repress the proud lift of his head. "I can look after myself. There's no better place for a dog than the city. I'll show you! There's food for the finding, and warm crannies to sleep in, and shelter from the rain—"

But is that still true?

For a moment he hesitated, letting his eyes rove over the smashed streets, the shattered walls and broken clear-stones, the tilting roads and abandoned loudcages. *This isn't safe,* Lucky thought. *We need to get out of here as soon as we can.*

Not that he was going to share that fear with Sweet; she was already so anxious. If only there were some distraction—

There!

Lucky gave a high bark of excitement. They'd turned a corner, and right in the road was another wreck. Lucky scented—*food!*

He broke into a run, leaping in delight onto the side of the huge overturned metal box. He'd seen longpaws throwing things they didn't want into these, locking them afterward so that Lucky was never able to feast on the unwanted food. But now the box was on its side, the half-rotten contents spilled out across the ground. Black crows were hopping and jabbing around the piles. Lucky held his head high and barked as loud as he could. The crows cawed, alarmed, as they half fluttered away.

"Come on!" he yelled, springing into the stinking pile. Sweet followed, barking happily.

As Lucky nosed his way through the mound of scraps, he heard the dull fluttering of wings as the crows descended again. He leaped and snapped his jaws at an indignant bird and it darted into the air, its wings beating strongly.

Lucky sent a final snarl after the departing crow as he landed back on the ground, his paws skidding in the dirt. Immediately his wounded pad howled with pain. It was like the fangs of the most vicious dog, biting all the way up his leg. He couldn't hold back his whimper of distress.

As Sweet dashed through the cloud of crows, chasing them clear, Lucky sat down and licked the hurt away. He eagerly sniffed the air, enjoying the scent coming off the piles of discarded items that had spilled out across the ground. Contentment began to settle over him again, and he was distracted from his pain.

For a while the happy mood lingered as Lucky and Sweet snuffed out the delicacies the crows had left. Sweet pulled chicken bones from a cardboard bucket, and Lucky found a crust of bread, but the pickings were poor, especially after they'd worked up such an appetite.

"We're going to starve in this city." Sweet whined, licking an empty box that had once held some food. She pinned it down with one paw as she poked her nose inside.

"I promise we won't. It's not all scavenging." Lucky's mind was flooded with an image of a place he used to visit. He nudged Sweet's flank affectionately. "I'll take you somewhere where we'll eat like Leashed Dogs."

Sweet's ears pricked up. "Really?"

"Really. This place will change your mind about cities."

Lucky trotted confidently down the road, his mouth already watering at the prospect of food. Sweet was right behind him. It was strange how happy he was with her company, how much he liked being able to help her. Usually by now, he'd be itching for solitude, but . . . he wasn't.

Maybe the Big Growl had changed more than just the city.

CHAPTER TWO

Sweet pressed close to Lucky's side as they walked through the deserted streets.

He had expected to see other dogs by now, and certainly a few longpaws. But the city was empty and far too quiet. At least they had found a few stale scent-marks; that was reassuring. He stopped to sniff at an upturned longpaw seat that had been marked by a male Fierce Dog.

"They can't be far." Sweet interrupted his thoughts. She bent her muzzle to the scent, ears lifting. "This is a strong message. And there are others! Can't you smell them?"

The fur on Lucky's shoulders bristled: Why was Sweet so determined to find a Pack? Wasn't his company enough?

"These dogs must be long gone now," he said, backing away. "We won't catch up any time soon."

Sweet raised her nose in the air. "They smell nearby to *me*."

"But this only smells strong because it was their territory. They marked it over and over. I'm telling you, Sweet, they're far away already. I can pick out their scent in the distance."

"Really?" Sweet sounded doubtful again. "But *I* could catch up with them. I can catch *anything*."

Why don't I just let her? Lucky wondered. *If she's so desperate to find a Pack, I should just tell her to run away as fast as she likes.*

Instead, he found himself rumbling a warning growl. "No, Sweet, you can't. *Shouldn't*, I mean," he added quickly as she bristled. "You don't know the city; you could get lost."

Frustrated, Sweet cast her nose around in the air, then barked angrily. "Why did this happen, Lucky? I was fine before. My *Pack* was fine! We were so happy in the open country, and we didn't do any harm to the longpaws. If they'd only left us alone, if they hadn't rounded us up into that awful Trap House—"

She'd come to a miserable halt, and Lucky sat down beside her, wishing he could think of something to say. But he wasn't used to being responsible for another dog. Already it gave him an ache in his heart that he would rather live without.

He opened his jaws to try to reason with her some more, but stopped, gaping, as a gang of fierce, furious creatures tumbled, yowling and squealing, into the street right in front of them.

Lucky felt fear tear through his hackles as his back stiffened. At first, he thought the fighting bundles of fur and teeth were sharpclaws, but then he realized they were different—very different. These animals were round and bushy-tailed, and they didn't hiss. They weren't dogs, and they weren't huge rats. Lucky gave an alarmed yelp, but the creatures didn't respond—they were too busy squabbling over a carcass that was so ripped and torn, he couldn't tell what it had once been.

Next to him, Sweet stood alertly, her eyes on the other animals. She took a moment to nuzzle his neck. "Don't worry about them; they won't hurt us."

"Are you sure?" asked Lucky. He'd caught sight of the face of one of them, a sinister black mask that seemed full of vicious little teeth.

"They're raccoons," Sweet replied. "We'll be fine if we give them a wide berth. Try not to show too much interest and they won't feel threatened. I bet they're as hungry as we are."

Lucky followed Sweet's lead to the far sidewalk. She shot the raccoons a fierce, bristling glare as she went. Lucky copied her, feeling prickles of anxiety in the roots of his fur.

We're not the only ones looking to fill our bellies, he realized. With everything torn from the ground and lying in ruins, easy pickings were a thing of the past. This was about survival now. He picked up his pace, keen to put as much space as he could between themselves and the raccoons.

A few streets beyond, Lucky tasted familiar air and gave a happy bark. It was the alley he'd been looking for! He ran forward a few paces, then sat down and scratched at his ear with a hindpaw, enjoying the moment, anticipating Sweet's delight. The delicious smell of food was getting stronger. Here, at least, he could guarantee a meal.

"Come on!" he yipped. "I promise, you won't regret this."

She padded up behind him and cocked her head quizzically. "What is this place?"

He nodded at the panes of clear stone. There were long tubes there. Normally they breathed chicken-scented steam into the air—but not today. Still, this was definitely right. Excited, he turned a couple of circles, tail wagging quickly.

"It's a Food House. A place where longpaws give food to other longpaws!"

"But we're not longpaws," she pointed out. "Who's going to give food to us?"

"Just you watch." Lucky jumped forward mischievously, dodging around tumbled trash cans and a small heap of rubble. He tried not to think about how ruined everything was, or that they hadn't seen a single longpaw walking the streets. "We'll do what Old Hunter does. He's the expert!"

Sweet brightened. "Old Hunter? Is he a Packmate of yours?"

"I told you, I don't have a Pack. Old Hunter is just a *friend*. Even Lone Dogs can find huntingmates, you know! Watch this. Copy what I do. . . ."

It was such an easy method of getting food, and it took no time to learn—Lucky was pleased to be able to teach Sweet something. He sat back on his haunches, tilted his head, and let his tongue loll out.

Sweet slowly slinked around him, studying the posture. Her head cocked. "I don't understand," she whined.

"Just trust me," Lucky growled.

Sweet whined again, then turned to sit down beside Lucky as she did her best to copy him.

"That's it!" Lucky barked. "Now, lift one ear a little higher. Like this, see? And a friendly mouth—look hungry but hopeful! You got it!"

Lucky wagged his tail as he gave Sweet an affectionate nudge with his muzzle. Then he turned his attention back to the Food House door, and waited. A longpaw would spot them soon. Slow moments passed and Lucky's tail began to wag more and more slowly until it came to rest in the dust. The door stayed resolutely shut, so Lucky padded over to scratch at it. Still no reply. He gave a small, respectful whine.

"How long do we stay like this? It's a bit—undignified," said Sweet. She licked her chops, then let her tongue hang out again.

"I don't understand. . . ." Lucky's tail drooped in embarrassment. Where was his friendly longpaw? Surely *he* hadn't run from the Big Growl. Lucky scratched at the door again, but still there was no reply.

Sweet's nose was back in the air. "I don't think it's working."

"The longpaws must be busy, that's all," Lucky grumbled. "This is an important place for them. They wouldn't have just *left*." He tried not to notice how high and anxious his voice had become. He trotted behind some bins and spoil-boxes and scratched his way through to a side door. Up on his hind legs, he put his paws against the wood and felt it sag and creak.

"Look! The Food House is broken." He tugged at a sagging hinge with his teeth. "That's why the longpaws are busy. Come on!"

The smells from inside must have been enticing enough to

31

make Sweet forget her doubts, because she helped him nose and pull and tug at the broken door until it cracked open. Lucky wriggled through ahead of her, his tail thrashing in anticipation of scrumptious food.

He slowed, glancing from side to side. This room was a strange place that he hadn't seen before, lined with huge metal boxes. There were snaking, shiny lengths of what looked like long worms. Lucky knew that these usually hummed with the longpaws' invisible energy. But nothing hummed now. Above him, water dripped from the collapsed roof, and broad cracks ran along the walls.

There was a blurred reflection of him and Sweet in the big steel boxes. Lucky shuddered as he saw how distorted their faces were. The food smell was strong now, but old, and he felt prickles of uncertainty.

"I don't like this," said Sweet in a low voice.

Lucky whined his agreement. "This isn't the way it normally is. But it should be fine. It's probably just a little bit of damage from the Big Growl." Tentatively Lucky pushed on through the rubble and mess. Sweet watched him, her muzzle wrinkling with uncertainty. "Don't look like that," he told her. "Come on!"

She lifted her slender paws high as she moved around broken, splintered shards of white stone that covered the floor.

There was another door, but it was easy to push open—almost too easy, because it swung wildly back and forth, nearly bumping Sweet's roving nose and making her jump. As it grew still again, Lucky sniffed the air.

The chaos was even worse in here, beyond the room of metal boxes; longpaw stuff was flung in heaps, sitting-boxes broken and listing together, thick dust falling from the broken walls to cover everything. Shivers rippled through Lucky's fur.

Abruptly he stopped, drawing his lips back from his teeth. *What's that smell? I know it, but . . .* He couldn't repress a frightened growl. Something moved in the corner.

Lucky took a few hesitant paces, crouching low to the ground. The scent felt strong inside his nose. He bounded forward and pawed at the fallen debris. There was someone here!

White dust stirred and swirled; Lucky heard a groan, and a breathless rasping of longpaw words. He recognized only one. "Lucky . . ."

The voice was weak, but it was familiar. Whimpering, Lucky sank his teeth into one of the huge broken beams and leaned his weight back on his paws, heaving. His whole body

33

trembled with the effort, and he could feel his teeth being pulled from his jaws. It was no good! He released his bite and fell back, panting with the effort. The longpaw lay still and unmoving beneath the beam, a trickle of dried blood tracking down his face.

Lucky drew closer, ignoring his instincts, which were telling him to run away as fast as he could. Behind him, he could hear Sweet pacing with anxiety. Lucky lowered his head over the longpaw's body. One arm was free of the rubble, twisted at an unnatural angle. The longpaw's face was pale as snow, his lips a horribly unnatural blue, but they curved in a smile as his eyes met Lucky's.

He's alive! Lucky licked at his nose and cheeks, gently clearing some of the coating of dust. If Lucky could just clean the longpaw up, he'd look much healthier—just like his old self. But as Lucky stepped back, he saw that the skin beneath the dust was gray. The longpaw's ragged breath was the faintest of whispers, barely stirring the fur on Lucky's muzzle.

The longpaw's eyes flickered open, and with a groan of pain he lifted his trembling free hand to pat Lucky's head. Lucky nuzzled and licked him again, but the hand fell away, and the eyes closed once more.

"Wake up, longpaw," Lucky whined softly, his tongue lashing the cold, pale face. "Wake up. . . ."

Lucky waited. But the lips were still and cold.

The whisper of breath was gone.

CHAPTER THREE

A yelp of despair shattered the silence. Turning hurriedly away from the dead longpaw, Lucky stared at Sweet. Every hair on her sleek coat seemed to bristle with fear. Stiff-legged, she backed away, tail tight between her legs.

"I don't want your city!" she whined. "There's death and danger *everywhere*. I can't stand it!"

She let loose a howl of disgust and sprinted, making the door swing wildly once again as she shot through it. Lucky scrambled after her, knowing he had no hope of catching a swift-dog.

But Sweet's speed did her no favors in the close quarters of the steel room. She was hemmed in, dashing desperately from reflection to distorted reflection, crashing wildly into the metal boxes, and skidding on the slick floor. When she slammed into a wall in her terror, Lucky lunged forward and pinned her to the ground.

She squirmed beneath him, panicking, but Lucky kept his

forepaws firmly on her sweating flank, his eyes fixed on hers. "Calm down! You're going to hurt yourself."

"I can't stay. . . ."

As Sweet's barks fell away to anxious pants, Lucky let his weight gently flop down on her. "It's nothing to be scared of, Sweet. He's only dead." He repeated what he was sure she already knew, hoping to calm her. "It's a natural smell: the longpaw's life force. Just like when we die—our selves leave our bodies, become part of the world."

Lucky had been taught ever since he was a pup that that was the way of life and death. When a dog met his end and his body went to the Earth-Dog, his self floated up to meet all the scents of the air, to mingle with them and become part of the whole world. That's what was happening to the longpaw now, Lucky was certain.

Sweet's flanks stopped heaving as her panting breaths subsided. Lucky could still see the whites of her wide, fearful eyes. He cautiously released her and she climbed to her feet. "I know that," she growled. "But I don't want to be anywhere near escaping longpaw spirits. I want to find as many dogs as we can. We need to track down other survivors, and get us all out of here *right now*!"

"But there's nothing we need to get away from—nothing will

hurt us now, Sweet. The Food House fell on the longpaw in the Big Growl, that's all. . . ." Lucky needed Sweet to trust him. If he could reassure her, perhaps all of this would make sense to Lucky, too.

"Where are the other longpaws?" Sweet barked, tossing her head. "They've either run away or they're dead, Lucky! I'm leaving this city, and I'm going to find a Pack. So should you!"

Lucky opened his mouth to speak, but the words dried up in his throat. He could only stare at her sadly. Sweet half-turned to leave, then froze with one paw raised and all her muscles tensed, eager to flee. She gazed at Lucky for a long moment, licking her lips uncertainly. "Aren't you coming with me?"

Lucky hesitated. The idea of a Pack didn't appeal to him one bit, but—for some reason—he didn't want Sweet to leave. He liked having her around. For the first time, he felt himself tremble at the prospect of being alone. And she was waiting for him, ears pricked, eyes hopeful. . . .

He shook himself. He'd spent his whole life on these streets. That's what he was—a Lone Dog.

"I can't."

"But you can't stay here!" Sweet howled.

"I told you: I'm not a Pack Dog. I never will be."

She gave a sharp bark of exasperation. "Dogs aren't meant to be alone!"

Lucky gave her a regretful look. "*I* am."

Sweet sighed, and padded back to him. Fondly she licked his face. Lucky nuzzled her in response, fighting down a mournful whine that wanted to erupt from his belly.

"I'll miss you," she said quietly. Then she turned to wriggle through the door.

Lucky padded forward. "You don't have to . . ." But with a flash of her tail, she was gone. Lucky found himself staring at an empty space.

For a while, Lucky didn't feel like moving. He settled down on his belly, chin resting on his forepaws as he listened to the click of Sweet's claws on the ground, fading into the ruined emptiness of the streets. Even when he could hear her no longer, her scent still clung to the air. He wished it would vanish—and take this terrible pang of loneliness with it.

Lucky shut his eyes and tried to focus his mind on other things.

But that just left the hunger.

It was like a set of sharp teeth, gnawing and chewing at his stomach. Lucky was almost relieved to feel the pain—at least it took his mind off Sweet. *That's why I don't let myself get close to other dogs,* he thought.

Back in the room with the dead longpaw, Lucky sniffed and scratched in every corner, licking at crumbs and grease. Some of the broken things on the floor held smears of food, so he lapped at them, trying not to cut his tongue; then he leaped onto one of the untoppled tables to find small scraps to nibble on. There was so little, and the tantalizing taste of it only made his stomach growl louder, the teeth bite harder. He didn't go near the longpaw, forced himself not to look.

I'm on my own now. This is the way it should be.

The steel room would have food, he was sure—that was what must be in the metal boxes lined up around the walls. But when he scratched at them, they refused to open. Whimpering in hunger, he tugged and bit at the metal doors. They stuck firm. He flung his body against them. Nothing. It was no use: He was going to have to wander farther, see what else he could find.

At least he'd be in the open air again, he thought: free and easy, the way he used to be. He had looked after himself just fine until now—and he would keep on doing that.

Lucky headed back out into the alleyway. It seemed so much emptier than before, and he found himself scampering as fast as he could across the rubble, until he reached the broad open space beyond. Surely he'd find something here? It had always been such a bustle of noise and energy, full of longpaws and their loudcages.

There were plenty of loudcages, sure enough, but none of them was moving and there was still not a longpaw in sight, friendly or otherwise. Some of the loudcages had fallen onto their flanks—a big, long one had crashed its blunt snout into an empty space in the wall of a building, shattered pieces of clear-stone glittering. Picking his way carefully through the shards, Lucky felt his hackles rise. The scent of longpaw was back in the air, but it was not comforting: It was the scent that had settled on the Food House owner when he had grown still. The silence was oppressive, punctuated only by the steady drip and trickle of water.

Above him the Sun-Dog, which had been so high and bright, was casting long shadows from the buildings that had withstood the Big Growl. Each time he passed through one of the pools of darkness, Lucky shivered and hurried back into the light. He kept moving, the patches of light growing steadily smaller, the shadows longer, and the ache of hunger in his belly sharper.

Maybe I should have gone with Sweet . . .

No. There was no point thinking that way. He was a Lone Dog again, and that was *good*.

He turned and trotted determinedly down another alley. This was his city! There was *always* food and comfort to be had here. Even if he had to dig deep for the leftovers in Food House spoil-boxes, or find another overturned smell-box in the road, there would be something the crows and the rats hadn't found. He was self-reliant, independent Lucky.

He was not going to starve.

Lucky drew to a stop as he got his bearings. This alley wasn't as damaged by the Big Growl as other places, but there was one deep, vicious crack running up the middle of it, and two spoil-boxes had been knocked flying. There might be a real feast there, if he rummaged. Lucky bounded up to the nearest one—then froze, nerves crackling beneath his fur. The scent was sharp and strong, and he knew it well.

Enemy!

Lips peeling back from his teeth, he sniffed the air to pinpoint the creature. Above him was a set of slender steps going up a wall, and his instincts pulled his eyes, ears, and nose toward it: That was the kind of place where this enemy liked to lurk, ready to pounce, needle-claws raking.

There it was: striped fur bristling, pointed ears laid flat, and tiny, glinting fangs bared. Its low, threatening growl was punctuated by vicious hissing as it crouched, every muscle taut for its attack.

Sharpclaw!

CHAPTER FOUR

The green-yellow eyes glared down at Lucky. He fought to suppress the tight ball of nerves in his belly even as his neck fur lifted. The sharpclaw would smell fear, he knew that; it would sense any hesitation—but Lucky would not hesitate.

His lips pulled back from his teeth and he raised his head to bark the most ferocious bark he could muster.

I'm dangerous, too, sharpclaw. . . .

It got to its feet, stiff-legged and swollen to what seemed like twice its size, fur standing on end all over its arched body. One paw almost lifted, claws unsheathed and ready to strike. Lucky told himself not to look away and trained his gaze determinedly on the other animal, deepening his snarl.

Its growling and hissing were ferocious now, and Lucky felt sharpclaw spit land on his nose. The creature launched itself from the rickety ladder, and Lucky forced himself to hold his ground as the sharpclaw landed lightly, perfectly, on a half-wrecked loud-cage. It drew itself up with a lethal glare.

And then the loudcage woke up.

Raucous wails ripped the air as it screamed and howled, flashing its orange eyes and its white ones. For an instant, both Lucky and the sharpclaw were startled into frozen silence. Then, at the same instant, they bolted.

Panic lent Lucky speed, despite his injured paw, but it made him breathless, too. He found himself yelping as he ran, the shriek of the loudcage almost drowning him out. Careening around a corner, Lucky ran as hard as he could away from loudcages and high buildings.

There in his path stood another sharpclaw. It was as black as no-sun, and as rigid as a tree.

Lucky didn't even slow down. The sharpclaw's ears flattened and it opened its mouth in a snarl. Lucky darted to one side, racing around it, growling, his hackles up. He had to end this fight—quickly. He launched himself into the air, landing on his enemy. Almost immediately he lost his footing and found himself tumbling with the sharpclaw, which yowled in panic. One flailing claw caught Lucky's shoulder with a glancing scratch.

Rolling to his feet, paws scrabbling, he saw the black sharpclaw racing down a nearby alley. It had clearly decided escape was more important than fighting—Lucky's attack had worked, however fumbling. Panting, his legs trembling beneath him, Lucky blinked and listened to the silence. The loudcage had stopped howling.

Well, *of course* it had. They always did in the end.

Lucky felt a pang of hurt pride as his flanks twitched and calmed. Lucky—Lone Dog, Street Dog, City Dog—scared of a loudcage howl! He was glad Old Hunter hadn't witnessed *that*! But he quickly shook it off. That was the reflex of a proper Lone Dog. The moment's slight embarrassment gave way to pride. He was still on his paw-tips, smart and streetwise as ever. No Growl, Big or Small, could take that away from him.

Lucky felt his muscles stop shivering. He trotted on; this road seemed to lead away from the once-crowded center, and that was a good direction for the moment. It was his own decision, his own choice: one of the big advantages of being a Lone Dog.

Lucky glanced around with curiosity as he walked toward the edge of the city where most of the longpaws lived; it didn't seem quite as bad here. There wasn't so much to shatter; these longpaw houses didn't have as far to topple.

At last he stopped, turning a circle and eyeing his surroundings. This was one of those streets where longpaws lived and slept.

And it wasn't the kind where the longpaws lived piled on top of one another in stone cages . . . no, here the longpaw houses were set in neat little squares of garden that were full of intriguing smells. And the most intriguing of them all was . . .

Lucky opened his jaws, pricked his ears, and eagerly sniffed the air. Elusive but distinct, the scent made his stomach churn with anticipation. *Food!*

He bounded toward its source. Meat! Meat was cooking on one of those metal longpaw fireboxes! The invisible fires that made the raw meat turn dark, that made the food-smell so strong and tangy and . . .

A bird clattered from a tree with a flap of black wings, bringing him to a startled halt. He needed to slow down. Hunger should not make him reckless. He knew from experience not every longpaw was friendly when it came to food. Some of them were reluctant to share, protecting their food the way Mother-Dogs protected their pups.

Still, he wasn't about to give up altogether. At a more cautious pace he padded forward, his fur bristling all over with longing. He could almost taste the food now, feel it filling his belly, warm and satisfying. Not far now! *Not far!*

He paused in the shadow of a stunted tree, his tongue lolling, jaw wide and grinning, his tail thumping the ground hard and fast. There it was: a rundown wooden longpaw house, set in overgrown grass and shaded by straggly branches. And there was the firebox, gently sizzling and steaming. And there was the longpaw—well-fed, by the look of him, with a belly that bulged right through his fur.

And there—also looking well-fed—was his Fierce Dog.

They were both snoozing in the shade, the longpaw sprawled on a raised surface by the firebox, the Fierce Dog lying at his feet. Lucky knew its kind from many a tussle over food. It wasn't very big, but it was deep-chested and heavy-jawed and, probably, short-tempered.

But maybe this one would be happy to share?

Lucky hesitated, catching a tiny whine in his throat. The food-smell was so tempting, but . . .

Why were they here? Weren't all the longpaws gone, or dead, like the friendly one in the Food House? Why hadn't this longpaw left, too? Dozing beneath the Sun-Dog like this, he seemed not to have noticed the Big Growl at all.

Or maybe this longpaw *was* dead, and so was his Fierce Dog? Lucky sniffed the air uncertainly. The strong tang of grilling meat could have been masking the death-smell. . . .

Warily Lucky took a pace forward, then two, his tail raised, his muzzle dripping with eagerness. He licked his chops. Neither the longpaw nor his dog moved.

He had to try. Close to the firebox now, Lucky eyed a chunk of sizzling meat. The distance and angle were just about right. . . .

He lunged.

The longpaw's eyes flew open, and he leaped to his feet, brandishing a stick. His barks stung Lucky's ears. The Fierce Dog had woken too, springing to the attack position, legs stiff as he unleashed a furious volley of fight-barks.

"GET BACK! It's MINE! Want to fight me for it? FIGHT ME OR *RUN*!"

Lucky was no match for the longpaw's stick, let alone for the Fierce Dog and its savage jaws. Turning tail, he bolted from the garden, sharp terror overwhelming the gnawing ache of hunger.

He leaped a crumbling wall and raced down the hard road. He was sure the Fierce Dog must be chasing him, but he didn't dare turn to look. If the Fierce Dog caught him, he wouldn't stand a chance. His paws skidded on the broken and uneven ground, almost tripping him. Panting, heart thrashing, fear biting hard at his guts, he bolted along a road that seemed never to end.

Until it did.

Blackness opened before him. He automatically flung his weight sideways, halting his momentum, his haunches scraping painfully on the rough road surface. His claws rattled against unyielding stone, his tail lashed over hideous emptiness, and at last he stopped, aching with terror and pain. His injured paw throbbed with each beat of his heart, and Lucky was sure the wound had opened again.

He raised his head. He was lying on his flank on the brink of a vast black hole in the earth. He scrambled to his feet and lowered his head to sniff fearfully at the crack in the road. It was wider than he was long, and the bottom was hidden by shadows thicker than clouds.

Bristling, he took a nervous step away, then shook himself, and risked another look. Was Earth-Dog down there, waiting for him as she once waited for Lightning? Would she spring suddenly from the darkness and drag him down? He was almost afraid to peer closer, but he found it hard to believe that Earth-Dog had let the Big Growl happen. Why would she let it destroy her own home? Perhaps Earth-Dog, too, was afraid of the Growl. . . .

Lucky found himself trembling, but there was no movement from within the black depths, no sinister snarling. Breathing deeply, he paced along the edge, feeling his courage return.

He had to get around this hole. He loped first one way, then the other. Panic began to rise in his chest again. There was no end to it: It extended through gardens as far as he could see in both directions. Even a longpaw house had collapsed into it, leaving rooms on each side open to the sky. Back and forth he ran again, yipping with desperation.

He didn't dare go much farther; there were trees ahead that obscured his view of the crack, but they were distant, and as far as he could see the gap only seemed to get wider. It was too big a risk. Street Dogs were more sensible than that.

Then, not far enough in the distance, he heard the Fierce Dog's voice.

"You! *Food-stealer!* I'll teach you a lesson! *Come back and try that again!*"

Lucky stood still, pricking his ears toward the furious barking. Thank the Sky-Dogs his new enemy liked to talk so much; if he had more breath to spare he might have caught Lucky by now. But the Fierce Dog was going to catch him soon. . . .

There was nothing else he could do. Lucky hurtled back the way he'd come, hearing his pursuer lumbering closer all the time. He had to give himself a good running start, because he would only get one chance to clear this chasm.

He had to hope he could live up to his name.

He spun to face the opening again, and began to race. Faster and faster, his paws flew across the ground. As the bottomless crack opened before him, he launched himself from the edge. Now, there was nothing below his belly but death and blackness. . . .

The Earth-Dog waiting to swallow him . . .

He landed hard. He tumbled and rolled, welcoming the pain he felt in his paw and bones. He was alive!

For long moments he let himself lie there, his flanks heaving as he shut his eyes and felt the deep relief flood him. There was no way the stocky Fierce Dog could clear that great rip in the earth. He was safe!

Safe . . . but starving.

Lucky's hunger returned, as painful as being kicked in the gut by a cruel longpaw.

Desperate and miserable, he laid his head on his paws and whimpered softly to himself. He was alone. Alone, lost, and scared.

Maybe he should have gone with Sweet. . . .

But then what? They might *both* be starving by now, and he'd have a second belly to fill. This way, Lucky had only himself to look after. And he had always been good at that.

As he rose to a shaky standing position, though, his ears were low and his tail was between his legs. He needed food, and soon. The shadows had lengthened even more, swallowing the last patches of light; the blackness of no-sun would soon be here, and he knew he shouldn't stay in the open.

Slowly, painfully, he slunk into an alley and began to hunt for a sleeping-place. As he sniffed at doors and gaps in the rubble, he couldn't help thinking about that terrible void in the Earth. Had Sweet, too, come upon such a crack? He hoped she hadn't slipped into the Earth's jaws, as he nearly had. . . .

He crossed three separate roads, all the while limping badly, before he finally found a wrecked loudcage whose door hung loose. Lucky barely had the strength to haul himself into it, but he was rewarded with a scrap of shiny silver paper that smelled of food. It felt tinny and strange against his teeth but when he peeled it open, there was a piece of stale bread with old-smelling meat tucked inside. A longpaw had taken a bite of it, no more.

It wasn't firebox steak, but it would calm the raging hunger just a little. Gratefully Lucky wolfed it down, then licked and chewed the last scraps from the paper, not caring that he was swallowing bits of that as well.

Lucky raised his head and closed his eyes, quietly thanking the Sky-Dogs for that small morsel of luck. Feeling a little better, he paced a tiny circle in his familiar sleep-ritual, then curled up, tucking his tail around him.

Please, Earth-Dog, keep the Big Growl silent during this no-sun.

Settling his head on his forelegs, he licked as well as he could at his sore paw until sleep overwhelmed him.

CHAPTER FIVE

That sound . . . what was it . . . ? The Big Growl—back to finish him off?

The noise filled his skull, stung his ears, made his head ache. Not just the howling and snarling that seemed to echo from every direction; worse, there was the savage ripping of flesh, the snap of vicious jaws.

The sound of dogs, fighting. Fighting to the death . . .

Could it be the Storm of Dogs? Was it here? No, it couldn't be—couldn't—

Pressing himself to the ground, lowering his ears, Lucky whimpered his fear and horror. It was coming to swamp him. Just like the Big Growl. There was no escape. He had to turn and face the Storm, and fight for his life—

But as he leaped to his paws and spun to face the savage warrior hounds, he saw—nothing. Nothing but more darkness, emptiness, as gaping a void as the hole in the earth that he'd leaped.

And all he could hear was a distant, fading, terrifying howl—

* * *

He woke with a start. *Sweet!*

No. Sweet wasn't here now.

And it was a dream. The Storm of Dogs had been nothing but a dream . . . except that it had felt so real. Sounded and smelled so real. Was it hunger-madness, or was it worse than that—a vision of something that was yet to come . . . ?

Nonsense. He couldn't afford to think of such things. Tired and stiff and sore, Lucky recognized the hiding place he'd crawled into last night. It smelled of hot metal, of tanned hide and the strange juice the longpaws fed their loudcages. The Sun-Dog was shining, but he still missed the warmth of Sweet at his back. The loneliness felt like a great stone in his belly. For a moment he wanted to bay his misery out loud to the empty blue sky.

He didn't know where he was or where he was going. Perhaps even a Lone Dog sometimes needed a traveling companion: someone to hunt with, sleep beside, someone to watch his back. Someone he too could protect.

No. He walked *alone*, and he liked it.

The heat in the loudcage was growing stifling, his hunger unbearable. Slinking out, he glanced once in each direction, then set off hesitantly down the side street. And just at that moment, something black took off above his head with a clatter of wings.

Pausing to pant and lick his dry chops, Lucky stared up at the crow; it didn't fly far. It flapped and perched on a broken metal pipe that led down from the roof of the longpaw home. There must have been water caught there, because it dipped its black beak to the pipe and drank. Then it cocked its head and eyed him directly.

It was just like the crow that had flown out of the tree yesterday, warning Lucky to be careful. It might even be the same one.

Don't be silly. All crows look alike! Lucky scolded himself. Still . . . that crow yesterday had appeared at just the right moment, or he'd have run headlong into the jaws of the Fierce Dog. Maybe it had been sent by the Sky-Dogs to warn him; it certainly seemed to be watching him very closely. He raised his gaze to the bird's, and yipped with respect.

It tilted its head to the other side, gave a caw, and flapped lazily away.

Half-sorry to see the bird go, half-glad it wasn't staring at him any longer, Lucky set off again, taking a shortcut through the narrowest of alleys and emerging onto a broad avenue. On either side were large longpaw homes that had crumbled into piles of dust and rock. The power of the Big Growl was displayed here for any dog to fear.

One longpaw house had had its roof sliced off. It now lay in front of it like a scrap of unwanted food. Two trees tilted crazily against each other, as if they were trying to wrestle. Around the next corner, another longpaw house had collapsed in on itself, and Lucky stiffened, backing away, his hackles rising and skin quivering. The smell of death was strong here.

Distracted and unsettled by the scent, Lucky stumbled over a hole in the ground, jarring his sore paw. As he tried to lick it better, a sound burst from the city silence that made him yelp with shock and dash for cover, forgetting the throb of pain. The noise was like a loudcage, but different—deeper, a resounding growl. Peering out from his hiding place between two tipped spoil-boxes, Lucky shivered and watched the street as the rumbling roar grew louder and louder—and stopped.

If this was a loudcage it was an Alpha. He had never seen one so huge and threatening, its flanks a dull green metal that looked strong and indestructible.

A door creaked open, and a longpaw stepped out.

Lucky felt his heart quicken. Had the Big Growl changed even the longpaws? Because this was like no longpaw he'd seen before. It moved like a longpaw, and smelled—vaguely—like a longpaw, but it was covered from top to toe in the strangest fur that Lucky had ever seen—a bright yellow that made Lucky's eyes water. Its face was blank, black, and flat.

There were tremors in Lucky's skin, but he was almost certain this was a longpaw. And who was to say it was a hostile one? He'd long ago discovered you couldn't tell with longpaws. A dog just had to approach with caution, and not be too proud to run away if necessary.

He crept from his hiding place, slinking low to the ground with his tail tucked between his legs, and looked beseechingly up at the blank, eyeless face. The longpaw didn't immediately kick him, so Lucky let his tongue hang out hopefully, and pricked his ears.

It glanced down at him. There was no food in its thickly covered hands, only a strange stick that beeped, so things did not look promising—and sure enough, the longpaw muttered some words in its language and swiped its arm, a gesture that Lucky knew meant, *Go away.*

It didn't sound very welcoming, but it didn't sound very hostile, either. It certainly didn't try to collar him with a long stick, so it couldn't be from the Trap House. Lucky gave it a hopeful whine.

It waved him away again, its tone harsher.

59

Certainly it was a longpaw, because it spoke like one, but there was no way of smelling its intentions beneath that strange fur. And Lucky couldn't read that eyeless face. *I guess I should give up.* He turned around, and loped back into the alley. It was strange. He'd sensed neither friendliness nor hostility from the longpaw—just a deep nervous tension. This wasn't the way that longpaws normally were.

The sound of the loudcage rumbling back into life sent fear down his spine again, and he ran, heading for the center of the city, where he knew most longpaws prowled. He tended to avoid these particular streets if he could. Usually there was nothing but noise: the constant growl of loudcages, longpaws barking at one another. But as he approached, the only thing Lucky heard was the moan of wind between buildings, the drip of water, the creak and groan of roofs, and metal bent to the breaking point.

In front of him the road was covered with tiny glittering pieces of clear-stone, and Lucky stopped. He knew he couldn't afford another cut paw. Instead he looked up at the building that had shattered in the Growl.

It had once been made of huge sheets of clear-stone; now its face was open to the still air. He started when he saw longpaws staring from the base, but then he remembered that these were fake longpaws, with no smell, no warmth, no movement. Cautiously he paced between them, sniffing at their brand-new furs; even those didn't smell of longpaw. Some of them had been stripped of their fur and knocked sideways, but they weren't hurt. They stared at him, empty-eyed.

Lucky slunk warily between the stiff and lifeless longpaws, but their eyes didn't blink and their skin smelled of nothing. This place was what they called their *mall*. Longpaws—real ones—had gone in and out of this building all the time, he remembered. Sometimes they'd carried food, but they'd never stopped to give him any. And when he'd tried to saunter in and find the Food Houses for himself, he'd been chased out by other longpaws, who all wore the same blue fur. He remembered all too well having to dodge their kicks.

But there were no angry longpaws to stop him now!

Lucky sniffed. Once this place had been a confusion of scents: cold air that blew like a constant wind through the rooms; strong unpleasant odors that the longpaws sprayed on themselves; strange sharp smells smeared on the floors by longpaws with long wooden poles that ended in a ball of rags. And there had been the new-made scent of untouched things set out for longpaws to gaze at. Those smells had mostly faded, and the clingy warm air of Outside had forced its way in. That, and the death-smell that haunted the whole city. Lucky shuddered. He had never smelled so much death in one place before; even the Earth-Dog would be offended by so strong a sense of ended lives.

He shook himself free of the horror. There was more than all that. There was *food*!

It smelled stale and maybe a little spoiled, but Lucky didn't care. Keeping a nervous eye open for the longpaws in blue, he made his way farther into the building. There were more broken clear-stones here, littering the smooth, shiny floor, and he was careful to avoid them, but he couldn't help staring at the deserted longpaw houses within the huge mall. Some seemed untouched; others had been stripped bare. In some places, piles of longpaw stuff lay abandoned. Lucky could smell both longpaw and dog, but the strong stench of fear and desperation overlaid both. His neck prickled.

Ah! he thought, pausing to sniff at a ransacked heap of bags made out of some kind of old preserved skin. They were polished, and not fresh, but the smell was strong and familiar. Longpaws carried their things in bags and pouches like these. Perhaps this was a place where they kept their precious things—like burying bones! They left them here, piled together, and came back for them later. Was that it? Longpaws had been here since the Big Growl, he was almost certain, taking the things away; he could see scuff marks on the floor from their covered feet. Apart from the skin-pouches, and some of the furs, nothing else looked familiar. The smell of food was growing stronger, so Lucky headed toward it, taking little notice of the racks of sparkling longpaw collars and studs, the scraps of longpaw fur hanging on plastic hooks, the stacks of paper and boxes. He even caught sight of a row of small imitation dogs, as unmoving and lifeless as the strange-smelling longpaws at the front of the building.

The rich scent of food was coming from above. Hesitantly he put his good paw on a ragged metal hill that led upward. It seemed to bear his weight, so he took a step or two farther; then he was suddenly too hungry and eager to be cautious. Taking a deep breath, he bounded up as fast as he could. There were grooves on the metal hill that felt odd beneath his paw pads, especially the wounded one, but he made it without mishap to the top.

And drew to a stop.

That wasn't only food . . . there was a dog-scent that seemed familiar, too: a musk of well-known sweat and skin and breath.

Old Hunter!

Lucky's heart leaped. He could hardly believe there might be friendly company ahead; there was no one he'd be happier to see right now. Lucky dodged and slunk through the longpaw sitting-boxes and small tables spilled across the floor as he followed his nose. The food-scent was strong now, reminding him of those things the longpaws ate—meat chopped up and made into round shapes like flattened balls; the discs that were smothered in tomatoes and cheese and spicy chopped meat. The smells were stale and old, but his chops watered just thinking about the prospects.

Clambering clear of the last tangle of longpaw sitting-boxes, Lucky stood and sniffed. There were openings in the wall, but they were covered by metal shutters. In one of the gaps, though, the metal was torn sideways, sagging, and it smelled strongly of meat. Lucky would have bolted straight for it—if it hadn't been for the low growling coming from below the counter.

But there was nothing to fear. If he'd been unsure about the smell, the tone of that growl had definitely convinced him.

Happily Lucky sprang up onto the counter, wobbling a little on his sore paw.

"Old Hunter!"

Lucky leaned down on his forepaws and lowered his shoulders and his head, opening his mouth and panting. Even if Old Hunter was a friend, it was best to look unthreatening.

Old Hunter's blunt muzzle was slightly curled as he stared up. He rose, standing tall on his powerful legs, and growled.

Then he sprang for Lucky's throat.

CHAPTER SIX

Lucky yelped in shock as he tumbled backward under the big dog's attack. Old Hunter stood over him, snarling. Lucky made himself lie still and submissive as drool from Old Hunter's jaws dripped onto his muzzle. Lucky whined softly, and a light of recognition dawned suddenly in Old Hunter's eyes.

"Lucky?"

Feeling a dizzy wave of relief, Lucky thumped his tail eagerly. The big stocky dog above him stepped away, relaxing and pricking his ears. He sniffed once more at Lucky's face, then grinned, panting.

"Lucky!" Old Hunter snuffled and licked affectionately at Lucky's ears as the smaller dog scrambled to his feet, trying not to slide off the countertop. "I didn't recognize you. You *stink*, my friend!"

Lucky yipped with delight. "I've been hunting."

Old Hunter wrinkled his muzzle. "Mostly in spoil-boxes, by the smell of you."

"There wasn't much else." Lucky's ears drooped, then he pricked them up again. "It's so good to see you!" It really was, he thought. Not that he'd been desperate for company, of course. If he hadn't run into Old Hunter it would have made no difference to him—but now that he *had*, well . . . it felt better than he'd have expected.

"It's good to see you, too. It's been a long time." All the same, there was a certain wariness in the big dog's eyes as he leaped back down to the meat scattered on the floor.

"Too long," said Lucky. "I'm ready to see a friend again!" He hesitated, not wanting to sound needy or weak in front of this independent old dog. "We can watch each other's backs, at least! Maybe now I can get a few bites of food without looking over my shoulder."

The excitement—and the sight and smell of the meat littered at Old Hunter's feet—were too much for Lucky, and he crouched to leap down off the counter. He was brought up short, though, when Old Hunter stiffened and growled once more.

"No offense, Lucky," he rumbled threateningly, "but it took me long enough to find this stash. It's not for sharing, friend."

Lucky stared at him, his shoulders sagging. What *was* a friend, if not someone to share meat with? Indecisively he sat down on the counter once more. "But—"

"I've been guarding this since the Big Growl. You know how hard I've had to work to keep it? You're not the first dog to come along. And there were foxes."

Lucky licked the drool from his chops, his flanks shivering. He was almost unable to bear the closeness of food. The door of the big silver box behind Old Hunter hung off its hinges, and as well as the meat at the big dog's feet, there was more piled on the shelves. The metal box must have kept the meat cold, because he could see water pooling around the plastic-wrapped steaks, and some of them looked frozen solid—like the injured rabbit he'd found last winter. The meat might be frozen, but it would still be edible, even before it melted. He knew that. And there was so much of it. . . .

"But there's plenty here. . . ."

Old Hunter growled again, more angrily. "There's plenty of it, but it could be the last meat left to find. I can make it last. I *will* make it last, Lucky."

Lucky felt his whole body tense with the shock—this was so unlike his friend! Old Hunter had always been willing to share before, and for such a fierce-looking dog, he was known for being slow to anger. The Big Growl must have spooked Old Hunter very badly.

Lucky lay down, lowering his tail but not his head: He kept that proudly raised. "We've known each other a long time, Old Hunter. You've always shared with me."

"Things change, Lucky."

"*We* don't have to. We're both survivors. We always have been! You and I, we're tough. You're tougher than any dog I know."

The big dog stared at him, lips still tugged back from his teeth, but his suspicion was wavering. The tip of his tail twitched with indecision. Lucky saw it was flicking close to something else: something that dangled from a broken cold-box, dangerously close to the pooling meltwater of the frozen meat. For the first time in a long time, Lucky sensed the invisible power of the long-paws, prickling in his fur and blood.

"Old Hunter!" He lunged, banging his shoulder into the bigger dog's side. Old Hunter staggered sideways, away from the snaking thing, just as its severed tip brushed the pool of water and sparked viciously.

If Lucky hadn't taken him by surprise, he knew Old Hunter would have fought him; as it was the big dog sprawled on his flank, staring in shock at the swinging, spitting cable.

"I'm sorry, Old Hunter, I—"

"No," he growled softly. "No, Lucky. Thank you. I should have known. Been more diligent. I thought the light-power was dead."

Cautiously regaining his feet, the old dog sniffed delicately at the water, then used a paw to swipe at the meat, knocking and dragging it safely away.

"Careful," said Lucky.

"I will be. The light-power snake would have bitten me. I'd be hurt or dead if you hadn't been here."

Now, decided Lucky, was a good time to stay silent.

"Know what?" Old Hunter said at last. "You're right, Lucky. The Big Growl's had everything its own way so far. Why should I let it beat me, too?"

He took a pace back from his guarded meat.

Lucky yipped with relief and leaped down from the counter, giving a wide berth to the water and the power snake. He remembered his manners, licking Old Hunter's face with gratitude and affection, and the big dog reciprocated, making a far happier rumbling noise in his throat. Then, respect properly shown, they both began to wolf down the meat.

The half-frozen food tasted better than anything Lucky had

ever eaten. He ate it quickly, noisily, messily. Only when he'd satisfied the worst of his hunger did he manage to slow down and gnaw at it more sociably with Old Hunter.

It was good to be eating with a friend.

"So," mumbled Old Hunter after a while, through a half-chewed bone. "Where were you when It happened?"

There was no need to ask what *It* was. "In the Trap House," said Lucky, shivering briefly at the awful memory. "They'd caught me a few no-suns before."

"Bad luck." Old Hunter shook his head.

"Not completely. The Big Growl freed me. Maybe the Earth-Dog took pity on me." He thought for a moment, becoming solemn. "I must remember to bury meat for her when I'm outside."

"A good idea. But leave enough for yourself. The Earth-Dog understands *that*."

"You're right." Lucky was grateful for Old Hunter's reassurance and his hard-earned wisdom. "And you? Where were you when It growled?"

The big dog grunted at a happier memory. "Hunting rabbits in the park. And catching them, I might add."

Lucky licked his jaws. Now that the ravening hunger no longer

71

chewed at his belly, he could remember the taste of fresh rabbit with pleasant nostalgia. "They're fun to chase," he remarked, "but hard to catch."

"You have to be wily," said the wise old dog, licking the last scraps of flesh off a bone. "Play friendly for a rabbit; make it think you're not a threat. Be calm and uninterested, however hungry you are. And then, when it's in paw range, pounce fast!"

"I've done that before, and it wriggled free."

"Let your whole weight fall on it. If you try and catch it with your paws, it'll squirm away and be gone before you know it."

"Thanks." All of Lucky's best hunting tips had always come from Old Hunter. "You must have been hunting in the wild since you were a pup! I really should practice proper hunting as well as scavenging and begging."

Old Hunter gnawed thoughtfully on the stripped bone, licking at the marrow. "I wasn't always in the wild," he murmured. He sat up and scratched at his neck with a hind leg, managing to part the fur a little. "See that?"

Lucky stared. The bare bit of skin, rubbed smooth and hairless, couldn't be what he thought it was. Could it?

"I spent time as a Leashed Dog."

Lucky couldn't believe it. "You lived with *longpaws*?"

"When I was no more than a pup," said Old Hunter gruffly. "It didn't last long, thank goodness. They moved away and didn't bother to take me with them. That's when I started to survive on my own. But it's true: Before then I was a Leashed Dog."

"What happened to it? The . . ." He found it difficult even to say the word.

"The collar? I took it off myself. It wasn't easy." Old Hunter's expression darkened. "I had no choice. I was growing, getting very big. It was cutting into my neck. Might have killed me in the end, but I chewed it off. Took me all day and half the night, but I did it. I swore I'd never wear another one."

A shudder rippled through Lucky's muscles. Collars were unnatural; dogs like him and Old Hunter should run free. That was the true way, the natural way.

What would a collar even feel like, locked around a dog's throat, choking and restricting? Maybe he knew. Something flickered in his memory. Was it possible . . . ?

Very, very dimly Lucky could recall his old Pup Pack. The other pups in it had worn collars; he was sure of it. So had he, too, worn one? A hated symbol of captivity, a sign of being in thrall to longpaws?

What had happened to him? Lucky wondered. What lay in his past that was so cloudy and elusive? He couldn't remember. More than that, he didn't *want* to remember, and it wasn't just the fear of some perhaps-imaginary collar. Just thinking about the Pup Pack made him feel sad, though he didn't know why. The memory brought with it other remembered sensations: warm bodies, small hearts beating close to his, the crush and comfort and noise of a crowded basket.

Lucky shook himself, unease lifting his fur. The half-forgotten images brought with them a horrible feeling: that dreadful, cold sadness, like a stone in his belly. He got up on all fours, stretched away the dull pain. Dipping his head, he licked Old Hunter's ear.

"Thank you, friend."

"You're welcome, young one. Good luck to you."

Lucky hesitated. *Good luck* . . . Didn't they both need more than that just now?

"Old Hunter . . . I've been thinking. It might seem crazy, but why don't we team up for a while?" At the mute astonishment in his friend's eyes, he rushed on hurriedly. "Just for a little while, I mean. Until we get used to—to all these changes."

Old Hunter still said nothing, only watched him a little sadly.

Not sure whether to take his silence as encouragement or not, Lucky rushed on. "I know we're both Lone Dogs at heart. I *know* that, and we belong on our own, in ordinary times. But everything's so strange and dangerous. The Big Growl has changed so much. Maybe it would be good to watch each other's backs for a little. We'd be a good team, you and I. . . ."

His voice trailed into silence. Old Hunter, too, stood up.

"I'm sorry, Lucky," he said gruffly. "It wouldn't do. It wouldn't feel . . . right. It's like I said: We can't let the Big Growl win. We can't let it change *us*."

"But—the light-power snake. Remember how it nearly stung you? If we're together, we can—"

His friend's eyes grew harder. "You probably saved my life, that's true. But we have to keep on surviving alone, like we always have. Understand? It's every dog for himself."

Lucky bowed his head in reluctant agreement, and gave Old Hunter a fond flick of his tongue. "I understand. But thank you again."

"Thank *you*. Here."

As he turned back, Old Hunter picked up a sizable chunk of meat in his jaws and dropped it at Lucky's feet. Lucky pawed it, surprised.

"Go on, take it. I won't miss it."

Lucky gave him a grateful whine as he seized the meat in his jaws. He threw Old Hunter a last look as he leaped up onto the counter, then bounded back through the broken mall.

CHAPTER SEVEN

It wasn't long before he slowed to a gentle jog, then halted altogether. He shifted the meat in his mouth slightly. A full belly had made him sleepy, and here, close to where he'd entered the mall, he was standing in front of a very tempting bed.

This huge inner House held far bigger longpaw things than the others, including a low, broad, squishy longpaw seat made of that same aged skin as the treasure-pouches. Lucky gazed at it with longing, and took a few paces toward it. He was so tired. He could rest, then eat when he woke, then move on again. . . .

A pungent earthy musk assaulted his nostrils, overwhelming the enticing smell of his prospective bed.

Oh no . . .

There were animals around; he'd known that. Animal scavengers and longpaws, too. But he hadn't taken much notice when he'd cared only about finding food, when he'd had nothing they could take from him.

Now he did.

Lucky tightened his grip on the chunk of flesh, growling softly. There was a high stack of wooden shelves behind the seat, and he sensed something hidden there. A sharp black nose twitched, followed by mean predatory eyes and huge pricked ears. Lucky's growl became louder, more threatening, as the gray fox eyed him.

Then, around the shelving, three more of them padded, thin and vicious-looking. They exchanged glances.

Their Alpha's yellow eyes glinted, and they stalked forward with arrogant snarls.

"Meat, dog. Give us *now!*"

Still gripping the hunk, snarling deep in his throat, Lucky sized up his enemy. Each fox was maybe half his size, but there were four of them and their eyes were sharp. A desperate fox was a dangerous creature—especially one in a Pack. As he watched them, all four crept forward, showing their fangs.

They were confident, he realized, and clever—dividing themselves into pairs on either flank. A cold knot of fear formed in his stomach. They were going to attack from two directions, and Lucky knew he stood little chance of fighting them off. He could drop the meat. Drop the meat, and run—

No!

He couldn't lose this food. He had no idea when he'd find more—and besides, they were *foxes*! He was a dog, and a tough Lone Dog at that—no scrawny fox was going to take what was his.

His eyes darted from side to side as he watched the foxes maneuver, slinking under small tables and edging around obstacles. They were forming a circle now, closing in, and Lucky felt a prickle of terror at his raised hackles.

"Silly dog, stupid dog," hissed the Alpha, its voice thick and distorted.

Another joined in. "No friends! No help! Ha!"

"Wish you stayed with *big* dog, *scary* dog," smirked a third. "Silly dog!"

He'd eaten, he reminded himself, and would have more stamina than these desperate creatures. What was more, hadn't he escaped the Big Growl? Hadn't he already dodged raccoons and sharpclaws and an angry Fierce Dog?

I can get out of this!

Lucky focused on the Alpha before him. Curling back his lips around the meat, he glared and growled. The other animal gave him a cocky grin.

Without warning, Lucky charged forward, straight into the

Alpha. The fox gave an astonished yelp as he knocked it flying into a broken longpaw sitting-box. Lucky kicked his back paws into its belly, and it gave a yelp of pain, winded. Lucky didn't waste a moment. He fled, bolting through the mall as fast as he could.

Lucky heard the leader scramble back to its feet, recovering fast. The rest were already screeching at his heels, snarling and squealing with rage and frustration. Lucky was fast, but desperate hunger was giving them an edge, and he was hampered by the meat in his jaws, hardly able to draw breath. He nipped between pillars and raced through the open area where longpaws used to sit and eat, crashing over tables and sitting-boxes. He skidded through water that leaked from a place he couldn't see, but the foxes wouldn't be shaken.

A rack of longpaw furs went flying; then Lucky was back on the metal hill and fleeing down, his claws scrabbling wildly as he tried not to fall head over hindpaws. At the bottom of the metal hill another big sitting-box loomed, and he leaped.

No! Midleap, the chunk of meat slipped from his panting jaws. He caught sight of it slithering beneath a broad wooden table with a loose blue fur hanging over it.

Lucky doubled back and skidded after it, the soft blue fur falling back to conceal him.

His flanks heaving, Lucky pricked his ears and panted as silently as he could. He could smell the foxes, sharp and earthy and coming closer. If they heard him, or smelled him—and he knew his panic and fear must be strong-scented—he was as good as dead.

He heard a low snarling and snuffling as they searched the air with sharp noses. They muttered to themselves and one another. Some of it was incomprehensible; some of it all too clear.

"Dog close," growled one. It spat the word *dog* with disgust in its rasping high fox-voice.

"*Meat* close," said another, and there was huffing, hungry fox-laughter.

Lucky wrinkled his muzzle. To think these scrawny scavengers were his cousin-kind!

He knew he didn't have long before they found him. Fear rippled down his spine, raising his fur. He had to force himself not to whine in terror. There was a fox at each side of the table.

"Noise! There!" yipped one suddenly. "Go see! Is dog?"

Heart thundering, Lucky strained to hear the clicking paws as they moved slowly, so slowly, away from his table. Any second now, they'd realize the noise was a false alarm—a rat, or a bird—and then they'd be back. . . .

Seizing the meat, he bolted, heading straight for the center of the mall. They were squealing behind him once more, giving chase, but at least he'd escaped the trap of that table. Lucky pounded on, pain jabbing sharply at his wounded paw, his lungs aching, his whole body feeling heavy and awkward now. He felt the first wrench of despair in his gut. The foxes were going to get him.

Close to the entrance the displays of longpaw treasure seemed more cluttered. No longpaw thief or scavenging dog had bothered to take the brightly colored beads and bottles. A whole rack of them crashed to the ground as Lucky slammed sideways into it, then veered around another high counter and leaped over a broken shelf. At least all the clutter was holding up the foxes, too; he could hear them stumbling and skidding behind him.

A rack of small bottles went tumbling and shattering, sending sickeningly powerful scents to assault his nose. *High ground,* he thought. *I should find high ground.* Somewhere to make a stand, somewhere to stay safe . . .

There. Lucky bounded toward a tall counter, scattering paper and strange metal machines, the biggest of which fell to the floor. It exploded open, paper and small metal discs scattering everywhere, and Lucky nearly followed it, sliding helplessly on the smooth surface. Scrabbling, he managed to halt on the countertop at last and spring to his feet.

Panting hard, he stared down at the circling, grinning foxes.

"Can't stay up," came a menacing growl. "No, can't, silly dog. Not forever."

"Must come down!" said another.

"Soon, boys. Soon." The hissing snarl was confident enough to send a thrill of fear through Lucky's shivering flanks.

They were right, he realized. He *couldn't* stay up here forever. He could take another flying leap, of course, over their heads and away, but the terrible pain in his paw had finally overcome the thrill of the chase. The stabbing of the wound was a pure white agony that almost made him dizzy.

Lucky's flanks rose and fell swiftly with his desperate breath. Had this really been worth it, for one chunk of meat?

The answer came straight from his wild instinct: a fury that raced through him, humming in his limbs and flanks, his muscles preparing for a last fight. *Of course it was worth it.*

He was bigger and better than these foxes. Submit to these creatures, and he was unworthy of being a dog.

Besides, in the new world after the Big Growl, it wasn't cowards who would survive. It was the brave, and the strong, and the determined. And he *would not* give up his rightful prey!

He laid the meat between his forepaws, prepared to guard it to the death—just as Old Hunter would. Lowering his head, raising his hackles high, and baring his teeth in a lethal snarl, he summoned all his energy for one last wild bark of rage and defiance.

And then he hesitated.

The strange noise seemed to come from nowhere. It certainly didn't come from him or the foxes. And yet it was there, swelling to fill the echoing hall.

A low, menacing growl.

Suddenly nervous, the foxes twitched their heads from side to side, ears pricked. In an instant, all four had sprung around to face the shattered entrance.

Scarcely able to believe what he was seeing, Lucky stared over the foxes at the group that was approaching. Dogs—more dogs!

A little crossbreed, short-legged and hairy-faced, her pink tongue poking out in excitement. A sleek black-and-white Farm-Work Dog, clutching a huge leather item in his mouth. A Fight Dog, with a long snout and a bushy coat, whose eyes were full of hectic fear. A small thing, with long white hair. And a giant, furry black dog with a broad head and determined eyes.

They barely gave Lucky a glance, all their nervous attention focused on the foxes. They were such a strange Pack. Then the last dog entered. She was handsome and long-legged, with golden-and-white fur. In fact, she reminded Lucky of his own reflection, before the city's clear-stone shattered. And her scent . . .

But there was no time to wonder anymore. The newcomers were facing up to the foxes, which formed a ragged line and snarled back in insolent defiance.

"A gang—very scary!" The smallest fox sneered at the lineup.

The Alpha laughed, a cackling yelp of derision. "Scary? You *think*?"

Lucky felt his shoulders start to droop. He'd been glad to see more dogs approaching, but now that he'd had a closer look . . . maybe the foxes were right to laugh. At least they had some sort of battle formation. The new arrivals looked more like puppies let loose without a Mother-Dog. The little crossbreed seemed brave for her size, but she appeared incapable of doing anything other than run in excited circles. The long-haired pretty one was yapping hysterically. The bushy Fight Dog was working hard to attack the foxes, but the big black giant was getting hopelessly in the way.

It was the dog who looked like Lucky, the handsome-faced golden dog, who kept her nerve, charging straight for the foxes. Behind her raced the Fight Dog, dodging the black giant at last, and the Farm-Work Dog, who at least had dropped his piece of padded leather.

The skirmish was brief and vicious. Teeth snapped and claws raked; from his position Lucky saw the Fight Dog grab for a fox's leg and almost instantly lose it—but not before he'd drawn blood, and the fox had yipped in shock and pain. The leader-fox sprang at the black-and-white Farm-Work Dog, jaws slavering, but the golden dog spun with surprising agility and raked its scabby gray flank with her teeth, knocking it off balance. Even the pretty little longhair was standing her ground, barking furiously, though she flinched at an attack; the big black dog pounced to protect her flank, sending a fox tumbling across the slick floor. A paw lashed out, drawing blood from a fox's muzzle, and its head snapped sideways, trailing a sliver of drool.

The foxes had a wiry ferocity, and they were willing to fight, but they were too smart to stand up for long to a Pack of dogs, however chaotic. When it became clear they were outnumbered and outsized, the leader-fox gave a high and vicious bark.

"Go, boys! No point!"

With a final vicious snap and snarl, the last fox turned tail and bolted after its escaping companions.

"Brave in a Pack!" it sniggered, making a mocking face at Lucky as it scampered away. "Coward dogs!"

As they vanished into the chaos of the mall, Lucky breathed easily for the first time since he'd left Old Hunter. Thrashing his tail in wild gratitude, he gave the newcomers a brief, friendly bark.

"Thanks. You saved my hide!"

Panting, they all turned to look up at him in renewed anxiety, as if they'd only just remembered he was there. The Fight Dog took a couple of paces toward him and sniffed. Although his body was big and burly, his stance was nervous.

"You're welcome," he rumbled gruffly. "Foxes indeed. Ha!"

"I thought I was done for." The flood of relief made Lucky almost weak with gratitude to this motley Pack.

"Happy to help!" yipped the crossbreed, almost falling over her own feet as she spun.

The dog that looked like Lucky said nothing at first. She leaped up onto the counter, and though Lucky moved instinctively to protect his food, she ignored the meat altogether. Instead, she sniffed hesitantly at him. Their eyes met, and Lucky's heart leaped inside his chest.

Something in his gut tugged at him, stirring sense-memories, sparking images in his head. He knew this dog. . . .

She blinked her dark, friendly eyes, and nuzzled his face.

"It's really you!" she barked softly. "Dear Yap, it's *you*! Hello, my brother!"

CHAPTER EIGHT

Yap...!

A pang of memory twisted inside Lucky, and the heavy stone-feeling of loneliness in his belly lifted just a little. *Yap!* How long had it been since he'd heard his Pup name? And hers came back to him in a tumble of sounds and images. A snuffling nose, an insistent squeaking, a body nestled close to his, tiny paws shoving him, golden skin and fur pressed cozily against his own ... and yes, again and always, that constant talkative squealing. . . .

"Squeak! It's you!" Overcome by happiness, he licked at her face, and she crouched playfully on her forepaws to nibble at his throat.

"I'm not Squeak anymore," she yipped. "I have a new name. Bella!"

"Bella," Lucky repeated, getting used to the sound. "That's beautiful," he decided.

There was a snorting yelp from the pretty white dog, and a *shut up!* growl as the crossbreed beside her nipped her nose. Lucky realized the whole motley Pack was sitting there, ogling him and his newfound litter-sister. They looked both fascinated and expectant, though the Fight Dog had a defensive expression. They might be an odd assortment of dogs, but they all looked very fine in their own way. Their fur was sleek, their bellies round, their muzzles free of fleabites and scratches, except for the few scrapes the foxes had managed to inflict before they ran. Poised on three legs, one forepaw delicately raised, the pretty dog might have had her long glossy hair brushed by a longpaw just that sunup.

Despite her pert confidence, though, she seemed a little ashamed of her outburst, and Bella was giving her a stern glance of disapproval. "It's what my name *means*, Sunshine. Bella means *beautiful*."

Lucky nudged Bella's muzzle with his own, as much to calm her down as to show affection. "I have a new name, too," he told her. "I'm Lucky."

She washed his ear with her tongue. "The name fits! You're certainly lucky we came along just now!'"

"You're right about that." Lucky stepped back and studied Bella's friends. "Hello," he said.

Sunshine seemed too intimidated to reply, and quite off-balance with her paw in the air. The Fight Dog grunted some inaudible answer, but he was standing up on his hindpaws and sniffing hungrily at the meat Lucky had left on the counter.

"Oh, Bruno." Bella gave him a playful growl and a nudge with her muzzle. "You're always hungry. Even at the end of the world, you're thinking of food."

Don't all dogs think of food and how to get it? The end of the world wasn't a joke—it was real, he thought, remembering the terror of the Big Growl, the horrible endless depths of the crevice in the road. Getting and keeping food wasn't a *joke.* He knew that. But perhaps these sleek, well-fed dogs didn't.

As if to prove him right, Sunshine flopped onto her plump belly, her white coat spreading on the ground. She gave a whine. "I wish you wouldn't say those things, Bella. We don't *know* the world's ended."

Bella's answering whine held a touch of irritation, though she licked reassuringly at the black button nose. "If the world hasn't ended, Sunshine, where do you suppose our longpaws are?"

Lucky stiffened. *Our* longpaws? In disbelief he studied each dog, all so very different, except for one thing. Every single one of them wore the ownership sign of the longpaws.

Horrified, he couldn't help exclaiming out loud.

"You're *Leashed Dogs!*"

They all stared at him, and then at one another, bemused.

"Yes?" said the Farm Dog, cocking his head curiously.

"It—well, that explains—I mean, the way you all—" Lucky fell silent, his mind a turmoil. *Leashed Dogs. Pampered* dogs. Tame, silly, *pointless* dogs . . .

They'd let longpaws buckle collars around their necks. They relied on longpaws for food, for fun, for exercise, for a place to sleep. Without their longpaws they were helpless, hopeless. . . . The horror of it was beyond belief. How were *Leashed Dogs* supposed to survive the end of the world?

Lucky shook himself free of the shivers in his fur. He couldn't think about it just now. Besides, what did it matter at this moment, when they'd come to his rescue with such good timing?

Lucky glanced back at Bruno, still snuffling at the meat with his muzzle. "Come on. Let's share this." He leaped up onto the counter and grabbed it in his jaws, then jumped back down and dropped it. "You saved me *and* this meat. I owe you a share. It's the least I can do."

And it's all you'll get if you can't hunt by yourselves. . . .

For a while there was only the contented sound of tearing

and chewing as the odd little Pack shared Lucky's spoils. Wolfing down his own portion, Lucky murmured to Bella, "Your friends are . . . interesting."

Bella lifted her head and gazed at them fondly. "They're not like us at all, are they? I used to think all dogs were sheltie-retrievers!"

Lucky blinked. "Is that what we are?"

"Yes. Don't you remember our sire and Mother-Dog?" Her expression was filled with conflicted emotion—relief, deep happiness, regret at their long separation—but there was amusement in her voice, too. "Most of us have proper kind-names, names the longpaws gave to all of us."

Lucky grunted disapprovingly. "Things aren't *proper* just because the longpaws invented them."

Bella ignored that. "Now, Bruno there, his Mother-Dog was a German Shepherd. And Mickey's what the longpaws call a 'Border Collie.' He's very smart, likes to herd us! Daisy's sire and Mother-Dog were a 'Westie' and a 'Jack Russell.' Little Sunshine, there—she's a 'Maltese.' *Very* delicate," she added.

"And this one?" Lucky nodded at the biggest, black dog.

"Martha? She's a 'Newfoundland.' Look at the size of her next to Sunshine!"

Lucky eyed the pair. Martha was much taller than Lucky, and Sunshine didn't even reach up as far as her knee joint. The foxes had been right about one thing: This really was the most unorganized Pack he'd ever laid eyes on. Were they even a real Pack at all? Who was their Alpha? Bella talked a lot, and she was kind but brusque with Sunshine, but she didn't act like a Pack leader. She didn't have that air of unquestioned authority; she didn't expect to be obeyed at her first bark or nip, and even when she seemed decisive, she looked to the others for approval or advice. The collie-dog, Mickey, seemed intelligent, and Bruno looked like he could handle himself in a fight, but neither of them had played the Alpha with the foxes. Sunshine—certainly not! And Daisy seemed brave, and scrappy, and feisty, but she was barely out of puppyhood, no Alpha dog, either. . . .

Who was in *charge* of this Pack?

Lucky's bewildered thoughts were interrupted by a high panicked howl. Sunshine had leaped up, abandoning her last delicate morsel of meat, and was running in tight circles, long hair floating, claws skittering in panic.

"I'm hurt! I'm hurt!"

"What—" began Bella.

"The foxes! *I got bitten!*" Sunshine's yelping was becoming hysterical, and she lifted one paw pathetically off the ground. It was the forepaw she'd been favoring since the fight, and now Lucky realized there was a reason—one she'd only just discovered herself. Waving her paw in the air, flapping it as though she was still trying to run, Sunshine instantly fell over. She got up on three paws, still panicking, and flew in circles again.

"My longpaw! I need my longpaw *now*! *I need to go to the vet!*"

Lucky saw that Bella looked anxious, her eyes wide. He was taken aback by a sudden scornful disdain. No, his sister *really* wasn't an Alpha dog.

But the others were no better. Mickey had sprung to his feet, staring. Daisy was yapping wildly in sympathy, and suddenly the others joined in.

"We'll go back to the longpaw houses!"

"No, we can find a vet! Find a vet!"

"Where? Where will we find a vet? They're ALL GONE!"

"The *longpaws* are all gone! What will we *do*?"

Snapping out of his disbelief, Lucky jumped to his feet and gave a single angry bark.

"Calm *down*!"

Falling silent, they stared at him. He thought back to the longpaw he'd seen with the vivid yellow coat. Should he tell the dogs about his encounter? But that longpaw had been so . . . strange. No, it would only confuse matters—make them think there was a longpaw around to help.

He stood straighter. "I don't know what a *vet* is, but I'm sure Sunshine doesn't need one. Let me see."

Tentatively, her flanks quivering, Sunshine crept forward and shyly offered him her paw. Lucky sniffed at it. There was a smear of blood, sure enough, but it was no more than a tiny tear in the skin. He touched it delicately with his tongue.

"Here, it's just a scratch. That's all. I'll show you." Lying down, Lucky stretched out his own wounded paw, turning the pad up for their examination, and there was a collective gasp of horror.

"That's terrible!" squeaked Sunshine. "You need a vet more than I do!"

"No I don't," said Lucky in exasperation. "It's only bad because I haven't stopped long enough to tend to it. Look." He licked carefully at the wound. Sure enough, it felt better already. *Maybe if I had given it more attention before, I would have had an easier time getting away from those foxes,* he thought. He licked at it again. "Come on, Sunshine. Try it."

Obediently Sunshine bent her head and licked rather dubiously at the scratch on her own paw. When nothing terrible happened, she tried again, and was soon washing it quite pains-takingly.

"You're right," she whispered in awe. "It doesn't sting as badly. It *does* feel better." She stopped licking to gaze admiringly at Lucky. "He's right, everybody!"

"You see?" he barked. "You don't need a silly longpaw vet!"

They were all staring at him in respectful silence. He met their eyes, feeling a ripple of unease in his fur.

"That's wonderful," murmured Martha, lowering her big black head and tilting it to study Sunshine's paw.

"Fine job. Fine job!" growled Bruno. "Splendid!"

"You're so *clever*!" exclaimed little Daisy. "I can't believe you knew that!"

Mickey said nothing, but he looked profoundly impressed. Even Bella was gazing from him to Sunshine and back again, with delight. Six tails wagged and thumped.

Oh no you don't! thought Lucky. *I'm not your Alpha!*

Hastily he rose again, and backed off a step. "Listen, I—I'm really grateful you helped me out there. You were the best!" He retreated another couple of paces, his hackles rising. "But I've got to go. Thank you, again. And good luck!"

Before any of them could react, he had turned and was trotting

97

as fast as he could out of the mall. He could feel their stunned gazes, could almost sense those drooping tails and ears, but he wouldn't look back. Would *not* look back—

Lucky came to a halt. Outside, the sky had turned a dark charcoal gray, heavy with water. Even as he hesitantly lifted a paw to leave the mall, brilliant light lit the street for a fraction of an instant, and then a colossal bang shook the world.

Lucky froze.

Lightning!

In a second there would be battering water, falling in torrents from the sky. The shattering crash of a terrible war in the clouds, where Sky-Dogs fought to the death over and over again, and Lightning the swift dog hero teased Earth-Dog by tearing through the sky leaving fire in his wake. There was very little that frightened Lucky, but he hated to be outside when the sky burst its clouds. . . .

He'd hesitated too long, and he could feel Bella's warmth, her flanks close against his. She didn't look at him, but watched the warring black skies, too.

"Stay with us, Lucky," she said at last. "Just for a while?"

For a long moment he couldn't answer. He thought about the loneliness he'd felt when he woke this sunup, and the empty realization that Sweet was no longer there. He remembered the warmth and tumble of the Pup Pack, the smell of Squeak cuddling up beside him as they slept. And now Squeak was Bella, and she was beside him again, different but the same. . . .

"Okay," he said at last, slowly. "Just for a little while, though."

She gave a loud bark of delight, and suddenly she was down on her forepaws, then leaping up, tumbling into him. Unexpected joy fizzed through Lucky's body and he rolled with her, jumping up and spinning in a circle, then letting her chase him back toward the little Pack.

The others looked thrilled. Daisy darted forward, yapping and colliding with Bella, and solid old Bruno knocked the little dog playfully sideways so that she and Sunshine fell in a heap. Then they were all chasing and barking and play-fighting, as if they didn't have a care in the world.

An empty longpaw mall was the best place in the world for a game, Lucky decided as he dodged Martha's lumbering pounce. Mickey dropped his precious leather item to grab a fallen longpaw fur, shaking it like a rat, and then Bruno had seized it, too, and the two dogs were rolling around in a chaotic tug-of-war.

Lucky watched happily until he felt Bella cannon into him and the littermates wrestled in a squirming heap.

"Are you all right?" panted Bella breathlessly.

"Of course! Come on!" Lucky sprang for her again.

Even Sunshine joined in, yelping wildly and spinning, trying hopelessly to jump on Martha and knock her over. Chasing Mickey in circles, Lucky spotted piles of the metal pots the Food House longpaw cooked with. He'd always liked the noise of those! Lucky plunged into the middle of the stacks, and the pots went flying with a most satisfying, deafening racket.

At last, exhausted, the dogs lay down panting one by one. Sunshine had found a pile of silk cushions; Mickey lay contentedly beside her. Lucky stretched out on the cold, hard floor, watching them all. As Daisy flopped beside him, he gave her ear an affectionate lick.

"Lucky, come up here!" Bella's head hung over the edge of a longpaw seat, her ears pricked.

Uncertainly he rose and put first one paw, then the other, against its soft cowhide body. He sprang onto it and curled up beside Bella, who gave a happy little whine and licked his nose.

Lucky closed his eyes, tilting his head up to wish for a good sleep. *Moon-Dog, watch over us. . . .*

"What are you doing?" Bella's surprised voice broke into his reverie.

"What am I—?" Lucky paused, dumbfounded. "I'm getting ready to sleep. . . ."

"You *are* ready to sleep." She stared at him as he turned three times.

Lucky stopped turning and cocked his head at her curiously. Didn't Bella prepare for rest properly? He lowered his head, sniffing dubiously at the longpaw seat, then met her eyes.

"Stop fidgeting, Lucky," she said softly.

"I can't help it." He shifted position, trying to settle. "This is just too comfy. . . ."

"No such thing." She yawned. "You'll get used to it quickly, believe me!"

Lucky thought about that for a few moments. "You must have been happy with your longpaws," he said softly.

"I was. . . ."

"Where are they now? What happened, Bella?"

"Oh." She laid her head on her forepaws, lifting her ears as if hearing something in her memory. She sighed. "It was such a rush, when the Big Growl came. Such a terrible panic. They left in a great hurry. Piled all their possessions into their loudcage, and drove away. All their possessions," she murmured sadly, "except me."

Well, what did she expect? They were longpaws, weren't they? She shouldn't have relied on them, shouldn't have built her happiness on a Leashed life . . . but Lucky nuzzled his sister's head and licked at her ear. "I'm sorry, Bella."

"That's all right, Lucky. I don't miss them. Not much, anyway. I can't be that sad—they left me behind, after all. *They* abandoned *me.*" There was bitterness in her voice, but she shook herself.

Now you're beginning to understand, thought Lucky. He was sorry she'd been hurt, but the sooner she hardened herself against her old life, the happier she'd be. There was hope for her.

"Besides," she went on, "I have other things to think about. My friends, for a start. They need someone to take charge. I don't have time to mope."

"Good for you," said Lucky, glad his litter-sister was so practical and unsentimental. Just like him, in fact. She'd make a good Free Dog. . . .

"But what happened to you, Lucky?"

"What do you mean?"

"After the Pup Pack."

"Oh . . ." Lucky closed his eyes. What was the point in dragging up those memories? They weren't happy ones. Still, Bella was his sister. He could tell her. If he could recall it . . .

The memories were hazy and half-blurred, like looking into a pond for small prey that kept dodging out of view. But slowly, haltingly, they began to take shape.

"I remember them taking me . . . the longpaws. They smiled, looked happy . . . oh! I didn't wriggle." He raised the muscles above his eyes, surprised. "I didn't try to get free. That's so strange. Why didn't I run away?"

"We didn't," said Bella. "Not then. Not as pups. Go on."

"I remember the longpaws' house." Beyond the broken clearstone at the mall entrance, lightning lit the world for an instant, followed by the crash and thunder as the Sky-Dog battle resumed. The dreadful sound echoed the unhappiness of Lucky's memories, and a shudder ran through his flanks. "The longpaws didn't smile so much, there, in their home. There were small longpaws, like pups. They never left me alone. Chasing me, picking me up, teasing me. I remember being so tired, just wanting to be left alone . . ."

"Longpaw pups are like that," Bella said, nodding. "But they're not so bad once they get used to you."

"No, but the big longpaw was. He was strange. Sometimes he toppled over, like an old tree, and he smelled so wrong. Like the longpaw fire-juice, but stale. When he smelled very badly of it, he couldn't stay on his legs. And he would get so angry. I remember . . ." Lucky closed his eyes more tightly, not liking the effort of recollection. "I remember his paws more than anything. Kicking out at me. Sometimes getting me. He shouted and kicked and was always angry, even when he didn't smell of that fire-juice."

Bella nuzzled him. "Your longpaws don't sound like mine at all."

"Some longpaws are good, that's true." Lucky thought of the Food House longpaw with a twinge of sadness. "But not this one. All I wanted to do was get away from him. He scared me. One day the door was open—by mistake, I think—and I made a run for it. I ran and ran and . . ."

"And?"

"And I never went back." He sighed, relieved the story was over. "Things have been good for me ever since then. I've been happy on my own, and I've learned to take care of myself. I don't have to be scared of anyone anymore, and I never will be, ever again."

Bella nestled closer against him.

"Do you remember the stories Mother used to tell us when we were pups?" she asked.

"Of course," said Lucky, thinking of the flash of lightning he'd just seen.

"I'm thinking about the story of Omega Wind and the Forest-Dog. Do you remember it?"

Lucky frowned. "Not completely," he said. He licked his litter-sister's ear affectionately. "How did it go?"

"Well, there was once a little dog called Wind who was the least important dog in her Pack. They called her Omega and made her fetch and carry for them and do everything they said. The Alpha of the Pack was a cruel Fierce Dog who always bit Wind whenever she was too slow in carrying out his orders.

"But Wind dreamed of leaving the Pack and being free from all her duties, and she used to sneak into the forest and hunt small creatures by herself. Omega dogs were forbidden to hunt, so she always ate half of her prey and left the rest as a tribute to Forest-Dog.

"Then the Storm of Dogs arrived, and the world turned upside down. Wind's Pack was one of the first to be attacked by the giant dogs who came down from the mountains. Wind ran away into the forest, with one of the giant dogs on her heels, and she thought she would be caught and torn to shreds.

"But Forest-Dog had been watching Wind since she started to leave him her tribute, and he loved her because she was cunning and she wouldn't give up, just like the Sky-Dogs loved Lightning for his speed. So Forest-Dog helped her to climb into a tree so that the giant dogs couldn't find her, and she was saved from the Storm of Dogs.

"From that day on, Wind was a Lone Dog, going wherever she pleased and never obeying any Alpha dog's command again. You'll never see her, but sometimes when you're in the deep forest you can hear her, howling in the trees with her friend the Forest-Dog."

Bella nuzzled Lucky. "You remind me of that story," she said. "You escaped, and it made you a strong, free Lone Dog. I'm just sorry your longpaw Alpha was so cruel."

Lucky laid his head down beside Bella's. Of course he didn't need the sympathy she was offering him, but just lying next to her again, after all this time, felt reassuring. The fear and the loneliness of this sunup seemed very distant with his litter-sister here. Huddled against her warm side, listening to her tell one of their Mother-Dog's stories, it was as if something unlocked in his mind. The happy times flooded back into his head as he thought of his days with the Pup Pack, that misty muddle of sensations: safety and affection and fullness in his belly. And companionship . . .

They had been good days. But that was a long time ago, Lucky reminded himself. The company of other little dogs was natural for a puppy—as natural as needing his Mother-Dog beside him, looking after him and loving him. But he wasn't a puppy anymore. He was a grown dog, a Lone Dog.

Lucky didn't think he'd ever be able to sleep on this too-comfortable longpaw seat, and he lay for a while listening to the snores of Bruno, the small dream-whimpers of Sunshine and Daisy, the low, soft breathing of Bella beside him. All the same he must have dozed off, because the next thing he was aware of was shafts of late sunlight reaching into the broken mall, making the other dogs stir and stretch and whine.

The roar and clash of the Sky-Dog battle in the sky had ceased altogether, and water no longer battered down. From outside came the beautiful scent of a fresh new day, washed clean by the cloudwater. Bella raised her head as Lucky got to his feet and stretched his forepaws.

"The Sky-Dogs have destroyed the clouds," he mused. "That's good."

"It's *very* good," cried Daisy. "Time to go home!"

"Yes!" yipped Sunshine. "Come on, then. Let's go!"

"Wait a minute." Lucky looked at them all, perplexed. "Home? Where's home?"

"Where we come from, of course!" Bella licked his face.

"Come with us!" Sunshine jumped up against his flanks, panting with adoration.

"Our longpaws are gone," said Martha mournfully. "But our homes are still there."

Bruno nodded sagely. "They're quite right, Lucky. Shame to be on your own. You're tough, I dare say, but even you probably need someone to watch your back now and then." The dog flexed his muscles and leaned forward on his long, strong forelegs. "Bit of a fighter myself, you know? Handy in a tight corner. How about it, hm?"

In their varying ways they all had that pleading look. Bruno was trying not to appear too eager, but he wasn't hiding it well. Mickey, his precious belonging still in his jaws, was gazing at him with beseeching eyes, as was Martha. As for the two littler dogs, they were jumping up and down at him till Lucky felt like swatting them with a paw.

He sighed, and glanced at Bella. She, too, was looking at him with a combination of kindness and fervent hope, and he remembered how good it had felt, waking up at her side.

Old Hunter was right—the Big Growl didn't have to change them—but perhaps Lone Dogs could make temporary concessions in a strange new world. There would be no longpaws in this "home" they talked about, but there might be a few comforts. The decision was simple, when he thought of it like that.

"Yes, all right," he said. "I'll come with you. For now!"

Bella yipped, dancing with delight, and the others gave in to a volley of happy barks, Daisy spinning on her hindpaws till she fell over. Lucky watched them, flattered that he was the source of such excitement.

Lucky still wasn't a Pack-dog, and he never would be. But who in their right mind would call *this* a proper Pack?

CHAPTER NINE

"Oh, we were friends long before the Big Growl," explained Bruno as he muscled his way to Lucky's side. "Isn't that right, everyone?"

They'd left the mall far behind now, and Lucky was conscious that the territory was growing far less familiar. He'd usually haunted the bustling parts of the city where scraps were plentiful—as were hiding places. Now the views were opening up, and the streets grew broader and leafier. Remembering the longpaw's firebox yesterday, and the Fierce Dog who'd guarded it, Lucky's senses bristled with alertness.

The shadows were lengthening again, and the ruins of high buildings were haloed in brilliant light. Fountains of water still gushed from broken pipes, the droplets glittering prettily, and around him Lucky recognized the kind of once-neat houses where longpaws lived and slept. Uneasily, he wondered when those long-paws would return—and whether they ever would. Surely they'd come back for their lost companions? He knew longpaws didn't like to leave their friends to dissolve naturally into the earth, that they liked to bury them as if they were preserving precious bones. So why hadn't they returned yet?

But Lucky didn't have time to brood and wonder. The other dogs chatted constantly, vying for his attention, and once or twice he almost tripped over little Daisy as she scuttled in front of him.

"That's right!" she exclaimed now, and Lucky shortened his steps to avoid standing on her. "We've been friends for ages. We all live on the same street."

"And play in the same dog parks!" added Mickey. "Do you think the sandpit's still there, Bella?"

"I don't see what harm could come to the sandpit," observed Martha. "One day our longpaws will be back, and we'll all go there again. Maybe Lucky could come, too!" She gave him a hopeful glance.

A *sandpit*? Lucky tried not to let his muzzle curl. Perhaps these dogs had never grown out of their Pup Pack days. He ignored Martha's expectant eyes for the moment. "So you're ... friends. And so are your"—he hesitated, confused by the unfamiliar notion—"so are your longpaws. But, it's not like—well, it's not *exactly* like being in a Pack, is it?"

"No!" Sunshine shuddered. "Not like a *wild* Pack."

"Although it *was* a sort of a Pack," mused Bella. "We played together, and sometimes ate together, and we all knew one another."

There's more to being in a Pack than that, thought Lucky.

"And our longpaws—they were in a kind of Pack of their own," added Mickey. "They were always together, too. That's why it was so much fun." His eyes grew wistful.

"It'll be fun again, just you wait!" yelped Sunshine. "My long-paw will be back for me, I know she will. She'll come back for the Frisbee-throw—she *always* took that with her—and she'll come back for me."

Lucky caught Bella's eye. He didn't want to say anything to spoil Sunshine's moment of optimistic joy, and he was relieved that Bella, too, said nothing. But his litter-sister's eyes were sad, and her ears drooped a little. She at least was beginning to under-stand how much had changed. If only they'd *all* listen to what the Earth-Dog was telling them. If only they knew how to tune their senses into the world. Perhaps that instinct was lost to them?

He nuzzled Bella's face, sure that no one else would have noticed her fleeting expression of foreboding. After all, the dogs were all licking one another's faces now, cheerfully wishing one another farewell and happy dreams. . . .

What? Lucky stared around at them as they bid him good night and set off in different directions, each dog trotting happily into a different longpaw house. What in the name of the Sky-Dogs were they doing? They knew nothing of Pack rules—like staying together, like obeying the Alpha, like watching one another's backs. . . . Lucky had never felt like such an expert on Pack life before.

And it wasn't only the splitting of the Pack that worried him. Here on this street the longpaw homes were still standing, but only just. Some of the walls had vicious wounds where the Big Growl had snapped at them. Many of the windows were broken, and water escaped beneath doors, collecting into a growing pool in the middle of the road. There was a smell of longpaw waste, too, from beneath the ground, but the strongest scent in Lucky's nostrils was the scent of danger.

"Are you sure you should sleep here?" Lucky paused behind Bella, bringing her to a quizzical halt.

"What? Oh, it's safe now, Lucky. Don't worry. The Big Growl's faded away."

"It could come back," he reminded her. "Some of these longpaw homes are damaged. Look at that wall—it's leaning. And those things wriggling out of the wall like snakes—don't you feel the invisible power? Can't you hear it singing?" He shivered, remembering how close Old Hunter had come to being struck down. Lucky didn't want to have to rescue anyone else from the brutal force. "There's still danger here, Bella. And who knows if the Big Growl will leave us alone?"

"Oh, Lucky." Bella licked his face affectionately. "No wonder you're nervous, after what happened in the Trap House. But these are our *homes*. Real, proper longpaw houses."

"I don't know." His hackles were still bristling. "I think we should sleep outside. And why are you all going into different houses? I may not know much about Packs, but isn't the whole point that you stay together? Then you keep one another warm at night, and protect one another."

Bella glanced back at the others, confused. "But, Lucky, these are our homes. We have to be here when our longpaws come back. Don't you see how important that is?"

No, thought Lucky. *No, I really don't.* But he couldn't say so to Bella—and besides, there was a determined gleam in her eye that he couldn't help respecting. He knew he'd end up helping her, going with her into the longpaw house. It was the least he could do for his litter-sister.

When he padded inside, Lucky could understand Bella's reluctance to stay outside. It was true that some of the longpaws' belongings had been tipped over and smashed, and there were ominous wounds in the walls, running from floor to ceiling. But mostly the rooms were dry, and there was no doubt it was a comfortable place to be.

For a Leashed Dog, he reminded himself.

As he padded around, Lucky was surprised to see how big and sprawling the longpaw house was—nothing like a cage. He felt almost free as he explored the rooms. His claws clicked on the hard floor of the food area as he nosed around the cupboards. There was a distinct, though faint, smell of food—raw meat, soft cheese, and stale bread—but frustratingly, though he pawed at the cold-box door, it refused to open for him. Scenting Bella behind him, he turned to see her standing sheepishly in the doorway, head lowered.

"I couldn't get into the cold-box, either. And there were bits of food around the longpaw house, but I ate them. I should have left some, I know, but I was so hungry."

"Don't worry." It was true, she *should* have thought ahead; she should have avoided bolting everything down the first day—but Lucky reminded himself yet again that Bella didn't know any better. She was a Leashed Dog. Once again, he found himself grateful that he'd learned to survive and look after himself. He wondered what would become of dogs like Bella in this new and hostile world.

"But it *was* stupid," she went on, ears drooping. "I should know better, Lucky. I *do* understand, even if some of the others don't."

"They have a lot to learn," he remarked.

"Please don't think too badly of them, Lucky." She gave him a beseeching gaze. "It's all they know—being carefree, never having to worry. I've never had to worry about my next meal, either, but I do understand that's not how it is for every dog. I know things are different now." She turned and slunk out of the kitchen.

Unsettled, Lucky sat down and gave his ear a comforting scratch with a hindpaw. When he felt better he spent a few more moments sniffing and scratching at cupboard doors. He had another go at the cold-box, raking at it with his paws and tugging with his teeth until it felt as though they'd tear from his jaws, but it refused to open for him. He was wasting his time and energy. *I might as well make myself comfortable until tomorrow,* he thought, going in search of his litter-sister once more.

He didn't have far to look. Bella was just in the next room, which was furnished with tables and lamps and a longpaw picture box—though the hum of invisible power was absent. There was one of the large, soft longpaw seats that he'd made himself comfortable on before. But his litter-sister was crouched in a corner, sniffing mournfully at a small pile of longpaw things between her paws.

Lucky padded across to her. She barely stirred, only snuffled and whimpered at the scent on a burst cushion. There was a longpaw fur, too, crumpled and smelling of sweat, and a leather leash like the ones he'd seen attached to Leashed Dogs. The very sight of it made him shiver with distaste, but Bella was nuzzling it longingly.

She must have been entirely wrapped up in the memories the scent-things stirred, because when he licked her ears sympathetically, she jolted and scrambled to her four paws, avoiding his gaze.

"I'm just tired," she said gruffly. "These things. They help me sleep. That's all."

Lucky said nothing. How could a few longpaw trinkets help a dog sleep? Perhaps the loss of the longpaws really was hard for her. If that was true, he had a notion she'd be too embarrassed ever to admit it.

"Come on," he said, touching her muzzle gently with his own.

"We have to get some sleep. Who knows what a new sunup will bring?"

It was obvious where she usually slept: Beside the pile of treasure, nestled in this cozy corner, was a squashy cushion covered in shed golden hair and smelling strongly of Bella. Lucky waited for his litter-sister to tread a languid circle on it, then settle, head on her paws. Only then, with a polite whine, did he turn his own three careful circles, and close his eyes with a silent wish to the Sky-Dogs. He snuggled down beside his litter-sister and rested his head on her back.

It was warm in this corner, and the cushion molded perfectly to their bodies, but Bella seemed unsettled, and her restlessness infected Lucky.

Lucky raised his head, opening his jaws a little to taste the air, and beside him Bella gave a soft whimper of unease. The atmosphere tasted familiar, somehow, and not in a good way. He recognized it, suddenly and horribly, as the way the air had tasted and felt before the earth had shuddered so violently. Before the Growl. There was that prickling sensation again, and the metallic smell of danger.

"I can't sleep here, Bella. I can't," Lucky whined, glancing around. "What if the longpaw house falls on us?"

"No. It won't happen. The Growl has gone." Bella flattened herself on the cushion, as if willing herself to go to sleep. "Don't be silly, Lucky. We'll be fine."

She was wide awake, though; Lucky could sense it. Again she fidgeted, and at last she got to her feet, head lowered, ears pricked for trouble.

"On the other paw . . ." she murmured.

Lucky stood up, determined. He knew this warning in his bones; he knew this urge in his gut. "Higher ground, Bella. *Higher ground.*"

"Yes. You're right, Lucky. *Yes.*"

No sooner had she said it than the floor rippled beneath their paws. It felt like nothing more than the shiver of skin beneath fur, but the two dogs bolted for their lives. Crashing together as they leaped from the cushion, they stumbled, and Lucky took a moment to make sure Bella was back on her feet. They scrambled through the hallway, barged out of the open door, and raced outdoors to safety. The Big Growl had left many of the doors hanging at awkward angles. Longpaws would have hated it, but it made it easy for the dogs to move around— thank goodness.

"We have to warn the others!" cried Bella.

But before they could so much as bark, the rest of the Leashed Dogs were running from their longpaws' houses, too, darting into the open patch of grass in the middle of the houses. Unsure of themselves, afraid to make a further move in any clear direction, they circled, whined, scratched at the earth. Martha gave a deep bark at her own longpaw's house, and started back toward it. Daisy yelped frantically and began to race back to her home.

"No!" barked Lucky. "Stay together! Stay here!"

It wasn't much of a strategy, but it seemed like their safest option. Once again the other dogs looked at him in that trustful, appealing way that made his skin prickle. *No time to worry about it . . .* thought Lucky.

"Everyone together. Come on!" Lucky gave the most commanding bark he could muster, but no one protested. The dogs crowded around him in a huddle, seeking safety and protection in the warmth and numbers of a . . .

. . . *Pack,* thought Lucky with a jolt.

The ground felt so terribly disturbed beneath his paw pads. It shook and quivered still, as if it were trying to throw them off. Was the Earth-Dog afraid of the Big Growl, too? Or were the two of them part of each other? Lucky didn't know. *Please,* he thought, *please, Earth-Dog, keep us safe. . . .*

Maybe the Earth-Dog listened to him, because the Big Growl didn't return—not the way it had that terrible night. This could have been its smaller earth-brother, turning restlessly the way Bella had, but going back to sleep in its underground den. The ground stopped grumbling beneath his paws, and the crackling sensation left the air. For the first time in ages, Lucky breathed properly. Around him the other dogs, too, were shaking the fear out of their fur, standing up more confidently, looking around for the next danger. They weren't assuming that all was well again, and they weren't trotting straight back to their longpaw houses, but they weren't panicking, and that made him absurdly proud of his whole . . .

Don't think it, he told himself. *They're not my Pack.*

Yes, he'd helped them, and maybe he'd found it reassuring to huddle together with other dogs. But that didn't mean a thing! They wouldn't have been much use to him if the danger had worsened.

Time to strike out again, Lucky told himself. *Alone.* His fate was in his own paws and he'd better remember it. Warm flanks were one thing, but there was a lot more to Pack life than a bit of company. A *lot* more, and some of it he couldn't bear to imagine. . . .

And then he stopped worrying, because a new, deadly rumble

filled the air. There wasn't time to huddle together and protect one another. The rumbling instantly became a tremendous crash, a chaos of stone and screeching metal, and the air filled with blinding dust.

Lucky froze, crouching against the ground, and so did the others. He gazed ahead, his jaw hanging slack. Where a longpaw house had stood, right next to Bella's, now there were only billowing clouds of smoke.

The echoing thunder seemed to go on forever. No one moved until the dust began to thin and clear and settle. Sunshine whimpered uncertainly, and Mickey's growl was a frightened one.

Nothing had fallen on them; he'd gathered Bella's friends in exactly the right place, he realized with pride.

His sense of achievement was swept away as the hairs stood up on the back of his neck and shoulders. The sound that came from the ruins was horrible: an unearthly howl of terror and pain and desolation. For a few seconds he stood stock-still with the rest of them, uncomprehending, as chills ran through his belly; was the Earth-Dog herself mourning and whining at this further disaster? Was this the final straw: the destruction of all that was left?

Then, at his side, Bella lifted her muzzle and gave a hysterical

SURVIVORS: THE EMPTY CITY

howl. Lucky watched in amazement as she stood there, trembling, the others joining in her cry of distress.

"What?" he snapped desperately. "Bella! Tell me!"

"Alfie!" she whined. "He's trapped in that house!"

123

CHAPTER TEN

"Alfie! Alfieeeee!" Sunshine was running in frantic circles. "Lucky, do something! *Pleeeease!"*

Lucky turned from one dog to the other, nearly tripping over Daisy again. The others were all frozen to the spot. "Who's Alfie?"

Bella shook her head miserably. "A little, brave dog. He wasn't with us when we found you. He'd stayed behind to guard his longpaws' house!"

"I knew we should never have left him," Daisy muttered, her nose drooping into the dirt.

"There's nothing we can do." Mickey's whine was bleak.

"If we go in there we might be killed." Bella took a shivering step backward as she stared at the wreckage. A faint breeze lifted a billow of white dust, and another piece of wood creaked, fell, and shattered. The howling rose again from the longpaw house: a small dog, lonely and desperate and afraid.

Martha raked the ground with one huge paw, unwilling to look at anyone. "Poor Alfie. He wasn't really one of us. He always kept to himself."

"Martha's right." Bella crouched on her belly, pawing dust from her eyes. "He wasn't one of our Pack, Lucky. Not really. Oh, poor little Alfie. If he'd only come with us . . . but he hardly ever did. . . ."

Lucky looked from the collapsed longpaw house to the other dogs, and back again. Why were they talking about Alfie as if he were already dead?

He had to bark loudly to make himself heard over the miserable sound from the ruins. "What are you saying? There's a dog trapped in there! He's still alive!"

"But we can't help him." Bella's ears flattened even closer against her skull, and she growled resentfully. "We can't do anything!"

"We have to *try*!" snapped Lucky. Daisy was staring up at him with wide eyes.

Sunshine whined and spun frantically. "We can't leave him there, can we, Bella?" Her ears drooped. "Can we?"

A deep, gruff bark came from his side. Lucky turned, surprised, to see Bruno, looking belligerent.

"Lucky's right." Bruno glared at Bella and the others. "Alfie's one of our Pack whether he knows it or not. And I'm going to help!"

"Thank you," Lucky said. Bruno, at least, understood what it meant to look out for other dogs. "You'll make a good Pack member. Now, come with me."

As they both turned and loped toward the ruin, Sunshine's whimper rose behind them, high and frightened. "I'd come, too. I'd come, but . . ."

Lucky shook his head. *They treat me like I'm some expert on being a Pack leader,* he thought, *and they don't even know what being in a Pack means!*

But if they wanted leadership, he'd give it to them; he'd show them this one last thing before moving on. Whatever else lay ahead of them, they'd have to find out for themselves, the hard way. *One last favor. No dog deserves to be left to die. Then I'm off—they can look after themselves!*

"Look at the front of the longpaw house," rumbled Bruno. "If he was in there, he'd be a dead dog already. He must be in the back, in the kitchen. The cold room, you know? That's where his basket was."

"Right. Good thinking, Bruno." Lucky inspected the ruins, pacing carefully through the debris. The walls were reduced to rubble at the front and sides of the longpaw house, and the roof had caved in completely. "There's still a wall standing around the back. Let's try there."

Lucky picked his way to the back, moving carefully on his injured paw pad. He could still hear Alfie howling pitifully somewhere under the rubble.

"Alfie! Can you hear me?" Bruno barked. Alfie's yelping didn't stop; his friend's calls to him had gone unheard.

They clambered over fallen bricks and pieces of twisted metal into the backyard of the longpaw house.

Lucky sniffed at the ground. No invisible power here; its source must have been destroyed. A huge and creaking old tree overshadowed the yard, and he glanced up at it nervously. It leaned at a slight angle, its trunk cracked where the lower branches began to spread, and he didn't like the groaning noise that came from within it, as if it was in pain.

Just in time, he spotted the broken shards of clear-stone on the ground in front of his paws. He trod a delicate path around them, followed by Bruno. A window had fallen out of the back wall. In the empty space left, some crisscrossed wire was torn and sagging, but still intact.

"That's our way in." Lucky nodded at the window.

127

He put a paw against the wire mesh, but quickly drew it back. It felt so sharp, reminding Lucky of his Trap House cage. He couldn't afford a second wound—but Alfie's howls were a tormenting racket. The sound made Lucky's bones ache and his blood pound. *I can't give up!*

Lucky scrambled up on a pile of rubble, Bruno at his side. Together they tugged with their teeth, and Lucky tried scratching the wire aside with his claws, but it was no use. Lucky got a good grip on a sagging piece of mesh, but it sprang back, giving his nose a stinging blow. Lucky jumped away and tilted his head, frustrated.

"This is no good. What should we do now?" Bruno frowned.

Lucky realized that the proud old dog was deferring to his experience. He felt a flush of confidence surge through him. *I can do this.*

"I got it!" Lucky turned and bounded down from the pile of blocks. "I know what to do!"

"Lucky, look out!"

Lucky heard Bruno's shrill bark of alarm. He looked up in terror as the groaning tree gave a crack like the war of the Sky-Dogs.

He couldn't falter. He dashed on, dodging sideways as the massive branch above him plummeted to the earth. It missed the tip of his tail by a hair's breadth; he felt the rush of air on his hindquarters.

As the crash of leaves and branches faded, he paused to glance back at Bruno, catching his breath. He gave a sharp bark of gratitude for the warning. Then he was running hard for Bella's house.

Bella and Sunshine barked something he didn't catch as he sprinted away from Alfie's home. The rest of the Pack was still huddled together on the grass patch in between the longpaw houses. Were they encouraging him, or trying to get him to stop? He didn't have time to think about it now. He reached Bella's door and hesitated, his heart thrashing.

This longpaw house might collapse, too. Lucky's forelegs trembled with nerves as he eyed the cracked walls.

I'd better be quick. . . .

Darting through the doorway, he found Bella's sleeping corner and snatched up her soft-hide in his jaws. It was big and thick, and awkward to carry, but it was perfect for what he had in mind. He dragged it out through the door, his muscles trembling with relief as he reached the open air once more. He paused, letting the pounding of his heart calm a little—and giving quick thanks to the Earth-Dog for her tolerance—then raced back to where Bruno waited, to where Alfie still whined pitifully for help.

"We're coming, Alfie," growled Bruno reassuringly. "Not long now! Stay calm."

Please, Earth-Dog, Lucky took a moment to beg, *will you help me again like you did in Bella's house? Please let us get Alfie out. Please don't let the Big Growl come for us. . . .*

With the soft-hide between their teeth protecting their soft gums from the tearing spikes of wire, Lucky and Bruno tugged as hard as they could. Lucky felt his body jerk back as strands of wire weakened and tore apart. One last tug—and a whole section of wire was ripped aside.

Yes! We're in!

There were jagged spikes of broken clear-stone around the wooden frame, but the soft-hide cushioned those, too, and both dogs managed to squirm through and into the longpaw house.

Bruno stood on the rubble-strewn floor, panting from the exertion. "Alfie! Where are you?"

There was a soft whine from beneath one of the longpaws' sitting-boxes. Lucky tugged at it with his jaws, loosening a tangle of broken wood and metal till they could reach the dog trapped beneath. Bruno squirmed between the wooden legs, grabbed Alfie's collar, and dragged him free.

The little dog lay shivering for a few moments before getting shakily to his paws. He glanced nervously at Lucky. Alfie was short and stocky, and his face was blunt and covered in wrinkles. His fur was a mottled pattern of brown and white.

"Thank you," he whispered, and glanced around mournfully at his ruined house.

"Come on," grunted Bruno. "Let's get you back to the others."

Lucky led the way carefully back across the rubble-strewn floor and through the broken window. Bruno had to give Alfie a nudge up with his head just to help the little dog reach it.

"You'll have to stay with us now, Alfie," Bruno said when they were safely outside.

"Yes . . . oh, my poor longpaws!" He whined with distress as he stared at the wreckage of his home. "Where are they, where *are they*? Look at this place! What will they do when they come back?"

Lucky blinked. Why were these Leashed Dogs so anxious about their longpaws' feelings? It wasn't as if the longpaws had given them much thought before they ran. "Don't worry about them," he growled. "You have to take care of yourself for now."

Alfie's head was hunched into his neck as he looked up at Lucky, and he blinked anxiously. "Who are you?"

"He's Lucky," broke in Bruno. "And so are you. It's amazing

you weren't crushed in there. Now come on."

The others were waiting, tense, ears pricked as they picked their way back to the grass in the middle of the avenue. Lucky gave each one of them a disdainful stare.

We saved him, no thanks to any of you. . . .

Bella came forward and tentatively licked Lucky's ear. "I'm glad you're all right," she murmured guiltily.

He made a rumbling sound in his throat, not quite ready to forgive her. The others were avoiding his eyes, blinking around at the skewed walls of their longpaw houses, the dust clouds raised by a tiny breeze. The surroundings looked almost as forlorn as they did.

Sunshine was the first to recover. She trotted up to Alfie, licking him in apologetic welcome. Soon the others joined her, nuzzling the friend they'd nearly abandoned out of fear.

"You see, Bella?" whined Sunshine. "I knew Lucky would get him out! I knew he could do it!"

"I got him out, too," grumbled Bruno.

"Of course you did! Brave Bruno!" Sunshine was beside herself with admiration. "It was the right thing to do, Bella! You shouldn't have tried to stop them."

"Hey!" objected Martha. "You didn't want to help, either, Sunshine!"

"Wait a minute." From the milling group of dogs, Alfie pushed forward, tilting his head to the side. "Bella?" he squeaked in disbelief. "Were you going to leave me there?"

The happy growls and yelps faded to a guilty silence. Bella hung her head.

"Alfie, you mustn't be angry with Bella," said Mickey. "She was right to be careful." He padded up beside her and nuzzled her neck. "We didn't know how dangerous the longpaw house was, and anything might have happened. Bruno and Lucky could have been killed, too. It was a tough decision, and she was thinking of everybody. Let's just be glad it worked out, and you're safe."

Bella licked the dog's brown-and-white face gratefully and Alfie gave a reluctant nod. Lucky, though, kept silent, thinking.

What Mickey said was true. Bella's attitude had made sense. And yet . . .

Hearing Alfie crying for help like that, Lucky couldn't have left him—the other dog's distress caused an urgency in his bones and blood, something he could not resist. There was an instinct, a dog-spirit deep inside him, and he was growing more aware of how much he relied on its strength in times of danger.

So where did that leave Bella . . . ?

Lying down, head on his paws, Lucky watched his litter-sister sadly. The dog-spirit inside her was quiet, repressed, buried so deep she had forgotten it long ago. There were times when a dog had to rely on his inner spirit to tell him what to do—but Bella thought like a longpaw.

Anxious, he got to his feet and padded closer to her. She seemed uneasy, but then all of them did. Mickey pawed at his glove—Lucky finally recognized it now; it was like the ones he'd seen when longpaw pups played ball in the streets. Martha sat beneath the wilting tree, ears drooping. Sunshine nibbled at a few blades of grass, disconsolate, while Daisy padded back and forth, gazing at her creaking longpaw house and sniffing anxiously. Alfie simply lay with his head on his paws. He looked as though he was thinking hard.

They failed their first test as a Pack, thought Lucky. *And they know it.*

Lucky gave a soft growl and drew Bella aside.

She glanced at him, her tail wagging low to the ground.

"Don't even say it, Lucky." She sounded bitter. "It's not that I didn't care. I didn't want any harm to come to Alfie. But I was afraid for the others. I was afraid for *you.*"

"You don't have to make excuses to me, Bella." He'd meant it to sound kind, but she bristled.

"I'm not making excuses! I made a perfectly sensible decision, and you went against it. If you had been killed inside that longpaw house, it would have been your own fault."

"You don't need to worry about me! I can *always* look after myself—I'm used to it."

"But Bruno isn't. None of us are!" she snapped. "You have to understand, Lucky. We're not like you. I need to make my *own* decisions. You made the right one in the end with Alfie. But it might have been the wrong one! It could have been disastrous. So you don't need to tell me I was *wrong.*"

Lucky stared at her, exasperated. "I know. The thing is, I think it's important that you—"

A wailing whine cut through the air, and all the dogs' heads snapped around to stare at Sunshine.

"Daisy!" she cried, turning one way, then the other, on the verge of yet another panic. "Where's Daisy? She's gone!"

CHAPTER ELEVEN

What trouble has Daisy got herself into? wondered Lucky.

Sunshine was dashing in frantic circles; Martha paced back and forth as Mickey tried to herd the group around Lucky. But the other dogs were too frantic to obey.

"We've got to look for her," Bruno said. "We've *got* to. But *where?*"

"We can't just stand by!" yelped Sunshine, and her ears drooped with sudden shame as she muttered, "Not like last time."

"Bruno's right!" exclaimed Bella. "We need to think!"

Yes, thought Lucky, exasperated, *but none of you are!* He leaped up onto a tumble of bricks and gave a commanding bark.

"Calm down, all of you!" As they turned to gaze at him, Lucky shook his head. "Be quiet—all that noise doesn't help Daisy! I'll try to sniff her out. She can't be far away."

There was a line of longpaw houses to his left, low and neat behind trimmed lawns; they seemed to be less badly damaged than the others, though their windows were cracked and bits and pieces of walls had crumbled away. He took a few paces toward them, sniffing and cocking his ears, straining to find Daisy's trail. He was sure he'd seen her yearning toward one of those longpaw houses while he and Bella fought: that one with the broken swing in the front garden and a lifeless stone rabbit on the doorstep, one ear snapped off.

Bella and Mickey were right behind him. *They don't want to be seen hesitating again.*

The others held back and watched, eyes beseeching. That didn't make it easier to concentrate—but there was something else, too, interfering with Daisy's scent. It was a sharp and strange odor that drifted in the air, sickening and dizzying.

A suggestion of Daisy pricked his nose, but he couldn't pin her down—not with that acrid smell making his head sway and his stomach churn. Lucky lifted his muzzle into the faint breeze, going absolutely still. That smell. It was coming from . . .

Daisy's house!

"Stay back!" he barked sharply. His hackles bristled; there seemed to be something treacherous about that sharp, sickly scent. It wasn't the death-smell, but his instincts screamed at him to avoid it as if it was.

Padding cautiously toward Daisy's house, the smell grew overwhelming. His eyes watered, his stomach turned, and for an instant he was so light-headed he nearly stumbled.

But Daisy's scent was definitely there—almost buried beneath the dreadfulness. . . .

And there she was! Swaying, but standing determinedly square, Daisy blinked at him from the skewed shadows of the cracked porch. Her eyes were unfocused, and she looked as if she might collapse at any moment.

Darting forward, Lucky snatched at her collar, his eyes streaming now, his sense of smell dead to everything but the sick-stench. She gave a little whimper as he lifted her by the scruff of her neck and turned, bounding back to the others. Even as he ran, Lucky felt his body wobble and sway, but the smell was already growing fainter as he bounded unsteadily back to the tight group of anxious dogs. When he could smell it no longer he let Daisy fall to the grass and stood over her, panting and staggering with dizziness.

She was asleep now, motionless on the ground, her flanks barely moving. Lucky began to lick her fiercely, and Bella moved to join him as the others looked on with fear.

"Why is she sleeping?" yelped Sunshine. "What were you running away from?"

"Come on, Daisy," Bella whined. "Wake up."

Her body lay as if lifeless, her sides moving almost imperceptibly with her breaths. They seemed to rise and fall less and less. How long would it take for her to stop breathing altogether? Her eyes had rolled back in her head and white flecks foamed at the corners of her mouth. Martha reached out with one of her giant paws. With more gentleness than Lucky could have imagined from such a huge dog, she wiped the foam from the corners of Daisy's mouth.

"Don't die!" Bella said, more urgently. She gently poked Daisy's body with her paw. Nothing.

"Come away," Lucky told his litter-sister. "It's best to leave her now." Whatever fighting spirit had been in Daisy had gone now. He started to turn away, his head bowed, when . . .

"Wait!" Bella cried, drawing closer to Daisy. "Look!"

She was right. The little dog was trembling back into life. Her eyelids opened, and a shiver ran through her fur. A paw twitched, her tail thumped feebly, and her dark eyes opened. They were still blurry and distant, but Lucky felt a huge wave of relief as he sat back and watched Bella wash Daisy's face.

139

"Oh, Daisy. You're all right!" Bella nuzzled her. "What on earth happened? Where did you go?"

Unsteadily Daisy sat up, tilting her head from side to side as she tried to get her balance back. "I'm sorry. You were all fighting and I didn't want to listen."

Mickey paced forward to lick her nose. "What a time to go wandering!"

"I just thought, well, I'll look and see if my longpaw's house is all right, and . . . I smelled something odd. . . ." Daisy shook herself, a little shamefaced, but her eyes were brightening once more, her ears were pricked, and she looked steadier. "It was worse than anything I'd ever smelled before—even worse than the time I got sprayed by a skunk and had to sleep in the garage. I didn't know what it was but I thought if I found out, I could tell you all about it." Daisy looked sheepish. "It was coming from the kitchen. I went closer to get a better sniff at it, and . . . I felt so sick and dizzy. I thought you'd know what to do—but I couldn't seem to walk straight. I felt so awful."

The Sun-Dog was starting to come up over the broken roofs of the longpaw houses, and as Lucky looked around at the cracked and tottering walls and broken road, his fur bristled and he stood straighter.

"Listen, all of you." He looked around at them, meeting their eyes with determination. "You have to leave this place. Now. And for good."

"What are you talking about?" Bella barked, showing her teeth. "We can't leave!"

Lucky took a pace back. "Bella—"

"This is our *home*!" she snarled. "We have to wait for our longpaws. I don't expect you to understand, but we can't go. Not yet."

Lucky couldn't speak for a moment. No, he *didn't* understand. But her bark was so fierce it made his stomach clench.

The others' tails drooped, and they lowered their ears, looking from Bella to Lucky and back again. Bella looked ferocious, her hackles raised.

"But, Bella . . ." whispered Daisy.

"No. Don't listen to him, Daisy! Lucky's a smart dog, but he's a Lone Dog. He doesn't understand about longpaws; he doesn't understand why we can't leave!" Bella bared her teeth at her brother. "I know you don't approve, Lucky, but we're loyal to our longpaws, and we can't abandon their homes."

"Bella!" he barked angrily. "In the name of the Sky-Dogs! Don't you understand? It's dangerous here—that smell nearly killed Daisy. Alfie's house collapsed. And it *isn't* Alfie's house," he added savagely. "It belongs to Alfie's longpaws, and Alfie's long-paws left him—like they left you all!"

Bella yelped in frustration, but she stood up to him defiantly. "They didn't mean to!"

Lucky stalked forward, curling his muzzle. "Oh, yes they did. These longpaw houses are falling down, Bella." He turned his head to give the buildings a look of distaste and fear. Against the dimming sky they seemed even more ominous, skewed and loom-ing as if they'd crumble at any moment. "They won't be here for long, and that smell is a death-smell. It's like the breath of the Earth-Dog herself!"

Martha shivered with fear, and Sunshine gave a pitiful whine, but Bella scraped her claws along the earth for silence. "You are so superstitious, Lucky! The smell is—I don't know, but it's not the Earth-Dog."

Lucky shook his head, hackles bristling. "How do you know? How do we know what goes on down there in the darkness? If we're lucky, the Earth-Dog will protect us from the Big Growl. But what if she thinks we aren't worth protecting—that we're stu-pid mutts who aren't clever enough to sense danger? She might abandon us altogether!"

"You're talking nonsense!" Bella snapped.

Lucky growled. "This place could kill you. You can't stay here. Don't you all trust me, after everything we've been through? Haven't I gotten you out of trouble? Did *your longpaws* stay to do that?"

Someone whimpered in the silence that fell. The dogs' heads drooped and seven tails tucked between their legs. Even Bella looked downcast and, for the first time, uncertain.

"But where would we go?" Bruno asked.

"I don't know." Lucky sat down, scratching his ear to dispel the aggravation he felt. "I suppose you could come with me, just for a bit. Or you could lead your friends somewhere else, Bella. I know you could do it."

"I don't," she murmured.

"But whatever happens," he went on, "you have to find a new place to live. You understand, don't you?"

Daisy's tail thumped slowly and pitifully on the grass, raising puffs of dust. "But if we go—if we leave here—how will our longpaws find us when they come back?"

Lucky gave a bitter snarl. "You need to *give up* on your longp—"

He turned to glare at her—and saw that her eyes were dark and huge. Beside her, Sunshine looked just the same—miserable,

143

needy, and desperate for reassurance. Lucky breathed out, forcing himself to calm down. He was asking a lot of them, after all. Their comfortable lives had spoiled them. They weren't just Leashed Dogs—they were Spiritless Dogs.

Lost dogs.

Quietly he growled, "If the Earth-Dog is still angry, if the Big Growl might return, we need to leave. You know it's true—feel it inside you. Stop thinking like longpaws—feel the dog-spirit. It's there somewhere, I promise." Affectionately he licked Daisy's face, and put more confidence into his voice than he really felt. "You'll be fine. You're strong dogs, I know it. One day, your longpaws might come back. When you see other long-paws returning, and this place feels safe again, you can come back, too."

Inside his belly he felt a twist of guilt at his lie. He was certain that their longpaws would never return—why would they? Their homes were ruined and belongings destroyed. But for now, he knew these dogs needed to believe the longpaws were coming back for them. Pricking his ears with confidence, he gazed at them.

One by one, they whined, lowered their heads in acknowledgment, and thumped their tails sadly.

"Yes," said Bella at last. "You're right. This place is dangerous. We'll come with you. But there's something we need to do first. Things we need to get."

She nodded to the other dogs, who all turned and padded toward their longpaw houses. Only Mickey stayed where he was at Lucky's side, silent and patient.

Lucky watched them go. Hadn't he convinced them yet? What in the name of the Sky-Dogs could they be doing now?

"Daisy!" he barked, as he realized that the little dog was heading for her own foul-smelling yard. "What are you doing? You can't go back in there!"

"I just need to get something," Daisy yapped back. Lucky watched in astonishment as she took a deep breath and then ran across the grass into the longpaw house. He couldn't help but hold his breath until she reemerged, clutching something in her mouth.

One by one, each dog came out of its longpaw house carrying something. Not one of the objects looked as if it would be of any practical use. Martha's powerful jaws now gripped a red square of cloth. Sunshine had retrieved a yellow leather leash studded with sparkling stones, and Daisy a longpaw treasure-pouch like the ones he'd seen stacked in the mall. Unable to

145

go back into his collapsed longpaw house, Alfie had lifted a rubber ball sorrowfully from his littered front yard; Bruno's pointed muzzle dripped drool, wetting the peaked longpaw cap he held.

Now he could see why Mickey hadn't gone with the others: He had simply kept hold of his padded glove.

As for Bella, she gazed defiantly at Lucky as she set down a tattered stuffed bear-toy at his forepaws. "These things still smell of our longpaws," she told him in a low growl. "We need something to remind us."

Hesitantly Lucky eyed each object, then nodded. They were at least trying to do what was right; perhaps he needed to make allowances for them and their sad Leashed pasts.

"Of course," he said, licking her nose to show that he understood. "Of course you can bring them along. Now follow me. Mickey—you bring up the rear, you're good at that. We'll head into the hills."

As they padded silently through the outlying streets, Lucky tried not to look back at the city where he'd run happily free. Bad enough that the other dogs halted, now and again, to gaze back mournfully at their old lives. That bustling, lively place of the longpaws was wrecked and gone, and they were leaving it forever.

Distantly a loudcage howled; in a far street iron groaned and clear-stone shattered as another wall fell. Otherwise there was only silence and the death-smell.

There was no looking back. No looking back at all . . .

CHAPTER TWELVE

As their surroundings grew less citylike, and the longpaw houses were scattered farther and farther apart, Lucky's spirits lifted. He'd forgotten how much he enjoyed the freedom and space of the wild—on the rare occasions when he ventured there.

He'd gone past the city limits only a few times: for the chase of a rabbit hunt, or when the longpaws from the Trap House were on the streets and he needed to make himself scarce for a few days. Now, he felt excitement growing in his belly and tickling his spine. He could try proper hunting again—rabbits, squirrels, even gophers!

This wasn't wild country just yet, but it was getting that way. A scrubby field lay before them, rough-grassed and fenced with broken wire. Not the wilderness, but not a longpaw park, either. Running through the gorse and weeds was a small, sluggish river, perhaps two dog-lengths wide, its surface calm and smooth and slow. Lucky's ears pricked up and he panted with pleasure as the other dogs came to his side.

"Water!" he said, and bounded toward it.

He was still many dog-lengths away from it when he scrabbled to a halt, hair bristling all over his body, the river-smell stinging his nostrils. A growl rumbled in his throat.

Bella slowed, too, and stopped beside him, one paw still raised. She sniffed the air, suspicious, as the others joined them.

"There's something wrong," she whined.

"Something *very* wrong," Lucky confirmed, backing slowly away from the glistening stream.

"What could possibly be wrong?" With a howl of joy, Alfie darted past them all, nearly knocking Sunshine over in his haste. "Come on!"

"Alfie, no!" Lucky sprang after the squat little dog. Alfie was dashing at his top speed, but Lucky was faster.

Good thing Alfie has short legs, he thought as he bounded almost on top of the smaller dog and seized him by the scruff of the neck.

Alfie struggled and wriggled in shock, paws flailing at the river. "Let me go! Let me go!"

Grimly Lucky turned and trotted back to the frightened group of dogs. They had come a little closer to the water, alarmed for Alfie's sake, but they were all sniffing the air now, shivering, their hackles high. He dumped Alfie unceremoniously at their paws, and the little dog scrabbled to his feet, shaking himself rid of the indignity.

"Don't you smell it, Alfie?" Martha shook her head at him. "That water isn't good."

"When is water ever bad?" he said indignantly. "My longpaws' water was always perfectly good!"

"Your longpaws' water was made safe and delivered in pipes," growled Lucky. "Come here. But *don't* touch the river."

He nudged Alfie to the river's edge, followed by the rest, who held back nervously from the odd sharp scent of the water. "You see? Look at it!"

Beside him he felt Alfie shiver. "That can't be right."

The river looked even more sluggish and stagnant up close, and its water wasn't clear, but a dense, impenetrable gray-green. Worst of all, it had grown a skin with pools of odd colors, like the stripes that lit the sky after a heavy rainfall. Lucky had seen this kind of water before—when a loudcage had been wounded, and bled onto the road and into puddles—but this was much worse. And though he disliked the scent of loudcage blood, it was nothing as bad as this—a thick sickly stench that burned his nostrils.

"That's not a river at all," said Martha, shuddering.

Lucky glanced at the big Newfoundland in surprise, then back at the river. *She's right,* he realized.

"I think it's one of the scratches the Big Growl put in the earth. I nearly fell into one." Lucky trembled at the memory. "But this one's filled up with water from somewhere. It only *looks* like a river."

Bella growled with fear. "Let's get away from here. And don't be so impulsive again, Alfie! You've got to *listen*."

Alfie looked suitably cowed by his scolding. "All right, Bella. I'm sorry."

They all turned and trotted back across the field, but they were only halfway to the tumbledown fence when Bruno pricked his ears and pulled up short.

"Longpaws!" he exclaimed.

All the dogs stopped at once, cocking their ears to hear what Bruno had heard. Lucky could pick up longpaw voices, coming from somewhere across the scrubby field. There were quite a few of them, but what kind of longpaws would be gathering in a pack near that poisonous river?

His heart raced and he longed to run in the other direction, but the others didn't look worried at all. They were sniffing eagerly in the direction of the voices.

Sunshine yelped with delight. "Let's go say hello!"

"Where are they? Where are they?" That was Daisy, spinning with overexcitement.

"Calm down," barked Lucky anxiously. "Don't draw attention! Be careful, all of you. Calm *down*!"

They ignored him. Martha, Mickey, and Bruno were all giving deep, joyous barks, and Bella was yearning toward a corner of the field, panting, her ears pricked forward with enthusiasm.

"There! There they are! By that big tower!"

Lucky froze. Yes, longpaws—yellow-suited, black-faced longpaws! He remembered them from the encounter in the city. They were *not* friendly, and their strange hides and eyeless faces made him prickle with nerves. "Wait—"

Too late.

"Oh, hurray!" Daisy gave a volley of barks, then raced toward the longpaws.

"Daisy!" yelped Martha in alarm.

All the dogs chased after her, Bella in the lead, but Daisy had a huge head start, and her excitement gave her short legs an astonishing speed. The others weren't halfway to the longpaws when she reached them and bounced and leaped, yapping, around their booted feet.

The longpaws didn't pay attention to her, Lucky noticed with relief as he ran. Maybe she would take the hint and leave them alone. . . .

Daisy was not to be ignored, however. When her friendly yelps got no reaction, she took hold of the shiny yellow hide on one longpaw leg, and tugged and shook it playfully.

The longpaw jumped back, shocked—and before Lucky could bark a warning, he had roughly shaken the little dog off. Daisy howled and tumbled onto the ground.

"Daisy!" Sunshine yelped.

Stupid longpaws! Lucky suppressed a growl and put on a burst of speed. He could see Daisy quivering as she tried to get back to her paws.

The yellow-hide longpaws were already turning to leave, talking urgently among themselves and comparing their beeping sticks. Lucky dashed up to Daisy, who was scrambling shakily to her feet.

"I have to . . . but . . . the longpaws . . ." She took a step forward, her eyes on the retreating longpaws. Lucky's heart sank as he realized she was still trying to follow them.

"No, Daisy!" He planted himself in front of her, blocking her way.

The little dog looked bewildered and shocked rather than hurt. "Why did the longpaw do that? I have to—"

"No, don't follow!" Bella was beside her now, too, licking her side where she had hit the ground. "Leave them!"

The other dogs drew close, forming a cluster around Daisy, all of them sharing dazed and shocked glances.

"That's not how longpaws behave!" cried Martha.

"I don't understand," whined Sunshine mournfully.

"I've never seen a longpaw try to hurt a dog," said Mickey, shocked.

Lucky shook his head, astounded at their naïveté. "I have," he growled darkly.

Bella gave him a worried glance, but she was more concerned with Daisy, who was sitting up now and whimpering. "Don't worry, Daisy. Those weren't our longpaws, or anything like them. Did you see their strange fur? Their faces?"

"Let's get away from here." Martha gently nudged Daisy away.

Lucky began to follow the others as they padded dejectedly back the way they'd come, but he noticed Mickey wasn't following. "Mickey, come with us!"

Mickey turned to him. "There's something behind those longpaws being here all alone. I can feel it." He walked up to Lucky and growled in a low voice, "What were they doing?"

"I don't know," admitted Lucky. "I've seen hundreds of long-paws in the city, but I've never seen those beeping sticks before. And it looked like they wanted to find out about the strange river—why else would they stand so close to the bad water?"

"I don't like it." The black-and-white dog shook his head. "Those are the only longpaws we've seen since the Big Growl! Where are all the others?"

"They ran away. . . ."

"But they didn't come back. *Those* longpaws did, but no one else. It's very odd, Lucky, and I don't like it."

I don't like it, either, Lucky admitted to himself. *But who can explain longpaws? They aren't like us, whatever these dogs think. . . .*

"I don't have any answers," he said at last, "but I do know one thing: We need to get as far from here as we can. Come on, Mickey. The sooner we get well away from the city and into the wild, the better we'll be."

CHAPTER THIRTEEN

This is my home now, Lucky thought as he padded determinedly farther from the city. *The wild.*

They'd been walking for a long time since leaving the field of the longpaws and the poisoned river.

Only when he'd reached the crest of the first foothill did he turn, panting as he gazed back at what was left of the city. He'd rarely seen his former home from this distance before. It looked so strange now—its remaining buildings leaning forward dangerously, water spraying from angry cracks, and huge, glinting shards of metal piercing the sky. Craters had opened and taken great gulps of his city. Were there other Leashed Dogs back there, trying to survive among the ruins? They didn't stand a chance without their longpaws. *Everything has changed forever.*

It was just as well he'd allowed himself that one pause to look back, though. His odd gang of followers was having trouble keeping up, straggling in a long line behind him. Sunshine caught his eye, far back at the rear. For perhaps the sixth time she'd got her long white fur—not quite so white now—tangled in a thornbush. Exasperated, he bounded back to her and pulled at the branches with his teeth to free her. As a strand of her fur tugged loose, she yelped.

"That hurts!"

"Calm down. It's not the end of the world!"

"Oh, so you're *happy* my fur's falling out? Just *look* at me!"

Ignoring her, he trotted back to his lead position. It wasn't just Sunshine. These dogs, he thought, whined a *lot*.

"You're doing fine!" he barked at them. It was a lie worthy of cunning Forest-Dog himself. "Keep going. Don't give up."

Lucky barked to encourage them. He was worried that they were completely at a loss out here in the wild. Had a single one of them ever had to find food or shelter? *They wouldn't last for more than a few hours without me,* he thought. *First sign of a rainstorm and they'd scamper back to their ruined homes.*

Even as he hesitated and glanced back over his shoulder, he saw Alfie stumble to a halt yet again and flop to the ground.

"Is it time for a rest?" the little dog yelped.

"Look at my *fur*!" wailed Sunshine, scratching hopelessly at her belly.

"Sunshine, shut up!" snapped Bella. "This is no time to be whining!"

"Now, now," said Mickey, plodding tiredly up to the others and dropping his glove so that he could nudge them together with his nose. "We're all together. One, two, three . . . yes, yes . . . and Daisy. Good! Lucky, could we stop a little more often? It's hard keeping everyone together . . . and my paw pads ache. . . ."

Lucky sat back on his haunches and glared at them. He'd been delighted that Mickey was helping—guarding the rear, rounding up the stragglers. And now even he was complaining!

"We have to keep moving!" Lucky barked.

"But *why*?" whimpered Alfie.

Standing up, Lucky shook himself, trying to get rid of his frustration. His instincts were screaming at him to keep going. "We can't stop for any old reason—just because some dog's paw aches, or you're a little out of breath! This isn't a stroll on a leash—this is getting as far away from danger as we can. Do you want to live or die? Stop for a rest and you'll soon meet Earth-Dog, I promise you that."

Some of the dogs let out low whimpers.

"Lucky's right," said Bruno encouragingly. "Come on, then."

They were still whining softly as they set off once more, gripping their longpaw things in their mouths, but Lucky tried his best to push their moans to the back of his mind. It was becoming harder and harder to feel sorry for them, even for Bella, who was on edge with everyone. She was curt and short-tempered with Lucky, snapped out orders at Mickey and Martha, and scolded the smaller dogs relentlessly.

"Sunshine! If you can't stop getting tangled, stay away from the thorns, you silly dog!"

Lucky might have tried to defend Sunshine—if he hadn't been so annoyed with her himself. He did his best to ignore both her and Bella. At least his own paw wound was feeling better, and he could set a good pace and example. If he'd been struggling, too, they never would have gotten out of the city.

Bella had the energy of a bad mood to keep her going, and for a while Lucky was content to let her take the lead. She trotted ahead, her leg muscles working fiercely. He could almost hear the angry thoughts tumbling around inside her head. He fell back to keep an eye on the others, trotting beside Mickey.

"Thanks for herding everyone together back here," he said. "We can't afford to lose anyone."

"No worries. It's what I do," Mickey mumbled through the glove in his mouth. He shifted it slightly so that he could talk more easily. "It's good of you to lead us like this."

"Only for a little while," said Lucky quickly. Anxiety prickled through him—he couldn't let Mickey start thinking of him as Pack leader. He needed them to be strong without him. "You know, you'd all do much better without these longpaw things."

Mickey nodded, but he kept his grip on the glove. "I know. But I can't leave this. My young longpaw . . . he . . ."

When Mickey looked around at him, there was such sadness in his brown eyes that Lucky could almost feel it, too. He shook his head. "I'm glad my longpaws gave me up," Lucky said softly to the older dog. "I'm glad I didn't have a life like yours. All your longpaws have done is break your hearts." Lucky knew he was being harsh, but Mickey deserved to hear the truth.

"But they never meant to, Lucky. If my longpaws left me, it was because they had no choice. I know that."

Lucky sighed. "All the same. I'm glad I never got the chance to be attached to mine."

Mickey gave him a sympathetic look. "Bella told me about what happened to you. They don't sound like any longpaws I've known."

"Hmph," growled Lucky.

"It's true. Most longpaws are good. My longpaws took care of me when I was sick. They fed me treats from the table, they took me to the dog park every day, and played with me. The youngest pup—I slept in his bed every night, since I was a pup myself. I was on duty, you see, to stop him from having nightmares. But I had nightmares, too. And then they stopped, because we both helped each other. That's what most longpaws are like. They're our friends."

"Good for you," growled Lucky. It did sound nice, he thought, if you liked that sort of thing—but why did they abandon Mickey?

The city was fading into a haze behind them, the crumpled buildings and broken metal no longer visible. Lucky couldn't help feeling satisfied that despite all the whining, they'd managed to walk so far. If there were any more Earth Growls, they'd be far from those dangerous snakes that buzzed with energy or the falling blocks of stone that could crush a dog's body. The Sun-Dog was beating hard, and all around was the sound of crickets, but farther ahead he could see pools of shade and scrubby patches of woodland. He lifted his muzzle, sniffing the faint breeze.

Could it be?

Yes! He knew that fresh scent, the teasing deliciousness of it. Water! And not bitter, rotten, gray-green water. Suddenly his throat felt dry, and the vision of a bubbling spring was too much to resist. He bounded ahead, barking.

"Come on! Come on! There's a river ahead!"

As if the Sky-Dogs had suddenly given them wings, the Pack burst forward, breaking one by one into an excited run. Lucky, racing side by side with Bella, crested a low rise—and there, glittering in the sun-high light, a clear stream flowed over stones.

"Is it safe?" barked Alfie anxiously. "Do you think it's poisoned?"

"Not this one," cried Lucky. "Use your nose! It smells fresh."

"He's right. I can smell the fish wriggling," said Sunshine. Lucky blinked at her in surprise. He could smell it, too, but he wouldn't have expected the inside dog to recognize the scent. Sunshine must have a better sense of smell than he'd realized. . . .

"Come on," he barked, and joyfully sprang for the deepest pool he could spot, plunging in up to his neck. He called to the others. "Look! This will make you feel better!"

Bella splashed in beside him, her temper forgotten. She and the other bigger dogs entered the water up to their bellies, lapping happily, shaking their fur free of dust and easing the ache of their paw pads. Alfie trotted deeper, sending up fountains of spray to splash the others, but no one minded. Little Daisy and Sunshine were more hesitant, but they paddled into the shallows, flicking droplets at each other's faces, panting and lapping and standing dreamily with water dripping from their jaws before wading farther. Sunshine even let herself sink up to her shoulders, so that running water could wash her fur clean of the dirt. "Oh, this is lovely! Much better than that poisoned river!"

"Careful," warned Lucky. "River-Dog can be tricky, even when she's bringing you wonderful clean water. The stream's deeper when you go farther in, and the flow looks fast."

They were far enough away from the city to stop and rest for a little while, he decided. Wading from the water to join Bella on the pebbly shore, Lucky shook himself dry in a spray of cold droplets, and let the dappled light warm his fur.

Sunshine had splashed back out of the river, and was examining her paw doubtfully. Lucky sniffed at it with her.

"It's nearly healed," she said, sounding surprised.

"Clean it again," Lucky told her. "Just to be sure. Give it a lick. That's what I kept doing."

Gratefully she licked at the little scratch, as Alfie shook water from his short brown-and-white fur and watched with interest.

"I can't believe Sunshine has a battle scar!" exclaimed Alfie. "I

163

missed so much excitement!"

"You had quite a bit yourself," Bella reminded him.

"That's probably why I'm so hungry!" Sitting back on his sturdy haunches, he wagged his tail and looked expectantly at Lucky.

Alarmed, Lucky averted his eyes from Alfie's—which were big and hopeful—and studied the others instead, jumping and clambering out of the river. But they, too, were watching him with hope, tongues hanging out.

Oh no . . . thought Lucky. "I don't have food! Don't look at *me* like that!"

"Of course not!" panted Mickey, cocking his head to smile at Lucky. "But you can hunt!"

"Yes!" squealed Daisy. "You're a hunter! You can teach us!"

A chorus of barking approval greeted this statement, and Lucky felt his stomach shrink inside him. "I'm—I'm not a teacher! I don't know how . . ."

"All you have to do is show us!" barked Mickey excitedly. "We'll copy you!"

"Yes!" squeaked Sunshine. "Go on, catch something!"

Dumbfounded, Lucky licked his chops. He was hungry, too, and though he wasn't a skilled hunter, he probably knew more than they did. He had all Old Hunter's teaching to fall back on. At the very least, he could make something up; it wasn't as if the Leashed Dogs would spot his mistakes. . . .

He took a deep breath. "Well, it's not that easy, Sunshine, but let's see . . ." Lucky glanced around, deciding to start with the likeliest hunters. That would be Mickey, and Bella, and . . . "Where's Bruno?"

They heard the splash. It wasn't the light, happy splash of a dog playing in water. It was a great disastrous explosion of water.

"Bruno!"

They all raced to the water's edge. Daisy was yapping like crazy.

"I told him it was deep there! I told him he was too big and heavy!"

Lucky took a few steps into the rushing current, feeling it dragging at his paws. Out in midstream and already washed quite a way down, Bruno surfaced, his head struggling to stay above the water, his paws and body thrashing wildly against the strength of the flow. His eyes rolled over toward them, silently pleading; then he sank and lurched up once again, gasping for air.

"Bruno!" barked Lucky. As he waded toward the deeper water, the current almost pulled his paws from under him. He froze, bracing himself on the slippery pebbles, and watched Bruno's struggles in desperation. They might both drown, and then what would happen to the Pack?

Oh, River-Dog, please help me! Don't take Bruno like this!

Just as he was about to fling himself into the deep center of the stream, he saw a huge black shadow pound past him, scattering pebbles and plunging into the water, sending up a great fan of glittering droplets as her body submerged.

Martha!

They were all barking now, urging her back to shore, but Martha had surfaced midcurrent and was swimming toward Bruno. The speed of the water was carrying her quickly, but she showed no sign of panic, her body cutting strongly through the foaming waves till she was alongside him. Lucky watched in awe.

Bruno didn't seem to notice, too focused on keeping his head above the surface and snatching gasps of air as the water tumbled him helplessly. But Martha snatched the scruff of his neck and dragged him through the water.

His eyes opened wide in surprise, but Lucky could tell that he was exhausted and panic-stricken. He gave only a brief startled wriggle, then went limp in her broad jaws. Even against the current, Martha swam powerfully to the bank downstream and tugged Bruno after her onto dry land.

The others raced down the stony riverbank, leaping logs and bushes to reach the two sodden dogs. Bruno lay panting and sneezing and coughing, head on the stones, his forepaws sprawled in front of him. Martha, though, barely showed a sign of strain. She was standing up, all concern for Bruno, shaking the water off her coat and licking the brown dog dry.

She's a real fighter, Lucky thought, impressed.

"Martha?" Bella had skidded to a halt. "Are you all right?"

"Of course I am," rumbled Martha. "Do you think Bruno's okay? Is he hurt?"

"He'll be fine." Lucky snuffled and licked at Bruno's muzzle, then stared again at the huge black dog with awe. "You swim. You swim *so well.*"

"Yes, that was amazing!" Daisy said. The other dogs were staring at Martha, slack-jawed.

Martha wagged her tail and let her tongue loll as she looked at her paws. Lucky looked at them, too, and felt his eyes widen. Between her claws, spread on the uneven pebbles of the beach, he could see . . .

Is that, is that . . . ? It's webbed skin! He'd only ever seen skin like that on the waterbirds that lived on the water in the longpaw

167

parks. He glanced back up at her face, but she didn't seem to see anything wrong as she stared awkwardly at her own paws, embarrassed by the praise.

Bruno was struggling to stand now, licking Martha's chest and lowering his muzzle in gratitude.

Well, River-Dog, Lucky thought, sending his thoughts out toward the bubbling water. *You may not have come to my aid yourself, but you must know Martha well. . . .*

It was the best sign he could have had. Martha had knowledge of the River-Dog that he couldn't have guessed at, and she clearly had her respect, too. She could survive out there. Maybe the others, too, had their own hidden links with the Dogs of Nature, connections just waiting to be reawakened.

For the first time since leaving the city, Lucky felt happy. He wouldn't be bound to these dogs forever, because there would come a time when they wouldn't need him. This funny, temporary Pack of his was going to make it—however much the world had changed. There'd come a day when they didn't need him anymore, and then he'd be free again. Truly free.

CHAPTER FOURTEEN

The whimpering. Why didn't it stop? Why did it have to go on, and on . . . ?
Lucky couldn't bear it.

Yes, he was a coward! Yes, he should beg the Sky-Dogs to forgive him. But
what could he do? Surely they couldn't expect him to sacrifice himself. River-Dog
couldn't expect him to die, when...when Bruno—

No! This wasn't right. . . .

This wasn't Bruno! Those whimpering dogs weren't drowning. They weren't
in the water at all! They were trapped in the rubble, caught and crushed when the
Trap House fell. There was nothing he could do. He and Sweet were helpless. If
they went back for the others, they would die, too. . . .

—Come on, Lucky!

Sweet! He ran blindly after her, his legs working hard, his heart pumping.
He was desperate to block out the whimpering, the dying howls. . . .

But there was something else. Another set of paws. Something behind
him, pursuing him, running him down. It was angry, vengeful, merciless,

and it was almost upon him.

This couldn't be right!

Lucky risked a glance behind him, even as he fled, lungs aching for air, muscles screaming for rest.

There was nothing behind him. Nothing but darkness in the city streets, shadows and broken light and destruction.

Then, out of the corner of his eye . . . glinting eyes and teeth. So many savage dogs, hunting him down. Howling, baying, they were almost on him, almost at his tail, jaws snapping, reaching out their jaws to seize him and tear him—

The Storm of Dogs—

Terror sent Lucky leaping to his feet so suddenly that he stumbled and almost fell. His chest and lungs heaved, and he panted, his throat parched. In his head he could still hear that ferocious baying, the sound of hate. It felt so real—but nothing like this had ever happened to him!

It wasn't a memory. But what *was* it? It didn't feel like a normal dream—it was too real.

As the fear drained from his body, his trembling slowed and he watched the Leashed Dogs sleep. They'd settled down in a low hollow by the river—a sheltered spot, well hidden by the dip of the ground, but with no nearby rocks or gullies for enemies to lurk unseen. The dogs were far enough from the water to be safe, but close enough for the whispering rush of its voice to soothe them. Now the dawn was turning the river's surface pearly, and as Lucky watched, a fish jumped, then splashed beneath the rippling waves. Pale light glowed between the tree trunks, picking out the horizon in gray and pink and orange.

Gradually Lucky's breath calmed, and he licked his chops self-consciously. He felt ashamed of leaping to his feet, of being scared by the pictures in his mind. The other dogs all slept so peacefully, none of them haunted by ghost-hounds and demon-dogs. *It's just me. I'm the only one stupid enough to be fooled by my dreams.* Shame flooded him. Perhaps missing a meal last night had been foolish, but they'd all been too exhausted to hunt or eat. They'd all collapsed in a heap, but maybe Lucky's empty stomach had given him bad dreams.

Perhaps those memory-objects were helping the other dogs after all—those longpaw belongings. Perhaps they protected their dreams. Or perhaps it wasn't so surprising they didn't have nightmares since they were so far detached from their own dog-spirits.

It was true that Lucky himself wasn't exactly an expert on the natural world after his life spent scavenging for food in the city, but he was far closer to his dog-spirit than they were. And he felt it wakening more and more out here in the wild, thrilling in his belly and bones, keeping him alert and safe.

Lucky shivered. All his optimism, all his positive thoughts about Martha and River-Dog had dissolved with the dream. *How could I possibly expect them to cope alone?*

It was a bleak thought, but he felt a new determination. He couldn't save the Trap House dogs when the Big Growl had first hit. But he *could* help these dogs. He could teach them to look after themselves. Perhaps that was what the Spirit Dogs were trying to tell him when they sent these dreams. . . . If he helped Bella and her friends, maybe the bad dreams would stop.

It's worth a try, he thought. *Anything to stop the visions.* But even as he considered this, he knew it was too simple. There was more to those dreams.

There was a message.

He had to look after the Pack. No one else would. He had to look after them because something bad was coming; Lucky knew it in his marrow. He gave an involuntary shudder that wiped away any doubt about the startling dreams. They weren't just dreams; he'd been right to trust in them. They were warnings of something terrible, and not just for him: for all dogs. *The Storm of Dogs . . .*

Lucky could hear his Mother-Dog's voice, from long ago: *"When the world turns upside down and the rivers run with poison . . ."*

He shivered again, looking over at the Leashed Pack. They were barely able to survive in the wild . . . if the Storm of Dogs was really coming, they'd never make it. He needed to help them learn to survive, and quickly!

Lucky let the others sleep on; why shouldn't they enjoy a few moments of peace? But soon the Sun-Dog had risen, glowing through the branches of the scrubby trees, and he couldn't wait any longer. Nudging at the dogs with his nose, whining gently, he goaded them all to their feet.

"Wake up! If you want to learn how to be good hunters, you need to get used to early starts."

Sunshine protested, covering her eyes with her paws as she tried to snuggle back under Martha's belly, but the big black dog stood up and licked the little white one till she was awake and grumbling. Daisy woke with a start and almost immediately began to spin, panting with excitement. Bruno stretched his limbs tentatively, as if testing for injuries, but his soaking seemed to have done him no harm. Mickey and Alfie shook off sleep as Bella affectionately nudged Lucky's muzzle.

"I'm hungry," complained Sunshine, blinking dismally.

"If anyone wants breakfast," Lucky pointed out dryly, "we're going to have to catch it."

To his surprise, they accepted that without a murmur, and set off purposefully, after leaving their longpaw things carefully hidden beneath rocks or behind clumps of grass. The trees became sparser as the dogs trotted up the shallow slope away from the river, and as they crested a ridge, the woods gave way to a broad, rolling grassland dotted with scrub and small rocks, and pocked with promising burrows.

The sight was encouraging—as was the swift movement of creatures disappearing belowground—and Lucky felt a flicker of pleasure pass over him. Today had a purpose: the tricky business of teaching these dogs, soft from longpaws spoiling them, how to hunt. The task would be sure to chase away the last clinging horrors of his dream.

"Now," he told them in a low voice as they sniffed hopefully at the breeze. "Try to be quiet and still—no sharp movements. That means you, too, Sunshine! Stay out of the eye line of those burrows if you can—we need the gophers to think they're safe so they'll come back out of their holes."

"That makes sense to me!" said Mickey eagerly.

"Keep your noses alert for anything we can eat—gophers,

rabbits, mice, anything—and try to hold on to the scent as you follow it to the source. Really open your nostrils—like this, see?" He flared his own, taking deep breaths, casting around in the wind. "It's easy once you start. Let's go."

It wasn't as if he was the most natural of hunters, but Lucky felt like the favored pup of the Forest-Dog as he led the others in search of prey. Sunshine, despite his special warning to her, was incapable of doing anything quietly, yelping every time she so much as caught her fur on a twig. Alfie darted ahead, his little white paws flashing as he ran.

Mickey, Bella, and Bruno were doing their best—slinking low to the ground, avoiding twigs and rustling brush as they snuffed the air for clues—but they weren't used to staying unseen. Though he didn't like to say so, Lucky knew they didn't have a hope of creeping up on the small prey they needed to catch. As for Martha, she was simply too big and burly to be inconspicuous—though Lucky couldn't resent her for that, not after what she'd done the previous day. They were such a varied bunch, he would simply have to accept that they all had different talents.

In the meantime, though, he had to give up any hope of rabbit or squirrel, any of which must have scarpered long ago, or of the gophers coming out of their holes. The land spread before them, not a mouse stirring, the only sound the breath of the wind in the grass.

We're wasting our time, he sighed inwardly. Calling them together again, he decided on a change of tactic.

"Let's start small," he suggested. "We'll practice with bugs and beetles."

"Bugs and *beetles?*" Sunshine's wail of horror must have frightened away any remaining prey. Lucky took a deep breath and reminded himself to stay patient.

"Yes. You don't have to eat them if you aren't that hungry," he said.

That quieted the little dog down.

"Here." Lucky pawed a rock, hooking it with his claws till it tumbled over to reveal fresh wet earth. "Catch, Martha!"

She bounded forward, slapping both huge forepaws down on the beetles that scurried in a panic for the grass. Tentatively she lifted a webbed paw, and yelped with delight when two bugs tried to escape. Quickly she caught them again.

"Two!" exclaimed Lucky. "Well done, Martha!"

All the same, she eyed them doubtfully. "You can really eat these?"

Daisy bounced forward. "I'll try one if you will!"

Lucky watched as the giant dog and the little one crunched a beetle each. Their expressions of uncertainty gave way to a brightening of the eyes and a pricking of the ears.

"That's not bad at all," observed Daisy.

"Really rather nice!" said Martha, in a tone of elegant astonishment.

That was enough to reignite the whole Pack's enthusiasm. At Martha's recommendation, they all bounded off in search of rocks and branches and roots, and foraged beneath them.

This, Lucky decided some time later as Alfie pounced with delight on a green beetle, was a much better idea. It gave the dogs some practice in stalking, with a reward at the end of it—however much Sunshine wrinkled her little black nose. Even she was hungry enough, eventually, not to mind the taste and the crunch of spiders and insects, and Mickey in particular was getting the hang of slinking low along the ground, snuffling at the rough grass, then pouncing.

"Well, Bruno," said Martha with amusement as the brown dog chewed on a particularly plump spider. "Did you ever think we'd be doing this?"

"No indeed." He chuckled as he gulped it down. "No indeed!"

They'd come close to the edge of a belt of trees as they

worked, and now Lucky sniffed the air. There would be larger prey in here, the kind that didn't disappear down holes. Squirrels, and birds, perhaps—even a nest full of eggs if they were lucky. Maybe they were ready for a bigger challenge. It was getting later in the day, and bugs only went so far toward filling hungry stomachs.

Mickey had come to his side with surprising quietness, and now he said hesitantly, "Lucky . . . I've been thinking."

"What?"

The other dog looked a little awkward. "I know you're the expert, but . . . these rabbits are so fast. What do you think . . . I wondered"—he looked at his paws—"suppose Bruno and Alfie go to the other side of the trees, downwind. And you and I and the others could drive out any game from here . . . let them smell us? Then when they run, they'll run right into—"

"Bruno and Alfie!" This was an inspired idea! Lucky was impressed. "It's worth a try. Come on, let's suggest it to the others."

Some of the dogs were doubtful, but Bruno and Alfie were more than willing to trot a cautious wide circle to the far side of the copse, and despite their inexperience, managed to do it without too much noise and disturbance. These dogs, who he'd thought so spoiled and soft, were learning quickly. Three birds took frightened flight, clattering up through the branches, and a mouse scuttled into a hole in a tree trunk, but there was no mass stampede of prey. The Sun-Dog had bounded to his highest point in the sky; perhaps most small creatures were dozing now, sleepy with warmth.

Mickey was proving to be a natural. He slunk into the undergrowth, sniffing for possibilities, and though his first find was a squirrel that scurried out of reach up a pine trunk, he didn't waste time and energy barking at it. Daisy, overexcited by the prospect of meat at last, put her forepaws on the trunk and yapped, but even that was no disaster—alarmed into unwise flight, a rabbit bolted from the grass.

Mickey and Daisy were after it at once. Lucky had to force himself not to spring after it, too—this was a challenge for the Leashed Dogs, not him. There was a slab of rock at the edge of the wood, and he leaped up onto it, watching the chase. The rabbit Daisy had scared scuttled into a hole, unreachable, but another instantly panicked and ran—straight toward the place where Bruno and Alfie were waiting. Lucky felt a flicker of excitement. *This might work!*

Bella and Mickey raced after the rabbit, and even Sunshine

joined in. Little Daisy wasted energy barking her excitement—*Not again!* thought Lucky. *She needs to calm down!*

But just as Bruno and Alfie burst from the undergrowth ahead, forcing the rabbit to double back, it was Daisy who was in the right place. As the rabbit ran almost between her paws, she made a wild pounce-and-grab—and caught it!

It struggled so hard she'd have lost it right away, except that the other dogs were on it in an instant. Martha slapped her big paws onto its back, holding it firmly, and Daisy gripped a hind leg desperately between her teeth. Now that it was immobile, Bruno grabbed it securely and finished it off with a shake of his powerful jaws.

For a moment they stood panting, staring at one another with delight.

"We did it!" squealed Sunshine.

"Well done, Daisy," rumbled Bruno, dropping the dead rabbit to the ground. "Well done!"

It wasn't enough to fill all their bellies, thought Lucky as he put a paw on the still-warm body and began to tear it into portions, but it was a start—and more than that, it had once again given him hope for the future. Mickey's instincts had been right back there—and that was further proof that the Leashed Dogs must still have some instincts left that could help them survive. Mickey's dog-spirit was waking inside him, and Mickey was listening to its voice. If all the dogs followed his example, they had a chance of becoming a true Pack—a free, wild Pack!

CHAPTER FIFTEEN

The hollow by the river was an excellent location to settle and make a proper camp. The place they'd slept last no-sun had been fine, but Lucky knew they needed to find a more permanent base, one that could protect them.

There was a broad plot of grass shielded both by the rising ground that stretched away from the river and by a tangled thicket of bush that would give shelter if it rained. With their hunger lessened somewhat by the rabbit and bugs they had eaten, the dogs could sit, heads cocked, and listen to the soothing trickle of water over stones, and watch the light play on the rippling surface.

"It's perfect," sighed Sunshine happily. "Who'd have thought we'd find a new home so quickly!"

"And not too far from the longpaws," added Mickey. "We'll be able to go back to the city quite easily when they come back for us."

Lucky couldn't help giving a small growl of despair, but he

managed to keep it to a muffled rumble in his throat. "Don't get too comfortable," he warned them. "We have to stay alert."

"Oh, nonsense," yapped Alfie. "Why would we ever move from here? It's so clever of you to find this place, Lucky!"

Best not to say any more, Lucky decided. Instead he gave a more cheerful bark. "The ground is good, but you'll soon feel every single pebble against your bones. Let's gather some leaves. It'll be much more comfortable than lying on grass."

The other dogs were enthusiastic enough not to grumble at this task, and they bounded energetically into the trees, seizing jawfuls of soft fallen leaves and bringing them back to scatter on the ground beneath the scrubby bush till there was a messy heap of them. Bella and Martha scraped the pile together into a good thick bed, broad enough for all of them if they lay snuggled close together.

Stepping back, Bella examined their work with satisfaction, though Sunshine had now flopped down, panting.

"Being a wild dog is such hard work!"

Bella licked her ear. "And we haven't finished yet."

"Bella's right," Lucky agreed. "We have to organize ourselves. We all have different talents. Let's make use of them."

"I don't think I'm good at anything," said Sunshine

mournfully, her ears drooping.

"That isn't true," said Lucky heartily. "You have sharp eyes and a good nose. You can patrol for dangers. You and Daisy!"

Daisy gave an excited yap. "Oh, yes! I can do that, Lucky!"

"You think I can do that?" Sunshine pricked her ears doubtfully. "All right, Lucky! I'll try my best. And I can look for more leaves. . . ."

Lucky felt his eyes twinkling with amusement. "I think we have enough of those at the moment, but you should keep an eye out for anything else we could use. Alfie could scout for that sort of thing, too. Mickey? You should be in charge of looking for food."

"Yes," agreed Bella. "Mickey's the best hunter. He should come with me."

Mickey positively swelled with pride, yelping proudly through his mouthful of glove.

"And Bruno and Martha can stand guard?" Bella looked questioningly at Lucky.

"Yes! Martha, you'll be especially good at watching for trouble from the river side."

Sitting around Lucky in a semicircle, the dogs gave him looks of pride and gratitude, and he found himself touched by their trust. He yelped encouragingly and pawed the ground. "Let's get started!"

Sunshine bounded after Lucky, along with Daisy and Alfie, as he trotted out of the makeshift camp.

"We could go back toward the field where we saw the long-paws," suggested Alfie. "What do you think, Lucky?"

At his side Daisy shivered nervously. "Maybe not exactly that direction," Lucky said, with a swift reassuring nuzzle at Daisy's head, "but we could take a wide circle around it. I don't want to run into any of those yellow longpaws again, but there might be things they've left behind, things we could use."

"Good idea!" yapped Alfie, and bounded ahead, up a shallow slope and onto the grassy plateau.

They weren't nearly as far from the city as Lucky would have liked, but there were advantages to being around old longpaw places. It wasn't long before they came in sight of a small wooden longpaw house that looked deserted, tucked between a rough field and a copse of trees. Was it a longpaw house—or something else?

Lucky sniffed the ground very carefully, but couldn't find a fresh scent. "Can you help, Sunshine?" She placed her yellow leash on the ground and the two of them worked together, their noses close to the earth, but they couldn't find any clues. "Let's have a look around," he murmured.

The four dogs edged nervously around a broken wire fence and began to explore. A scruffy-looking building leaned against the house like a longpaw who'd been drinking fire-juice. Pawing the splintered wooden door, Lucky felt it give abruptly, and he jumped back as it creaked and groaned and collapsed inward.

Hackles high, they sniffed the dank air inside. There was a sharp smell of the liquid that longpaws gave to their loudcages to make them run, but the loudcage that squatted in the shack, apparently asleep, didn't look as if it had run anywhere for a long time. It was dented, and rusty, and its round rubber paws were flat against the stone floor. Its big round eyes didn't flash, even when Lucky pushed the loudcage's door with a paw, and one of them was broken into sharp shards.

"This loudcage hasn't been used for a long time," announced Daisy, proud of her knowledge.

"I don't think it'll howl. . . ." said Lucky doubtfully.

"Of course it won't howl," said Sunshine. "It's dead."

Well, these dogs know more about longpaw things than I do . . . Hesitantly Lucky pawed at the loudcage's door, but it didn't swing open for him the way the broken loudcage in the city had, when it let him sleep inside.

Alfie barked at a small bar of metal set into the door. "That bit. Pull that, Lucky!"

More determinedly Lucky scraped at the metal lever till he felt it give under his paw; as soon as she heard the loud *clunk*, Daisy grabbed the edge of the door with her teeth and pulled it wide.

Lucky gave her an admiring glance, then sniffed at the inside of the loudcage. "That was clever, Daisy."

She wagged her brown tail with pleasure. "Let's look inside!"

The loudcage smelled of old and acrid longpaw smoke. The tanned skin of its seats was torn and moldy, and Lucky wrinkled his muzzle. Alfie, though, squeezed past him and began to tug with his teeth at the skin.

It must be dead, Lucky thought. *Otherwise it would definitely be wailing by now!*

When he was quite sure of that, Lucky joined Alfie in tearing at the skin till it was coming off in strips with an awful, but rather satisfying, ripping noise. "We can't eat this," he pointed out curiously.

"I have," said Alfie mischievously. "I've eaten it lots of times. It doesn't taste very good, but it's fun."

Sunshine gave a little giggling yelp of agreement. "My longpaw was so angry when I chewed hers!"

"I bet she didn't smack you," said Daisy.

"Of course not," said Sunshine smugly. "She never smacked me, but I didn't get a treat before bedtime. Still, it was worth it."

"The thing is," Daisy told Lucky, "this stuff is terribly comfy to lie on."

Lucky pricked his ears and wagged his tail hard, looking from face to face. "Well done!" he exclaimed proudly, and tore at the seat-skin with renewed enthusiasm.

"*And* there's a soft-hide in the back," pointed out Sunshine, putting her paws on the seat-back and panting eagerly as she peered over. "It doesn't look very clean, but it'll be cozy."

By the time they left the shack, they held in their jaws a magnificent haul of soft loudcage skin-strips and one tattered soft-hide. It was awkward carrying it all back to the camp, but even Sunshine didn't complain. Their reception from the rest of the Pack made the small dogs lift their heads and trot with pride.

"Daisy!" exclaimed Bella. "All of you! Where did you find those?"

It took Daisy and Sunshine a long time to tell the story, they were so breathless with excitement. While they explained their adventure, Lucky and Alfie were left to pull the soft-hide and the pieces of skin onto the leaf-bed. But Lucky found he couldn't mind. *They're taking pride in their dog-spirit.*

Bella gazed admiringly at their new and splendid sleeping-place. "We had good luck, too," she told Lucky. "Mickey found a squirrel, and we caught another rabbit!"

"That's wonderful." Lucky licked his litter-sister's muzzle. "Did you keep some for us?"

"We haven't even started it yet," she told him, mock-indignantly. "As if we would!"

Well, he thought to himself, *you haven't been really, truly hungry so far. . . .* But all he said was, "Thank you, Bella! That's good Pack work."

"And there's something else." She nipped gently at his nose. "Come and see what Martha found."

Bella led him over toward the river. Martha and Mickey were pawing energetically at a boulder on the banks of the stream, and Lucky and Bella had to wade into the water to watch them properly.

"Look!" Martha turned to him, panting. "Isn't this perfect?"

Lucky peered at the big flat rock, and saw right away that of course they weren't trying to dig away at solid stone. Beneath the rock there was a small cavern formed by thick tree roots, and Mickey and Martha had hollowed it out. It now formed a deep hole beneath the bank, and the very edge of the stream rippled across its entrance. Martha gazed at Lucky expectantly as he explored it with his muzzle.

"We can keep extra food here—if we have any," she told him. "It'll stay cool so it'll still taste good, and it won't go bad so quickly. Like a longpaw cold-box!"

Lucky stepped back into the stream, deeply impressed. "Martha, that's brilliant."

"Isn't it?" agreed Bella. "It was Martha and Mickey's idea." She sounded terribly proud of her Leashed friends' initiative. Although Lucky doubted they'd ever have much food to spare, it was the kind of practical, longpawish idea that would never have occurred to him.

As if reading his thoughts, Bella said, "I think we should try to keep a little food back whenever we can. It'll be difficult, but it'll mean we always have something to keep us going if—well, if we can't catch any food one sunup, for instance."

"That's a smart idea," Lucky told her approvingly. "In the meantime we must all be hungry. Let's share Mickey and Bella's prey."

It was a popular suggestion, and the other dogs watched admiringly as Mickey and Bella divided up the rabbit and the squirrel, tugging them into bits of fur and flesh and nudging the pieces to their friends. As they worked, Lucky glanced at the sky, feeling the hairs on his back prickle. Things looked gray and bleak up there, as though Sky-Dog was getting ready for something. They should make their offering and eat quickly, Lucky decided. Then he hesitated.

"It's a long time since I shared my food with the Earth-Dog," he said, ashamed. "I've been so busy trying to survive, I haven't been able to spare even a scrap. She's brought me this far, and I have to give her some prey, too."

"But—" Bruno opened his jaws to protest as Lucky began to scrape a hole in the earth. He noticed Martha shoot Bruno a warning look.

Lucky picked up a rabbit leg in his teeth, and dropped it reverently into the hole. For a moment he closed his eyes, thanking the Earth-Dog, then scraped soil back over the chunk of flesh.

When he looked up, all the other dogs were staring at him, but at least they knew better than to say anything. *They'll learn*.

"Now," Lucky said. "We can eat!"

The rest of the dogs exchanged glances, their shoulders sagging with relief and their tongues flicking out to lick their chops as Lucky shared out the meat. When each dog had a chunk to

191

gnaw on, there were two haunches left over, and Mickey put his paw on them.

"Let's put these in our cold-box. For tomorrow, just in case."

"Yes." Lucky paused in chewing at his tender piece of rabbit flank. Despite his approval of Mickey's forward planning, he felt a little tremor of distaste. "But can we call it our 'river-store'? Instead of a cold-box?"

Bella gave an amused bark and licked his ear fondly. "Well, I don't see why not. That's a much better name anyway. More . . . more *doggish*."

"Yes," agreed Lucky, relieved. At that moment he felt something wet splash onto his ear, and he shook his head, only to feel two more cold spots on his skull and his other ear. "It's going to *pour*—"

Sure enough, they all raised their heads and heard the distant rumble of the Sky-Dog growling, as the rain suddenly spattered harder on their hides. Sunshine crouched whimpering beneath Martha's flanks.

"Not thunder!" she whined.

"Another Sky-Dog fight." Lucky shivered. "It's time to test our shelter."

Together they crept onto the sleeping space beneath the

tangled branches of the thornbush, and huddled in a heap of warm bodies, Sunshine and Daisy tucked safely in the middle. Each of the dogs had pulled their longpaw things close beside them—Mickey settled beside his glove and Daisy rested a paw on her leather pouch. Lucky could feel Sunshine trembling against his flank, and the warmth of Bella's throat where she rested her head across his shoulders. The closeness, the strong beating hearts of other dogs, sent visions of the Pup Pack flashing through his head again, but it no longer made him uneasy. Now, the memory was comforting.

The storm was over soon. Lucky raised his head as the sky lightened, and watched the black, thundering cloudbank drift out over the ocean.

"You know what was happening, don't you?" Lucky said, almost to himself.

"No," Sunshine said, her voice full of misery. Lucky knew he could make her feel better if he shared a story. The little dog edged out slightly so that she could train her eyes on Lucky's face.

"The Sky-Dogs sent out Lightning to tease Earth-Dog. But the Sun-Dog growled his displeasure—they were the rolls of thunder—and sent the Sky-Dogs and Lightning packing. Now, the Sun-Dog blazes once more and the wet leaves glitter. See?"

Hesitantly Lucky crept across the shivering bodies of the other dogs and nosed the air. It still tasted of battle and lightning, but the sky was clear and bright once more.

Lucky glanced back at the others' nervous and expectant faces. A few drops of rain had leaked through to their sleeping-place, but the overhanging bush had protected them all remarkably well. Lucky barked happily.

"Come on! It's fresh water from the Sky-Dogs!"

He bounded into the open, where a puddle of new rain glinted in the hollow. He leaped wildly into it, and Bruno and Mickey followed on his heels, rolling and barking with glee. The rest were quick to join them.

The clear puddle was soon a splattered patch of mud, and their legs and bellies were black with it; Sunshine was the first to escape the puddle, trot toward the river, and splash delicately into the calm eddying pool at its edge, letting the water wash her white fur. When they'd all swum themselves clean—Bruno with some trepidation, though Martha stayed protectively close to him—they clambered from the stream and shook themselves dry. Each dog, Lucky realized, was thoroughly wetting the others with every shake, the scattering showers of water glinting in the sun-high light.

Panting, he flopped onto the flat rock at the edge of the river and watched Mickey roll blissfully in the dry sand on the shore. The Sun-Dog's rays were deliciously warm on his heaving flanks, and Bella soon came to join him, followed by the others. Only Martha still stood in the river, lapping at the water, enjoying its flow around her legs.

Sunshine was right, he realized. *It really is perfect here.*

Carefully he licked his paws. Perhaps, soon, they would take him bounding across open land again. . . .

But he couldn't think about leaving the others—not yet. These dogs were getting better at listening to their dog-spirits—so much better—but they had a long way to go. When they could look after themselves, when they could hunt and survive and thrive alone: *That* would be the time for Lucky to leave.

CHAPTER SIXTEEN

"Look! Look what I caught!"

Lucky opened one eye and pricked an ear. It had been his waking routine for the last several days. The late sun-high was warm and humming with bees, and he was almost too comfortable to move. But Daisy loved to impress him; sleepily he wondered what she'd brought him this time. It was hard work feigning enthusiasm over her latest beetle, but he was fond of the young dog and he didn't want to disappoint her, so he hauled himself to his feet and sniffed eagerly as she came bounding toward him.

At his forepaws, she dropped the prey. It was a good bit larger—and furrier—than a beetle.

"A mole? That's terrific!" Lucky licked her nose admiringly, and sniffed delicately at the tiny prey's big flat paws. They could tunnel so fast, these silky black creatures, burrowing swiftly out of reach when a dog had barely started to dig. Why, he'd only ever caught two of them himself, in his entire hunting life!

Daisy was swelling with pride, her tail thrashing furiously as Bella, Bruno, Alfie, and Martha gathered around to admire her catch.

"Daisy, that's wonderful!" said Bella. "*I've* never caught a mole!"

Lucky exchanged an affectionate glance with his litter-sister. She knew how important it was to encourage a dog like Daisy, barely more than a pup and so excited to learn. Bella had a great deal of good sense and instinct, thought Lucky warmly. She would be a good leader once he had moved on.

They were getting more organized as a group, and that made Lucky even more hopeful that they would thrive in the wild. In the last few days, he had stepped back a pace to let Mickey gain some leadership experience. With the herding dog in charge and Lucky supervising, all the Leashed Dogs' hunting skills had begun to improve. Working together, herding prey toward two or three of the Pack, they'd caught a few more rabbits and even a squirrel. It was enough to keep the hunger pangs at bay, together with bugs and grubs and the remains of a deer carcass—an old deer, Lucky supposed, that must have died of weakness and exhaustion rather than a longpaw loudstick. Even Sunshine had developed a taste for raw wild meat. They'd be able to look after themselves soon.

But niggling at the back of Lucky's mind was always the horrible echo of his bad dreams. If something bad was coming, the Leashed Dogs had to be as ready as he was.

Lucky put a paw on the mole and let Daisy divide it with her teeth. *Earlier on in our journey,* he thought with pride, *she could never have done that!*

There was barely a nibble for each of the dogs, but Daisy solemnly nudged the biggest piece to Lucky with her nose.

"I don't know where we'd be without you, Lucky. I can hunt now!"

"You certainly can," agreed Bella solemnly. "It'll be a rabbit next, you'll see."

"Yes!" yipped Daisy, and turned, about to race off in search of one. But the party was interrupted by a sudden volley of high-pitched barking.

Their heads turned toward the sound, hackles raised and ears pricked forward. Lucky recognized the voice even before Martha barked, "That's Sunshine!"

Sure enough, the little dog raced through the trees and came to a skidding halt beside them. She was panting with exertion and panic, but she managed to gasp, "Mickey! Mickey's trapped!"

"Calm down, Sunshine!" yelped Bella. "'What do you mean, trapped?"

"His collar—oh, please come, Bella. He's choking!"

Lucky sprang toward the trees, the other dogs at his heels, and let Sunshine lead them through a shallow glade and into a thick undergrowth of thorns and tangled branches.

"Here! He's here!" Sunshine pawed at the scrub.

Mickey's nose was sticking out through leaves, and now Lucky could see his eyes in the shadows, filled with fear, wide enough to show the whites. His tongue hung from his jaws as he tried to rasp air into his lungs.

"Don't move, Mickey!" Lucky barked urgently. He tried to rake aside the thick branches, stinging his paw pads on thorns. The others gathered behind him, not crowding around and panicking as they usually did but with eerie worried calm. They were giving Mickey and Lucky some space, but they couldn't help barking some rather useless advice, too.

"Pull him, Lucky!"

"Bite the branches off!"

Sunshine scraped the ground nervously with her front paws. "Oh, Lucky, please help him. He was only teaching me to hunt.

I'm so hopeless and he's been so good. . . ."

"I'm trying, Sunshine. Hush. Bella!"

She was at his side in an instant. "What do you need me to do, Lucky?"

He was thinking fast. Mickey didn't have long if they couldn't stop that collar from choking him. He was trapped tightly by the thicket of thorns, and he couldn't seem to move forward at all, but if . . .

"Here, Bella, your head is narrower than mine. Can you get a hold of his collar?"

Bella nudged and forced her way into the bushes, getting scratches on her muzzle and ears, but she managed to take Mickey's collar carefully between her teeth.

"Hold still! That's it—now, Mickey, you have to go backward."

Mickey looked up at Lucky with frightened eyes. "Backward?" he gasped. "*Deeper* into the thorns?"

"Yes. Wriggle backward. Trust me!"

Mickey needed no second telling. Lucky just wished he could be as sure as Mickey that he knew what he was doing. . . .

Planting his forepaws as well as he could on the ground, the dog wriggled and shoved desperately backward, flinching as the thorns dug harder into his hide. But the branches were giving, gradually. Despite Mickey's awkward struggles, Bella managed to keep a tight hold of his collar, her paws scrabbling for purchase on the sandy soil.

"That's it! Well done," cried Lucky. "Just a little more, Mickey. Turn your head—Bella, *pull*!"

Mickey shot backward into the bush, yelping as the prickles caught his haunches. But the collar was off, dangling loose in Bella's jaws, and it took him no time to scramble free of the thornbush. The others clustered around him, yipping their relief and delight.

Sunshine bounced on her hindpaws, licking Mickey's jaws. "Mickey, you're all right! Oh, thank you, Lucky. I *knew* you'd be able to do it."

"Mickey and Bella did most of it," Lucky pointed out. "Mickey, are you hurt?"

Mickey stood squarely and gave himself a violent shake, sending twigs and leaves flying. "Just a few scratches. I'm sorry, Lucky, that was stupid of me."

"It could happen to any of us," Lucky consoled him. "Those of us wearing a collar, anyway," he added dryly.

"My collar!" Mickey started. Glancing left to right, he caught sight of the brown leather strap, still gripped in Bella's mouth.

Mickey licked her nose gratefully. "There it is. And it isn't even broken!"

Lucky couldn't believe his eyes as Bruno padded up and took the other side of the collar in his jaws, so he and Bella were holding it between them, stretching it out to its full extent. Mickey shoved his nose into it and tried to wriggle back in.

"What are you *doing*?"

Bruno gave him a surprised look. "Helping, of course."

"Helping him do what?" Lucky sat down on his haunches, flummoxed. "Put it back *on*?"

"Of course." Mickey gave him a nervous glance, while Bella looked a little apologetic. "It's my collar. Why wouldn't I wear it?"

"Because of what just happened!" barked Lucky in exasperation. "If we hadn't been here, you'd have been strangled!"

"But you *were* here," pointed out Mickey reasonably.

Lucky raised his head and barked angrily at the sky. "You should get rid of those collars altogether! They can trap you, choke you. And if you ever got into a fight with some other dog—well, you wouldn't have a chance!"

"That's not true!" snapped Bruno. Proudly he squared his shoulders and jutted his head forward. "Not have a chance? I've got the blood of fighting dogs in me! My collar doesn't change that!"

"Bruno's right," yelped Sunshine, and the others barked in agreement.

Lucky's temper flared, lifting his hackles on his back and curling the skin of his muzzle. These dogs were making him crazy—one minute, they showed all the instincts necessary to live and thrive in this broken world; the next they were behaving like puppies, pining for their longpaws' restraints.

"I'll prove it to you!" Lucky growled, charging at Bruno. The brown dog was so startled he flinched back, and in that moment Lucky seized his thick leather collar between his jaws. Bruno fought to keep his balance, but it was no use; he was dragged over by Lucky, who twisted his neck, flinging the other dog around. Bruno was heavy and thickset, but it was easy for Lucky to use the collar to gain leverage and throw him sideways.

The rest of the dogs were barking in protest and fear now, and Bruno was yelping, trying to fight back but unable to get leverage with his paws. Lucky shook him like a huge trapped squirrel.

"Oh, Lucky, please!" cried Daisy above the scared racket of the others. "Please don't hurt him!"

Lucky released Bruno and let him flop to the ground, panting for breath. He put a paw on the brown dog's chest; that was too much for Bruno, who rolled over with a growl and staggered to his feet, then shook himself from head to tail. Lucky returned his glare, and it wasn't long before Bruno dropped his eyes.

"You see?" said Lucky. "Do you see now?" He kept his voice low and averted his eyes to prove the fight was over. He felt guilt prickling under his fur. He'd worked out all his temper on poor, gutsy Bruno. *I shouldn't have done that....*

But they *had* to learn, and he was the only teacher they had. "You see how vulnerable a collar makes you? I bet Bruno could beat me in a fair fight," he said, with a glance at the strong dog, "but with his collar on, I could do what I liked. Trust me. You should take them off."

The Pack exchanged shocked glances, and one or two of them stared at their paws. It was little Daisy who finally summoned up the nerve to answer him.

"Lucky," she whined softly, "I know how you feel about this. We all do. But—but my collar? I can't take it off. I *won't.* I'll do anything else you ask me, but please don't ask me that. It shows I'm bound to a longpaw, that I'm owned and loved and that I have a longpaw to look after. It's so important. To *all* of us."

Lucky stared at her, bewildered at such a long, firm speech from this pup.

"But, Daisy," he said, "you don't have a longpaw now. They're gone."

She whimpered and averted her eyes.

"I don't care if I don't have longpaws just now," Mickey said. His dark eyes met Lucky's, respectful but determined. "I'll find them again. If I have to learn to fight better, that's what I'll do—but I *will* put my collar back on. I won't give up on my longpaws."

Lucky realized he was wasting his breath. He turned and padded away over the beaten earth and back toward their camp. He couldn't bear to watch as Sunshine and Martha joined in the efforts to replace Mickey's collar.

He heard the sound of paws behind him, and glanced over his shoulder. There was Bella, her eyes beseeching.

"Lucky, you have to try to understand. Collars are important to us. They're part of who we are."

They're part of who you've been made to be, he wanted to say. But there was no arguing with his litter-sister at the moment, so he kept quiet, shaking himself and padding on.

A distant yelping and whining startled him. *Alfie!* Lucky picked up speed and turned toward the sound of his barks, but realized with relief that they weren't the cries of danger and distress—Alfie just couldn't find the Pack.

"Everyone? Bella! Lucky, Bruno! Where *are* yooooou?"

Bella was behind him as he trotted back into the camp, and he could hear the rest following behind in a racket of broken twigs and scattering stones. Hunting-craft was all but forgotten for today, then.

When Alfie caught sight of them emerging from the trees, the short, squat little dog bounded across to them with delight, yapping his welcome, oblivious to the recent frictions. *Every dog has something to bring to the Pack,* Lucky thought. They were lucky to have a dog like Alfie to lighten tense moments.

"You're here! I thought you'd forgotten me!"

"As if we could," barked Bella in amusement as he jumped to lick her nose. "Did you have any luck with hunting?"

"No." Alfie's ears drooped, but only for a moment; then he was dancing on his paws once more. "But I found something else!"

"What?" asked Martha, pricking her ears.

"Tell!" yelped Daisy, clearly relieved to have a distraction from the quarrel.

Alfie sat back and scratched at his ear. Lucky could see he was delighted to have a story to tell and determined to make the most of it. "I walked a long way. All on my own. I like to be alone some- times," he added with a glance at Lucky as if seeking approval. "I investigated the little valley, there—and those hills. I even went beyond them!"

Lucky was startled. The valley that sloped gently away from the grassland, up beyond the trees, was quite broad, and the hills beyond it were rocky and steep. He'd investigated the area a little himself, on one of the nights he had prowled the territory checking for enemies, but he certainly hadn't gone beyond the hills. The squat dog must have explored a long way.

"That could have been dangerous, Alfie," Lucky chided him gently, though he could relate more than ever to Alfie's need to be alone. "But what did you find?"

"Dogs!" he announced triumphantly. "Lots of *dogs*!"

The others yapped and barked at the news, and Daisy performed her spinning-in-a-circle trick, bouncing with excitement. "What were they like, Alfie?" she yelped. "Are they friendly? Can they help us?"

"I don't know. I didn't go that far. But I heard them! And I smelled them, too—and there was something else!"

Lucky's skin prickled with unease, but the others were too excited to worry.

"What?" yipped Sunshine. "What was it?"

Alfie's eyes gleamed. "Food. Lots and *lots* of food!"

CHAPTER SEVENTEEN

"Let's go," yapped Sunshine. *"Let's go* there now and introduce ourselves!"

"That's a wonderful idea," said Mickey warmly.

Lucky took a breath as the others barked and yelped with the eagerness to investigate. He was uncomfortably aware that the questions he was about to ask could cause another squabble. "Alfie, what kind of dogs were they?"

"I don't know. They were dogs! Like us! But with food!"

"Not all dogs *are* like us. What if they're hostile? What if it's a Wild Pack? They'll defend their territory if they are. You shouldn't mess with a Wild Pack—and they won't choose to share food with you."

Sunshine was crestfallen, but Bruno interrupted. "There's no harm in looking."

"There could be plenty of harm in it," growled Lucky. "I don't like this. I'm sorry. It sounds dangerous."

"Oh, Lucky," yipped Bella fondly. "You think everything is dangerous! You're a wonderful leader, but perhaps you should stop being quite so cautious."

"If there's food for the taking, we can't *not* look," added Bruno. "This could mean we wouldn't have to tire ourselves out by hunting!"

Lucky realized Bruno was still aggrieved about the fight demonstration. He sighed. "We don't know anything about these dogs," he protested.

"But we can find out. The least we can do is look," suggested Martha.

"I agree," Bruno said.

"And if they're smaller than us," said Bella, throwing Lucky a challenging glare, "there won't be a problem."

"Bella's right," put in Mickey. "Why don't we at least go and investigate?"

"It would be easier than hunting beetles," said Sunshine mournfully, sitting down and tapping the ground with her tailtip.

What's wrong with beetles all of a sudden? Lucky pawed at one that was clambering over a grass stem, but he'd lost his appetite. He didn't like the way Bella was looking at him: She was drawn up to her full height and her ears were turned back, almost as if she was spoiling for a fight. When a squirrel in one of the treetops chirruped angrily at them, she didn't even flick an ear, just went on staring at Lucky with her head slightly tilted.

"Tell you what," Bella suggested. "Some of us can go and investigate. The rest will stay here, as a sort of backup team, and guard the camp while we're gone. A small group will be less noticeable anyway. I'd suggest me, Daisy, Alfie, and Lucky."

Lucky studied the hopeful eyes and the pricked ears of the little group. *I have a bad feeling about this,* Lucky thought. But he knew that if he was going to leave these dogs to cope on their own one day, they had to start making their own decisions—and he had to trust them. "All right. But at the first sign of trouble—turn tails! The rest of you, stay close to the camp."

Whatever happened next, Lucky would just have to be ready.

Alfie seemed happy to be lead dog for a change. He'd found a path through the brush, beaten down by small animals, and there was plenty of shade dappling the way, at least till they reached the beginning of the slope. As they stepped out from beneath the tree cover, the late Sun-Dog's rays beat down on them, and by the time they'd climbed to the ridge they were all moving sluggishly. When Alfie paused in the shadow of a tree even Lucky flopped down.

"We should rest," he told them.

"It's not far now," panted Alfie, still eager.

"We'll get moving again soon," promised Bella, wagging her tail. "When I say so, be ready to go."

She'd raised her voice to be sure it would reach Lucky. He laid his head on his paws and turned away, glaring down into the valley. She was making sure her so-called Pack knew who was boss; that was all.

Let her! It's not as if they're my *Pack!*

Lucky followed Alfie as he led them down a winding rabbit path. His mind was a tumble of conflict and uncertainty. How would a Wild Pack react to the approach of a bunch of Leashed Dogs? Would they be driven off with their tails between their legs? How would Bella's leadership skills stand up if she had to talk her way out of a fight?

Suddenly Alfie squeaked, "There. Look!"

Lucky halted with the others and sniffed the air doubtfully. Yes, he could scent them—dogs, a good many of them—and he was fairly sure he didn't like it. The scent was dark, bitter, and musky, and it reeked of anger—not that it seemed to bother the others. From the shade of a small scrubby tree, they gazed out at the scene below.

The valley was broad and dotted with longpaw buildings, but these longpaw buildings didn't look like the longpaw homes that Lucky had seen in the city. They were too short, for one thing. In fact, their doors looked dog-sized. The walls were plain, and the windows had metal bars across the holes where most longpaw buildings had clear-stone. They seemed less damaged than the buildings in the city, but there were a few vicious cracks running up some of the walls.

There was something unnatural about the sight, something frightening that would have made Lucky want to run away as fast as he could in any direction—if it hadn't been for the scent of food.

It was a strong, tantalizing odor. Not longpaw food like the Food House owner had given him, Lucky decided—but very definitely food made of meat. Lucky felt his mouth water and he licked his chops. His stomach grumbled. There was no sign of movement below—not that that made Lucky feel any better.

So where were the dogs he could smell? Lucky's heartbeat quickened. He'd worked so hard to look after the Pack, and he couldn't put them in danger now. But his stomach was telling him something different. If these were friendly dogs—friends with food . . . perhaps Bella was right, after all, and they would share what they had. It had to be worth exploring.

"All right," he said slowly. "Let's go closer. Stick together and try not to draw attention to yourself. Not until we know what type of dogs are down there."

Creeping forward, then running low, they scampered toward the fence and peered through. Bella put her forepaws up against the wire, snuffling.

"Look," she breathed in awe. "Look at all that food!"

In front of the low houses there were metal bowls, some with a thin puddle of water in them, some brim-full of dry-looking nuggets of meat. Once again Lucky licked saliva from his jaws. It wasn't like live rabbit, but it did smell good. And there was so much of it. . . .

"I think it's . . ." whispered Alfie haltingly. "It *smells* like . . ."

"Like our home-food," agreed Bella in a murmur. "It's like the food the longpaws used to give us."

"Oh . . ." Daisy breathed a nostalgic, hungry sigh. "I'd love to taste that again. . . ."

Even as they watched, they heard a loud click. All the dogs froze, limbs stiffening and muscles tensing to run, but no one appeared, longpaw or dog. Instead, more of those nuggets poured from holes in the wall into the metal bowls, making some of them overflow, and fresh clear water streamed into every second bowl.

It was too much for Bella. She hopped on her hindpaws, sticking her nose desperately through the wire, whining and scratching at the fence with her claws.

"It's amazing! Food that comes from nowhere! We *have* to get in!"

Lucky cocked his head, staring at the bowls as the others nuzzled and poked their noses under the fence, searching for gaps and scraping at the earth. Certainly it seemed quiet enough, he thought.

So why was the dog-spirit inside him telling him to run?

"Here!" yelped Alfie. "I found a hole!"

The others bounded toward it, but Lucky approached more cautiously, watching the dark entrance to the closest building for any sign of movement.

He could smell dogs, and he could see their food. So where were they?

His hackles bristled, and he took a pace back. The Leashed Dogs were surviving on the food they hunted; did they really need these overflowing bowls of extra food?

"Lucky, come and see!" cried Daisy. "I can dig deeper. Just you watch—I'll make us a way in!"

"No." Lucky shook his head. "This doesn't feel right. There's danger here. Can't you sense it? We should get away while we can. You can hunt now—we don't need others to give us our food."

"Don't be silly," snapped Bella. "Why should we hunt, when all this is here for the taking?"

Lucky's skin prickled all over as he looked at the late Sun-Dog glinting off the shiny metal bowls. "That's the point. Don't you see how much food there is? How big those bowls are? How big do you think the dogs are that live here? Do you think you'd win a fight? We haven't seen them, but why? Are they hiding?"

Daisy glanced nervously at Bella, but the bigger dog growled, "We can look after ourselves."

Lucky whined. Every moment he spent in this place made him more uneasy. He was wrong to have let the Pack come here. The sensation in his hide had become a tingling, an almost unbearable sense of threat, similar to the way he felt before a Sky-Dog battle—or before the Big Growl shattered the world. And worse, it was waking the memory of his terrible dreams: the dreams that didn't make sense. The Storm of Dogs . . .

They had to get out of here.

"Please, Bella!" he started to say.

Springing up onto a higher hillock of earth by the fence, Bella snarled. "That's it! *I'm* the Alpha of this Pack, Lucky. *I* brought you in. You might be very clever on your own, but this is *our* kind of place. And I say we're going in!"

Lucky bared his teeth at her. "Stop acting like a spoiled puppy! You've no idea what being an Alpha is all about!"

"Oh, and you do?" Legs stiff, hackles high, Bella stalked around him, growling. "We were doing just fine before we met you. You're the one who's showing off. Pretending you know it all!"

"I know a lot more than you do, Leashed Dog!" snarled Lucky. "You don't know anything about staying alive! You're all soft, and you've got no sense. No—no *dog-spirit*!" That was about as bad an insult as he could find to throw at her. Guilt plunged through him, but it wasn't enough to overwhelm his anger. *How dare she! After everything I've done for her!*

There was something else in Lucky's heart, too: a fear that pounded through him with every breath. These dogs looked up to Lucky as a leader because he knew the lay of the land and could teach them crafty survival tricks. But it did not matter how crafty Lucky was; he knew what happened to dogs who lost challenges. He had seen it happen before. It was like their dog-spirit had been slashed, wounds ripped open, and their essence, their bravery, their courage all seeped out. A defeated dog would duck his head in the presence of others, and keep his tail low, limp between his legs.

Lucky's instincts urged him to fight against this.

Bella barked in anger. "You talk a lot of nonsense!"

"Dog-spirit is what's inside us all," he snarled. "Or it should be! That's what protects us—along with the Sky-Dogs and the Forest-Dog and—oh, why am I bothering with you? You don't understand any of it!"

"Well, your so-called dog-spirit is making you a coward, Lucky!" growled Bella. Her lips were pulled back from her teeth as they circled each other. Alfie and Daisy watched fearfully, crouching close to the ground. "There aren't any other dogs here! Worse, there aren't any longpaws, either."

Lucky shivered with anger and frustration. He thought of the Fierce Dog who'd driven him away from the firebox. Had Bella ever had to face a dog like that? Of course she hadn't—because she'd been protected by longpaws all her life. "There *are* dogs here! I can't see them, but I can smell them!"

"You can smell dogs that used to be here, maybe. It doesn't matter. I'm in charge, and I say we go in!"

Lucky gave a bitter snarl, and snapped the air. "You may be in charge of these *Leashed Dogs*! But you're not in charge of me, *Squeak*, and you never will be!"

Alfie gave a groan of protest, and Daisy whined, but Bella and Lucky ignored them. Lucky knew their barks were getting loud, but he no longer cared. He half hoped they *would* be overheard and chased away from here before Bella did something stupid.

"I order you, Lucky!" she yelped. "I order you to come with us!"

"You can order all you like." Lucky curled his muzzle and sat down, scratching his ear with casual disdain. "You're not my Alpha. I'm not coming."

Daisy gasped.

"I'm the Alpha of this Pack!" growled Bella.

"And you're welcome to it!" He gave her a furious bark.

Bella fell silent, flanks heaving, saliva dripping from her jaws.

"Be that way, and see where it gets you, Lone Dog." Turning, she stalked off along the side of the fence, tail high. "You're not as smart as you think you are. There won't be any food for dogs who won't help get it!"

He shook his head in disbelief as she squirmed under the fence, followed by Alfie. They paced away toward the low houses. Daisy gave Lucky a mournful glance of longing, but she'd obviously taken Bella's declaration seriously.

"I'm sorry, Lucky," she said, then wriggled through the fence after them.

He watched the three dogs trot away, his heart pounding harder with every step they took toward those food bowls, until he couldn't watch anymore. He walked a little distance back, then turned and lay down with his head on his paws, heaving an unhappy sigh.

They were in danger. He was sure of it. At every snap of a twig, every cry of a bird, his ears twitched and he lifted his head.

He couldn't leave them. Bella was his litter-sister; he owed it to her to see that she was safe—and she wasn't safe here. Maybe his fears were just the result of his solitary life, when he had to be alert for danger at every turn. On the other hand, he felt certain there was something deeply bad here, however much it seemed like a perfect place for a new camp. He could smell it in the air.

Slowly he climbed to his feet.

Oh, Sky-Dogs, he thought to himself, *I hope I'm not making a stupid mistake. . . .*

Turning back toward the strange Dog-Garden, he headed for the hole in the fence.

CHAPTER EIGHTEEN

Daisy had done a good job of scraping out the earth, and once Lucky forced his shoulders through, his haunches followed easily.

When he was on the other side he paused, crouched against the ground, seeking some clue as to the whereabouts of the unfamiliar dogs that he could smell. Were they really gone? Perhaps they'd escaped in the Big Growl, or crawled through the gap under the fence. Maybe they'd preferred the freedom of the wild to the easy source of food.

A crow flapped into the air with a raucous caw, making Lucky jump with alarm. As his heart calmed he watched it as it settled on a branch, cocking its beady black eye at him.

The grass inside the compound was lush and green, cropped neatly short. *Longpaw work,* Lucky thought. Were there longpaws still alive here? He could smell nothing but dog. Beyond the grass loomed the dark shadow of the central big house, and Lucky narrowed his eyes in Sun-Dog's dying light, trying to make out what might lurk there.

He could see almost nothing from his position near the fence, and he knew with a lurching sense of fear that he was going to have to move farther in. He couldn't make sure the others were all right if he stayed where he was. Gathering his courage, he set off, slinking so low to the ground his belly almost scraped the grass. He picked up speed and made it to a tree with spreading branches. It wasn't the best cover, but it would have to do.

He could see the others now, right in the shadow of the dog-houses. Lucky's heart lurched with fear and anger. They weren't even trying to be quiet or careful. All three of them were wolf-ing down the food in the nearest bowls, and no one was keeping watch.

"It's delicious!" squeaked Daisy through a mouthful of nug-gets.

"Mmmph," was all Alfie could reply for a moment. Then he gave a loud yip of pure excitement, and plunged his muzzle back into the bowl.

Bella gulped down a half-crunched mouthful. "We must try to take some back for the others," Lucky heard her announce. "Maybe I'll even take some back for Lucky," she added haughtily.

Lucky's spine tingled with resentment. He'd only been trying to keep them safe. Still, it was hard to watch the others gorging themselves while he could only look on, his belly growling. Lucky looked around. Nothing—no sign of dogs or longpaws. *Were they right?* he thought. *Was I too cautious? Bella will be very smug if I admit it, but . . .* Lucky began to slink forward.

And froze.

Around the corner of the biggest house stalked a group of sleek, ferocious-looking dogs.

Lucky's fur stood on end. He'd seen their kind before: dark lean bodies, pricked ears, pointed snouts that were bared more often than not in a snarl. He'd come across these dogs as guardians of longpaw homes and work-houses, doing the bidding of longpaws with harsh voices and glowing light-beams and vicious sticks.

Lucky backed swiftly behind the tree. They hadn't seen or scented him—their attention was focused on the others. At the clatter of paws on gravel, Alfie, Daisy, and Bella stopped gobbling and raised their heads in alarm; the fierce Pack had come from downwind, and had approached unnoticed. Now the big dogs spread out in a frighteningly disciplined circle, trapping the Leashed Dogs.

Bella and Alfie exchanged anxious glances. Daisy did the smartest thing under the circumstances, and rolled onto her back, whimpering as she exposed her throat and belly. *Good, Daisy!* thought Lucky, impressed. *That was quick thinking—and sensible.*

Alfie gave Daisy a nervous look and then followed her example, submitting to the other dogs. But Bella, stiff-legged and proud, curled her muzzle defiantly at the huge dogs.

Panic chilled Lucky's body, making breathing hard and sending his hackles bristling. *No, Bella! Don't be stupid. You don't stand a chance!*

He wanted to dash from the shelter of the tree, take her by the scruff of the neck, and shake some sense into her. *She's so puffed with arrogance now that she's decided she's the Alpha,* he thought. *Please, Bella, don't be reckless.* His muscles trembled with the effort of not rushing to her side. But there was nothing he could do. . . .

"You dare defy us?" One of the Fierce Dogs finally spoke in a low vicious sneer. He sounded rather pleased that she was going to resist. The attack-dogs started to close their circle around Lucky's friends.

It was Daisy who came to Bella's rescue, whimpering desperately. "Bella. Please?"

Bella gave a small yip that told her to be quiet, but after a few moments she took a breath and dipped her head in defeat. As if it cost her a huge effort, she lay down awkwardly, submitting with the others.

Briefly Lucky closed his eyes, letting relief flood his limbs. He opened his eyes again to see that the Fierce Dogs had relaxed a little, pricking their ears and growling their approval. Thank the Sky-Dogs: Bella had come to her senses in time.

"How did you get in here?" The biggest, sleekest of the Fierce Dogs growled. Her voice was dark and deadly. She must be their Alpha, Lucky decided. Her legs and body were powerful with sinewy muscle and the others lowered their heads as she spoke, deferring to her. The evening light made her coat gleam. On the side of her neck was a patch of white fur in the shape of a fang.

Lucky watched the Leashed Dogs exchange glances, and for a moment the frightened Daisy seemed about to blurt a reply. But Bella interrupted.

"We jumped," she told the bigger dog, her bark nervous but quite steady. "Over the fence."

Lucky wanted to put his paws over his eyes. How could she imagine the Fierce Dogs would fall for that one? As soon as they compared Daisy with the height of the fence, Bella was in for a sharp bite at best. . . .

But perhaps the Fierce Dogs' brains weren't quite as sharp as their teeth, because the Alpha nodded slowly, still growling in her throat.

A big male snarled at Bella. "Steal our rations, would you? Impudent rats."

"Indeed." The Alpha peeled her lips back from her teeth, showing how deadly they were. "You're our prisoners now. And you will be until we decide what to do with you. Mace? Bring them."

The male dog opened his jaws and barked. It was the loudest, most threatening sound Lucky had ever heard from a dog, making him cower in his hiding place, and he wasn't surprised when Bella, Alfie, and Daisy huddled obediently together and ducked their heads. Trembling, the Leashed Dogs were herded by the Fierce Dogs toward the big house, the bigger dogs occasionally snapping at their paws and tails. Daisy yelped with fright, and one of the guard-dogs loomed over her, barking and snapping his teeth in her face.

"Quiet! Keep moving!"

Daisy scurried on, tail between her hind legs and ears drooping miserably. Alfie made a brave attempt to stay protectively at her side, but at a warning snarl he licked her ear and dropped reluctantly back.

Oh, Earth-Dog, who are these Fierce Dogs? wondered Lucky unhappily. The powerful black dogs were so ferocious, so unfriendly. They would surely shred the Leashed Dogs without much effort.

Please, Earth-Dog, Lucky willed. *Don't let Bella and the others die here. They were foolish, but they didn't mean any harm. They will learn. Let them get free. . . .*

He had to get closer to the big house. If he was quick, he could make it while the dark dogs' backs were turned. After that? Well . . . he'd just have to take his chances.

None of the Fierce Dogs glanced back, too busy watching their prisoners with glinting eyes, and Lucky seized the moment. *Now!* He darted out from the cover of the tree. *Quickly!* Crossing the horribly open space in the waning daylight seemed to take forever, but at last he scurried close to a cracked wall and slunk into its shadow.

Breathing more easily, Lucky panted his relief and crept forward, keeping the group of dogs just in sight. He couldn't even see the Leashed Dogs now; the guard-dogs were packed tightly around them. His hide prickled with heat and fear, and his fur stood up all over his body, but he was still protected by the wall when he saw the Fierce Dogs herd the others through a door in the side of the big house. Its walls were cracked in several places, but it looked solid and strong enough to hold them till the end of the world, when the Sky-Dogs would fall to earth.

It was hopeless. Lucky felt his tail droop, and his head dip as if a longpaw hand was forcing him to sniff the earth. His fear for the Leashed Dog Pack mixed with his sense of resentment at finding himself caught up in other dogs' problems. This was why he didn't want to be in a Pack—too many dogs couldn't move quickly. Too many dogs could get into trouble. A Pack-dog was responsible for his Packmates. A Lone Dog only had to rely on himself.

Sitting down to rest, but not daring to scratch his bristling neck fur, Lucky peered cautiously around the corner of the wall.

This is the best chance I'll have to get clear.

It made sense. All he could do now was save his own fur. Every instinct was telling him to run, quickly, while he still had the chance, and get as far from this sinister place as possible. There was nothing he could do to help dogs trapped in such a forbidding prison and guarded by hostile and deadly enemies. They should have listened to him before.

And yet . . . he thought as he half turned to go. *They are my friends. . . .*

He thought of the challenges they'd faced together, the small achievements of every day as they learned to fend for themselves.

He thought of Daisy's mole, and her pride and pleasure as she'd presented it to him. . . . The way that Martha had launched herself into the river to rescue her friend. How Mickey had helped to herd his friends out of the city.

Lucky's decision was made.

He pressed close to the wall as he rounded the end of it, then raced across the last stretch of open ground. Blood thundering in his veins, he huddled against the wall beneath a barred, cracked window, panting as quietly as he could. He couldn't let the Fierce Dogs smell him, or hear his thrashing heart.

Then, for an instant, he thought his heart had stopped. The Alpha Fierce Dog, her voice as silky as it was vicious, was growling at her captives.

"Where is the other dog?"

Lucky's blood ran cold, and his skin tightened. The *other* dog?

He heard Bella's submissive whine, her frightened protestation. But the Alpha wasn't interested in denial. "You know very well, Pet Dog. The one like you. *Where is he?*"

"I don't know who you mean . . ." whined Bella, then gave a yelp of shock as jaws snapped audibly.

"Oh yes, you do . . ." snarled another Fierce Dog.

Lucky, listening beneath the window, was stiff with horror.

The knot of fear in his belly had swollen till it felt as if it filled his whole body.

They can smell me!

The Fierce Dogs hadn't spotted him but they knew he was here anyway; they'd picked out his scent from the other dogs and matched it to that of his litter-sister. These terrifying hounds must have stronger noses than any dog Lucky had ever known. How was he supposed to rescue his friends now?

CHAPTER NINETEEN

The big house was raised farther off the ground than the low doghouses that surrounded it, and a flight of wooden steps led up to the main door. They were the best cover Lucky could hope for just now, and he crouched beneath them, ears pricked for the first hint that he'd been discovered. He'd taken care to roll in some mess that he'd found in the grass—at least now he would smell of the Fierce Dogs. He hoped the deception would be enough.

He wondered what chance he'd have if they did detect him. He certainly couldn't outfight them, or even stare them into a stalemate. Could he hope to outrun them? Sweet could, if she were here. Despair gnawed at his guts. *I'd be caught and torn to pieces before I was halfway across the grass.*

He'd waited for hours now, as the sky darkened and the air cooled and the moon rose, and still he didn't see what he was going to do. He knew his friends had been fed a little; he'd heard the

Fierce Dogs carry in bowls of food and drop them, clattering, to the floor, dry nuggets spilling and rolling. He knew, too, that they were held captive in a tiny room, with a guard at all times—and he knew it was small because he'd heard Daisy's muted whine of complaint. If Daisy thought it was cramped, he dreaded to think how Bella was feeling. He had to do something soon, but his head seemed—for the first time in his life—completely empty. He had no ideas, no ways out. No crafty tricks. It was as if he'd never been a Lone Dog in control of his own destiny.

But I was a Lone Dog, he told himself. *And I was the* best.

He felt as if the Forest-Dog was whispering in his ear, steeling his dog-spirit. Yes, he'd need cunning and stealth, and those were the gifts of the Forest-Dog. Breathing quietly, Lucky shut his eyes and begged.

The Fierce Dogs hadn't spoken much to their prisoners—only to order them around—but they did talk to one another when they prowled outside the house or stood sentry in the deepening darkness. Their actions were precise and controlled, and they seemed to anticipate one another's movements. They were frighteningly disciplined, and they never relaxed their vigilance for a moment. These must have been the prized Fierce Dogs of their disappeared longpaws. Lucky shuddered, remembering with dread his few previous encounters with dogs like these. The only sensible thing to do, ever, was run. . . .

But Bella, Daisy, and Alfie didn't have that option. So Lucky wouldn't run, either. In the shadow of the steps, barely daring to breathe, he lay and listened.

Three of the Fierce Dogs came out of the big house. Lucky shrank back, hoping they wouldn't see him, but they didn't come down the steps. They sat above him, unseen, talking in loud sneering voices about their captives.

"We should kill them, Blade," grumbled one of the three, staring out at the huge moon. They were so close; Lucky struggled to keep his breathing silent and his heart steady in his ribs.

"Dagger's right," growled the second. "We should leave their bodies by the fence, so no one else will dare trespass. And besides, they're too much trouble."

"And they eat," added Dagger. "A *lot*. They're as greedy as if every meal could be their last. A waste of rations is what they are. Pathetic mutts."

"Or we could give them a beating and send them on their way," said the other, with less enthusiasm. "It would be another kind of warning. They'd be sure to spread the word."

"They're not going anywhere." The third dog, the one they'd

called Blade, growled her opinion. Lucky recognized her silken voice—she was the Alpha. "Not until they tell us how they found us and how they got in. They're all sticking to this story about jumping the fence, but I don't believe it, do you, Mace?"

"Don't worry, Blade. We'll get the truth out of them," said Mace darkly. "They'll be sorry they ever tried to steal from us."

"Indeed," growled Blade smugly. "I imagine it won't take long to persuade the mangy little mutt. And she'll tell us where the fourth dog is, too. I know he's here somewhere—I can scent him."

Beneath them, Lucky shut his eyes, trying to summon the nerve to act. These glossy, terrifying dogs might be ferocious and ruthless, but they weren't the brightest of creatures. If he'd been in Blade's position, he'd have thought of a hole in the fence as soon as Bella told her ridiculous lie, and sent one of their patrols out to check. It would've been sealed and safe by now.

As he'd expected, the guile of the Forest-Dog would be his salvation—if there was any salvation to be had.

Stealthily he crept out from his hiding place under the steps. He could hear the Fierce Dogs muttering above him, secure in the knowledge that their captives weren't going anywhere. One of them rose and stretched—Lucky heard his claws click and scratch on the wood—and he stopped still. But the dog settled again, grunting and sighing.

It was a nerve-shattering task to cross the grass, moving silently between the shadows. Lucky placed each paw carefully, praying to the Forest-Dog that they wouldn't catch a stronger whiff of his scent—not just yet.

He was a little more than halfway to the fence when he stopped, breathing in and out, calming his jangling nerves. Was this far enough? If he went too far, they wouldn't be tempted to come after him; on the other hand, he had no desire to misjudge the distance, and end up in a Fierce Dog's jaws. . . .

I can do this. Hunching his shoulders, filling his lungs, he gave a wild, deafening bark, and leaped into the air. Spinning, he dropped to all fours, then dashed in a circle, halted, and howled.

The Fierce Dogs got to their feet, staring at him in the moonlight, but they looked too dumbfounded to move for a moment. At his howl, more Fierce Dogs stuck their heads out of the house. Lucky lifted his head and howled again, the sound cutting through the still night air. "Hey, *stupid!*"

Blade lowered her head, snarling, but she only raised a paw, hesitating. Clearly his behavior was too frenzied not to raise her suspicions.

"Mad dogs, sad dogs, stupid crazy bad dogs! *Ha!*" Lucky racked his brains for the worst street insults he could remember from his days in the city. "Your mothers had worms! Your fathers were *foxes!*"

"You little—" roared Dagger, but Lucky barked over him, well into his stride by now.

"You were born in spoil-boxes! You taste so bad, the fleas spit you out! Your mothers were tailless! *You hear me, mange-breeders?* Your fathers licked sharpclaw spit!"

They sprang at him, howling with rage. Lucky hesitated only for an instant, his eyes wide as they raced across the grass, drool flying from their jaws. The insults had done their work, and all of them were after him.

Good!

And . . . bad!

Lucky spun on his hind legs, and ran as fast as he could.

He raced for the fence, doubled back, spun, and dodged—just as one snapped its teeth close to his tail. They were fast, but Lucky knew that his insults had upset them. They lunged for him angrily, more erratically than a Pack of Fierce Dogs should. This gave Lucky an advantage. His biggest advantage, though, was his fear of the Fierce Dogs. It made him dodge and duck and fly. Panting, he hurtled along the fence away from the hole Daisy had scratched out. He had to draw them farther away. Hopefully his friends had heard the commotion. *Now, Forest-Dog,* he thought, *please let Bella be smart enough to make a move....*

Lucky slid to a halt on his haunches, tumbled into a quick reverse, and bolted between two pursuing Fierce Dogs. They were enraged now, howling with hate. Saliva from snapping jaws whipped across Lucky's face and he ran again, his heart in his throat.

He was running out of ideas, and they were getting wise to him. Maybe it was time to make his own escape? If he could just dodge through the bushes, keep ahead of them long enough to reach the hole under the fence—

Oh no!

Lucky bounced off wire he hadn't seen in the dark, shocked enough to slide onto his flank. Sure enough, the fence took a sharp turn here, right in front of him.

As he scrambled to all fours, shaking and gasping for breath, the semicircle of Fierce Dogs hemmed him in.

He blinked and panted, staring wildly at the sleek Fierce Dogs. They were calm and controlled now, muscles bunched as they regained their discipline and formed a moving, snarling trap around him. Slowly, slowly, they stalked forward, stiff-legged, fearsome teeth bared. In the darkness their eyes glinted with hatred.

"Who's clever now, stinking mongrel?" snarled Mace.

Fur bristling, Lucky backed up till he could go no farther, the wire of the fence biting painfully into his haunches.

But that was nothing. There would be worse biting in a minute, far worse. These savage dogs were going to rip him to pieces, limb by limb.

CHAPTER TWENTY

"Blade! Blade!"

Blade's elegant head snapped around, and Lucky realized, with a chill in his blood, that although there were several Fierce Dogs waiting to kill him, one seemed to be missing. Despite her fury, Blade must have sent one of them back to check on the prisoners. And now . . . ?

"They're gone, Blade! The prisoners are *gone*."

Blade whipped her attention back to Lucky, her muzzle curling back from her white, deadly teeth. Unable to help himself, Lucky shrank against the fence, shivering.

"Where are your friends?" the Alpha hissed. "Are they still in the compound?"

Lucky swallowed. He hoped not.

Blade took a menacing pace toward him. "Tell me, Street Mutt. Where are they hiding? They can't have gotten out. Not even with one of their miracle jumps," she sneered.

Lucky managed a hoarse, brave bark. "I don't know."

"You don't know? Well, let me see. I could tear you into pieces right here, or you could help me round up your miserable little friends."

"Yes," snarled Dagger. "And then we won't hurt you. Not too much, anyway."

"That's right." Blade wore a horrible grin. "It'll be better for all of you if you tell us where they're hiding. You know, don't you? You've been hiding from us since we caught your little *Pack*"—she spat the word with derision—"so you know where they are now. Speak, stupid dog, and you'll live. You *and* your inferior friends. Submit as you should, and we won't kill you. I think that's as fair as I can be, isn't it? You can hardly ask for a better deal."

Mace sniggered at his leader's side.

Lucky stared into Blade's eyes, trying to control the trembling of his limbs. There wasn't a hint of mercy in those dark depths.

This dog was going to kill him no matter what he did. She was going to kill them all, if she got the chance.

At least the others had escaped. Lucky raised his gaze to look beyond Blade and her cohorts, away into the trees beyond the fence. *Thank you, Forest-Dog,* he thought. *You couldn't save us all, but you saved my friends. . . .*

A distant clatter of wings.

Lucky blinked.

A crow had flapped up from the tangled branches of the wood, and now circled in the sky, cawing.

A crow, in the dark hours of no-sun? He'd seen the bird before. It was the same crow, the crow that he'd seen in the city, calling to him when he needed a kick of courage. There'd been one in the Fierce Dogs' garden, too.

These sightings were a message, surely, reminding him of where he'd come from and what he was: He was a Lone Dog. A Street Dog, cunning and dirty and wise. It was time to start acting like one.

Lucky followed his instincts. He dived straight between Blade's forepaws. She was shocked motionless just for an instant, staring down; then Lucky rolled, snapping his jaws at her soft underbelly. His teeth closed satisfyingly on skin and flesh, and he tasted blood on his tongue as he heard the Alpha's bark of pain and rage. He squirmed out from beneath her, his teeth still tearing free. Then he was past them all, and racing for the fence.

Surprise had won him a snatch of precious time. There was no ducking and dodging now; just a desperate headlong race for the hole. The big dogs were slow to turn, chaotic in their fury; but now they were after him. He could hear their pounding paws, their wild, enraged howls. But above that, there was his own desperate ragged breathing.

He burst through bushes, his muscles and chest burning. His legs felt as if they wouldn't carry him any farther, but he forced himself on, running till he thought his heart would burst. The hole in the fence was so close now, so close, and the Fierce Dogs were crashing through the bushes behind him.

Don't stop. Don't stop. I don't want to be Fierce Dog dinner. . . .

He could almost feel their hot breath on his haunches as he blundered through the last branches and scrabbled for the hole. It wasn't there—*no!*

Lucky pushed on, sensing the jaws of Blade and her Pack right behind him. How could he have missed it? *Had* he missed it? If he'd missed it he was dead—

There! The hole was ahead of him, a dark smear on the earth, smelling of Daisy and Alfie and Bella. Lucky dived, scrambled, kicked with his hind legs.

For suffocating seconds the hole was dark and horribly endless. Lucky pulled frantically with his forepaws, squeezing himself through the crushing earth. In a miraculous instant, his head was free, breathing the open air. Then the rest of him was free, too, and his tail was thrashing, scattering earth and dirt. Staggering to a trembling halt, he shook himself violently, then bolted away from the horrible Dog-Garden as fast as his shaking legs would take him.

Behind him, the Fierce Dogs crashed against the fence, flinging themselves in mad rage onto the wire. They couldn't have seen the hole, even when they were right by it. He'd outsmarted them after all. Blade and her cronies were the prisoners now—penned in by that high fence. He heard the crash of their bodies as they ran farther along the wire, searching furiously for his escape route.

"Pesky Street Dog!" Blade was snarling.

Lucky bolted farther up the slope, then halted and stood very still, panting hard and listening for strange, threatening sounds behind the darkness. At this height, the night was still, punctuated only by the song of crickets and the rustle of a faint breeze, and the aggressive hunting sounds of the Fierce Dogs, fainter now.

Where are the others? Have they gone? Lucky looked around him, sniffed the ground for any trace of Bella, Daisy, or Alfie. There was a faint scent of them, but they weren't close by.

They left me, thought Lucky. The others had run for it, leaving him to fend for himself. And that was fine. Finally they were thinking like sensible dogs, and running as fast and as far as they could. They'd be okay now.

The bark of delight was almost at his ear, and he jumped.

"Bella?"

His litter-sister charged out of the undergrowth, panting with relief. She put her paws on his shoulders, licking his face enthusiastically. A wave of embarrassed happiness surprised him. They'd been upwind of him; that was the only reason he hadn't smelled them. He must have used up all his Forest-Dog blessings escaping from the Fierce Dogs to have missed them.

"Lucky!" Bella barked. "You made it!"

Suddenly the others were there as well: Alfie, yapping his excitement, and little Daisy capering at his forepaws, trying to dislodge Bella so she could lick his ears, too.

"Daisy! Alfie!" He crouched on his forepaws, wagging his tail frantically as they exchanged happy greetings. "You waited for me!"

"Of course we did!" yipped Daisy, spinning a circle. "How could we leave you, Lucky? You saved us!"

Alfie's stubby tail thrashed the air. "You were wonderful!"

"You risked your life for us! *Again!*" Daisy was beside herself with gratitude.

"Oh, Daisy," he sighed, nuzzling her. "How could I desert you after you brought me that mole?"

Bella seemed calmer now, almost subdued, though her tail still wagged as she pressed her face to Lucky's. "I'm sorry, Lucky. I'm so sorry I didn't listen to you."

He blinked at her, sniffing her face, unable to speak.

"You were right. And I should have listened," she told him softly. "I won't make that mistake again."

His heart swelled. "It doesn't matter." He licked her forehead. "Don't worry, Bella. Right now we need to get moving. Listen."

The four dogs stilled, ears pricked to the night. Not far away they could hear the growls and snarls of the frustrated Fierce Dogs, hunting up and down the fence that stopped them from escaping. They weren't all-powerful—and they weren't Free Dogs, either. For all their acute sense of smell, they hadn't found the hole yet—and even if they did, it would take some digging to get them through it. But Lucky wasn't taking any more chances.

"It's time to go," he insisted quietly. "Come on."

This time there was no argument from the others. Alfie sped off into the night, finding the track they'd followed from the camp, and Daisy and Bella followed close at his heels.

Lucky paused to glance back at the fence. He knew the desire

244

for vengeance would be burning in Blade's chest. To be out-smarted would be far more than a humiliation for that proud dog: It would be a challenge.

This wasn't the last they'd hear of her; Lucky was sure of that.

CHAPTER TWENTY-ONE

When he woke, Lucky could make out a pale gray line on the eastern horizon, and their surroundings had taken on colorless but distinct shapes. Thorns and twigs pricked at his hide. The others must have had an uncomfortable night's sleep, too, but Lucky had insisted they lie low in the undergrowth until sunup. If they were tracked down, he didn't want to lead Blade and her Pack to the others back at the camp.

He blinked his eyes clear of the blur of sleep and stretched his stiff and aching muscles, languidly wagging his tail. He padded to the sleeping form of Daisy and nudged her ear.

"Come on, Daisy. Time to move on."

She jerked awake, still nervous after her adventures, and was soon yipping softly at Alfie and pawing him, desperate to get moving. At least, thought Lucky, they finally understood the importance of caution.

"I don't think those Fierce Dogs have found the hole yet," said Lucky quietly, "but we shouldn't hang around. They're bound to try again in daylight."

"Oh yes." Daisy shivered.

Alfie stretched and scratched before trotting on in an eager fashion. The other three followed him, keeping up a brisk pace. The more distance they put between themselves and the Dog-Garden, thought Lucky, the better it would be. They had to leave Blade and her Pack far, far behind them, and the only way to do that was to keep moving.

And, he realized with a heavy heart, it wouldn't even be safe to stay in the camp. He dreaded breaking that news to the others.

Walking was doing his aching body some good, but Lucky still felt sore and tired, and his dark thoughts weren't helping. Bella kept giving him anxious glances, but he wasn't ready to talk.

They came to the long open slope and were in sight of the camp sooner than he expected, but that only reinforced his certainty that they had to leave. They were far too close to danger here.

Mickey bounded to meet them, his intelligent face creased

with worry, and Sunshine was at his hindpaws, already barking with relief.

"You're back! Thank goodness! What happened?"

"I'll tell you about it when we're all together, Sunshine." Lucky licked her nose and butted her back in the direction of camp. He tried not to notice how Mickey was looking at him, the anxiety etched on his face.

The Leashed Dogs quickly gathered around, gently placing their longpaw things on the earth before them. When they heard what had happened—mostly in breathless snippets from Alfie and Daisy—they were simply glad to have their friends back. No one was disappointed at their failure to bring back food.

"I can't believe you got away from them." Martha shuddered. "They sound dreadful. And frightening."

"They were *very* frightening," declared Daisy emphatically.

"You should have seen Lucky run!" yipped Alfie. "I thought he was done for, but he got the better of them!"

"He was so brave!" Daisy panted, gazing adoringly at Lucky.

"Will they track us back here?" asked Sunshine.

"No," said Lucky, and took a deep breath. "They *will* track our scents to this camp. But they won't find us here, because we're moving on."

For a moment all the dogs were stunned into silence, tails and ears drooping.

"No!" wailed Sunshine. *"Already?"*

"Come on, Sunshine." Martha licked her affectionately, almost knocking the little dog sideways. "I know it's perfect here, but we'll find somewhere else that's just as good."

"Not easily," said Mickey bleakly. "But I do see what Lucky means."

"We're leaving." Bella's tone was brisk. "Unless you want to stay here and wait for Blade and her friends. And let me tell all of you, you do *not* want to wait for Blade."

"No," agreed Alfie with a shiver. "I'm sorry, Sunshine."

Sunshine gave a last mournful whimper, glancing back at the glade with its shade and fresh water. "All right."

"Let's just get going," Bella broke in. "Pick up your longpaw things."

Lucky sighed in frustration but decided not to make any comment. *Let them bring their things if it makes them feel better,* he thought. At least they were moving swiftly to organize themselves, and they'd all accepted they had to abandon this camp. That was a start.

As they headed out of the camp, first along a barren ridge and then down into a gully, Lucky saw the little Pack was doing well in other ways, too. They were barely recognizable as the nervous, inexperienced Leashed Dogs he'd led out of the city.

They no longer smelled of soap and longpaws, but of river water and trees, of earth and one another. It was a proper, wild smell. They were far scruffier, too; even Sunshine no longer looked as if she'd ever suffered careful grooming from a longpaw. To Lucky, the little dog looked much happier trotting along with tangled fur and muddy paws. She and Mickey seemed to be getting along well, and when Mickey suggested they hunt together while they walked, she agreed with enthusiasm.

"Don't go too far!" Lucky warned them.

"Of course not," agreed Mickey seriously. "We'll keep as close to the Pack as we can."

The Pack, thought Lucky as he watched the unlikely hunting pair set off into the bushes that lined the gully. Yes, it *was* nearly a proper Pack. There were hardly any complaints anymore, no one stopping to whine about thorns in their fur or bruises on their paw pads. They moved as a unit, watching out for one another without even realizing they were doing it.

Dog-spirits coming alive, he thought proudly.

Even Bella was listening to the spirit within her, though she might not admit it or know it. They were learning how to be Free Dogs.

Lucky moved more cautiously as they reached the brow of the next hill, slinking as low as he could to the ground and flattening his ears. Both Mickey and Bella noticed, and came close to him, one on each flank.

"What's wrong, Lucky?" asked Bella nervously.

"That field down there. It's where we saw those yellow long-paws. Let's be careful."

All the dogs eyed the land below nervously. *Good,* thought Lucky; *they're starting to think before they bark.* From up here he could see more of the field's surroundings: smoke rising from a huge longpaw tower; sluggish streams of yellow-gray water flecked with sickly curdled foam. Even the roads beside the field were stained with grimy suds where the water and foam had leaked, perhaps from that tower. Lucky shuddered, then shook himself. He was glad they'd gotten away from that terrible place while they could. It made him think of panic, and sickness, and death.

He picked up speed a little as they left. It was good to put these things behind them, and Lucky had started to relax, to feel free and easy once more as he listened happily to the chatter of Sunshine and Daisy behind him.

Then he heard a longpaw bark.

Lucky froze, one paw in midair. A ripple of fear went down his spine. The others, of course, pricked their ears, and one or two gave yelps of excitement, but it was Bella who snapped at them.

"Calm down!" Bella growled. "Be quiet! Have you forgotten what happened to Daisy?"

"Oh yes," whispered Daisy. "Let's be very careful."

Placing one paw cautiously in front of the other, Lucky crept through the trees and bushes ahead. There was a low building there, visible beyond its rusty wire fence, that reminded him of the Fierce Dogs' home. Even though they were far away from Blade and Dagger and the rest, Lucky didn't like it at all. Nervously he crouched and sniffed at the fence.

A crash of branches ahead and to one side almost made him yelp out loud; but instead he went as still as he could, cringing against a tree trunk and hoping he wouldn't be seen. The long-paw—the one who'd barked, he was sure—had burst from the thick bushes, but its shape seemed strange: bulky and uneven. Lucky realized instantly why—there was a dead deer slung over the longpaw's shoulder. In the longpaw's other hand was a loud-stick—and one that had recently spat fire and death, judging by the acrid, pungent smell. But there was another smell, too: the smell of fresh blood, wafting from the deer carcass. Prey. *Food . . .*

Lucky was slinking backward into the trees as the longpaw hauled a door open in the low building and began to carry the deer inside. It wouldn't have noticed the dogs at all, if the Pack had managed to stay quiet.

But then Bruno dashed forward, barking a greeting, and Mickey, Sunshine, and Alfie could no longer contain themselves, either. Bella growled at them to come back, but only Daisy and Martha remained subdued, the littlest dog huddled and trembling beneath her friend's legs. The rest were yelping their joy at the longpaw, running toward it, ears flying.

It spun around, dropping the deer in a thudding heap, and its eyes widened.

The longpaw gave another furious bark, and brought the loudstick to its shoulder, pointing it at the running dogs.

Lucky trembled as terror lifted his fur. Didn't the others *know* about loudsticks? Didn't they know what those terrible things could do? He was about to bark a warning when the loudstick exploded.

The sound was a crack as loud as the Big Growl. It echoed in the clearing, ringing in Lucky's ears, and it brought the running dogs to a terrified, skidding halt.

Lucky skittered forward, nervous, but worried for his friends.

He saw instantly that none of them was hurt; the loudstick must have been pointing over their heads when it exploded.

While they were cowering back, the longpaw turned and dragged the deer inside the building, then slammed the door with a thundering clang.

The four dogs gathered their wits—but Lucky could barely believe what he was seeing. Instead of turning tail and running for their lives, they were bounding toward the low building again.

Bruno flung his muscular body at the door with a crash, and immediately the others were scratching at it, too, whining and yelping and whimpering. Stopping only to exchange one disbelieving look with Bella, Lucky raced forward, his litter-sister at his heels.

"Come away, you fools! What on earth are you doing?"

"Bruno!" barked Bella. "Didn't you see the loudstick? Didn't you *hear*?"

Bruno shook her off, and scratched at the door again. "It's only a *gun*, Bella! My longpaw had a gun! It hunted deer, just like that one!"

"And don't you see, Bella?" cried Mickey. "It didn't shoot us! And it wasn't a *bad* longpaw. It wasn't one of the eyeless ones with the yellow fur."

"Oh," yelped Alfie. "Oh, Bella! The longpaw has a whole deer in there! If it lets us in, it'll share it. It can't eat a *whole deer*! We can help it!" Alfie yapped wildly at the door again.

A volley of angry longpaw barks from within made Lucky twitch.

Sunshine looked a little less certain than the others, and cast nervous looks back at Martha and the shivering Daisy. "Maybe Bella's right, Mickey. The longpaw did try to scare us, even if it didn't . . . hurt us . . ."

"It'll kill you next time," snarled Lucky furiously. "It gave you a warning with its loudstick . . ."

"Thank you, Lucky!" Bella interrupted. She waited for the look of surprise to fade from his face. "You're right, of course." She turned to the rest of the dogs. "I miss my longpaws as much as you all do, but *this* one isn't our longpaw. We can't chase after every longpaw we see!"

For the first time, Bruno, Mickey, and Alfie looked uncertain. "But, Bella . . ." whimpered Alfie.

"It's no good," scolded Bella firmly. "You *have* to stop and think. Hasn't Lucky got through to you at *all*?"

The others looked downright ashamed now. Lucky looked up at his litter-sister, pride and nervousness jangling together in his mind. He was truly impressed with Bella's leadership. The four runaways were certainly submitting to her, lowering their heads, tucking their tails between their hind legs, creeping back to their friends in the trees. Bella was going to make a good Alpha for this group.

They would not need to depend on Lucky anymore.

Daisy yipped softly with relief at their return. "Come on, Mickey," she begged. "Let's leave that longpaw here with its prey. That's all it's thinking of just now. Let's go on, quickly!"

"You're right, Daisy." Mickey sounded ashamed of himself. "I'm sorry. We're all sorry, Bella." He licked her nose apologetically. "We didn't think."

"It's all right," said Bella. "But from now on, we all have to be wary of longpaws. We don't *know* them. They aren't ours, and you must all remember that."

As they headed on up the valley, quieter now, Lucky padded at Bella's side. When he licked her jaw, she gave him a quizzical glance, but looked happy.

She's starting to understand, thought Lucky, with a warm sense of relief and pride.

They moved quickly after that, unnerved by their encounter with the longpaw and its loudstick. Breaks to rest, or to drink and eat, were brief, though Lucky took plenty of time to praise Sunshine in particular when she and Mickey returned from their foray with a rabbit. They needed encouragement now, after their shock and their fierce scolding from Bella.

But still, they were all coping much better than before. Even when they'd traveled over more land than he'd ever covered and the Sun-Dog was setting across the western hills, there were few complaints. It was Lucky, recognizing that Sunshine and Daisy were almost at the end of their endurance, who barked encouragement from the ridge of a hill.

"We're stopping to rest here. Look!"

All of them came right up beside him before flopping down, heads on paws, to gaze at the view.

"Oh my," breathed Martha.

"Is that our *city*?" gasped Sunshine.

From their vantage point, they could see more than even Lucky ever had before. The shoreline was a curved ribbon of silver and the ocean an expanse of blue that stretched to a brilliant horizon. The precipitous hill at their paws sloped down to fields and broad plains of grass, and farther on, neatly groomed stretches of grass, made tiny by distance.

And there, too, was their city. Lucky stared. Even more from this angle than up close in its streets, Lucky could see the changes in one great, sprawling vista. There were gaps, like patches of skin in mangy fur, where buildings had simply ceased to exist, and lakes of silver water shimmered where there should be none. There were great rivers of that poisoned gray-yellow water, too, running between the ruined buildings.

No one had spoken since Sunshine's outburst. Now, Bella stepped forward to face her friends.

"Listen to me," she said. "This is a different world." She gave Lucky a sidelong glance, and he nodded, giving her a soft woof of encouragement.

Bella addressed her Pack again, more confidently. "You can see almost the whole of it from here, can't you? The whole world. You can see how it's changed. And a different world"—she took a moment to gaze into each Pack member's eyes—"needs a different kind of dog."

Daisy whimpered uneasily. Solemnly Martha returned Bella's gaze. "You're not just telling us the world has changed, Bella. Are you?"

Bella took a breath, but the only nerves she showed were in the anxious thumping of her tail. "We have to survive on our own. We have to learn—we don't have a choice."

"But, Bella," whined Alfie, "we're trying. We really are."

"I know! We're acting like a real Pack! But we'll never truly be self-reliant if we don't trust ourselves." Bella pawed Alfie's long-paw ball where he'd let it drop. "We need to accept that we're alone, and we need to rely on ourselves and no one else. Not even our longpaws. We're going to"—Bella took a deep breath—"we're going to leave these things of theirs behind."

Mickey dropped his glove in shock and stared at it, then at Bella. "Leave them? Bella, we can't!"

"We have to! Don't you see? Until we leave these things in the past where they belong, we'll never truly trust ourselves or one another. We need to accept these are our old lives! For now, Mickey, at least. They were important, but they are *past*. Please believe me." Bella's ears drooped, and she added quietly, "Maybe Lucky's right. Maybe we need to try harder to listen to our dog-spirits."

Lucky had never felt prouder of anything in his life.

Mickey gazed mournfully at Bruno, who lay down with a great sigh, his bulky head on his paws. But Alfie broke the miserable silence with an angry bark.

"But Lucky doesn't understand. And I'm starting to think you don't, either, Bella!"

"Alfie's right," said Mickey, rising onto all fours. "I know it doesn't make sense to Lucky, but, Bella, you know how much this matters!"

What matters, Lucky wanted to yelp in frustration, *is that you give these things up!* But he knew how important it was, especially for Bella, that he keep quiet, so he said nothing.

"It matters," said Bella quietly, "but our survival matters more."

"You're only saying that because Lucky thinks it!" yelped Alfie. "You're just trying to please your brother!"

"That's nonsense!" snapped Bella. "I'm saying it because it's true."

"No, Bella!" squealed Sunshine, planting a paw on her yellow leash. "No, I won't throw this away! My longpaw bought it for me and it's *special*!"

"That's right!" grunted Bruno, taking the peaked cap back into his mouth as if Bella was going to snatch it away.

Alfie's eyes were alight with anger. "I'm surprised at you, Bella. We won't abandon our longpaws!"

"Then none of us will survive!" she barked. "We'll always be looking over our shoulders for help from our longpaws. And I know it now, and so do you if you're honest: *They aren't coming back!*"

As each of the dogs began snapping and yelping with indignation, Daisy suddenly sat back and gave a howl of misery.

The others looked at her, shocked, and then at one another.

"Please don't fight!" she whimpered. "I hate it when we fight!"

Bella turned to the small dog and licked her head reassur-ingly. "I'm sorry. You're right. It doesn't do any good to squabble." Determinedly she lifted her head to gaze once more at the others.

Lucky hardly dared to breathe as he watched the scene unfold. He couldn't interrupt. Not when so much hung in the balance. They'd already learned from their Fierce Dog escape that it was worth listening to Lucky—and now to Bella. Would that lesson be remembered?

Martha was the first to move. After a few long moments she bent down and picked up her red scarf. His heart in his throat, Lucky thought she was going to defy Bella, turn, and walk away into an uncertain, dangerous future.

Instead, she found a patch of soft earth and began to scrape at it with her forepaws. With her huge webbed paws it didn't take long to dig a small hole. The rest watched, silent, as the soil flew. When the hole was perhaps a foreleg deep, she lifted her scarf and dropped it gently into the ground.

The other dogs shared anxious glances. A little grumpily, Bruno followed suit with his cap, Alfie with his ball, and Sunshine with her glittering leash. Her expression was tragic as she slowly covered the sparkling stones with layers of soil. Daisy took longer to dig a deep enough hiding place for her battered hide pouch, but Martha helped her, and soon they had both pawed earth back over their longpaw things. Lucky watched them in silence, afraid to break the spell of their dog-spirits; surely now they were listening to those inner voices. Finally Bella picked up her own grubby bear toy, and buried it in the earth.

Only when she was done did she glance at Mickey, the last one left. Mickey placed a paw on his glove. "This was my longpaw pup's most precious possession, Bella. I know how much it mattered to him. He wouldn't have left it if he could help it. And I know for certain he wouldn't have left me, either."

Bella gazed at him, thoughtful. The other dogs looked from one to the other.

Fondly Mickey nuzzled the glove's worn leather, then raised his head. "I can't give up my faith in the longpaws. I don't think you have, either. I understand why we have to leave these things— truly, Bella, I do. I understand we can't rely on the longpaws to help us anymore. But one of us has to remember. One of us has to carry the memories for the rest of the Pack." He lifted the glove delicately in his jaws. "I'll do it."

Bella gave a soft, accepting bark. "Perhaps you're right, Mickey. And we can all help you carry it sometimes—that means we'll all have a part in looking after the memory." She nuzzled Mickey's face fondly.

Giving them a last brief time with their longpaw things, Lucky padded a little way down the hill and looked back. Each of the dogs stood over their mound of disturbed earth, howling at the sky. The sight and the sound gave Lucky a pang of mixed emotion. They were mourning their longpaws, certainly—but they were sending their cries out into the world! Whether they knew it or not, they were also making peace with the Earth-Dog. . . .

As Bella's voice raised above the howls of the others, he felt his heart swell in his rib cage with love and pride.

"Earth-Dog!" cried his litter-sister. "Earth-Dog, keep our things safe!"

"And us, too!" howled Mickey. "Earth-Dog: Bring the long-paws home to us, too."

Lucky couldn't share their sorrow, but he did feel an aching fondness for them all. His heart was sore with affection and sympathy, but at the same time he was light-headed with gladness that it wasn't like this for him.

He was free and easy Lucky.

A Lone Dog.

CHAPTER TWENTY-TWO

It was late the following day, after a long and tiring plod through forest and stream, when Lucky found the valley. Because of the sweeping angle of its slopes, it wasn't visible till his forepaws were on the edge of the steep ridge above it.

As the others padded up to his side, weary, their fur thick with the dust of travel, Lucky gazed out silently at the scene before him. A clear river flowed through the center of the valley, diverted by rocks and hillocks and clusters of tree and bush, but apart from those places of shade and shelter, the space was broad and open. A Pack of dogs in this valley would be able to see trouble coming from a long way off. And there were no huge trees or high rock faces to tumble and fall and trap them, should the earth Growl again. . . .

It was perfect. His friends would be safe here. He wouldn't have to feel guilty about leaving them, moving on, being a loner again.

He should feel happy about that—so why this twist of sadness in his belly?

At his flank, Daisy gave a whine, but it was a whine of hope, not complaint. The low, late Sun-Dog gilded the grasslands below and turned the river gold.

"Lucky! Do you think—could we—"

"I think you just might, Daisy," he told her softly.

"*We* might, you mean?" she yapped, confused.

He didn't have to answer, because Bruno was harrumphing happily at the view now. "This is great! Lucky, you genius!"

"It's beautiful," breathed Alfie. "Wonderful!"

"And there'll be plenty to hunt," Lucky pointed out as Bella and Mickey joined them. "That's ideal territory for mice and rabbits."

Bruno was shifting from forepaw to forepaw. "Lucky! Does this mean the Earth-Dog liked our offerings?"

Lucky was perplexed only for an instant. "Your longpaw possessions? Well, maybe . . ."

"I think Bruno's right!" yapped Alfie. "The Earth-Dog is pleased with us at last, and she's brought us here!"

Lucky agreed that it was piece of good luck. "It's a perfect place. You'll be happy here, and you'll hunt and eat well. But best of all, you'll be as safe as you can possibly be." He licked Alfie's nose, feeling a little pang of fondness for him. "I'm glad."

"But—" Alfie was dumbfounded.

Bruno broke in. "You can't mean you're going?"

Lucky averted his eyes, and kept his bark cheerful. "Of course I am. That was always the plan!"

The chorus of dismayed howls that greeted his announcement rocked him back on his hindpaws.

"You can't leave us alone!" cried Sunshine.

Lucky licked the top of her head. "I'm a Lone Dog. I have to be on my own."

"But you're part of *our* Pack!" whined Daisy.

"No! You don't need me! Look at how well you've been hunting. You can take care of yourselves, and you're listening to your dog-spirits—that's the most important thing. You're a team, a proper Pack, and now you have a perfect place to live!"

"Oh, Lucky." Bella padded forward, licked his nose, and sat down squarely in front of him, gazing into his eyes as her tail slowly thumped the earth.

Lucky felt his heart sink. *Please,* he thought. *Please, Bella, don't try to stop me. I can't bear to fight with you, not after everything we've been through just to survive. . . .*

267

"Don't worry." She touched her nose to his. "I won't argue with you again. But I'm going to ask you one thing. Stay one more night with us."

"Oh, *yes!*" barked Sunshine. "Lucky, do!"

"Oh, please!" Daisy's expression was pleading, and the others were barking enthusiastically in agreement.

"Just one more night." Bella's gaze held his. "If you feel the same at sunup, we won't try to stop you. Even *I* won't argue." She cocked one ear and tilted her head. "That's fair, isn't it?"

Lucky sighed and closed his eyes. He wouldn't change his mind and he knew it; he'd always felt this way, and it was how he'd still feel at sunup.

But could it really hurt? One more night sleeping curled up with his friends, feeling the warmth and companionship he hadn't known since the Pup Pack. One more night of comfort, and then, at sunup, his old life back: freedom and the wilderness, a solitary happiness. It was what he wanted, what he always longed for, and if there was a tiny voice inside him crying like a pup to stay with his friends, then it was only an ancient memory, an almost-dead instinct from a blurred time he could barely remember.

"Yes," he said at last. "All right. But I warn you, I won't change my mind."

* * *

Lucky lay, head on his paws, and watched in startled awe as the dogs of his temporary Pack worked around him, an efficient team under the confident direction of Bella. *They've come so far,* he thought with a twinge of affection.

Alfie and Sunshine had been sent to fetch mouthfuls of long, dry grass from the valley, which they had strewn across a large boulder by the river. They sat panting now, admiring their hard work. On top of the grass the others had carefully placed the results of their last hunting trip—which Lucky had not been allowed to join.

"You're our guest!" Daisy had yapped.

"So that we can say farewell," added Bella quietly.

It had been entirely different when he was staying out of the hunt to let them learn. Now Lucky felt very awkward not helping, but Bruno had given him an amiable snap of his teeth every time he'd offered.

"Lie down and wait in peace, Lucky!"

So Lucky did. He had to admit, once he'd relaxed, it had been a nice sun-high lying in the dappled shadows by the new river, listening to the flow of the water. Now they had all returned— Mickey trotting back last, a limp and bloody rabbit in his jaws—and one by one they placed their prey on the bed of grass.

Shyly Daisy laid down a rather crumpled mouse. Bella had caught another rabbit, and Martha had somehow managed to catch a squirrel. Bruno and Mickey between them had made the star catch: a small deer that they'd surprised and trapped. It lay in a place of pride in the center of the spread. Alfie and Sunshine had even brought back some beetles as well as their haul of grass.

There was a lump in Lucky's throat as they formed a semicircle around him and the food. Bella stalked forward and lowered herself onto her forelegs, then bowed her head.

"We've caught this prey for you, Lucky. For all you've done for us. Please, will you eat first?"

Lucky swallowed. He'd never seen anything like this, and he was embarrassed, but touched. Out of their own habits and rituals with their longpaws, they'd created this ceremony especially for him. He was grateful for the thought they'd put into their last meal together.

"Go on, Lucky." Sunshine pricked her white ears hopefully. "Take the first bite of everything!"

Obediently he paced up to the strewn prey, and took a beetle delicately between his teeth, then crunched and gulped it down.

Sunshine looked ridiculously pleased that he'd chosen her offering first, and her fluffy tail thudded the earth with delight.

Lucky took great care to tear small pieces from every single offering, chewing even as he whined his appreciation. Only when he'd tasted everything did they all come forward and join in. Soon they were all happily wolfing down chunks of rabbit and deer and squirrel.

"You're hunters," he said, pausing to swallow and gaze around at them. "You have a real talent for finding food. Thank you for this."

"Thank *you*, Lucky," murmured Martha. "It's you who made us hunters."

When they lay down at last in a contented huddle, their bellies full, Lucky closed his eyes with a long sigh. Bella once again lay against him; Daisy had flopped over his haunches, while Sunshine was tucked under his throat. Mickey's hind legs were tucked cozily under Lucky's flank, and as he drifted into sleep he felt them twitch. *Ah,* he thought with amusement, *so Mickey's dreaming of chasing that deer....*

Darkness. Again. But so different this time!

Lucky couldn't sense the wire of the Trap House. There was nothing hemming him in but this black emptiness . . . and the snarling, tumbling, thrashing bodies of dogs.

Dogs fighting one another! Fighting to the death, in a storm—the Storm of Dogs.

Turning, spinning desperately, he could see no way out. Claws raked at his flank; fangs flashed as they snapped. A huge dog crashed against him, then was gone, tearing back into the battle. The noise was dreadful: howling, screaming, snapping. All around him was fury and pain and terror. Wildly flailing fangs caught his ear and tore it; the pain seemed to pierce his skull.

It was like the final battle of the Sky-Dogs, the one his mother had told him would come one day. Yes! That was it; it had to be—the war at the world's end. And he was in the middle of it, cowering and ducking from the savagery of the warriors.

There were other dogs he knew—Bella, there close to his side, screaming as a huge red-eyed hound bowled her over onto her back and lunged for her throat. NO, he thought, NO—but he couldn't reach her. Paws and claws were pulling him down. There was Sweet, too, crippled and dying, unable to run. And Blade and Dagger, snapping, tearing, biting, but then they, too, were overwhelmed by the dark mass of dogs. Little Daisy vanished, howling, beneath the crash of bodies. And there was nothing he could do. Nothing!

He tried to lunge for Daisy's collar, but his paws slipped helplessly in water . . . . no. Not water. It was warm, slippery, dark . . . blood that rose steadily, lapping around his paws, clinging to his fur. The surface of it was sheened with something evil: a slick of poison like the one on the bad river. Terrified, he staggered and slipped and fell. Now his mouth was full of blood, the metallic tang of it. His teeth were coated in it, sticky and vile. And his eyes—they were filling with it, too, and all he could see was red.

Bloodred . . .

Lucky sprang to his feet, trembling from head to tail, gasping for breath. His heart thrashed inside his rib cage as if it would burst right through. The sky and the whole world was bloodred, and for horrible moments he could still taste dog blood in his mouth.

Then he realized: It was the dawn. The Sun-Dog was yawning, and stretching, and making the sky glow scarlet as he rose.

Lucky still couldn't control the beating of his heart, and he couldn't repress a terrified whimper. Beside him, Daisy stirred and stretched questioningly, half rising to lick at his muzzle.

"Lucky? Are you all right?"

He glanced down, shocked, as a wave of relief buffeted him. Daisy wasn't dead, then, crushed and torn beneath the weight of battling dogs; she was here with him, and safe. He licked her nose in return, swamped by gratitude.

"I'm okay, Daisy. It was . . . a bad dream. That's all."

She didn't have to know the details, he decided. He'd keep those to himself—even though the horror of the dream still clung to him, and fear shivered in his cold hide.

The others were stirring now, stretching in the beautiful rise of Sun-Dog, licking one another in greeting, yawning. As they stood up, shaking off sleep, they seemed to remember very suddenly, and as one, what the dawn meant for them and for Lucky. Their sunup yelps and growls quieting, they all turned sadly toward him. Martha padded close and nuzzled his face.

"Lucky," she whined softly, "what will we do without you?"

Firmly ignoring his own ache of regret, Lucky yapped with determined eagerness.

"You'll be fine! I have to look after myself. I'm sure you don't want to be responsible for me."

"I wouldn't mind that," whimpered Daisy mournfully.

"But, Daisy!" Lucky wagged his tail energetically, hating their distress and forcing lightness into his bark. "You're growing up so fast. You're a strong hunting dog, and you're going to be even stronger. Next time I see you, you'll be showing off, bringing me rabbits two at a time! And I will see you again, I promise. I'll come back to visit."

Daisy dipped her head and woofed sadly. "Oh, Lucky. I'll miss you so much."

"And I'll miss you," he told her fondly. "But just think, you won't have me nagging and bullying you!" He jumped up, thrashing his tail and bouncing in a circle, barking enthusiastically. "Aren't you going to say good-bye properly?"

They fell on him, barking and licking and nuzzling their farewells. Lucky licked and woofed and whined in return, crushing down the pang of regret in his heart and gut. He would not change his mind, so why feel any remorse? They'd be fine without him, and he'd be happy alone.

"Bruno, good-bye. Stay brave, stay strong. Martha, there's a river. You'll be able to swim again! Daisy, Sunshine, Alfie—I think you're twice your size, inside. Just you listen to your dog-spirits, because I think they're fiercer than any Fierce Dogs!" He turned to Mickey, accepting his solemn good-bye licks. "Mickey, you're a great hunter. Teach them well! And you, Bella—"

He quieted as his litter-sister padded up and pressed her face to his.

"Ah, Lucky," she murmured. "Do we have to lose each other again?"

"Oh, Bella." He felt a stab of hurt in his belly. "At least we can

275

say good-bye properly this time, not like when the longpaws took us from the Pup Pack."

"That changed you forever," she said softly.

"Yes." He sighed. "I'm not sorry, Bella. I'm glad my life has been like this. But I wouldn't have left you, you know. If we hadn't been parted by longpaws."

"I know." She licked his ear. "I know you're not like us. You're a different kind of dog, and you love what you are. That's good, Lucky. And you've helped us. *So* much. Thank you for staying with us all this time."

"No . . . thank *you* for being my friends. I'm so glad to have traveled with you." He was shocked by how true it was, by the sharp pain of loss he felt at leaving them.

"Good-bye, Lucky. But only for now." Bella gave him a last affectionate nuzzle, then took a pace back.

Lucky spun on his haunches and howled with happiness, drowning the ache of remorse that threatened to close his throat. "I'll see you again! Be happy! *Good luck!* I'll miss you."

Before he could change his mind, he bounded away, back down the hill, leaving the beautiful valley they'd found for a home. Racing fast, as if he could outpace the memories, he dodged trees and leaped fallen trunks, reveling in his refound freedom.

After all, the good-bye *wasn't* forever. He'd seen right to the ocean from that vantage point where he'd left his friends, and as far as the mountains to the other side. The world wasn't nearly as big as he'd thought. Eventually, he knew, his journey would bring him back to them. And how much they'd have to tell one another, of hunts and adventures and fun . . .

The Sun-Dog's rays dappled the forest floor in patches of green and gold, and the birds were singing unseen in the branches. Ahead of him he saw a crow perched, watching him, till it took off with a great flap of black wings, cawing what sounded like a greeting to a friend. The air smelled fresh and alive, full of growth and energy. He loved the forest; he always had! That was why the Forest-Dog had come to his rescue at the Fierce Dog place, with his gift of guile and cunning. Now he would be close to the Forest-Dog again. He would be solitary, free, and happy, hunting and living for himself alone. Just as he'd always loved to live.

A squirrel darted across his path, startled by his sudden bounding appearance and scurrying in a panic for the nearest tree. Lucky barked happily and made a halfhearted dash for it, not yet hungry enough to care if he caught it. As it fled into the topmost branches, turning to chatter angrily at him, he panted and barked with pure delight, spinning on his hind legs.

"Next time!" he yelped cheerfully. "Next time, squirrel!"

And then he froze, his tongue still hanging stupidly out. What was that sound?

One paw raised, he turned, uncertain.

There were frenzied howls and barks behind him, but it wasn't the unearthly, blood-chilling screaming of his dreams. So what . . . ?

Dogfight!

Back there, in the distance, where he'd come from. Where the others were. He'd left them, thinking they were safe. An enraged violent barking rose above the rest, and Lucky cocked his ears to listen, his bones thrilling with fear. It wasn't the Fierce Dogs, and it wasn't his friends—

"Our territory! This is our place! OURS!"

Lucky glanced at the crow in the branches ahead, as it watched him. He gazed around at the green-and-golden forest, so full of life, such a perfect place for a Lone Dog.

Then he turned and sprang back the way he'd come, racing through the trees. Jumping, dodging, leaping fallen branches, but always, always heading back to where he'd left his friends. They were in danger. They needed him. He had to go to them. *Now!*

He was conscious of only one thing as his muzzle drew back, baring his fangs for a fight. . . .

They were *his* Pack.

Lucky's Pack . . .

And they were in trouble.

SURVIVORS

A HIDDEN ENEMY

FOREST RIDGE

LONGPAW LOUDCAGES

LEASHED
PACK
CAMP
CAVES

FIERCE
DOG
GARDEN

RIVER

TO
THE
CITY

THE
WILD

PACK LIST

LONE DOGS

LUCKY—gold-and-white thick-furred male

OLD HUNTER—big and stocky male with a blunt muzzle

LEASHED DOGS

BELLA—gold-and-white thick-furred female, Lucky's littermate (sheltie-retriever mix)

DAISY—small white-furred female with a brown tail (Westie/Jack Russell mix)

MICKEY—sleek black-and-white Farm Dog (Border Collie)

MARTHA—giant thick-furred black female with a broad head (Newfoundland)

BRUNO—large thick-furred brown male Fight Dog with a hard face (German Shepherd/Chow mix)

SUNSHINE—small female with long white fur (Maltese)

ALFIE—small and stocky blunt-faced dog with mottled brown-and-white fur

WILD PACK (IN ORDER OF RANK)

ALPHA:

huge half wolf with gray-and-white fur and yellow eyes

BETA:

small swift-dog with short gray fur (also known as Sweet)

HUNTERS:

FIERY—massive brown male with long ears and shaggy fur

SNAP—small female with tan-and-white fur

MULCH—black long-haired male with long ears

SPRING—tan female hunt-dog with black patches

PATROL DOGS:

MOON—black-and-white female Farm Dog (mother to Squirm, a male black-and-white pup; Nose, a female black pup; and Fuzz, a male black-and-white pup)

DART—lean brown-and-white female chase-dog

TWITCH—tan chase-dog with black patches and a lame foot

OMEGA:

small, black, oddly shaped dog with tiny ears and a wrinkled face (also known as Whine)

PROLOGUE

Yap pawed excitedly after a shiny green beetle. *You won't defeat me, bug!* he thought. There was nowhere for his prey to hide now. He was Yap the Hunter, Yap the Swift, Yap the Brave! Fierce warrior of Lightning and the Sky-Dogs!

I'm coming for you. . . .

He was pawing at the wriggling critter, using his best scary barks to let the bug know it was doomed, when he heard an eerie howl. Fur prickled on the back of Yap's neck, and he cocked his head, a shiver running through him.

A dog? Is it another dog?

The beetle had vanished under the white fence, but Yap no longer cared. Getting away from the yard-boundary had suddenly become much more important than hunting. Tumbling back clumsily, he bounded across the grass and into the shed, where the warmth and smells were comforting and familiar. His littermates greeted his return with a wild chorus of yipping, and he squeezed in among them beneath his mother's belly.

At last their nuzzling and licking calmed his thumping heart, and he felt his courage creeping back.

"What was that noise?" he whimpered. "Did you hear it? Did you?"

"Yes! Yes!"

"We heard it!"

"A scary dog!"

"Now, now, little ones." Mother-Dog licked their faces fondly. "That wasn't a dog. That was a wolf, and he won't come here."

Wolf. The word sent a new tremor of fear through Yap's body, and he felt the same nervous prickling in the skin of his brothers and sisters. It did not sound like a nice word. It sounded like a word to be afraid of. . . .

There was amusement in Mother-Dog's soft voice as she continued. "There's no need to worry. Wolves are not so very different from us, you know. They have four legs, and fur, and teeth. They're fast and strong and fierce, but they're wild and cunning and crafty too."

"I bet I could outsmart a wolf!" announced Squeak.

"I certainly hope not!" said Mother-Dog. "That's not how

dogs should behave. Dogs are clever, but we're not devious. We are noble and honorable. You pups must always remember that."

"When it howled," said Snip timidly, "it sounded a bit like a dog."

"Wolves and dogs are connected, Snip, and that connection goes back a long, long time. But that does not mean they are to be trusted. If you ever see a wolf, keep your distance. Run away if you have to."

"Why?" asked Yap, his head cocked in confusion.

"Because a wolf will sink his teeth into your flesh the moment your back is turned. Never get close to a wolf. Nuzzle did, and she regretted it. Don't you remember the story? Nuzzle was always much too curious for her own good. She followed the wolves when she heard them howling, because she was brave as well as inquisitive."

"I'm brave too!" interrupted Squeak.

"There's brave and there's foolish, Squeak! The Wild Wolf-Pack caught and trapped Nuzzle beneath the First Pine, and their leader, Greatfang, would have killed her for spying on them.

"But Nuzzle was Lightning's grandpup, and even though Lightning had gone to live with the Sky-Dogs by then, he still watched over his kin. When he saw Nuzzle in danger, he leaped to earth and set fire to the First Pine and Greatfang both! The Wild Wolf-Pack fled in terror, and that's the only reason Nuzzle grew up to be the fierce Warrior-Dog Wildfire. The rest of us cannot rely on Lightning to come and save us, so we must learn from Nuzzle's mistakes."

Distantly the howling echoed again, and the pups cuddled even closer together as their Mother-Dog pricked her ears to listen. Yap felt himself relax. Mother-Dog's flank was so warm, and her heart beat a comforting *thump-thump* against his ear. She would protect them all.

Yap squirmed closer beneath her foreleg. "Even if the wolf came, we'd be all right, wouldn't we?"

Squeak gave a scornful yip.

"Don't be silly, Yap!" she said. "You heard what Mother said—the wolf can't get us here!"

"You're right." Amusement rumbled in the Mother-Dog's throat. "The wolf would never come here. You're all safe, so it's time you went to sleep."

Yap tucked his nose under his paw, cozy and comforted, but he couldn't help twitching an ear at the chilling wail of the wolf as it faded into the distance. *I'm going to be smart,* he thought. *Not like Nuzzle. I'm going to stay away from wolves.*

Safe and warm, nestled in the Pup-Pack: This was how life should be. Far from the Wild, and far from wolves, in the protective huddle of his family. . . .

CHAPTER ONE

"Our territory! Ours!"

Birds took off with an alarmed clatter and screech from the treetops, and disturbed leaves fluttered down around Lucky's paws.

He stood stiff and trembling, gazing back the way he'd come. That was his Pack in the valley—no, not his Pack, but his *friends*. And those ferocious barks told him one thing: They were in terrible danger.

Terrible danger he was not there to help them fight.

Lucky glanced around, torn. Since just after sunup, when he'd left his friends to fend for themselves, he had traveled a long way. He could make out the misty silhouette of the far hills in the distance, and now that he was a good way from the valley he was able to look down on almost the entire forest. Indeed, he'd nearly climbed clear of the trees, and close in front of him was the ridge he'd been heading for. The sight of it had been spurring him on, making his legs run faster and faster—but now he stood as still as a tree.

His friends needed him.

Heart pounding, Lucky bolted back the way he'd come.

Forest-Dog! Don't let them come to any harm! Let me get there in time. . . .

He raced toward the valley, leaping over fallen branches and scattering leaves. He should have trusted his instincts. Deep down he'd *known* that he was not supposed to leave the Pack. But he had trotted away like a Lone Dog, and now his friends were vulnerable.

Who will protect them if I don't?

He could still hear the howls of anger, dog voices that he didn't recognize mingled with the barks of his litter-sister and the rest of the Leashed Dogs.

"Our land, our water! Get out!"

"Everyone together! Stay with me!"

Lucky's powerful hind legs brought him quickly to the crest of a small hill and he scrabbled to a halt before his momentum could take him plunging down.

Wait, Lucky . . . find out the lay of the land before you dash into trouble.

Lucky's keen gaze searched the valley below. It opened out

into broad and lush meadows beyond the thick woods. It had seemed ideal for the Leashed Dogs. There were places for Mickey to hunt and for Martha to swim, plenty of shelter for Sunshine and Alfie and Daisy, wide ranges for Bruno and Bella to explore. He should have known that other dogs would have had the same idea. Of course another Pack had gotten to the valley before them, and now those dogs were defending their territory.

In the distance, silver light glinted on a smooth expanse of water; farther off and next to the forest's edge ran the river where he'd last seen the Leashed Dogs. Lucky bounded down the hill, heading toward it.

The hostile Pack's growls and barks made Lucky's fur prickle with anger and fear. But he knew if he burst out from the forest in broad daylight he'd be seen at once, so he made himself go carefully.

Something had changed about the river since he'd left his friends there. *A strangeness,* Lucky thought. And then he remembered the streams and pools close to the destroyed city. They had the same scent of danger that Lucky was picking up now.

Horrified, Lucky stopped and stared. There was a nasty green slick on the surface of the water. This was supposed to be a safe haven! The river was supposed to be clean, *pure*—and it had been, or they'd thought so when they found it yesterday.

But now, Lucky could see the deadly stain spreading downriver.

I led my friends to poisoned water!

Was there no getting away from the taint of death that the Big Growl had brought? At this end of the river, even the trees and bushes at the water's edge looked half-dead, shriveled and broken as if a giant dog had chewed on them. As he ran across the hillside parallel to the stream, Lucky's heart felt heavy in his chest. If the Big Growl's sickness could infect even this place, there might be nowhere else for the dogs to go. Nowhere they could be safe.

"Get out!"

A vicious howl split the air, and Lucky heard the panicked yelping of confused dogs and a sharp yip of pain. He raced along and down the hillside, claws skidding on stone. When he broke out of a line of thick scrub, he caught sight of them at last.

His friends looked small and vulnerable against the attacking Pack: a wild-looking band of large dogs, stiff-legged and snarling. Now and again, one would spring forward to give a brutal volley of barks.

"You've got it coming, Leashed Dogs!"

He could hear Bella's voice, too—quieter, more frightened,

but still brave: "It's all right, everyone. Stay together. Sunshine, get behind Bruno. Martha, help Daisy."

Skulking low to the ground, crouching in the shadow of a huge boulder, Lucky counted seven dogs in the enemy Pack. Blood surged through his body and he felt a powerful impulse to race right into the battle, but his instincts, learned on the city streets, held him back. He realized with a rush of relief that the fighting had stopped for the moment. The other Pack was just taunting and insulting Bella's Pack—if Lucky raced in now, the situation could become deadly again. The hostile Pack might decide to finish the smaller dogs quickly so they could concentrate on him.

Right now a couple of huge dogs were lunging and snapping at little Sunshine and Daisy, not biting to kill but making them flinch away in terror.

"Keep them off-balance," some dog said in a low growl. "Spring, watch your side!" One of the Wild Dogs leaped to her right, heading Sunshine off from escape as the small dog scuttled from behind Bruno toward the shelter of some underbrush. Lucky looked around for the dog that had given the orders, but couldn't see him.

Lucky knew that if any of the bigger Leashed Dogs dashed to Sunshine's and Daisy's defense, the rest of the hostile Pack would dart in at their flanks, biting and worrying till the defenders were harried and worn. When it came to the real fight, to claws and teeth and torn skin, Bella and the others would already be exhausted. He'd seen it before, sneaky but efficient, in the brutal bands of dogs he'd tried to avoid in his city days.

He would have to surprise these Wild Dogs, using tactics as cunning and dirty as their own. *Don't just jump in,* he told himself. *Be as wily as the Forest Dog.*

In the shadows, Lucky could get much closer before he pounced, so long as he kept downwind. He dodged through the trees, and as he crept from behind a ridge he caught his first sight of the hostile Pack's leader.

Their Alpha dog.

Huge and gray-furred, he looked lithe and graceful, yet powerful, too. He wasn't joining the battle, but kept giving his Pack sharp orders.

"Keep at their heels! Teach them nobody invades our territory!" He threw his head back and let out a long, snarling howl.

Lucky felt prickles of fear in his fur, his stomach clenching with foreboding as he crept forward.

That's no dog. . . .

No wonder the strange Pack's tactics were as cunning as a

wolf's. Lucky had never seen one of those distant dog-cousins close up, but from vague glimpses and half-remembered tales he recognized the pale eyes, savage teeth, and shaggy fur. And there was no mistaking that vicious howl; Lucky had heard something like it once, a long time ago. A memory rippled through his body—a memory not of something seen, but something *heard*.

This powerful gray dog must be half wolf! Lucky had heard of such dogs, but had never met one.

There were another two dogs keeping their eyes trained on the larger Leashed Dogs, though they occasionally looked to their leader and whined for his instructions. Lucky guessed they were directly below the dog-wolf in the strict Wild Pack hierarchy. One was a huge dark-furred dog with a brutally strong neck and mighty jaws. He was watching Martha carefully, but though she was the biggest of the Leashed Dogs, Lucky could see she was already limping on one leg, leaving bloody paw prints when she tried to get out of his way.

The other Wild Dog was a far thinner swift-dog who dodged and circled the fight, moving so fast Lucky's eyes could barely follow her, snapping out orders with a brisk efficiency. She was smaller than the dark-furred dog and fragile-looking, but she seemed very much in command of her underlings.

Maybe it was only her shape and coloring, but Lucky couldn't help being painfully reminded of Sweet, who had escaped with him from the Trap House when all their fellow captive dogs had died.

But this dog didn't have Sweet's good temper. Whoever she was, she would make crow's meat of the Leashed Dogs if her Alpha gave the order to charge.

Forest-Dog, I need all your skill and cunning. . . .

Lucky stalked forward, muscles bunched and tense, still careful to stay safely downwind. He was within a few dog-lengths of the fight now, and they hadn't scented him yet. If he could give them enough of a shock, the Leashed Dogs might have time to get away—yes, just a swift run and a sudden spring . . .

Then he froze again, one paw raised. Not five long-strides away, a small deep-chested dog had hurtled through the scuffle. Lucky's breath stopped in his throat.

Alfie!

The young Leashed Dog skidded to a halt right in front of the huge Alpha. His trembling hindquarters betrayed his fear, but his hackles were up and his lips were drawn back in a defiant snarl. The dog-wolf stared at Alfie, his head cocked as the smaller dog unleashed a volley of furious barks.

"You let us go! Let my friends go! Who says this is your land?"

For a moment, the Alpha seemed to waver between contempt and amusement.

Alfie continued his brave barking, his head whipping from side to side, as though he hoped the extra movement would make him look bigger, more threatening. "We're only looking for clean water—you attacked us! You're bad dogs!" Then his gaze fell between the straggly trees, and his eyes met Lucky's. Alfie seemed to swell to twice his size with happiness, renewed courage making his barks louder and more threatening. Lucky could almost hear the thoughts racing through the smaller dog's head.

Lucky's back. . . . Now we'll be fine. . . . We'll win this fight!

Lucky felt a fierce trembling in his flanks as he realized that he had given Alfie the courage to believe that he could stand up to the dog-wolf.

Alfie wrinkled his muzzle, baring his teeth at his massive enemy.

No!

Lucky's muscles bunched to spring forward, but it was too late. Alfie had flung himself at the huge dog-wolf. The Alpha barely moved. A single swipe of one massive paw slammed the brave Leashed Dog to the ground. Alfie rolled over once, and stopped, lying stunned and still. Blood spilled from a massive tear in his side.

Lucky stumbled to a halt. He wanted to howl with rage and anguish. If his friend hadn't seen him, he surely would never have had the nerve to charge at the half wolf.

Why did you have to see me, Alfie? Why—

Lucky's fur and skin prickled as the ground started shaking beneath his paws. It was as though the Earth-Dog shared Lucky's anger.

Then—*wham!*—Lucky was thrown forward, stumbling as the whole world shook again. He hit the ground and tumbled, but managed to jump back onto all four paws, his entire body trembling.

Another Big Growl!?

The fighting stopped as every dog crouched low, steadying himself. The Wild Pack all looked to their Alpha, who braced his legs against the trembling earth for a second before letting out a chilling howl.

"It's happening again! Pack, to me!"

A tree right beside Lucky creaked and groaned and started to fall. Lucky scrambled out of its path just before it slammed into the solid rock of the hillside and started rolling across the ground that was splitting apart at Lucky's paws. Soon, the air was filled with the shrieks of tortured wood as more and more trees fell, hitting the rocks with crashes that sounded like thunder.

Lucky fled in a panic, not knowing or caring what direction he was taking.

All that mattered was getting away from the Growl.

But the Growl was everywhere, above and around him. The whole earth seemed to slide treacherously beneath his paws. *No, not again! Don't let the Growl ruin this place too. . . .*

As he bolted, Lucky glanced back to see that the other dogs, both Wild and Leashed, were also fleeing in blind terror. The shuddering earth split, a wound tearing itself down the center of the valley. A bundle of pale fur was a blur at the edge of his vision. Someone was falling into the crack. Lucky snapped his head away and veered to the right, afraid to see the death of any dog. He spotted Mickey and Bruno struggling to drag Alfie's limp form toward shelter, and Martha limping painfully away from the crashing trees.

My Pack!

Instinct spurred him to run after them, but it was too late. Above him another gigantic tree was creaking and cracking, its roots lifting from the dirt as if it were trying to pull itself free.

Lucky leaped off the clod of earth and roots, tumbling awkwardly to the ground, and a jolt of pain went through his foreleg. For a moment, he couldn't move. But when he looked up and saw the great tree swaying, falling back into place, he thought he was safe—until the shifting ground heaved again, and the great tree toppled toward him.

Terror ripped through Lucky's bones as he lay on his side and stared up at the massive shuddering trunk, his brain rattled by the tree's tortured shriek of death.

He rolled onto his paws, trying to crawl away on his belly.

But there was no escape.

Earth-Dog wants me. . . . thought Lucky, as he heard the mighty tree falling. *I'm not going to get away this time.*

CHAPTER TWO

The tree was coming straight down on him. He heard the creaking roar, felt the rush of wind—

Then Lucky glimpsed the sharp blade of a rocky overhang. With a last surge of desperate energy he scrabbled and slid down a boulder, shooting under the jutting rock. He cowered in its shelter, trembling like a pup under its mother's belly.

For a long moment, all he could hear was the rumbling thunder of the tree crashing down onto the rocks, branches splitting and cracking as they hit the overhang, twigs and shards of bark exploding around him. He flinched as a splinter of wood struck his flank, but he knew he had to keep still. He could not jump up and run, no matter how strong the urge.

Please, Earth-Dog, he thought. *Be merciful.*

Slowly the deafening racket of the tree's collapse rebounded and echoed and faded. All that was left was a blizzard of pine needles. At last, the ground underneath him grew still. Earth-Dog had stopped growling.

Still trembling, Lucky crept out from his shelter, forcing his body through the thick branches and foliage of the dead tree. Its trunk was as broad as a loudcage, and shudders of horror went through his spine at the thought of how close it had come to falling right on top of him. *I'd be dead now. . . . My body would already be with the Earth-Dog.*

Lucky licked at his leg, but the twinge of pain had faded. He realized with a rush of relief that he wasn't hurt. He'd only just recovered from the slash on his paw from the last Big Growl. It wouldn't do to find himself with another leg wound.

The hillside around him was torn and devastated, as if a giant dog had scraped great gashes in it with its forepaws. Awed, Lucky crept carefully down the uneven slope, hardly daring to pick up his pace. But the area where the dogs had fought was not far below him now, and Lucky trotted more urgently when he reached level ground.

The air was a chaos of scents—damp, wounded earth, roots, blood, and splintered wood. Strongest of all was the smell of dog-fear, though the others had run away from the battle site now. Lucky's ears pricked as he glanced around, hoping he'd see one of his own Pack searching for him. He had no idea where they were now. Had any of the others seen him?

Or just poor Alfie?

As the image of the little dog, broken and wounded, came into his mind, Lucky heard a terrible keening noise. It was the sound of a dog in distress, hurt and helpless.

Lucky glanced around nervously, his fur bristling. Where was the noise coming from? It seemed close, but there was no sign of the dog who was making it.

As he turned, searching, he caught sight of the crack in the earth. Cold horror surged through his body as he remembered the blur of pale fur that he'd seen fall into the split in the ground.

Earth-Dog! he thought. She must have swallowed one of the dogs, showing them her fury at their fighting. Stiff-legged and shivering, Lucky began to back away from the chasm. If Earth-Dog was as angry as that with the battling dogs, who knew what she might do next, or who she might turn her wrath on?

He needed to get as far from the crack in the ground as he possibly could. He didn't know the distressed dog who was making the agonized sound. It wasn't one of the Leashed Dogs—he'd have recognized any of them immediately, even blurred and falling. The pitifully howling dog was a stranger—one of the enemy Pack.

None of that Pack can be trusted. Why should I rescue a stranger?

Still, Lucky's whole coat twitched and tingled. Something was drawing him back, an urge he couldn't resist. He pricked his ears high, straining to hear. Something about that desperate, pleading howl tugged at his recent memory. And the scent . . . it was tantalizingly familiar, but the mess of smells created by the Growl meant that he could not pick it out properly.

Lucky shook himself violently. Of course he couldn't walk away from a dog in danger! It didn't matter if that other dog was friend or foe. Lucky wouldn't be a dog at all if he left one of his own kind to suffer a terrible fate. What had Mother-Dog once said? Noble and honorable. He couldn't betray his own dog-spirit.

Taking a deep breath, Lucky loped carefully to the edge of the chasm. It was very dark but, as his eyes adjusted to the dimness after the bright sunlight, he made out the shape of a cowering creature.

The swift-dog.

It was one of the dog-wolf's lieutenants, the one who had darted back and forth and barked the orders to attack. Now she crouched on a narrow ledge of rock, quivering in fear. Her muzzle lay over the ledge as she stared down, wide-eyed, at the deadly drop; but as Lucky's claws scraped the loose rock on the edge of the crack, shards of stone skittered into the depths, and the swift-dog lifted her head. She stared up at him, petrified.

Lucky took a backward step in surprise.

Sweet!

His friend-behind-the-wire . . . his fellow survivor of the Trap House . . .

When she'd left him alone, in search of Pack companions, he'd wondered if she would be able to survive.

She had—and she was with the Wild Pack!

She was whimpering now, blinking her big eyes against the strong sunlight from above. As she made him out, she gave a sharp whine of shock.

"What are you doing here?"

They both asked the question together, and for a long moment gaped at each other. Then Lucky shook himself.

"Never mind that now, Sweet. You have to get out of there."

She crouched against the rock wall, trembling. "I don't know *how*."

Lucky took another hesitant step forward, bringing him to the edge of the chasm. He began to crouch, but loose stones slithered beneath his paws and a rain of tiny rocks clattered and pattered into the darkness. *Back!* Lucky stepped hastily away from the drop, his fur lifting.

"You're not far down. Can't you hook your claws over the edge, pull yourself up?"

"I don't think s͟o," she whined. "If I start to climb and lose my grip, I'll—"

"I'll help you. You have to try!"

Slowly, cautiously, Sweet got to her feet and turned in a tight circle, as if she were preparing for sleep. Her tail was tucked tightly between her legs, and her sleek coat seemed to tremble with fear. Hesitantly she rose up on her hind legs and caught the edge with her claws.

"Now kick with your hind legs. And pull! You'll be fine, Sweet—just pull—"

Gradually Sweet hauled herself up the sheer rock, hindpaws flailing. With a whine of terror she started to slip, but Lucky leaned into the crack to seize the scruff of her neck with his teeth, praying to the Earth-Dog that the crumbling stone would hold him. He could no longer encourage Sweet with his barks; he could only drag her upward, feeling her wriggle and thrash in his jaws.

Behind him, he heard a sound he recognized all too well. A violent, ominous creaking. With a desperate growl, Lucky scuffed backward, tugging Sweet hard as the swift-dog gave a final powerful kick with her hind legs. She was up and over the edge, and Lucky shouldered her sideways just as a wounded tree groaned and toppled, slamming into the ground with a crash.

They stood, panting with exhaustion and relief. Lucky blinked and gasped until he got his breath back, his heart hammering away at his belly.

Then they both yelped with joy, colliding as they sprang forward, tumbling over each other, licking and nosing and barking with delight.

"That's the second Big Growl we've outwitted!" said Lucky.

"Yes! Oh, Lucky, you are lucky!" Sweet barked.

"I didn't think I'd see you again!"

"I didn't think I'd see you, Packless Dog!" She nibbled his neck fur happily.

"Sweet . . . " Lucky drew away slightly, remembering the moment he'd laid eyes on her again—when he hadn't even recognized such a fierce, feral dog. "Why was your Pack attacking . . . those dogs?"

Sweet gave a yelp of derision. "Those what? They're barely dogs at all. Did you get a good look at them? How dare those disorganized mutts think of invading our territory?"

"That's—sort of what I mean." Lucky averted his eyes, licking his chops. "They didn't know how to fight, I could tell. Your Pack was"—*cruelly efficient,* he wanted to say—"harsh to them."

Lucky bit back a whine as he wondered why he'd pretended not to know his friends.

Am I ashamed of them?

"Leashed Dogs," snarled Sweet. "I don't know what they were doing here, but they certainly won't be invading real dogs' territory again. They'll know better than that now."

I used to worry about her, he remembered. *I worried that she wouldn't be tough enough to survive. Can this really be the same swift-dog who panicked at the sight of a dead longpaw?*

Catching Lucky's shocked expression, Sweet jabbed her head forward insistently. "It was a necessary lesson. The Leashed Dogs won't make that mistake again. That's best for them as well as us."

"I suppose you're right," Lucky whined, feeling a flash of guilt burn in his belly. *This was my fault.*

"Of course I'm right," said Sweet. "And I was right to go seek out a Pack! I have missed you, Lucky . . . but I found just the Pack I was looking for. They're strong, organized—" She stopped, cocking her head and giving him a quizzical look. "But what brings *you* so far out of the city? I thought you were determined not to leave."

"I couldn't stay," he told her. "There was too much danger . . . you were right about that."

Sweet gave him a playful nudge with her nose. "I'm right about most things."

He licked her jaw affectionately. "I left the city with a Pack"— he wasn't about to mention *which* Pack—"and I was just striking out alone again when I heard the sound of fighting." He dipped his head, giving a sad, but sharp, whine. "Dogs fighting each other! When we've all just escaped the Big Growl! It seemed . . . strange. I was curious." He fell silent, deciding he'd said too much already.

Sweet looked astounded. "*You* were with a Pack? But I thought you hated Packs! I thought that's why you wouldn't come with me."

"It wasn't like that, Sweet." He hesitated, wondering how to explain.

She didn't speak for a moment, her gaze focused on the ground between her paws. When she looked up again, her eyes were angry and full of hurt. "You said you were a 'Lone Dog,' that you wanted to be free and by yourself!"

Lucky felt prickles of regret as he remembered the things he had told her in the Food House, the day he had refused to travel with her.

"I'm not with a Pack," he said. "Not *really*. It just happened. Almost by accident. They didn't know how to get by, so I tagged along. They were strangers, but they needed my help, so I gave it to them. Just like I would have helped *you*, if you hadn't run off and left me behind like you did."

"I didn't want to leave you behind," said Sweet, her voice small. "But you wanted to stay in the city. And I *needed* a Pack. I wish I could make you understand, Lucky."

Inwardly he squirmed. He understood far better than she thought he did. "And you found one. You must have done well, Sweet. They were treating you like a leader during the fight."

"I've advanced quickly," Sweet agreed a little reluctantly. "It's the way of a Pack, that's all. Things change."

Lucky raised his head and sniffed the wind, which was rising again after the stillness that had accompanied the Growl. There were distinct smells of life—and death—creeping into the air.

"I have to get going, Sweet."

"Again? But where will you go?"

Lucky was silent as he thought about it. He was desperate to find Bella and the others, to find out what had become of Alfie, but he couldn't tell Sweet that. He had as good as told her that he had nothing to do with the ragtag Pack she had been fighting. He couldn't go back on that now.

Sweet nuzzled him. "Why don't you come with me, Lucky? Come and meet my Pack. You'll like us. You've just saved my life, so they'll like you."

"I don't know . . ."

"Lucky, you can't survive on your own. What if the next Growl catches you, and there's no one to help you like you helped me? And so many of the streams are poisoned! You might not find clean water to drink. You must come with me!"

A shiver went through Lucky's fur, and he gave himself a brisk shake to disguise it. "I'm sorry, Sweet. I'm still a Lone Dog."

"All dogs should stand together at times like these," said Sweet, her nose turning up. "You're strong, you're clever—you should offer all that to a Pack, not keep it for yourself!" Sweet sounded almost angry, but her voice softened. "You'd be happy, Lucky. I promise."

Lucky averted his gaze, feeling the old stubbornness back in his belly. "I'm happier on my own."

Sweet dipped her head. "I can't make you change your mind, can I? Then I wish you well. Please take care."

"I will." Lucky padded away, still feeling the tug of regret and unable to resist a last look back.

Sweet was already bounding across the broken ground, elegantly leaping over fallen trees. A memory struck him sharply: Sweet bolting from the cold room in the Food House, terrified by the dead longpaw inside, and the destruction of the city outside. Her speed was the same, but in every other way she seemed different. Her head was high and her ears were pricked. Her coat was sleek and the muscles beneath were strong and defined.

Lucky felt the strongest urge to bark after her, to call her back and ask if she'd come with him instead. She'd be a great addition to Bella's Pack. And what if he never saw her again? He was going to miss her. . . .

But it was too late. Sweet was already out of sight, and Lucky would never catch her now. There was nothing left to do but continue his search for the Leashed Dogs.

As he padded on, he felt flutters of fear in his fur. *They'll be all right,* he told himself. *They've survived one Growl already. Surely they'll have survived this one, too. . . .*

CHAPTER THREE

It wasn't difficult to follow the trail of Bella and the others farther into the shattered valley. All Lucky had to do was pad after the trickles and pools of blood that Alfie and Martha had left. The metallic scent of it made his bones and muscles cold; a terrible anxiety drove him on to leap cracks in the ground and force his way through thickets of fallen branches.

At least, he thought, the valley would recover swiftly. Saplings would grow again to replace the trees, and the cracked ground and uprooted bushes would soon be covered with new moss and grass and plants, hiding the damage.

Unlike the city, which would never be able to heal itself.

Leaping on top of a thick pine trunk, Lucky made out the river beyond, very close now. Like the streams near the city, the silver of its surface was tinged with that same iridescent sheen. The poison really had spread this far, even in the short time since he'd left Bella's Pack. Lucky's heart sank. Maybe the valley wouldn't recover as quickly as he'd thought. . . .

There was a ridge of ground that fell sharply toward the river, and tree roots half-exposed by the rush of water jutted out over the bank. When he jumped down it he found a sandy hollow beneath the roots. Huddled there were the seven Leashed Dogs, their hackles stiff with fear.

"You'll be all right," Daisy was saying, licking at Martha's torn leg. "But you shouldn't move around."

Bruno's sturdy body stood over Alfie, who lay still and broken on the ground. Sunshine stared at the little dog, shivering.

"He needs a vet! He really does!" Sunshine whined. "I wish my longpaws were here."

"We all do." Mickey gave her a reassuring lick, but his flanks were trembling.

Then Daisy looked up and caught sight of Lucky. Her eyes widened and she gave a frightened yelp. That set the others off, leaping and scrambling to their feet, falling over one another in their haste. *They must think I'm one of the Wild Dogs,* Lucky realized. He gave a soft reassuring growl, and came out of the deeper shadows so they could see him better.

"It's me," he barked.

Their shock was plain in their faces and their bristling coats, but then Bella's ears pricked and she sprang to meet him, pressing her face to his.

"You came back."

"Lucky!" The others trotted to join her, whining and licking him—all but Bruno, who stayed standing protectively over Alfie. Lucky heard him grumble, "It's a little late for a heroic return, Lucky."

Sunshine and Daisy jumped up to reach his nose, but their old enthusiasm was subdued. Sadness filled the little hollow. Even the acrid scent of the river was overwhelmed by the tang of blood. Hesitantly, Lucky paced forward to where Alfie sprawled, eyes half-closed, panting weakly. His flank rose and fell barely at all.

"Oh, Lucky," whined Mickey. "Is there anything we can do?"

They all fell silent as Lucky nosed Alfie's wound. The skin was split wide and Lucky could see red, glistening muscle like he'd seen on injured prey. The sight of it turned his stomach cold.

A faint whimper came from Alfie's throat, but he couldn't raise his head to greet Lucky. The sand beneath him was stained with thick, dark blood, but it no longer flowed from his side in a strong stream. It had been reduced to a limp trickle that seeped feebly in the slash.

Lucky closed his eyes briefly, hating to have to break such news.

"He isn't bleeding so badly anymore." There was a faint hope in Sunshine's voice that made Lucky's heart turn over.

He licked her muzzle. "Sunshine," he said. "There's nothing we can do for Alfie."

"But . . ." Daisy faltered.

Lucky held her gaze, his heart feeling as heavy as a rock. "There's less blood because the Earth-Dog has taken most of it already. Do you see Alfie's eyes?"

Martha took a hesitant step closer. "They're so blurry—as if he can't see anymore."

"Alfie's essence is flowing out of his body. It's starting to become one with everything else around us." Lucky gazed down at the little dog, his shallow occasional breaths barely lifting his flank.

The Leashed Dogs fell silent again, and Martha lay down to push her nose close to Alfie's. "Oh, my poor little friend."

"This isn't fair!" whimpered Sunshine, raising her pleading eyes to Lucky's. She let out a terrible, mournful howl. "Why did this have to happen?"

Lucky longed to look away, but he knew he couldn't; his friends were grieving. They needed him to be strong.

Bella raised her muzzle and whined, and then Mickey and Daisy joined in the Pack's howl. Even stolid Bruno gave voice to his misery.

Lucky dipped his head to tenderly lick Alfie's face.

"He was barely more than a puppy," Martha said softly.

Lucky licked each dog's muzzle in turn, trying desperately to give some comfort. "We just won't be able to *see* Alfie, that's all. But he will still be with us, *around* us—in the air and the water and the earth."

Sunshine jerked back from him, and he blinked in surprise.

"What use is that?" she barked. "I liked Alfie being here! In his own body. With us!"

Lucky had no answer. Despite his reassuring words about the spirit essence, he knew just how Sunshine felt. The painful memory struck him again: Alfie, given new heart by Lucky's arrival and desperate to impress him, charging bravely at the dog-wolf and paying with his life.

Oh, Alfie, thought Lucky miserably, *if only I'd stayed out of sight.*

He turned back to the younger dog, bending to lick his nose again very gently. No breath came from Alfie's muzzle now. Bella came to his side, nuzzling Alfie's ear. The others gathered around her.

"I'll miss you, Alfie," mourned Daisy.

"We all will." Mickey nudged his tail gently. "Safe journey, my friend."

"Into the world," added Sunshine, her whines heavy with grief.

Lucky took a small pace backward as he watched them say their farewells. He wished he could *see* Alfie's essence escaping his body. It would be reassuring to watch his spirit flow into the trees, and the air, and the clouds. It would make this so much easier for all of them if they could witness his final journey.

But there was only a lifeless little body lying on the dry earth, and the first faint suggestion of the death-smell. There was nothing inside Alfie's body anymore—no breath, no spirit, no life. Lucky slumped down onto his belly and added his whines of grief to the Pack's.

Sunshine was right: This wasn't fair.

He realized that Sweet had also been right: There was still so much he did not know about Pack life, Pack traditions. There had to be some kind of ceremony, he was sure, but he had no idea what it would be, or how it would go. When a City Dog died, the longpaws came and took him away. Perhaps he should have asked Sweet about that aspect of Pack life. He should have asked her about so many things.

Lucky stood up hesitantly. "I think the best thing—the natural thing—would be to leave Alfie here. Earth-Dog will absorb him when she's ready."

"Leave him?!" cried Sunshine in horror. "I don't want to leave him!"

"Certainly not." Daisy shuddered. "If we do, the crows and the foxes will eat him. We can't do that to Alfie!"

"Daisy's right," Mickey agreed. "When a Leashed Dog died, the longpaws would always bury him—sometimes, they would put flowers and stones on top of the ground, after they put him inside. That's the proper way."

"It's the *longpaw* way," muttered Lucky, but so quietly it was only to himself. The last thing he wanted just now was to upset his friends, who clearly still thought like Leashed Dogs when it came to these sorts of decisions.

"Daisy and Sunshine and Mickey are right." Bella stood squarely on a nearby rock, gazing firmly at them all. She looked like a *real* leader of a Pack. "We should bury him, like his longpaw would have done."

Lucky watched, impressed, as the grief seemed to lift slightly from the Leashed Dog Pack. They nodded to one another, shook out their fur, and stood up straighter. *Yes,* thought Lucky. *It's not about what's normal for Wild Dogs—this is what's right for them.* Alfie wasn't ashamed of having belonged to longpaws. They were doing this for him, so they would do it Alfie's way—the way he would have wanted it.

Besides, at that moment Lucky found himself angry with all the Spirit Dogs.

River-Dog! Forest-Dog! Sky-Dogs! Couldn't you have helped him? Couldn't you have protected our brave friend from that dog-wolf brute?

He was so small. . . .

There was softer earth a little way from the riverbank, and Lucky pitched in to help Bella, Mickey, and Martha make a hole. It didn't take long to dig enough space for Alfie.

Martha was right, Lucky thought, grief burning in his gut. Alfie was barely more than a pup. With all a pup's foolish courage, too. . . .

This would be the best possible place for him. If his spirit was in these trees and this cool earth, deep in the peaceful valley, Alfie would be happy, he decided. And even the river might one day be clean again.

"I wish we had his ball to leave with him," whispered Daisy. "The one he brought . . . the one he brought when—"

"When the longpaw house fell. When he nearly died." Bella's

eyes were glimmering with sadness. "We saved him then. Oh, Sky-Dogs, why couldn't we save him today?"

"We don't have his ball," Bruno growled. "Lucky made us leave the longpaw things behind." He sounded angry, but Lucky could not scent any *real* rage coming from him. The stocky dog was just covering his deep sorrow.

Lucky felt an itch of guilt, but he didn't want to scratch it away. It had been the right thing to do, but now it was feeling wrong. "Earth-Dog will take good care of him," he insisted, but there was a catch in his voice. It sounded like an empty promise, even to his own ears.

Martha picked Alfie up in her jaws, moving slowly and carefully—even though there was no way Alfie would feel pain now. Despite her bad leg, he wasn't much of a burden for her. As she laid his limp body carefully in the hole, the others helped to scrape and kick the earth back over him, until he was hidden from sight for the last time. All the dogs paused and gazed at his final sleeping-place, lit by the dying glow of the sinking sun.

"It feels wrong to leave him," whimpered Daisy.

"I know what you mean," said Lucky. To his surprise, he really did.

"Why don't we stay here, then?" suggested Bella. "Just until the Sun-Dog returns."

"What if those terrible dogs come back?" asked Sunshine as she pawed gently at the mound of soil above Alfie.

Lucky shook his head. "They ran from the Growl, too. I think we should stay with Alfie."

"I like that idea," said Mickey quietly. "We'll guard his body during no-sun. Our way of saying good-bye."

Lucky nodded, an odd heaviness in his throat.

"It feels right," said Sunshine, glancing up at the bigger dogs. "Doesn't it?"

Mickey licked her neck fondly, before scratching at the ground with his claws three times. Then he touched it with his nose. "Earth-Dog," he whined. "Look after our friend." He turned his muzzle to the sky and began to howl.

The sound was eerie and heartrending, and Lucky felt a tremor run through his skin. Then the others began to join in, raising their heads and howling.

"Take care of Alfie, Earth-Dog!"

"Guard him for us!"

"Keep his spirit safe!"

Lucky watched in respectful silence. This was something he

had never witnessed, and did not quite understand. Maybe it had never happened before. Maybe it was another way that dogs were changing along with the whole world.

The sky was darkening fast, and Alfie's sad little burial mound was fading into shadow, but still the mournful howling went on. It was the strangest ritual Lucky had ever seen, but he had to admit that it made him feel a little better. He was sure Bella and the others must feel that way too, however sad they were. There was something comforting about passing Alfie formally into Earth-Dog's paws for protection.

Lucky trod his habitual sleep circle, then lay down with his muzzle on his paws. He closed his eyes. The howling was almost soothing. . . .

Abruptly he blinked awake from a half dream, his fur bristling.

In his drifting dream he'd thought it was something else, a sound not of grief but of terrible menace. A memory stirred from long ago. *The howling* . . .

But it was only his friends, still grieving for Alfie.

Lucky closed his eyes again and let sleep wash over him.

CHAPTER FOUR

Lucky could feel the sun on his back. The warmth was comforting after the chill of the night.

Bella walked at his side as they followed the river upstream. Both dogs eyed the water with trepidation; the sinister colors on the surface gave it a strange loveliness in the morning light.

"We should scout around," Bella had said, not long after Lucky had woken up and stretched his back and neck. "See if there's been any sign of those dogs since yesterday."

Lucky sensed that it wasn't just sensible caution on his sister's part. She *needed* to be away from the others for a while.

His litter-sister had something on her mind.

"Tell me what happened when that fight broke out," he suggested at last. "I heard it from far away."

Bella sighed. "It was terrible. But I don't see any way we could have avoided it."

"But how did you cross those dogs? How did it start?"

"Martha was the one who noticed." Bella stopped and wrinkled her muzzle at the stained river. "She came down to swim, and realized straight away that the poisoned water had reached us, and it was still spreading. She ran back to warn us. She was so distressed, but then you know how close Martha feels to the River-Dog."

Lucky growled in agreement. "I noticed the bad water as soon as I saw the river. It's a dark omen, Bella."

"Yes." Bella sighed again. "We knew immediately we couldn't stay. But we thought, it's such a big valley, and so fertile—there *had* to be clean water somewhere close by. So we set off in search of it."

"And you found some?"

"There's a place with a lot of water not far from here. I've never seen so much water in one place—I don't think any of us had. It's strange, Lucky—like the pond at the Dog Park, but so huge, and very still and silent."

"A lake," Lucky said. "So what happened?"

"We were worried about drinking the water, because we'd never seen anything like it. But we were so thirsty. Martha paddled in first, and then Bruno, and suddenly we were all splashing and drinking to our hearts' content. I thought our troubles were over."

"But you'd moved into someone else's territory—"

"Yes." Bella's head and ears drooped. "We didn't even know it until we came across a guard. Just one, and there was a stand-off—he was as shocked as we were, I think. He was a long-legged dog and when he ran away, he was fast. We heard him barking an alarm, and he came back with his whole Pack."

"And they attacked you? Just like that?"

"Not right away." Bella came to a halt, lay down on her belly, and licked disconsolately at a paw. "I tried to reason with them. I asked if we could drink from the lake—if we could at least share that. There was so much water there—more than any dog could ever need!"

Lucky shook his head sadly. "That's not the way it works."

Bella gave an annoyed grumble. "But I couldn't back down, Lucky. I knew my Pack would die if we had to go back and drink from the river. I tried again. I did my best, truly."

"I know you did, Bella." Lucky felt a flash of anger at dogs who could be so unfeeling for anyone who wasn't in their Pack.

Bella's tail thumped the ground, slowly and heavily. "The more I argued, the more I tried to persuade them, the angrier those other dogs got. It was as if they were offended that I would even try. Finally, their leader gave the order to attack, and they went for us. We ran at first, but when we got close to the poisoned river again, we couldn't keep running. . . . "

"And that's where I came in." Lucky licked her nose. "I saw the fight from a long way off, and heard you from even farther. I wanted to help, but I knew I had to be careful. Rushing in could have made things worse. Then Alfie . . ." His voice caught in his throat as he remembered.

If I had been there, if I had been fighting with them, would I have been able to stop all this from happening? Would Alfie still be alive?

Lucky could not help thinking he'd have handled it differently, had it been him in the standoff with the angry dogs. He would never have tried to argue with that dog-wolf once he had refused them. Bella should have backed off humbly, thought of some other strategy—challenging the Wild Pack's Alpha was asking for trouble.

Maybe coming back *had* been a mistake. He knew the others didn't think so, but . . . the Growl had put a stop to the fighting without his help, and perhaps if Lucky hadn't shown his face, Alfie would never have made his stupidly brave attack on the dog-wolf. That guilt still pricked at him.

"Come on," he said at last. "We'd better get back to the others."

Bella rose slowly to her feet, her tail and ears still down, and the two littermates retraced their steps back to the dogs' makeshift camp. All the sunlight and brightness seemed to have been taken out of the day. Lucky almost wished he hadn't asked about the battle.

As soon as they came in sight of the rest of the Pack, Lucky realized how much work there was still to do with these dogs—how desperately they needed a streetwise friend. Mickey was licking so hungrily from an old rain puddle, he was down to the mud at the bottom.

Lucky nudged the older dog away with his nose. "You shouldn't drink that."

Mickey lowered his ears, ashamed. "There isn't any fresh water, Lucky," he said. "Surely this is safer than drinking from that poisoned river?"

Lucky tilted his head thoughtfully. He had to admit, Mickey had a point.

"We can't rely on the rain." He licked his chops uncertainly. "The Earth-Dog drinks it quickly, and what she leaves behind is fouled."

"But Martha's wounded," said Mickey, looking at the big water-dog, who lay washing the bite on her leg with her tongue. "She can't travel far."

"I know!" Daisy leaped up brightly, tail wagging. "Remember we made that offering before, to the Sky-Dogs? Let's do the same for the River-Dog now! If we send her a gift, perhaps she'll clean the water for us!"

The little white dog's head cocked and her tongue lolled. She looked so pleased with her suggestion, Lucky couldn't bear to contradict her. He had never known the Spirit Dogs to intervene as quickly or obviously as that, but who was he to say they wouldn't do so now, in these desperate times? The River-Dog might appreciate an offering, and if there was any dog in the Pack that she might have mercy for, it would be Martha, with her love of water and her big webbed paws.

"Well," he said slowly, "it's worth a try. But what will we give to the River-Dog?"

"Food!" Sunshine barked excitedly. "We'll give her a rabbit— or a squirrel!"

Lucky stared at her, skeptical. "Food? Do you have any to spare?"

Sunshine's ears drooped. "Well . . ."

"No," Bella growled witheringly. "We *don't*."

"We . . . we could try to find some?" Sunshine suggested, but Lucky could see that even she didn't think it was a good idea.

Daisy gave her a supportive lick on one long-furred ear.

"I think River-Dog would want us to use any food we find to keep ourselves alive. We'll think of something else," she said kindly. Sunshine dipped her head, embarrassed.

Lucky felt a little sorry for Sunshine. If she could suggest, even for a moment, giving their food supplies away so casually, she was still a long way from understanding survival in the Wild.

Mickey was lying with his head on the longpaw glove he'd brought with him all the way from the city, and he suddenly sniffed at it and looked up. "I have an idea. What do we dogs like almost as much as eating?" He glanced around at all of them. "Playing! My longpaw pup would always wear this while he played fetch with me."

"How does that help?" Bella asked.

"All dogs like a game of fetch, don't we? Let's find the River-Dog a really good stick!"

Bella cocked her head, thinking. "That might work."

Lucky wasn't so sure, but Mickey looked enormously pleased with himself. "Come on, then. I bet we can find something *really* special. We'll check with Martha before we offer it, to make sure we find something the River-Dog will like."

Bella gave a bark of approval.

To Lucky it sounded more like Leashed Dog logic—*Why would the River-Dog want anything to play with, as if she needed a longpaw owner to entertain her?*—but if it would make the others feel better, maybe it was worth a try. And perhaps the good intentions behind the gift would win over the River-Dog. Surely she would at least be pleased with the Pack's efforts.

Mickey was already bounding between the remaining trees, sniffing out fallen branches and twigs. The others darted to join him, nosing in the tangled foliage, clearly relieved to have something positive to do. Their excitement was infectious, and Lucky found his hopes rising as he too searched for a fine fetching-stick. It was nice to be moving *toward* something, rather than running *away*.

"How about this one?" grunted Bruno through a mouthful of birch branch.

They all stopped their searching to examine Bruno's find. It was a beautifully shaped stick, smooth and sturdy but bent just enough in the middle to give the best jaw-hold. When they brought it to her, Martha tilted her head, sniffing at the papery silver bark.

"It's beautiful," she announced at last. "I think the River-Dog will like it very much."

They were all yelping and whining with eagerness as they trotted to the riverbank, Martha limping slowly in front carrying the special stick, and Bruno padding beside her, his head proudly held high.

At the crumbling bank, Martha lowered herself onto her forepaws and gently released the gift. The whole Pack helped her nose it into the stream without touching the water. It caught on a tuft of grass but, with a last nudge, it came free and floated off into the deeper water, swirling in the lazy current.

"River-Dog!" whined Martha. "Please help us. We need clean water to drink."

The rest of the Pack yelped in agreement, watching as the stick slid smoothly between rocks and into a fast-flowing channel of white water. It bounced and tumbled in the rushing current, and Sunshine yelped with delight.

"The River-Dog's playing with the stick! See? She really is!"

The dogs panted happily, watching the stick drift downstream into calmer water, creating eddies of rainbow in the filmy green surface. Then it spun out of sight.

Martha's ears drooped. "Poor River-Dog," she said softly. "She must hate that her rivers are poisoned like this. Perhaps she's unwell herself."

"Let's just hope she likes our offering," said Bella, nuzzling her neck. "We've done all we can for now. We'll find out soon enough if there's any change."

Lucky caught his litter-sister's eye as they turned and padded back toward their camp. There was anxiety in Bella's expression. *She's no more certain of this than I am,* he thought.

But at least Bella was keeping the Pack's spirits up, and it made Lucky happy to watch them turning their ritual circles and sending their thoughts to the Sky-Dogs. He felt a little more optimistic as he settled to sleep himself, his head against his litter-sister's warm flank.

They were trying to connect with the ways of the Wild. If they were going to survive in this empty and broken world, they were going to have to learn to understand it the same way that Lucky had learned to understand the city.

It was going to take time, he knew. But as no-sun approached, Lucky felt a flutter of hope.

Maybe they can learn, he thought.

A crash woke him from a deep sleep. As Lucky jerked his head, his whole body tensing and bristling, he felt the spatter of cold raindrops against his fur. Flattening his ears against his skull, he looked up just in time to see a bolt of energy from Lightning's hindpaws crackle across the blackness of no-sun. The Sky-Dogs snarled again.

Beside him, Bella snapped awake, trembling. The others too were waking up, whining anxiously as rain began battering their bodies. Lucky cringed at the drops, which felt as hard as stones falling from the sky. Within a few seconds his fur was plastered to his skin. Again Lightning leaped, and this time the Sky-Dogs gave an enormous deafening growl directly above them.

Sunshine sprang to her feet, yelping and barking now, and the rest followed. Lucky stood in the center of the panicking Pack, turning on the spot to watch them and beginning to get dizzy as they ran in chaotic circles.

"What's wrong? Stop! Slow down!"

"A storm, Lucky!" howled Daisy. "We need to hide!"

Lucky barked his reassurance, but they took no notice of him. Even Bruno, usually so stolid, was whimpering as he dashed from tree to tree.

"It's just a storm!" It was certainly a fierce one, but Lucky knew he had to calm them down. He tried a jovial bark. "You're Wild Dogs now; you don't have to be scared of Lightning and the Sky-Dogs' bickering."

"But Sunshine's right," yelped Martha, pressing her body close to the ground as Lightning's bolt of power exploded yet again over their heads. "There's nowhere to shelter! Where do we run to?"

They were panicking. Lucky could understand—their longpaws must have protected them from every storm, coddling them in their baskets and kennels whenever Lightning bounded across the sky, whenever the Sky-Dogs tussled noisily. He'd gotten them through a storm before, but it hadn't been nearly this bad. The Leashed Dogs simply weren't used to facing a true storm by themselves.

"Listen to the Sky-Dogs," wailed Mickey. "They're furious!"

"They're only growling at Lightning!" barked Lucky, but his voice was lost in another chorus of thunder from the Sky-Dogs.

Martha cowered, trying to put her huge paws over her ears. "They've sent Lightning to burn the earth. They must be angry with us!"

Sunshine was a blur of white fur, dashing here and there, whining and howling her terror. At last, exhausted, she crept between Martha's legs, shaking violently.

"It's never going to end," she whimpered. "First the Big Growl, then those horrible Fight Dogs. And now the Sky-Dogs and Lightning are trying to finish us off! We've got the most awful luck! Nothing but trouble!"

"Sunshine, calm down!" Lucky tried to lick the little dog's black nose, but she had buried her head in Martha's fur, and the older dog's own whines and trembles did nothing to settle her.

Lucky feared this was going to lead to real trouble. The Leashed Dogs were working themselves into a frenzy. Mickey was backing away, staring in terror at the sky. Martha stood up and began to lumber blindly toward the river, her wounded leg threatening to give with every step. She seemed to have forgotten Sunshine, who started to bark wildly now that her shelter had been taken away. Elsewhere, Lucky could see Bruno making a sudden, clumsy break for the open ground.

They're running! Lucky realized with horror. The Pack was splitting up. He spun around again, not knowing which dog to chase after first.

They're going to get lost, scattered . . . Lightning will burn them. . . .

And the enemy Pack is still out there!

CHAPTER FIVE

Lucky was soaked to the skin. He raised his hackles, turned up his head, and waited for a pause in the Sky-Dogs' snarling and growling. When it came, he gave the loudest, most commanding bark that he could muster.

"Come with me," he ordered. "Now."

The Leashed Dogs grew still, looking about themselves in shock. Then they crept closer to him, shivering as they moved. Lucky gave a few barks and growls of encouragement as he began to guide them toward the thicker tree cover. There might be some risk of falling trees and branches, but it would be much more dangerous to let the Leashed Dogs go on working themselves into their panic out in the open, where any stray lashing of Lightning could kill them instantly. Lucky snapped at Sunshine as she hesitated, and she jumped to follow him. Heads low, and tails between their legs, the Leashed Dogs crept into the dark undergrowth after Lucky.

The belt of trees here was dense, though it thinned out into a clearing a few dog-lengths away where a single tall pine stood alone, higher than the others. Whining reassurance, Lucky gathered the dogs into the bushiest thicket of trunks, a good leap-stride from the clearing. He didn't know why, but he felt sure they had to stay here, concealed from the Sky-Dogs.

The thicker foliage muffled the rage of the storm, and even the rain couldn't pelt down so hard. Lucky could hear his friends' breathing beginning to calm down, their whining growing quieter and more subdued. They were getting ahold of themselves. Lucky let out a huff of relief. Mickey shook his head from side to side and growled, as if realizing suddenly how silly he'd been. All of them peered nervously up through the branches at the sky, waiting for the next outburst.

Then the sky exploded into brightness. Lightning hurtled to Earth, trailing his blinding energy. Lucky froze with terror as Lightning's hindlegs caught the lone pine. It seemed to explode into flames, the ball of fire almost blindingly bright.

For an instant, the dogs were stunned into silence by the heat and the light. No-sun had been driven away by the glare and roar of the flaming tree. Lucky bit back a whine of relief and fear. *I remember! Old Hunter had seen many storms, and told me that lone trees were always attacked by Lightning.*

"Wildfire!" Mickey howled, tail tight between his legs.

"NO!" Any control that Sunshine had gained was torn apart, as she fled from the safety of the trees with an anguished howl.

"Sunshine!" Bella barked. "Come back!"

The little dog was already a distance away, racing toward the water. "River-Dog! River-Dog! Protect us!" she howled.

"No!" Bella sped after Sunshine, and then Lucky spotted what his litter-sister had obviously seen.

The river in front of Sunshine looked strange, like no river he had ever seen before. It looked as if it was rising, bulging. Cold horror ran through Lucky's body as he raced after Bella, barking at Sunshine to stop.

Sunshine took no notice of either of them, and continued to bolt toward the swelling river. As Lightning slashed another path across the sky, Lucky saw the danger clearly, just for an instant. The water was higher than the bank. How was that even possible? It was a dirty, foaming line, and the river was coming toward them.

With a shock as sharp as if Lightning had run right into him, he realized. *The river's breaking free!*

Bella was on top of Sunshine now, holding her down. Lucky leaped in to help his litter-sister move the little dog. He grabbed on to one of Sunshine's forelegs while Bella took her collar between her teeth. Then they scrabbled into an abrupt turn, racing away from the looming water. Sunshine yelped—more in shock than pain—as they pulled her away.

Then Lucky heard the sudden crash and roar of the water. *So much for liking the stick; the River-Dog is furious!*

They burst into the trees as the other dogs stared past them, their eyes wide and their flanks heaving in horror. As he and Bella dropped Sunshine unceremoniously to the ground, Lucky spun on his paws.

The river was still rushing toward them, the clear water turned to a churning darkness. The River-Dog was baying his rage. The waves of water were racing closer, their tips edged with that sick-looking, creamy foam.

"Run!" barked Lucky.

The dogs didn't need to be told twice. Yelping with terror, they fled farther up the valley, while behind them, the menacing torrent thundered through the trees where they'd been standing moments before. Lucky heard the tear and crack of branches pounded by water.

"Higher ground!" barked Lucky urgently. "Keep going up!" Water could not climb hills—that much, he knew.

The dogs were panting and gasping by the time Lucky let them halt, high on the slope. Flanks heaving, they stared down at the sheet of dirty, choppy water that lay across the lower meadows. Many of the trees were half-submerged, small waves licking at their trunks.

Lucky glanced at the sky. Clouds were breaking up, letting the Moon-Dog gleam between their shreds, and the rain had slackened to a spitting drizzle. The battle above them was over, and the Sky-Dogs' rumbling growls faded in the distance. The pine was sending up clouds of sharp-scented steam, its top branches blackened, half its trunk submerged in the broken river. A few last flames flickered in its topmost branches, but Wildfire's trail had been swallowed by the water.

"It's over," breathed Martha. "The Sky-Dogs have stopped fighting."

"For now." Sunshine shivered. "I'm sorry, Lucky. I'm sorry, Bella. I didn't know what to do. I was so scared. . . ."

"Don't worry too much," said Lucky. Thinking his bark might have been a little gruff, he gave her ear a reassuring lick. "But try not to panic. Trust in your Packmates. They are who you need to rely on now."

The hillside seemed very exposed, but that didn't bother Lucky when he thought about what might have happened to them had they stayed lower down the slope. He picked his way farther up, through flattened grass and tangled twigs, letting the others follow at their own speed. They'd been barked at more than enough since his return, and any haste or urgency might cause one of them to make a wrong step in the dark. This was something they could not afford.

Still, they were close behind him when he paused on a ridge and cocked an ear. The ground fell away quite sharply, as far as a dog could safely jump, then leveled out into a shallow dip like a longpaw drinking bowl. It was sheltered, and the surface looked like it had not been wounded by the Big Growl.

"Let's sleep here," suggested Lucky.

"Is it safe?" Daisy was trembling, only partly from the exhaustion of the climb.

Lucky licked her ear. "It's as safe as it can be, I think. I doubt we'll find any other shelter up here."

"Lucky's right," agreed Bella. "Don't worry, Daisy. We'll look after you."

Lucky gave her an affectionate glance. He had a feeling that after what had happened to poor Alfie, Bella would be more protective of the smaller dogs than ever. "It'll be sunup soon. We should get a bit of extra sleep if we can."

Lucky was almost too tired to tread his ritual circle, and when he curled up by himself the tip of his tail flicked restlessly. The others soon fell into an exhausted sleep, but Lucky found he could not.

Wriggling, he tried to make himself more comfortable, but his fur was still sopping wet, and he could feel every little stone and twig against his body. He stood up to give himself an extra shake, but it didn't help much. The air was cold against his wet skin, and his ears and tail felt bedraggled and heavy.

Once more he curled on the ground, his head on his paws, and closed his eyes determinedly. *Please, Moon-Dog,* he thought. *Let me rest. . . .*

CHAPTER SIX

He must have drifted into sleep eventually, Lucky realized, because the Sun-Dog had bounded high into the sky by the time his eyes next blinked open. Rising and stretching gratefully, he gave himself a huge shake. His fur was dry at last, and he felt both warmer and much better.

The rest of the Pack was a little way down the hill, excitedly dashing along the river's new banks, sniffing at the water. Lucky stared. The river's overflow had become a lake. It had subsided quite a bit from its high point in the night, and now shone silver in the sunlight, lapping peacefully at the grass and tree trunks it had flooded.

Spotting him, Daisy barked a joyful "Good morning!" and bounded up the hill to jump and nip at his muzzle.

"Come and see, Lucky. You won't believe what we've found!"

"What is it, Daisy?" He could hear the fondness in his own

voice. He was glad the little white dog was happy again. She trotted down the slope ahead of him, tail wagging, and for a moment Lucky thought with alarm that she was going to plunge straight into the river. But she stopped right on its new edge, where it had eaten away the bank, and turned to face him again, panting happily.

Lucky peered past her, puzzled. "What is it?"

Bruno padded to his shoulder. "No, Lucky—*there*. Beneath the bank. The river must have washed away some loose earth. And look what it has uncovered!"

Still doubtful, Lucky dropped carefully to a flat patch of sand. He looked closer. Bruno was right—the rising water had washed away rocks, roots, and soil, revealing deep caves in the rock.

"That is amazing." Lucky padded closer, sniffing at the great holes. They looked as if a gigantic dog had scooped them out of the high bank. Lucky frowned, thinking this must have been a very careful dog, because all the holes looked the same. Each one was as high as a fully grown longpaw, and the walls inside were of smooth stone, dry and clean and . . .

Unnatural.

His flanks tingled as memories drifted through his mind. Uncomfortable memories of rooms in the Trap House—long cold-rooms between the cage-rooms—but these caves were smaller, and of course there were no cages inside them.

They did look like excellent shelters. . . .

"The River-Dog must have done this," announced Martha. "He wasn't angry last night at all. He answered us, and dug these holes for us to hide in. Your idea worked, Mickey!"

"Thanks to you, Martha," he said a little shyly.

"We asked the River-Dog for clean water," said Sunshine, "and he's given us that, too!"

Lucky cocked his head in surprise as he watched Bruno stride to the water's edge. He dipped his head toward the water, gulping happily. Then he raised his dripping muzzle to look proudly at him.

"Are you sure?" Hesitantly Lucky padded forward and sniffed. "It does smell a bit better," he agreed. But he wasn't sure the river was entirely pure yet. There was a lot more water after the storm, and it had spread. Maybe the poison was hiding, preparing to come back and strike them later?

He wouldn't give voice to his doubts for now. It was nice to see the Leashed Dogs looking happy and confident after their terror in the storm. Their certainty in the River-Dog's help could do nothing but good for their mood.

Martha plunged into the water, right up to her shoulders, looking delighted to have a chance to swim once more and bathe her injured leg. Daisy and Sunshine watched happily from the shallows, less inclined to fling themselves in. Leaving them to their high-spirited splashing and lapping, Lucky wandered back to the exposed caves.

Bella came quietly to his side, sniffing and gazing at the great holes with him. "They look like they might be useful," she murmured. "But I'm not sure I'd want to stay in them for very long."

"Just what I was thinking," Lucky agreed. "After all, there's no saying the river can't rise again. If it does, it might wash away anything inside these caves."

"Just like it washed away the mud that was here," said Bella with a shiver.

"Still, they'll make a good temporary camp." Lucky ventured inside one, and pawed gently at the wall, leaving shallow scratch-marks. "It will do the others good to rest for a while."

"Yes." Bella averted her eyes. "I'm sorry about what happened during the Sky-Dogs' fight, Lucky. We . . . I panicked."

Lucky nodded. There seemed to be nothing to say. Bella obviously understood how dangerous their pointless frenzy had been.

She'd know to stay calm next time, he thought. At least, he hoped so. "I wonder where you should go after this though, Bella—" He froze, interrupted by a dreadful sound: a sickening, choking, heaving growl. As he and Bella turned, another guttural noise rattled his ears—a monstrous retching.

"What is—"

"Bruno!" Bella cried.

As they bolted toward him, the thickset dog gave one last ghastly heave, spewing thick, evil-smelling chunks from his mouth. Then he collapsed onto his side, his paws flailing weakly. The rest of the Pack crowded around, and Lucky shouldered his way through, shoving them aside. Standing over Bruno, he stared down in horror. The burly dog's lips had turned a ghastly color, and lumps of the foul chunks clung to his mouth and gasping jaws. He was drooling nasty-smelling foam. His breaths made it sound as though his throat was twisted and knotted.

There's rottenness inside him! thought Lucky, feeling a burn of dread in his body. *Like a spoil-box—but a living one!*

He knew what to do, although he had never done it before. Lucky lunged for the struggling dog, slamming his head into Bruno's heaving belly. Before the others could object, he did it again. Then the Pack was pawing at him, yelping and barking.

"Lucky, don't!"

"Leave him alone! What are you doing?"

Shaking them off, Lucky growled and head-butted Bruno again, making the dog thrash and squirm. Again and again he slammed his skull into Bruno's gut, ignoring the protests.

Then Bruno gave a great, retching cough, spraying more foul chunks from his mouth. The mess hit the ground like rain as the sick dog's head lolled back.

Lucky drew back, trembling. Bruno's eyes had lost their glazed, dead look, but he didn't stir from the ground, and his weak breathing was still a horrible hacking rasp.

"What was that?" whispered Bella. "Lucky, what did you do to him?"

Lucky shook his head. "The sickness had to come out of him, and that was the only way to do it. Old Hunter told me the secret. I never had to use it until now."

Daisy looked stunned. "But what—what would it have done to him?"

"It can kill a dog," said Lucky. "But not if he spits it out. Haven't you heard of this?"

The others exchanged embarrassed glances, and Lucky sighed. "No," he said. "Your longpaws would just take you to that vet of yours, wouldn't they? The longpaw-healer?"

"Yes." Mickey seemed dazed, too. "It's a good thing you were here, Lucky."

Bella nuzzled him gratefully. "It is. Or we'd have been giving Bruno to the Earth-Dog along with Alfie."

"Bruno's still very sick," Lucky pointed out, as Bruno tried and failed to lift his great fierce head. "We'll have to take care of him for a while." He added quietly to Bella alone, "And Martha's leg is still healing. Which means we should not be doing any difficult traveling, anyway."

Bella whined in agreement. "That's true. But what made Bruno so sick?"

"It must have been the water he drank."

"I was afraid of that." Bella's head dipped for just a moment, but Lucky's litter-sister was not going to be sad for too long. She picked it up again and addressed the Pack. "Everyone, remember you mustn't drink the river-water. It is still not safe for dogs."

The atmosphere was subdued as the others slowly dispersed to investigate their new, temporary territory. Lucky wished there was something he could say to make them all feel better, but what could that be? Without him, they would not have a chance of surviving at all. As long as they needed him, he would have to stay.

However long it takes, he promised himself.

"Lucky! Bella!"

Daisy had wandered away, unwilling to watch poor Bruno's agony, but now her bark was urgent.

What now? thought Lucky, as a thrill of fear rippled through his skin. If they were under attack, with Bruno so sick and vulnerable, and Martha injured, they were in big trouble. . . .

CHAPTER SEVEN

Lucky's tense muscles sagged with relief as he turned to see Daisy's head sticking out of one of the caves. She looked a little excited but unafraid.

"Look in here, quick!" she barked. "And bring Bruno. There's clean water—really clean. There's a sort of bowl in the rock, and some rain has gathered."

"Well spotted, Daisy," said Bella. "Now let's get Bruno into the cave. You too, Martha. You need to rest that leg."

With some difficulty they managed to drag Bruno's limp bulk into the cave; his claws scrabbled on the cave floor as he tried to help them, but to little effect. Once inside, they managed to roll Bruno onto his belly so that he could lap at the pure rainwater. Only when he and Martha had drunk their fill did the others line up to do the same.

Mickey poked his black-and-white nose out of the cave. His ears were pricked high with excitement. "Lucky, come and see what I've found!"

Lucky trotted over curiously to where Mickey was nosing at small objects on the cave floor. He heard Bella walking after him.

Mickey's eyes were shining brightly. "Do you see?"

"I'm not sure." Lucky wished he could be as enthusiastic as Mickey, if only to make the whole day more cheerful for everyone, but all he could do was paw at a piece of twisted metal, cocking his head to the side. "What are they?"

"Bella, you see it, don't you?" Mickey nudged a stone bowl, making it roll and clatter to Bella's feet. "These are longpaw things!"

Bella cocked her head and gave a happy bark. "You're right! Look, here's one of those skin covers that they would put over their bottom paws before they went for walks." She picked it up delicately in her teeth and showed it to Lucky.

"So what?" asked Lucky, bewildered. "We're not very far from the city—"

"Don't you see?" yelped Mickey. "When the water washed the mud away, and showed us all this—it wasn't the River-Dog at all. It was our longpaws—they're still watching over us!"

Lucky gave a soft growl of disapproval. He hadn't always been very good at keeping in touch with the Spirit Dogs, and sometimes he'd been less than respectful, but what Mickey was saying sounded like an outright insult to the River-Dog.

Still, the others didn't seem to notice that. They were beginning to crowd around Mickey. Martha, still favoring her injured leg, limped over as fast as she could. When she'd had a thorough sniff at the longpaw relics, she confirmed exactly what Lucky had been thinking.

"You shouldn't doubt the River-Dog, Mickey," she said. "He's been good to us."

"He made Bruno sick," grunted Mickey, but he didn't meet her eyes.

"I'm not sure either." Daisy sat back on her haunches, inspecting Mickey's haul. "If our longpaws were near, wouldn't they come to get us?"

"Maybe they can't," objected Mickey, gathering the longpaw things into a tidy pile. He had moved his own longpaw glove to lie with them, Lucky noticed. "Maybe this is their way of telling us they still care, even though they can't come for us. And they've given us shelter, and water! See? Even the hollow in the floor looks like my old longpaw bowl that they gave me to drink from!"

"I've never heard such nonsense," muttered Lucky, and Sunshine and Daisy gave him uncertain looks.

"And I still trust in the River-Dog!" declared Martha firmly.

But Mickey showed no sign of being swayed by her argument. "They're protecting us," he growled, "and they're watching over us. That means they'll come back!"

"Oh, Mickey—do you really think so?" Sunshine yipped.

Daisy barked excitedly. "Perhaps it is true! Yes, maybe the longpaws still want to keep us safe!"

Lucky shook his head as the two small dogs bounced and yapped with happiness. They clearly wanted to believe that Mickey was right, that the longpaws were looking after them even from far away. He sighed to himself. There seemed to be no convincing these Leashed Dogs that they were on their own now. He might have said this out loud, but Bella nudged his shoulder before he could.

"Come with me, Lucky," she said softly. "While the others are distracted. There's something I want you to see."

Lucky paced after his litter-sister as she led him out of the caves and away from their camp. There was a thin copse of trees a few paces up from the bank, where the ground was soft and wet.

"Here." Bella stopped and sat down, nodding her head at something on the ground. She looked very solemn—almost afraid.

Lucky bent his nose to the paw prints. He felt a shiver of nerves, and couldn't help jerking his head back, but then he sniffed again.

The paw prints were from a small dog, and that at least was reassuring. What was more worrying was that they seemed fresh, as if they'd been made only hours ago, but try as he might, Lucky could pick up almost no scent at all, just the smell of river-water. He took the deepest breath through his nostrils that he possibly could, but still there was nothing.

The print had not been made by one of his own Pack, but that was all Lucky could figure out.

It's as if some kind of ghost dog has passed by, he thought.

But ghost dogs did not leave prints in the mud. Lucky shook his head and growled with frustration. He had no idea if the dog was still close, even, or if it was long gone and far away.

So perhaps they had better not hang around. . . .

"Lucky, I'm scared." Bella, beside him, echoed his own thoughts too closely, and his neck prickled.

"There are other dogs nearby," he said. "That's for sure."

"Bruno has been poisoned, and Martha is still hurt. Our two best fighters. And even if no one else drinks the river-water, they will probably still get sick from having nothing to drink at all! There isn't enough water gathering in that cave—if it doesn't rain tonight, we'll be right back where we started. And we haven't hunted for a while. We're going to need food soon!"

This wasn't just Bella's cry of despair, Lucky realized; there was the gleam of an idea in his litter-sister's eye. With a sense of foreboding, he licked his chops. "What are you suggesting?" he asked her.

Bella lay down on her forepaws. She gazed up at him with determined eyes. "We have to get to that other Pack's water supply. And we have to be able to share it. We have to have water, and we have to be allowed to hunt in this valley!"

This was typical Bella thinking, thought Lucky, half in admiration and half in sheer irritation. His litter-sister always wanted to do the impossible thing, always sure she could have her way by sheer force of will. Stalling for time, he gave the prints another sniff.

Still nothing.

"Bella," he told her, trying to keep his tone as reasonable as possible. "Don't you remember what happened to Alfie?"

"Of course I do!"

"Then *think*!" he yelped. "The dogs in that Pack aren't going to change their minds just because one of us has fallen sick! All that means to them is there's one less dog that they have to fight!"

Bella glanced over her shoulder, as if checking to make sure no one else had come close. When she turned back, her eyes had that stubborn look he dreaded. "And that's exactly why we need to insist on *sharing* the lake and the hunting."

"No—it's why you need to get away from here. That Pack is vicious and ruthless. There is no way you will ever persuade them to share their territory. That's how Packs work in the Wild. Bella, you have to figure out how to tell when you're picking a fight you can't win."

Her lips curled back over her teeth. "I won't let them drive us away. We've survived this long, out in the wild without any longpaws to take care of us! I won't give up now. We can do this."

"But you don't need to be so stubborn!" Lucky didn't want to lose his temper with her, so he concentrated for a few moments on scraping sandy earth across the mysterious paw prints. He didn't want anyone else seeing them and panicking. "You wouldn't be letting them drive you away. You'd be steering clear of them so that they won't kill you and the others. You would be making the *smart* decision."

"No." Bella's face had that stubborn look about it, the one Lucky remembered from their days in the Pup-Pack. "This time it'll be different."

Lucky barked at her. *"How?"*

She didn't avert her eyes from his. "Because now, we will go in with a *plan*. Last time I couldn't think straight to argue properly with that Pack leader. But I will make him listen to me."

"He won't wait to listen," Lucky growled through his own bared teeth. "He will just drive you off, no questions asked or answered. That's if he doesn't kill you first."

"No." Bella sat up, staring directly at him. "I said I had a plan, and I do. It's a good one, Lucky."

"Don't be ridiculous—"

"One of us needs to infiltrate that other Pack," she interrupted. "To become a member, so that they can speak for us as one of them. Do you see now, Lucky?"

There was triumph in her voice, and Lucky let out a low growl.

"The other Pack never laid eyes on you, because you weren't in the fight." Bella paused, her eyes narrowing as she stared at him. "Because you had left us."

Lucky's jaws clenched. Part of him resented that Bella was trying to make him feel bad about that, but another part of him felt that she was right to be angry with him. After all, he had his own guilty secret. How could he explain to her that one of the dogs from that other Pack had seen him? And that this dog knew *exactly* who he was, and maybe even knew him as well as Bella did?

There was no way to explain this to his litter-sister now, not without raising questions to which Lucky was not sure he had the answers. Perhaps if he had told them at the very beginning, when he found Bella and the others under that tangle of roots, but now?

Impossible.

Lucky fell silent, torn by conflicting loyalties, but Bella seemed not to notice his sudden unease. He could sense her hide prickling in excitement as she pondered her plans, her tail thumping the ground enthusiastically.

"You'll make friends with them," she continued. "You'll earn their trust. You're good at making dogs like you. Once they do, you'll be able to get them to let us share their water. If that doesn't work, you're clever enough to find a way for us to get at the lake without them realizing! It's a good plan, Lucky!"

"It's a crazy plan," he grumbled. "How long do you expect me to spy for you?"

"Oh . . . just until we're back to our full strength," she told him airily. "When Martha's leg has healed and Bruno's feeling better, we can make our move—if the other Pack still doesn't want us here, we'll be able to go somewhere else. It's only for now, Lucky. You know how desperate we are. You will do it, won't you?" She looked at him with pleading eyes.

Would he? He hated the idea. He didn't want to be a spy; he didn't want to pretend he was something he was not. But if he refused Bella's request, he would be letting down his litter-sister, and the rest of the Leashed Dogs.

If he agreed, he would have to deceive Sweet.

Bella was right. Martha and Bruno *needed* food and water and a place to rest, and how else were they going to get it? And there was no other member of Bella's Pack who could do this. Not only was he the only dog the Wild Pack hadn't seen, Lucky was the only one of them who had a chance of succeeding.

He was a cunning street dog.

Lucky sighed and sat down, ears drooping. "Yes, Bella. I'll do it. You know I will."

"Great," said Bella. "Now, I spotted something before that other Pack attacked us. Farther up the valley—about five or six rabbit-chases—there's an old longpaw camp. It's just like the ones I used to go to sometimes, with my own longpaws. They went there to play and eat—you know, there were places for dogs to chase balls, and wooden tables, and big pits where the longpaws made fire."

"No, I *don't* know," Lucky reminded her, thinking of the long-paws he'd seen playing in the city parks with their pups, their food baskets, and their ball games. Would he be running the risk of encountering any longpaws? The only ones he had seen since he left the city were those with the yellow-fur, and they hadn't seemed interested in dogs at all.

"Oh, don't look so alarmed, Lucky!" said Bella. "It's long abandoned."

Lucky cocked his head doubtfully. "How can you tell?"

"All the longpaw things had been broken up by the first Big Growl, and nobody's come to fix them. You can't miss it," Bella went on. "You'll smell old fires and burned food, and longpaws. I'll go there every night, as soon as the Moon-Dog rises, and I will wait for you until she's right overhead. As soon as there's a no-sun when you think it's safe, slip away from that Pack and meet me there so you can tell me what you have learned."

Lucky let his head dip slowly to show that he agreed. If Bella wanted to go ahead with her outlandish plan, this did seem like the safest way to do it. "All right. Every no-sun, wait for me there. I'll come as soon as I can."

She licked his nose. "Thank you, Lucky! I knew you would help us."

Without another word she turned and trotted back toward the camp, tongue lolling, head and tail held high. His litter-sister looked like a real Alpha now. The trouble was, she didn't yet have a Pack leader's wisdom or wiles, only impulsive schemes. He couldn't blame her—she was doing her best, and she wasn't used to this life—but he was worried she would plot herself into big trouble before long.

With a sigh, Lucky padded after her, feeling a tingling ball of nerves in his belly. He was a clever dog—sneaky and cunning and crafty, he thought, remembering uneasily what their Mother-Dog would have had to say about that—but surviving in the city was so different from life in the wild. In the city, if he had tried to steal food from longpaws, he would have been chased off. If he got away, he was safe—free and clear. Longpaws eventually gave up and went back to their homes.

If the dog-wolf caught him trying to cheat his Pack, thought Lucky, he wouldn't just chase Lucky away. Lucky would be in real danger.

CHAPTER EIGHT

"There! A mouse!" Daisy shot off after the little rodent, her burst of speed bringing her swiftly on top of it. With a snap of her jaws, she tossed it into the air, limp and broken, caught it, and brought it proudly back to Lucky.

"Well done, Daisy!" She was turning into a natural. Prey had been hard to find this morning, and Lucky suspected the torrential storm had drowned or driven away much of what the Big Growl had left behind.

The Sun-Dog was racing higher and ever swifter into a clear blue rain-washed sky, which meant the best time for hunting was over—but Lucky found himself reluctant to give up and return to the caves. Daisy had caught their third mouse, and Mickey had surprised a fat brown bird dozing on a low branch, but it would be good to get something more—and besides, Lucky was almost dreading the end of this hunt.

This sun-high would be when he would leave the Leashed Dogs and try to wrangle his way into the enemy Pack, and even the thought of seeing Sweet again couldn't make him feel any better.

A bird scolded the dogs from high up in a pine, too far away for Lucky to do anything more than give it his best threatening glare. Soon there would be nothing to hunt but beetles and bugs, and then he would have no excuses. Stopping to sniff the air, Lucky saw Mickey slinking through the trees off to his left, low to the ground. Another ripple of pride went through his blood.

"Look!" cried Daisy. A rabbit leaped from the grass almost at Mickey's feet, hurtling toward Lucky in a panic and swerving aside at the last moment. Sunshine cut it off and drove it back toward Lucky, but it was Mickey who intercepted it with an agile sideways leap, and his jaws crunched down on its spine.

"Well done, Mickey!" Sunshine was jumping up and down and spinning with excitement.

"You did well too, Sunshine," Lucky pointed out, giving her ear a lick. "This was a real team effort!"

The little dog looked about to burst, and Lucky remembered with amusement her early dislike of hunting, her fear of getting her beautiful white fur caught on twigs. Now she looked grubby and her coat was matted, but she bounced with pride.

There was no putting off the moment anymore; their haul of prey was excellent for such an unpromising sunup. Lucky barked to bring the others back to him. Then, together, they carried their kills back to Martha, Bruno, and Bella.

They weren't quite in sight of the river and caves when Lucky halted, a scent bringing him up short. His hackles rose as he stood stiff-legged, sniffing the still air.

"Lucky? What is it?" Sunshine laid down her mouse and looked up at him quizzically.

"Nothing, I hope," he growled softly. "You three go on. I'm going to do a quick scout around here."

Sunshine looked uncertain, but obediently picked up her mouse and trotted toward the caves with Mickey and Daisy.

Lucky waited until they were out of sight over a slight rise, then lowered his muzzle to the ground, his sense of threat making his coat bristle all over. He hadn't wanted to say anything to the others, not yet; but he was certain of it. . . .

A Fierce Dog had passed this way.

It couldn't have been one of the enemy Pack led by the dog-wolf. Lucky hadn't seen any of those sleek black Fierce Dogs among them, and besides, there was something familiar about this particular scent. A picture came to his mind as the smell filled his nostrils: the strange doghouses where the Leashed Dogs had been caught and imprisoned by the violent Fierce Dog Pack. If Lucky had not been there to help them, he remembered with a shudder, Bella, Daisy, and Alfie would have probably been torn to pieces.

A nervous whine escaped Lucky's lips. Surely the Fierce Dogs would not pursue them all the way here, just for revenge for their wounded pride? The female Alpha, Blade, had been especially arrogant and savage, but would she really leave her easy, spoiled existence in the Dog-Garden to come after a Pack of mangy Leashed Dogs?

Lucky wasn't sure. And, in a way, that was worse than having something terrible but definite to fear.

He took his time snuffling around the trees, using his nose to nudge aside stones and branches. At last he felt a little more reassured—the scents were old and had not been refreshed recently, so whoever the Fierce Dog was, he had just been passing through. Still, he felt uneasy as he followed the others back toward the caves. There were far too many signs of danger around this place, too many traces of unfriendly dogs. Bella and her Pack could only move forward now. They could not turn around and walk back the way they had come—not when they were caught between two fierce, hostile Packs.

They needed to find a territory all their own. *Somewhere.*

The others were waiting for him, so happy and excited at the prospect of a good meal that Lucky decided not to mention his misgivings, or tell them about the strange and alarming Fierce Dog scent he had picked up. Any apprehension he felt was defeated by his appetite, which had been sharpened by the hunt and the clear air. He fell on his share of the prey with enthusiasm.

Afterward, he sprawled in the Sun-Dog's light and heat, his belly full and his ears tickled by the soft breathing and contented grunts of his friends. At last, he rose up to all fours, stretching and shaking himself from head to tail. Much as he would have liked to, there was no sense putting this off any longer. As he paced toward Bella, the others raised their heads and got to their feet one by one, nervously gathering around him.

"I should be going." Lucky nuzzled Bella's ear, wanting to stay angry with her, but too aware of how much he would miss her, as well as the safety and companionship of this odd Pack, while he was away on his dangerous mission.

"I wish you didn't have to go," said Daisy.

"We've only just got you back," Sunshine whined. "And those other dogs are so scary. Are you sure you'll be safe?"

Lucky licked her black nose. "It's for the best. You have to trust in Bella and me. That's what Pack's all about." He wished he felt half as confident as he sounded. "I'll be back again soon, and by that time I hope we will have clean water to drink. I'll do my best for you all."

"We know you will, Lucky." Mickey nuzzled his neck. "Just . . . be careful."

Suppressing a shudder, Lucky wagged his tail cheerfully. "Of course I will." He turned to give Bella a last glance.

She was watching him with a solemn look in her dark eyes. More and more, he thought, she seemed to fit naturally into her role as Alpha, and more and more he wished he could be sure she was capable of this responsibility. All the same he licked her nose fondly and pressed his face to hers before forcing himself to turn away and begin his journey.

He did not look back as he bounded up the valley's steep side. The air was warming rapidly, and he panted with the exertion, but he wanted to follow a high route toward the shining lake so that he would not be vulnerable to surprise attacks. There could be other dogs in the valley besides the enemy Pack.

He was glad his belly was full, because his thoughts were focused on what lay ahead, not on hunting. The prey seemed to know it, too; birds sang cheekily close to him and a mouse had the confidence to scuttle across his path and under a log. Lucky was not altogether sure if his anxiety was due to the angry enemies ahead or the thought of seeing Sweet again.

He almost wished the other Pack's guards would make their appearance so that he could stop worrying. The land was evening out, and as he crested a small ridge he saw the lake spilling away before him, brilliantly reflecting the Sun-Dog's shine. Surely, now . . .

There! Lucky jerked his head up at the sound of a ferocious bark, just as three dogs leaped out to confront him. Even as his hackles rose instinctively, Lucky felt a strange flutter of relief.

"What are you doing here?" A lean brown-and-white chase-dog, like a smaller swift-dog, stood squarely in front of him, baring her teeth. "This is our territory!"

Our territory! Lucky remembered their savage barks and howls on the day Alfie died. *Ours!*

"Leave this place now," snarled a long-eared black-and-tan dog. "Or face the consequences."

Lucky forced himself to hold his ground; if he turned tail, they might well chase him down and maul him, or worse. He crouched, keeping his haunches high and his forepaws low. He swung his tail nervously to signal that he was not here to threaten or challenge them on their territory.

"In the name of the Forest-Dog, I want to talk to your Alpha!" he barked.

The brown-and-white dog drew back her muzzle in a contemptuous snarl. "Why?"

Lucky took a deep breath and lowered his head even farther. He disliked bowing before these Pack Dogs. They had attacked his friends, and killed one of them! But he had no choice. And besides . . .

"Sweet the swift-dog is one of your Pack," he said. "We survived together in the city, after the Big Growl."

"And?" sneered another long-eared dog, a female who looked so much like the male that Lucky wondered if they were littermates.

He cocked his ears and let his tongue loll. If it worked for Food House longpaws, maybe his charm would even work on these dogs. "I want to join your Pack. Take me to Sweet and she'll vouch for me."

"Why would we want you in our Pack?" The brown-and-white dog's voice was full of disdain.

"Because I'm a hunter," Lucky replied. "I can be useful to you."

"We don't need scavenger city dogs who think they can hunt."

Something about the female long-ear's bearing sparked a memory in Lucky's mind—he'd seen this dog during the fight, following the Alpha's orders. This was the one the dog-wolf had called Spring.

Lucky clenched his teeth against a snarl. He knew he mustn't rise to the taunts, however tempting it was. "I would be valuable to your Pack. You would be stronger with me on your side."

To Lucky's relief, the male long-ear looked up at the brown-and-white chase-dog uncertainly. "I don't know, Dart. If he does know Sweet . . ."

"I doubt it, Twitch," snarled Dart, and turned back to Lucky. "I can smell the stink of the city on you. What is it you hunt? Food wrappers?"

The three dogs laughed scornfully. Lucky tried not to show how close the barb had come to the truth. He'd learned a lot since those days, after all. Besides, he was secretly pleased to hear that the city's stench still clung to him. It told him he was still his old self, still a City Dog and a Lone Dog.

He was still Lucky.

His quiet pleasure was shattered when the dogs began to advance again. Still refusing to back away, Lucky flattened his whole body against the ground, but he couldn't stop his muzzle from curling. If they insisted on attacking, he would fight back. Even if it only made things worse for himself.

I may still smell of it, he thought despairingly, *but I'm a long way from the city now. And I don't have any friends here. . . .*

There was no sign of these dogs giving any ground, he realized. And there was no point submitting if they were simply going to tear him to bits anyway. Baring his teeth in a warning snarl, he leapt abruptly to his feet, standing stiff and tall.

I won't be easy pickings. . . .

The male black-and-tan called Twitch was limping slightly, and Lucky was bigger than each of them, but he knew he couldn't outfight three brutal dogs all at the same time.

"Take him, Spring!"

The female black-and-tan went for him, charging low for his neck. She moved with unexpected speed, and Lucky just managed to leap sideways. But this only took him into the path of Dart, who lunged for his scruff. Lucky yelped as he felt her teeth sink into his flesh, and then Twitch sneaked in and bit his foreleg. Lucky squirmed, throwing Dart off, snarling and gnashing at Twitch.

But now Spring was back. She seized a mouthful of his neck fur and gave it a fierce tug.

Were they actually planning to kill him? Lucky didn't think so, but they were certainly going to hurt him badly—make sure he fled and never returned. And if he couldn't get the upper paw against these three mangy brutes, there was no way he would ever get into their Pack. The rest wouldn't dream of accepting him— even Sweet.

Sharp fangs sank into his flank and he howled with pain and rage, twisting to snap at his attacker but only catching her ear. At the same time, the black-and-tan male got a grip on Lucky's own ear, tearing at it. Lucky felt a sharp pain and warm blood spreading through the fur over his skull. Dart still had hold of his neck fur, her teeth now sinking into Lucky's flesh.

Lucky felt panic begin to overwhelm him along with the rage. She was going to do serious damage if he could not shift her soon.

"Enough! LEAVE HIM!"

The bark sounded savage, but also familiar. Lucky stumbled when he felt the pressure and pain at his neck fade away. Still snarling, his three attackers backed off, their hackles bristling and their teeth bared.

Panting, Lucky gave them a defiant snarl in return, but his eyes hungrily sought out the newcomer. That scent he knew so well tickled his nostrils, and his heart thudded hard and slowed as he caught his breath.

"Sweet," he gasped.

She did not bound forward to greet him, but simply stood there, her head held high as she studied him with narrowed eyes. Her ears pricked forward and she sniffed imperiously at the air around him.

"He's an invader!" Dart barked.

"So I see." Sweet stood very still, cocking her head only slightly, never taking her eyes off Lucky.

"We were trying to get rid of him," snarled the limping male, Twitch.

"You should let us finish!" said Dart.

"No," Sweet growled. "I know this dog."

Dart lowered her head and tail. She looked submissive, and not happy about it.

"I'm going to take him to Alpha. Any objections?" Sweet looked around her Packmates, clearly not expecting any disagreement— and none came. "I shall propose him as a new member. He would be an asset to the Pack."

"Yes, Beta." The others were deferential now, though they shot venomous glances at Lucky.

Beta? Lucky thought. He knew that every Wild Pack had an

Alpha, a leader, and an Omega, who had the lowest rank in the Pack—but what was a Beta? *Just how well has Sweet settled in to this pack?* But this wasn't the time to start questioning her. "Thank you, Sweet," he began as he scrambled back on all fours. "I'll—"

"That's enough." Any warmth in Sweet's eyes was gone altogether, and a faint shiver of apprehension went through Lucky's bones.

"Sweet, I'm sorry—"

"Just follow me. And don't use my name. In fact, don't say another word."

CHAPTER NINE

Sweet led Lucky around the shore of the lake into a deep bay fringed thickly with trees. Under the branches the light was green and cool, the ground soft underpaw. After the dazzling sun-high brightness of the valley, Lucky's eyes took a little time to adjust to the shade as he followed Sweet's narrow hindquarters closely through two lines of straight trunks.

Where the trees opened out to the shallow dip of a clearing, Sweet paused. The Sun-Dog's light pierced the pine canopy here, sending spears of dusty light to the grassy ground, and Lucky could see several distinct hollows strewn with soft leaves and moss—proper sleeping dens, carefully arranged. It was a long way from the rough camps his own Pack had managed to set up.

Still, he had a feeling that comfort was not the only advantage of this camp. On most of its edges it was hemmed in by thick thorn scrub that would be impossible for any large animal to penetrate without giving themselves away. Even Daisy would struggle to make her way through this dangerous undergrowth. Lucky would have liked to stand at Sweet's side, but he respectfully held back by her flank, constantly aware of the three smaller dogs at his rear who blocked his escape route. One of the shafts of sunlight fell onto a large flat rock near the center of the clearing, warming the hide of the huge sleeping dog-wolf. Of course the most prominent part of the camp, and the warmest, had been reserved for the ferocious Alpha.

Lucky held his breath, while Sweet casually swished her tail. Three more dogs had come forward to greet her, and to sniff suspiciously at him. One was the huge brown dog he remembered from the fight, almost as big as Martha but without her gentle face. The others were a tan-and-white smaller dog and a long-eared, shaggy-furred black dog with soulful eyes but a nasty expression.

"Who is this?" growled the big dog, snuffing the air. "Don't tell me it's another of those pathetic Leashed Dogs."

Lucky bristled at the insult but he stayed quiet. The Forest-Dog would think him stupid, and unworthy of protection, if he lost his temper in this situation. But he wasn't going to cringe. If he showed too much submission, a dog as arrogant and powerful as this might simply kill him for fun.

Sweet was not intimidated, even though the black dog was nearly twice her size. She gave him an imperious twist of her muzzle. "He's with me, Fiery. Do you have a problem with that? If so, we can take it up with Alpha."

The huge dog glowered, but he clearly did not want to take his argument to Alpha. Before he could say anything, the nearby undergrowth rustled.

Lucky flinched aside as a female black-and-white Farm Dog—not unlike Mickey—poked her nose out of the scrub. "What's the commotion? My pups are trying to sleep."

"I'm sorry, Moon." The old softness was back in Sweet's voice as she lowered her nose to the Mother-Dog's. "Go back to your pups. We'll try to be quiet."

"I'm sorry, too, Moon." It shocked Lucky to hear the massive Fiery apologize so meekly. Clearly the Mother-Dog commanded a lot of respect around here.

"Well, since I'm here . . ." Moon stretched out her forepaws, and Lucky caught the scent of warm milk and squirming pups. "I'm very hungry; the pups are growing fast. Someone get me some food, please."

Instantly Sweet turned and barked toward a little dog skulking at the edge of the clearing. "Omega! Bring food for Moon at once!"

Nervously the small dog trotted out of the shadows; he was a stocky, oddly shaped creature with tiny ears and a wrinkled face. His beady black eyes were suspicious as he paused to stare at Lucky. Something about his sly expression gave Lucky a ripple of unease in his bones.

"I said, at once," Sweet reminded the little dog darkly, and he shot off across the clearing.

Sweet didn't bother to introduce Lucky to any of the other dogs, but beckoned him forward with a haughty motion of her head. "Come. I shall present you to Alpha."

She paced forward, confident but respectful. Lucky followed with rather more reluctance, still taking in his new surroundings. The Pack was larger than Bella's, at least eight dogs strong not counting Moon and her pups. This unnerved him. Not only that—the dogs seemed very comfortably placed in this sheltered camp—the clean lake was close by and, from the scents drifting out of the trees, he could tell these woods were teeming with prey.

Even at full strength Bella's Pack would be no match for this one, so well fed, well disciplined, and strong. If the Alpha couldn't be persuaded to share, Lucky would have to convince Bella that the Leashed Dogs must move on.

"Wait here." Sweet's newly commanding voice broke into his thoughts. "Don't come forward until Alpha summons you."

Lucky stared at the dog-wolf, sprawled on his rock, nothing twitching but the very tip of his tail. Perhaps he was dreaming, or perhaps he was not quite so fast asleep as he wanted to appear. Sure enough, as Sweet approached him, one cold, yellow eye blinked open.

Lucky could hear nothing the two dogs said to each other, but Sweet did not seem meek in her leader's presence. She showed respect, but she did not act submissive. She spoke quietly, and Alpha cocked his gray ears to listen closely. At last he turned his head and stared piercingly at Lucky.

Sweet turned too. "Come here, Lucky."

Under the dog-wolf's chilly gaze, Lucky felt anger swirl in his belly as he walked slowly forward. This was the monstrous brute who had killed Alfie, and Lucky wanted to snarl at him, insult him, even to lunge and bite and let *him* know how it felt. But that would be suicide. He remembered Alfie's life force seeping away, the little body going still and cold as the Earth-Dog claimed him.

I am here to help the rest of Alfie's Pack, to save them from the same fate. I must not forget it.

Close up, Alpha looked even bigger and wilder, and his yellow eyes were extraordinarily frightening. His huge paws, with their vicious nails, were webbed like Martha's, but his savage face was nothing like hers. This, thought Lucky, was a true Wild Pack leader.

"So," the dog-wolf growled. "You want to join my Pack."

There was scorn in his voice, but Lucky kept his gaze level and brave.

"Yes," he said. "I'd be a valuable Pack member. Sweet can vouch for me."

"Yes. *Beta* already has."

That title again. And the way everyone deferred to Sweet: Did it mean she was this huge dog-wolf's second in command?

Alpha sounded bored. "I have no need of another dog in my Pack."

Lucky sensed that pleading would not have any effect on this creature. He would not respect weakness or submissiveness, yet there was no sense challenging him on his own terms.

He lowered his tail, tilting his head mischievously. "You don't need any more *ordinary* dogs, but what about one as strong and fast as me? I catch a good rabbit."

Alpha yawned widely, showing every one of his teeth. "So does

Mulch. And Beta can bring down a deer. But then you know that, don't you, City Dog? Since you know her so well."

There was a distinct menace in the dog-wolf's eyes now. Lucky swallowed, then let his tongue loll. "Seems to me you have a lot of brute force in this Pack. But I am *clever*. That's what comes of city life. And I can survive in the wild, too. The Forest-Dog favors me."

"Is that right?" Alpha rose up on his forepaws, stretching, muscles rippling with malevolence.

Lucky ignored the dog-wolf's tone. "I can be very useful. I can bring a fresh . . . attitude. I see things differently. That can be helpful in a Pack."

"Do not tell me what's good for my Pack," snapped Alpha, and Lucky took a backward step. He had to tread carefully.

"I would not dream of it," he said, more meekly. "I was just . . . explaining my experience. The ways I think I can help. You have such a fine Pack here, I want to be part of it."

Alpha seemed slightly mollified, but the long-eared black dog gave a shrill bark of objection.

"Throw him out, Alpha! He smells *wrong*. He stinks of long-paws and stone and metal. Chase him away!"

Alpha turned his cold eyes on the black dog. "Mulch," he

growled. "Are you telling *me* what to do?"

The massive dog called Fiery whacked a paw across Mulch's head.

Mulch yelped and ducked, backing off. "Of course not, Alpha. I was just—"

"Then keep your jaws shut. Or I will have Fiery give you a proper beating."

Lucky glanced around at the other dogs who had gathered. It was not only Mulch who cowered, subdued and scared. All of them looked terrified of Alpha, their eyes wary and nervous.

Except for the brutish Fiery. And Sweet.

Because Mulch had not tried to run away, Lucky assumed this was not unusual behavior from Alpha. Despite how harsh and cruel the dog-wolf seemed, none of his followers seemed desperate to leave. Lucky's old dislike of Packs swelled in him again. The little band of Leashed Dogs traveled together because they *wanted* to—because they knew one another, liked one another.

What was binding this Pack together?

Lucky's thoughts shattered like rain on stone when he saw Sweet leap gracefully up onto Alpha's rock to stand beside the dog-wolf. He did not smack her down or scold her, and she stood with her flanks close to his, proud and strong. If anything, Alpha seemed to stand taller in her presence.

Lucky's gut twisted with dismay and jealousy. Was Sweet the dog-wolf's mate?

His horror melted into gratitude, though, as she began to speak.

"I knew Lucky in the city," she declared. "He was my only Pack when I escaped from the Trap House, and I would be dead if it was not for him. Several times over." She paused to look at each of the Pack in turn, and let her words sink in. "He is loyal, brave, strong, and smart. He would be a fine member of this Pack. In fact I asked him to join us before. He said no." She turned her head to watch Lucky, expressionless. "If he has changed his mind, that is a piece of good fortune for us. You should welcome such a dog, not"—she gave Mulch a contemptuous twist of her muzzle—"chase him away."

Alpha gave a curt nod. "He may be all those things, Beta, but this Pack is at full strength. We don't need another dog."

"Moon will be nursing her pups for at least another full journey of the Moon-Dog. We are one good fighter short. Lucky could take Moon's place on patrols, and Spring could go back to hunting. Then you can judge for yourself what kind of Pack member Lucky'll make."

Slowly Alpha nodded again. "You talk sense as usual, Beta." She dipped her head in acknowledgment as Alpha went on. "And if you vouch for this City Dog, then he can stay for now." The cold eyes swiveled to Lucky, and Alpha's lip peeled back from his teeth. "But he must prove himself of use. If he does not succeed, we can still throw him out—with a beating for his impudence. What does the Pack say?"

Lucky watched the Wild Pack as they reacted to Alpha's decision. Despite their earlier fierceness, Dart and Twitch looked at each other and their tails quivered in agreement.

"We can use another Patrol Dog," Twitch said.

Spring muttered something Lucky didn't hear, shaking her head a little.

"I say welcome," said the small tan-and-white female beside Fiery.

"Well said, Snap," said Twitch.

Fiery stayed silent, though his face showed he wasn't at all convinced. Mulch was looking away, as if he couldn't trust himself not to earn another whack from the big dog.

Lucky let out a breath for what felt like the first time since he had arrived in the clearing, lowering his head humbly. "Thank you, Alpha."

"You'll join the Pack in the place everyone does: at the bottom, superior only to Omega. Your immediate commander is Twitch." The dog-wolf jerked his head at the limping black-and-tan dog. A smug look crossed Twitch's face.

"As you say, Alpha." Lucky faked gratitude by lowering his head even more. He had anticipated that he would join the Pack with low status, but to be placed at the very bottom—above only the Omega—was nevertheless a surprise.

He couldn't help glancing at Sweet. He couldn't think of her as Beta. He'd picked up plenty of information about the way Packs worked over the years, from Wild Dogs who came into the city, but it seemed there was still a lot he didn't understand. It was strange to realize that. He'd gotten so used to being the one in the Leashed Pack who knew about the wild . . . but he was still a City Dog who'd never had to think about rank or status before.

Still, his status was something he could work on. He was smarter than Twitch—and Mulch too, he suspected—and he was sure he could swiftly rise to something better in the hierarchy.

Something closer to Sweet's rank . . .

"While you're all gathered . . ." Alpha's bark became brusque and practical. "Make sure you keep your eyes open for that pathetic gang of Leashed Dogs. I don't want them regrouping and trying another attack. If you see them, chase them off. If they won't be chased, kill them. Understood?"

"Yes, Alpha," came the chorus of yelps and barks.

"You. Lucky. Did you see a band of Leashed Dogs on your way here?"

Lucky felt every pair of eyes fall on him, and his heart tripped and raced. Would it be wiser to admit he had run into the Leashed Dogs—even that he knew them from the city? None of that was a lie. And despite her newfound confidence and status, he felt he could still trust Sweet.

But she is Alpha's mate now. . . .

"I'm not sure." Lucky hoped his lie did not sound as obvious to their ears as it did to his. "At least, I *think* I saw them—a ridiculous bunch of useless pets?—but I have no idea where they were heading."

"Then let's find out if they're anywhere near," Alpha growled. "They tried to steal from our water supply. That won't happen again. Lucky, you go with Twitch and Dart and let them show you how we do things in this Pack. Go."

With that, the dog-wolf slumped back down onto the rock, his eyes narrowing to slits as he watched them leave. Lucky glanced back over his shoulder and noticed that the yellow eyes were still fixed on him. A tingle of apprehension went through his skin, lifting the roots of his fur.

If Alpha ever found out that he had run with the Leashed Dogs, what would happen then? How would he explain his lie? *You'll need all the guile of the Forest-Dog for that one, Lucky,* he told himself. *And even that might not save you. . . .*

Then he was troubled by a second, even more horrible thought. Sweet had vouched for him, had guaranteed his worth in front of the whole Pack—a Pack in which she had real status. What would Alpha do to her if he discovered Lucky had lied, and that she had fallen for it? If Alpha thought, perhaps, that Sweet had *deliberately* deceived him?

That she was conspiring with a dog from her old life in the city?

Lucky did not like to think about what punishments Alpha would inflict on dogs who betrayed him. He was prepared to take risks—he had done so his whole life in the city.

But he did *not* want to guide anyone else into danger.

CHAPTER TEN

"Keep up, Lucky," Twitch barked, *as* he limped hurriedly along.

Lucky felt a flash of irritation. When he had hung back to sniff right inside that hollow log, he was only being thorough—a lot more thorough than Twitch and Dart were being—and he didn't think Twitch needed to be quite so bossy. If Pack status could be changed, as he suspected, he might one day be in charge of Twitch. So it wasn't very clever of Twitch to throw his weight around now.

"Don't worry about me keeping up," said Lucky. "But do stop if you feel tired." He stopped himself from saying, *If your bad leg gives up on you.*

Twitch growled. "Careful what you say. Respect is very important in this Pack."

If that were true, Lucky thought, *you'd show more of it.*

An early mist had lifted from the lake's shoreline, revealing its brilliant glitter. Pine trees were outlined in silhouette on the distant shore; there was certainly plenty of forest, and that meant plenty of prey. Once again Lucky thought how unfair it was that this Wild Pack would not share food even when they had more than they could eat. If they would, he wouldn't be in this position of having to deceive other dogs.

As they ventured into a dense copse of pines, Lucky took care to notice not just possible dangers or likely prey, but any cover that Bella and her Pack might use, to stay unseen. He wondered if his two companions thought there was something odd about the way their new recruit was sniffing the surroundings, but they said nothing more. Neither Twitch nor the brown-and-white female Dart were as alert as they should have been.

That's just my good luck.

So far, Lucky hadn't seen anything that suggested Bella would have an easy time getting what she wanted from this Pack, but then this was only his first patrol. There was plenty of time for him to snoop around some more, although he hoped he would finish this mission quickly. He did not want to be a spy dog for long.

In his head Lucky dismissed the rocky outcrop as too obvious a hiding place, but he sniffed it over carefully for possible dangers to the Wild Pack. Lucky cast an eye back to Twitch and Dart, swallowing down an arrogant rumble.

Twitch really should be noticing how nosy I am, but he seems completely clueless. Even though they're sloppy, I shouldn't take too many chances.

"That's good, Lucky. Well done," Twitch yapped.

Lucky was dragged out of his thoughts, his ears pricking up. Twitch and Dart were both watching him with a sort of superior approval. Though his fur bristled at their smugness, he found himself relieved at the same time. Twitch's hostility was obviously melting away and, though Lucky wasn't sure why this was so, he had to admit it would make his task a lot easier.

The trees opened up and suddenly there was the lake again, shining brilliant silver in the light of the Sun-Dog. Lucky gazed, mesmerized by its glitter.

"The poison hasn't spread here," he observed.

"The river-poison?" Dart yapped. "No. Anyway, it would take a lot to make this amount of water undrinkable." There was arrogant pride in her voice, and Lucky cocked his head.

"No wonder the Leashed Dogs were desperate," he murmured.

"True." Dart laughed. "Still, that isn't our problem. You shouldn't feel sorry for them."

"They should have stayed at home doing tricks for their

longpaws," agreed Twitch contemptuously. "You may be a City Dog, Lucky, but at least you know about true dog-life, life in the wild, living by your wits and surviving. Those dogs do not *deserve* to survive."

Lucky could find no answer to that, so he dipped his muzzle to the cool, clear water and, playing for time, took a long drink. He had never truly appreciated clean water before. In this new and dangerous world, on a bright, hot sunup, there was something blissfully refreshing about a simple drink. Dart and Twitch were still bantering with each other, poking fun at Bella's Pack, but he took no notice. He did not need to hear their opinions about his friends.

"Anyway, they'll have moved on, if they know what's good for them." Dart padded along the lakeshore, sniffing, then glanced back and barked in horror. "Lucky! We do not indulge ourselves on patrol!"

Lucky lifted his dripping muzzle, astonished.

"A quick lap, that's all," said Twitch sternly. "Alpha says if we eat and drink on patrol, we will not see properly. Indulging our own appetites is disregarding our duty."

Disregarding our duty? Lucky was shocked to his core. How did these mutts ever come to think like this?

Still, as much as their attitude horrified him, Lucky didn't want to cause any trouble. He backed away from the water and followed them again. Clearly Alpha was serious about discipline—and he had to admit it was true: With his tongue lapping the clear, delicious water, and the lovely coolness of it in his throat, he had been unaware of what was going on at his back. Danger could have fallen upon him, and he would have been completely caught off guard.

"One of our Pack dogs learned that lesson recently," said Dart. "Found a rabbit corpse while he was out on patrol. Ate it himself."

Twitch shuddered. "Alpha did not take kindly to that."

Lucky felt his own skin shiver. "Which dog was this?"

"He is not in the Pack anymore. We do not mention his name." Dart seemed nervous, and she gave her coat a massive shake before she trotted on. Lucky guessed that whoever the nameless dog had been, he was not in anyone's Pack now.

"Lucky, check that hillock," commanded Twitch. "Three dogs could hide behind that rise."

He had been going to do it anyway, but Lucky kept his jaws shut and did as he was told. To be truthful, he was glad of a moment's breathing space in the wake of that story about the nameless Pack member. He could not let himself forget that he was playing a very, very dangerous game. There were chills in his spine as he shoved his muzzle into hollows, pawing aside long grass to look for anything that might be hiding, ready to attack. The sharp odor of raccoon made him tense up with alarm, but when he followed the trail a rabbit-chase or two, he realized it was too old to worry about.

He looked back toward Twitch and Dart, a strange thought tugging at his fur. When those two dogs sniffed at the air, and at the ground, their tails stayed down. Nothing they scented excited them, even though Lucky knew they *had* to be teased by the scent of prey, old and new. But they stayed calm at all times.

I don't understand that.

Loping back toward Twitch and Dart, he said, "Is there anything particular we're looking for? There are so many scents, so many traces . . ."

"Alpha wants to know about anything at all that might be a threat," Twitch replied. "Other dogs, obviously, and of course, foxes and raccoons. Sometimes there are sharpclaws, and they can be sneaky." He shivered, perhaps at the memory of an old attack; Lucky, too, knew just how much a sharpclaw scratch could sting, and how quickly the wound it left could become poisoned.

"If there's a small threat, we handle it ourselves, just the patrol,"

Dart grumbled. "And if we need support, I head back to the camp to gather the hunters. That's why there are always at least three dogs on patrol. There has to be one to run back while the others fight. There is no getting the better of *our* Pack. Spring was patrolling with us while Moon looked after her pups, but now you're here, so Spring can go back to hunting. More food for all of us."

"That was good work you did, Lucky," said Twitch. Lucky couldn't be sure, but he thought he saw approval in the mongrel's eyes. "I saw how thoroughly you . . . *checked*."

He's testing me, Lucky realized with some annoyance. Then it struck him why Twitch was acting like a strict but indulgent Mother-Dog.

Lucky had taken Twitch's place at the bottom of the Pack hierarchy.

Being low in this Pack's order clearly made life even harder than it had to be. Once again Lucky found himself longing for Bella's scrappy Pack. They might have needed a lot of teaching in the ways of surviving but, when it came down to it, the Leashed Dogs pulled together. They cooperated because they *cared* about one another. They shared food and tasks equally because they thought of themselves as friends and equals, not as rivals for Pack position or as possible threats. Lucky felt a sudden urge to confront

Twitch and Dart, to force them to question the savage rules they were living by. He wanted to tell them that their way was not the only way, that a Pack did not *have* to exile or kill dogs just for making a single mistake in a moment of desperate hunger. . . .

But Lucky clamped his jaws together and kept his silence. It would not do to start questioning the ways of Alpha's Pack so soon after he had begged to join them.

Besides, he had not *just* pleaded to join—he had lied, too. *I'm playing tricks on these dogs—and they are not the kind of tricks my Mother-Dog would have liked.*

He could hardly lecture Twitch and Dart about friendship and honor. . . .

Ahead of him, Dart had finished a long lap of the bay and was now absently sniffing the length of a huge driftwood log. For all their talk, Lucky thought, his companions' inspection of their surroundings seemed a bit brief. Dart had barely gotten to the end of the log before she jumped down and trotted straight toward a copse of pines on a small headland. Twitch was winding through tree trunks at the forest's edge, checking the roots of each, but to Lucky's eyes he seemed more concerned with following the trees in the right order than with actually examining them properly.

Lucky took a last careful sniff at the rocks under a sandy bank, then leaped up it to join Twitch and follow him into the next stretch of woodland. "Moon would usually lead this patrol, is that right?" he asked. Alpha had said that Moon wasn't patrolling because she was caring for her pups, and the respect the other dogs treated her with made Lucky think the Mother-Dog must be higher in the Pack hierarchy than Twitch or Dart.

"Yes," Twitch replied. "When she's on patrol, nothing escapes her. She could be a hunter, but she's so good at tracking and scenting—the best in the Pack." Twitch's voice held an awe and respect that told Lucky a lot about Moon's status. "But of course she's nursing her pups now—hers and Fiery's. They are such strong dogs, that pair, and so experienced. They've been running with Alpha for a very long time."

Lucky tilted his head as he walked beside Twitch. "And has Sweet—Beta—been with him a long time too?" He was very curious to learn what had happened to his friend since he'd known her in the city. . . .

"Beta? No. She's the newest member of the Pack!" If possible Twitch's eyes grew even bigger and rounder. "She joined maybe half a Moon-Dog journey after the Big Growl. But she is so fast, and clever—and ruthless. She became Beta *very* quickly!"

"That's . . . impressive," said Lucky, feeling a strange twist of pain deep in his belly.

"Enough," said Twitch, putting his paws up against a tree and sniffing thoroughly at a hole in the trunk. "It's *really* important we check the boundary just the way Moon would, or she'll have something to say to us about it later."

Lucky cocked his head thoughtfully. *But how would Moon know if you had done your job well or not? Is she really so terrifying that you think she can see you from back at the camp? You are so afraid of Moon and Fiery and Alpha—and Sweet—you don't dare do anything even the tiniest bit different. . . .*

The tree shadows had shortened since they had set out. Lucky followed carefully in Dart's and Twitch's tracks, but as he sniffed and peered, he noticed that they were following *old* paw prints. When the other two stopped to scent-mark, a stale, similar odor was easily detectable in the same place. As his nostrils flared, Lucky tasted the same scents on his tongue, but even older.

They're following the same tracks they follow every day, Lucky thought, astonished. *The same routine, every time. This is crazy!* When Dart glanced up anxiously at the Sun-Dog and yapped, "sun-high," they turned back toward camp as if ordered by an invisible Pack leader.

Now their route took them deeper into the forest, where there were hollows and hillocks and thick scrub to check and double-check, and Lucky had time to think. He doubted that Moon would approve if she knew how slavishly these two followed her old example. Any strange dog who watched the patrol for two or three Sun-Dog journeys would notice the pattern and know how to avoid it.

Alpha had created a disciplined Pack and provided them with a secure and comfortable home, but perhaps even that had disadvantages. Lucky and Bella and the Leashed Dogs had always been alert, always ready to flee or defend themselves at a moment's notice, simply because they felt so insecure. In contrast, Alpha's Pack felt too safe, *too* confident. They must have been here for a long time, perhaps even since before the Big Growl.

It seemed likely. Twitch and Dart were not on constant lookout for trees crashing down, and there certainly was not the kind of devastation here that there had been in the city—or even farther down the valley. One or two fallen trunks blocked their way, but Twitch and Dart bounded up and over them quite dismissively, taking little notice, and showing no sign of nerves. Perhaps, thought Lucky with a small shiver, this Wild Pack was simply too tough and hardened to be bothered by an occasional shake or snarl from the Earth-Dog? On the other paw, perhaps they simply didn't recognize the danger.

From the top of a rough, sandy ridge, Lucky panted as he pricked his ears and stared across the next bay. Yes, it was as he had thought—if Bella and her Pack kept clear of this jutting tongue of land, and the bay to this side of it, there was a shallow gully that they could slip along unseen. If they kept quiet, and stayed careful, and avoided a windy day when their scent might carry far enough for Alpha's Pack to catch it, he thought they would be able to sneak down to the farther side of the lake, and drink there.

Lucky felt a surge of satisfaction. His friends had a good chance.

"Come on!" yipped Dart imperiously as Lucky hesitated on the ridge.

Reluctantly Lucky followed.

The trees were thinning again as they got closer to the camp. Across a broad green meadow Lucky could see the dense, dark line of another forest, one that seemed even vaster than Alpha's territory. A little way ahead, prey-creatures burst from the grass in a panic, hurtling for deeper cover as they scented the dogs, and Lucky's heart leaped with the thrill of the hunt. Almost at his feet, a small shadow flickered in the grass, and Lucky pounced, his paw catching the mouse's tail and pinning it.

He was about to bark his success to the others when he felt a weight slam into his side, knocking him onto his flank. As he hit the ground, Lucky saw the terrified mouse scuttle and vanish, and he stared after it in disbelief. Then he rolled to his feet, hackles up, and glared at Dart.

"Why did you do that? I had it!"

"You had no business having it!" snapped Dart.

Twitch hobbled up. "We do not hunt," he said sharply. "Not on patrol."

Lucky panted in disbelief. "What are you talking about? Why would you not hunt when food walks right in front of you?"

"Maybe you hunt alone in the city," said Dart scornfully. "But *we* are a Pack, and the Pack tells us when to hunt. And that will be when we have earned our place as hunters!"

"Your place?" Lucky yelped, unable to believe what he was hearing. These dogs seemed . . . *trained.* "All dogs hunt! It's *natural.*"

"Not patrol dogs. If we get promoted to the hunting den, it will be because we have earned it. Hunting is not our job, and it is not our right, either."

Lucky looked from one to the other. They stared at him with such disapproval, he could not help his head dropping. "But I was not going to eat it straight away. I was—"

"The hunters will come out later," Twitch told him. "Fiery

will lead them out just as the Sun-Dog starts to yawn. That way the patrols are back in camp to support Alpha and guard Moon, and the food is brought back to camp to be shared at no-sun." As Lucky opened his jaws to object, he snapped, "That's how it works! Don't bring your city ways to *our* Pack, Lucky."

Lucky scratched fiercely at one ear, then shook himself and followed the other two obediently, with just one longing look after a last fleeing mouse. He supposed it was natural that the Pack would wish to defend their food source, and ensure that all the food was shared equally by all. If dogs hunted individually— like that nameless one who had eaten the rabbit—they might be tempted to take more than their share.

Oh, Forest-Dog, he thought dismally, *I have so much to learn about Wild Pack life. Don't let me make another mistake like that. . . .*

He could not help a heavy sense of sadness in his gut, though. Twitch and Dart had been perfectly content to let all that prey elude them, which meant that there had to be a *lot* of food in this territory. Yet Bella and her Pack were farther up the valley, desperately hungry and unsure how long they could survive without taking serious risks, like stealing from the Wild Pack. If Alpha had been willing to share, there would be more than enough for all the dogs. It seemed such a waste, and so unfair.

There was no point in Lucky suggesting such a thing, though. One word in favor of the Leashed Dogs, and his new Packmates would be instantly suspicious.

And Lucky had a feeling that Alpha would need no more than a twinge of doubt to throw him out of the Pack, or worse. *Do not let them get the faintest scent of what you really are, Lucky,* he told himself.

He was treading on the shakiest of river-stones. He did not want to fall and be swept away—and become just another dog the Pack was afraid to name.

CHAPTER ELEVEN

By the time the Moon-Dog was stretching lazily on the horizon, Lucky was regretting the loss of the mouse more than he'd thought possible. Hunger bit at his stomach. He lay with his head on his paws, licking his chops and trying not to seem impatient in front of the others. At least, from what Twitch had said, the Pack did *share* the prey that the hunters would bring.

Finally, the hunters returned. The other dogs in the Pack rose to greet them, ears pricked and jaws wet with eagerness, and Lucky took the chance to glance around the camp.

Yes, all the dogs were here—all the ones he knew about, at least. Only Moon was out of sight. She had to be with her pups in their cozy nest. With the whole Pack waiting eagerly for food, this would be a perfect time each day for Bella and the Leashed Dogs to creep down unseen to the lake's far shore. As the undergrowth rustled with the sound of returning dogs, Lucky stored away the knowledge for later, feeling pleased with himself.

Bella's plan might actually work.

The big brown dog—Fiery—advanced into the center of the clearing and dropped a small corpse of prey. He turned his head, sniffing the air, proudly howling to Moon: "We have mice and voles, rabbits and gophers." *And a fat game bird,* Lucky thought, his mouth watering. *And a couple of squirrels. Not a bad share for each of us.*

Spring dropped her catch onto the pile, growling at the broken body of a rabbit. "That one was slippery," she panted. "It almost got away."

Snap gave her ear an affectionate lick. "But you caught it in the end!" Lucky noticed the little dog's fur was stained with mud and blood.

The hunters joined their friends, sitting down to relax. Spring trotted over proudly to Twitch, her head high, and began telling him about the hunt as the limping dog listened appreciatively, his eyes wide with admiration. Mulch and Dart began to tussle, the long-eared black dog rolling the brown-and-white smaller dog over in the dirt as she snapped irritably at his paws. Lucky's stomach growled. He was so *hungry.*

At last, Alpha stalked forward, sniffing approvingly at the prey, and Lucky rose and started eagerly toward the gophers.

He swallowed a yelp when he felt a hard nip on his flank, and turned to see Dart baring her teeth in a warning.

"Not yet!" she growled in a low voice.

Mistake! None of the others had made a move, so Lucky quickly backed down and lay beside Dart and Twitch. "Sorry," he murmured. "Does Alpha divide the food himself?"

They watched as Alpha selected the plump bird along with the best of the rabbits, and settled himself down to pluck and tear at the prey with his teeth.

Lucky glanced around at the other dogs, but none of them had moved at all. They either lay with their heads on their paws, or sat patiently, with their tails flicking the grass, while Alpha ate his fill. On the other side of the circle, Fiery was deep in conversation with Sweet.

Lucky's stomach rumbled. "I don't understand," he said. "Don't we all get to eat?"

"One at a time," said Dart, her eyes glimmering in amusement. "Who in the name of the Moon-Dog taught you manners?"

"It was different in the city," Lucky grumbled.

"We have *rules* here," said Mulch, his nose tilted arrogantly. "We're not greedy scavengers."

Lucky decided not to answer. He had a feeling that, whatever he said, Mulch would scoff.

Alpha was taking his time, cracking the bones with his jaws and licking them clean of meat and marrow. Only when he had filled his belly, stretched, and padded away did Sweet step forward; and only when she had eaten a gopher and two whole voles did Fiery approach the prey. The huge dog tossed a whole squirrel toward the cowering Omega, who barked a humble "Thank you" before taking it away toward Moon's nest in the undergrowth.

Drool slowly fell from the little dog's jaws, but Omega didn't even dare lick at the prey in his mouth. He dropped it at Moon's paws. Lucky realized Omega thanked Fiery for nothing more than the "privilege" of taking Moon's food to her. As he watched three squirming pup noses sniff curiously at the meat even though they weren't old enough to eat it, Lucky pondered how odd the rules of Pack life were.

Could I ever get used to living like this?

Lucky's dismay mounted as he watched the heap of food shrink. The game bird was gone, as were all but one of the rabbits. There were far fewer mice, too. *What's going to be left for me?* He had never really considered it before, but now he keenly felt how rotten it was to be bottom of the Pack.

Fiery was still gobbling down a gopher, licking his red muzzle before tearing into its rib cage again. Lucky's tormented stomach was growling like an angry Alpha, so he almost missed the slinking shadow off to his left. Then he started, and turned.

Mulch was creeping through the twilight shadows, targeting a mouse that had fallen away from the main pile. His paw reached out, almost as if he was only stretching his muscles. . . .

But Lucky wasn't the only one who had noticed Mulch. As one of his claws caught the mouse's tail, Sweet lunged for him, biting his long black ear savagely. Mulch dropped the mouse with a yelp.

"What do you think you're doing?" snapped Sweet. "Stay back until it's your turn! One more trick like that and you will be demoted."

Mulch whimpered an apology, scuttling backward as blood dripped from his torn ear. Lucky felt his heart sink inside him. What had happened to the shy, gentle Sweet he'd known in the Trap House?

"Snap," the swift-dog announced. "Hurry up, or we'll be here until the Moon-Dog goes to sleep."

"Coming, Beta!"

Sweet's new aggression wasn't all that dismayed Lucky. What

would remain of the night's hunt for the dogs who held the lower statuses? There wasn't much left in the way of gophers now, and the remaining squirrels were all scrawny. Once Snap had taken her share, it was Mulch's proper turn. Subdued, the black dog snatched up a mouse and a squirrel's leg and scurried back, as if afraid of more punishment.

"Go on, Spring." Sweet broke off her conversation with Fiery to snap another command.

Spring, the hunt-dog who looked so like Twitch, stepped up hungrily and began to feed as Lucky glanced at Twitch.

"Is she your litter-sister?" he asked.

Twitch nodded. "Of course, *she* wasn't born with a useless paw," he growled, holding up his own. "But that's luck for you. That's why she's higher than me in the Pack."

Lucky tried not to let his sympathy show; he had a feeling Twitch wouldn't thank him for it. "But Pack status can change, can't it? You could move up in the ranks?"

"Yes, and you can move *down*," Twitch pointed out gruffly.

Lucky licked his lips nervously, watching the dwindling mound of prey now, sensing tingles in his flanks that felt oddly close to dread. "How does it work? I mean, how does Alpha decide?"

"Alpha and Beta, you mean," Twitch grumbled. "She advises

him a lot. There are all kinds of ways to change your Pack-place. If you do something stupid or wicked or rash—something that puts the Pack in danger—you will be demoted. Do something really stupid or rebellious, and you'll be lucky if demotion is all that happens to you. But if you do well, or serve the Pack, you will rise. That can take a long time, though." He sighed, ears drooping. "It always seems to be a lot easier to fall down than it is to climb up."

Lucky could imagine that. "Can a dog *ask* to be promoted?"

"Of course. But that involves challenging one of your Pack-mates to a fight. That's why I'm stuck where I am. I've tried a few combats . . ." Twitch glared resentfully at his lame paw. "But I never win. The only dog I could beat in a fight is Omega, and who couldn't? I'm just glad he's around to do all the dirty work. Oh, good! Dart has finished. My turn, finally."

Twitch limped forward to the diminished food-heap and began to eat the scrawnier of the squirrels and a leftover piece of rabbit. Waiting his turn, Lucky stole a glance at the miserable Omega, who stood on the very fringe of the Pack, shivering— from the cold, or hunger, Lucky could not quite tell. He felt sorry for the wretched dog, but at the same time deeply grateful there was a dog lower than he was in this Pack. Guilty as it made him, he could understand Twitch's feelings completely.

His thoughts wandered back to his own friends. Who would have been the Omega Leashed Dog, if Bella had run her Pack by these rules? Not Daisy; she was too spirited. . . . Sunshine? He shivered to think of poor Sunshine being treated this way, with her hopelessness at living in the wild, and her obsession with her silky fur. Or maybe it would have been little Alfie?

If Alpha hadn't killed him.

When Twitch had finished and Lucky padded forward, he felt a huge rush of relief. There was most of a gopher left for him, along with a half-chewed haunch of squirrel. It was no kind of feast, but it would be enough to satisfy his gnawing hunger. And for Omega, there would still be . . .

A scrawny shrew.

Lucky stared at it, his stomach burning with guilt. Catching Omega's mournful eyes as he cracked the rabbit's thigh bone, he pushed aside a detached foreleg with his paw, shoving it surreptitiously closer to the dead shrew. He could manage without that mouthful, whereas Omega . . .

Teeth snapped harshly, right against his ear. Lucky flinched, nearly dropping the rabbit leg.

"Next time, I will bite it off," growled Sweet in the silence.

Lucky gazed up at her, dumbstruck. "But—"

"No pity in this Pack, do you hear me? Fill your belly. You are a patrol dog, and I will rip your ear off if you let us down because of weakness. Eat your fill or leave this Pack right now. Do you understand?"

The eyes of every Pack member were on him. Lucky heard murmurs from some of the dogs, who seemed unable to believe what had happened. He heard Mulch growl, "That must be his City-Dog ways."

Desperately Lucky searched Sweet's face, looking for some trace of fellow-feeling, some hint that this display was only for the Pack's benefit. But her gaze was unforgiving. She wasn't doing this for show; she meant it.

So this was how she'd risen so far and so fast in the Pack. There was a ruthlessness in his friend that Lucky had not seen when they were captives in the Trap House, and she had clearly learned to use it.

"Your pity won't do Omega any favors," said Sweet, with a disdainful glance at the ugly little animal.

"I know. I just—"

"It seems that you need a lesson in Pack life, *City Dog*."

There were muffled sniggers from some of the other dogs at

Sweet's words, and Mulch in particular seemed to be enjoying his humiliation—probably because it took the focus away from his own bad behavior. "Indulge this pathetic dog's weakness— pamper him with food he has not earned—and he will never rise any higher in the Pack. Will he?"

Alpha watched her approvingly, and Lucky felt his belly burn with jealousy as well as shame. "I understand . . . Beta," he said.

"Good. If you do not give him a reason to, he will never better himself. Will you, Omega?"

The little dog snuffled and nodded, submissive. "Yes, Beta. You are right." He gave Lucky a resentful glare. "I don't want your pity."

Alpha gave a growling laugh. "Well said, for once, Omega. The City Dog would be holding you under his paw, not helping you." When the dog-wolf's unsettling eyes turned on him, Lucky found himself cowering inwardly. "You are not yet fully *accepted* in this Pack, Lucky. It would be wise of you to remember this—and do things our way from now on."

Sweet gazed at Lucky, her anger replaced with a sort of thoughtfulness. "He will learn, Alpha. I guarantee it."

With those words, Lucky's telling-off seemed to be over. He was grateful to Sweet for bringing it to a close. As he settled back to his food, subdued, he felt a reluctant admiration for her. Deep inside him—right there in his dog-spirit—he understood she was right. Sweet was not simply being harsh; she was being fair, and true to the Pack. Omega would not be allowed to starve, after all—the Pack needed him too much for all the lowly jobs. And Lucky sensed the Forest-Dog would approve of Sweet's savage discipline, the spur that would make Omega try harder to improve his rank.

All the same, none of that made Lucky feel any better. His appetite gone, he turned back to his rabbit and tore at it without enthusiasm, gulping down meat that tasted bitter.

"Wonder how much he'll leave for Omega now," he heard Mulch say.

"It's his first meal with us," said Snap, her voice low and even. "I'm sure he'll learn our ways soon."

Lucky swallowed another mouthful of tough meat, wondering at how this Pack of dogs could work so well together in some ways, even as they seemed to have regular disagreements. Snap wasn't exactly standing up for him, but she was still quick to tell Mulch he was wrong. And yet, there was a sense that everyone was pulling in the same direction, hoping to achieve the same goals.

Packs are just strange, I suppose, he told himself, thinking about Bella and the Leashed Dogs. They may have been clumsy hunters who pined pathetically for the security of their lives with the longpaws, but none of them would have willingly seen a Packmate go hungry. This Wild Pack, on the other hand, were content to talk lazily among themselves as they watched Omega creep forward to nibble on his scraps, stretching out his time with the shrew to make it last longer, chewing down even the tiny bones.

Neither Pack was where Lucky belonged. More than ever he wished he could be on his own again, free and easy, with responsibilities to no one: no dog to lord it over him, and none that he could bully and boss himself. He could barely stand to watch as Omega bit hungrily at the last bare bones.

The Pack dogs were stretching now, getting to their feet, shaking themselves, and licking the last traces of blood from their chops. Almost before Omega had gulped his last sliver, they were gathering in a new circle, away from the prey-tree, and Twitch whined to beckon Lucky over.

He was rising to join them when a new sound swelled around the clearing. Lucky's breath caught in his throat and he paused, his misery forgotten as he listened. The sound seemed to echo in the marrow of his bones before it broke on the air. He raised his head, a thrill lifting his fur.

The Pack had turned their eyes to the darkened sky. The noise that came from their throats was high and wild and haunting. As Lucky stared, he caught sight of Omega's small shadow slipping past him. Two of the dogs in the circle made way for him and the little creature took his place between them, lifting his muzzle and singing out a long howl to the stars.

Shivering, Lucky crept forward. Just as it had for Omega, a space opened for him in the circle, and he found himself next to Sweet, her slender head aimed toward the sky as she howled.

For a moment she grew quiet, pricking her ears to hear the song of the Pack, and she turned her head to Lucky, her eyes distant and solemn. There was no trace now of the arrogant Beta dog.

"At night we howl to the Spirit Dogs," Sweet told him softly. "Sing with us, Lucky. Join the Great Howl."

Those words were like a spirit-force inside him, filling his bones and guts and muscles—something mystical that had to be released into the air, into the sky . . . into the world. His spine tingled with an unfamiliar longing, a need. Lucky tilted his head to the night and howled with the other dogs.

On the opposite side of the circle he saw the black-and-white shape of Moon joining the circle, and the round, fat shadows of her three pups. Even they, with their half-blind eyes, opened their tiny, soft jaws and whimpered little cries to the sky. Though he had never had a glimpse of them beyond their noses before, a surge of fierce pride and protectiveness filled Lucky's body and he howled longer and louder: for the Pack's pups, for Omega, for Sweet and Alpha and the rest.

The stars seemed to whirl above him, breaking and reforming into the shapes of running dogs. Not just the stars, though: As if imprinted on the inside of his eyes he saw other dogs, shadow-dogs, flickering across his mind. The ghostly silhouette of a great hound raced between the slender pine trunks of a huge forest; another tumbled through a surging river, but not drowning or fighting: It was part of the torrent, swift and joyful. Clouds drifted across a bright sky, and between them leaped slender, ferocious Warrior-Dogs, springing from cloud to cloud, their leader a bright slash of light that hurt the eyes.

In his very bones, Lucky was aware that the dogs around him were howling to particular Spirit Dogs. There was a high, silvery note to Moon's howling that her pups did their tiny best to echo; Lucky wondered if she was crying out *only* to the Moon-Dog. Dart, the brown-and-white patrol dog, let out a cry to the Sky-Dogs, so fierce and clear that it somehow seemed to echo as far as the horizon. Fiery's deep rumbling howl was as rich as rocks and soil; and though Mulch's cry was thinner, it too was filled with love of the landscape. The two of them were calling, each in his own way, to the Earth-Dog.

And the Spirit Dogs answered them.

Was he imagining the phantom hounds that raced across his vision? Lucky hesitated, opening an eye and breaking the spell for a fleeting instant. Were the other Pack members seeing them, too? It was impossible to tell. Closing his eyes, he resumed his howling, higher and fiercer than before, and he thought he heard an answering song within him: the great ghostly dog that hunted through the dream-trees in his mind's eye.

Lucky felt like he could howl forever. The Spirit Dogs were inside him—they were inside all of them, joining with the Pack and leaping in the shadows around them.

But slowly, gradually, the Great Howl died away as the ghostly dogs faded from his vision. Lucky wasn't quite sure when the last faint howl was swallowed up by the night and the silence fell, but he blinked as if he had awoken from a dream—a dream he did not want to end. The surge of loyalty still tingled in his flesh, and he felt a huge, irresistible tug toward every member of the Pack. He forgot his feelings of only moments ago: his resentment, his shame and humiliation. These were his brothers, his sisters, his hunting-and-fighting friends, and he would never leave them, never. . . .

It was fleeting, fading, but the intensity of that Pack-spirit lingered in his brain and heart. Now he saw what bound these dogs together, despite the brutality and harshness of their lives. For the first time, he could truly understand what Sweet had told him.

Lucky felt dizzy with the echo of the Great Howl as he padded silently to the patrol den, where Dart and Twitch were already yawning and treading their ritual circles. The leaf-strewn space was close to the entrance of the clearing, and Lucky knew that no enemy could get past them, not with Twitch and Dart on guard there with their ears pricked and their eyes shining. A fierce certainty raced through him: No dog would get past him to his leader, to his Pack and the Pack's pups. No dog would dare. . . .

As he lay down, his head on his paws and his ears still alert for any threat, he gazed at the softest hollow of all—the sheltered glade that was Alpha's sleeping place. The dog-wolf was curled up there with Sweet, his massive tail tucked close to her slender muzzle.

Something other than loyalty and protectiveness was shivering through Lucky's flesh now. It was not Pack-love that prickled his neck and raised his hackles . . .

It was the sharp fang bite of jealousy.

CHAPTER TWELVE

Jaws, snapping and tearing . . .

The screaming barks and yelps of wounded dogs . . .

The howls of battle-rage as teeth tore into flesh.

Two shadowy leaders howled their hate at each other, commanding their Packs to rip and kill. . . . And they did, two armies destroying themselves, dragging each other down, down to the Earth-Dog. Sharp fangs sank into Lucky's ear, just as Sweet had threatened that hers would do, and he felt that ear ripped from his skull. But when he spun around to defend himself he could see only darkness, could feel only the spatter of blood in his face. There was no enemy for him to fight, no way of battling to survival.

There was only a raging torrent of savagery. . . .

The Storm of Dogs—

Lucky started awake with a terrified growl. The muzzle that

nudged and nipped him was no horrifying phantom. It was just Twitch. The black-and-tan long-eared dog's weak leg was shaking with weariness as he limped to lie down near Lucky.

"Wake up, Lucky. It's your turn on watch."

Lucky got to his feet, his own legs trembling. He took deep breaths to calm his fear. There was no battle—no dying and killing—only the same forest hollow where he had slept for five no-suns now. The woods were silent around them but for the whisper of branches, and the rustle of beetles and other small prey.

"Go on, Lucky!" Twitch insisted. "I need to sleep."

Stretching, shaking his fur, Lucky let Twitch slump into his sleeping place with a tired sigh. "I haven't been on watch before. Are you sure—"

"Beta says you're ready. She says that you fit in now, and that you show commitment to the Pack." There was approval in Twitch's voice. "She says that she trusts you. That means we *all* do."

Lucky gave a soft growl of acceptance and pleasure. "Where should I patrol? And who will be with me?"

"At night, we patrol alone," Twitch said. "You just have to pad around the edge of the camp, and keep your eyes open for anything that should worry us. Since you'll be by yourself, it's safer to keep moving. Don't stay in one place too long."

Still bleary, and a little shaken by his dream, Lucky made his way to the clearing's entrance. He was tired, but he was grateful as well for being woken from that terrible dream. And he could not deny a glow of pride that Sweet thought him so worthy of trust. He had been with them now for only four full journeys of the Sun-Dog, yet he was being given responsibility for guarding the whole Pack.

He would not let them down.

Just as he was thinking this, his gut turned over with realization. For a moment, in the blurry aftermath of sleep, he had forgotten the real reason he was here. Each night, the Great Howl drew him in and wound its spell tight around his heart, bonding him closer to the Wild Pack. Each morning he woke, remembering the thrill in his blood, and the memory was always followed by a sting of shame and disgust. How easy it was to forget, to be drawn in—to feel his blood singing that he was one of them, a Wild Dog, forever.

But the shame grew less each morning.

No! Again he reminded himself that he was *not* part of this Pack. He was here on a mission, and now was the time for him to fulfill it. He might not have a better moment to slip away, to reveal the Wild Pack's weak points to Bella. And once he was gone, he would not come back. Not ever.

The Wild Dogs might never even know it was him who had betrayed them.

Lucky shook himself violently from head to tail. He shouldn't be feeling this sadness, this crawling regret, in his belly. Twitch and Dart would miss him on patrol. He wondered what they would think had happened to him. At least he wouldn't have to face any of them again. Not even Sweet . . . A sick sensation filled his belly.

He shook it off angrily. He couldn't let Bella and the others down. With a last glance over his shoulder at the silent, sleeping camp, Lucky slunk away into the shadows of the forest.

Good-bye, he told them silently. *I'm sorry that I had to do this to you.*

The Moon-Dog was high overhead as Lucky picked his way cautiously through scrub and tree trunks, and he found himself wondering if Bella would still be at their meeting place. He barely liked to admit what a relief it would be if she had already left. Maybe she had given up on him altogether, after waiting in vain the last few no-suns. He could go on alone . . . or return to the Wild Pack. . . .

As he crept into the great open space, he could smell the longpaw-place, all old fires and burnt food as Bella had described it. He saw the strange shapes of tables and benches, silvered by the Moon-Dog's light. Beneath one of them, a cracked and over-turned board of nailed planks, he saw curled shadows that moved slightly: flanks that rose and fell with breath.

Bella and Mickey, huddled together and fast asleep. Lucky padded to them on silent paws and licked gently at their faces.

"Bella? Mickey?"

They were awake in an instant, leaping to their feet, hackles high and snarling. Lucky saw the bright glint of their wide eyes.

"It's me. Lucky."

Both Bella and Mickey relaxed, their breaths coming out in a relieved sigh. Tails lashing, they yipped soft greetings, exchanging licks with Lucky. He was so happy to see them again; it felt like an age since he had left his friends to join the Wild Pack. And he was shocked to realize just how much he had missed his litter-sister. Fondly he nuzzled her ear.

"It's good to see you safe," he murmured. "How are Bruno and Martha?"

Bella seemed to hesitate for a moment, but Mickey shook his head and barked gruffly, "Not good. We've given them the best of the food and the cleanest of the water, but they don't seem to be getting any better." The Farm Dog's eyes were downcast, as if he was ashamed to give Lucky such bad news.

Lucky's heart sank. His friends could not be eating or drinking well if there had not been much recovery; he felt bad now for resenting his small share of the Wild Pack's prey. At least he had been able to eat. . . .

Again he felt his loyalties shift, and the guilt gnaw at his belly. "I'm sorry it's taken so long. I did not dare creep away before now. There were always dogs watching."

"We understand. But the poison creeps farther and farther downriver," said Bella quietly. "And the hunting is poor. I suppose the prey is all moving away from the bad water, too. And every time it rains, we have to get out of the caves quickly, in case they flood. I can't afford to have that river water touching anyone else."

"That's sensible." Lucky licked her. "But it must be very difficult."

"Please, Lucky." Bella raised her golden eyes to his. "Please tell me you've found a way for us to get to the lake."

"Yes, I have." Lucky did his best to look cheerful, for Mickey's and Bella's sake. "Listen, the Wild Pack still will not let you share."

"But—"

"No, wait. I've scouted out a way we can get to the lake without them seeing us, and I know the best time as well. There's a gully—I'll show you where it runs—and we need to follow it around the long way to the far side of the lake. The patrols do not go that far, and if it's a still night there won't be enough wind to carry our scent to them. I think it will be safe for us to drink then."

"You think?" Bella looked doubtful, and Mickey gave her a worried glance.

"The best time is sunset," Lucky went on. "Not only is that a good time to travel—because the dusk gives good camouflage—but that is the time the hunters come back to the Pack. The whole Pack eats together, so no dog will be patrolling."

He did not want to mention the Great Howl, though he could not say why this was. Perhaps because the very thought of it gave him that ache of Pack-longing in his belly. . . .

Mickey pawed the ground, and Bella furrowed her brows. "I'm not sure that Bruno and Martha will be strong enough," she said.

"That'll be all right," said Lucky. "We can take all the fit and strong dogs down to the lake, and that should leave enough clean water back at camp for the sick ones. See?"

The Leashed Dogs exchanged a glance—one that he did not like, though he couldn't say why. Mickey shuffled some leaves into a pile with a paw, the pointless task seeming to fascinate him. Bella peered at the stars above her, as if searching intently for the shape of the Rabbit or one of the other star-creatures their mother had pointed out to them when they were just pups.

"I can't tell you how glad I am to be coming back." Lucky's voice was too bright; he could hear it himself. "I've missed you all!"

"Lucky?" With a great sigh, Bella raised her eyes to meet his. "You shouldn't come back . . . not yet."

"What?" He was startled. "But I've found the way—"

"No." Bella shook her head determinedly. "You have done a wonderful job, Lucky, but don't you see? That Wild Pack trusts you now. You can slip away without anyone suspecting anything is wrong. You might be able to find out more! Stay with them a little longer, Lucky—for us."

Lucky stared at her. The thought of going back to the Wild Pack after betraying them like this filled him with shame as well as guilt. And what if they had noticed his absence? He did not like the idea of having to explain himself to Alpha—or to Sweet, who had trusted him to watch over the camp. Would she get in trouble for what he had done?

Yet he did want to see Sweet again. And not just because of

what he had to do for Bella and her friends.

I can take part in the Howl again. . . . I can feel the power of the Earth-Dog and the Sky-Dogs. I can feel like I'm in control of myself, my destiny—rather than rushing around, simply trying to stay alive.

His fur bristled with sadness at that thought. Without him, would the Leashed Dogs be *able* to survive? His litter-sister was becoming stronger and more confident—he could see that—but even she seemed not to understand the world around them in the way that the dogs in Alpha's Pack did. They would always need his help.

"All right," he said at last. "I will go back. But, Bella . . ."

"What?" His litter-sister's voice sounded sharp, almost on edge.

Lucky shook himself. "Nothing. I just want you to know I don't like this. *Any* of it."

As he turned and walked away, he was almost sure he caught a guilty look passing between Bella and Mickey, but he shrugged it off. He did not mind if they had to share a little bit of his own unhappiness.

Moon-Dog was already settling down to sleep through the day, and Sun-Dog would soon replace her on the horizon. Lucky felt a fearful urgency to get back to Alpha's camp before they realized he was missing, but he was nervous, too. He stopped every few paces to listen, and to sniff at the breeze. One sign of an early patrol and he would have to take to his paws and run back to Bella. There was no excuse he could think of for abandoning his watch until sunup.

Birds were beginning to sing in the branches above him, and one took off with a flutter of wings. Lucky halted, his heart in his throat, but the bird settled; there was nothing else, no bark, no howl of alarm or anger. His paws shook slightly as he went on. He noticed there was a scent that clung to his coat, and recognized it as Bella's. A shudder went down his spine; how had he imagined the other dogs would not notice that?

He plunged deep into a pile of dead leaves that had rotted almost to mulch, rolling over and over until he was sure he had rid himself of her smell.

Finally he reached the outskirts of the Wild Pack's camp. Unable to suppress the tingle of fear in his skin, he padded silently closer, listening for the stir of dogs waking up.

Silence. Lucky was in his post by the clearing entrance just in time to see Spring stretching and rising, yawning at the morning, her long brown-and-black ears dangling, her keen nose twitching as she picked up the scents all around them. Lucky tilted his head and watched her expectantly as she trotted up and licked his ear.

"Any trouble, Lucky?" she asked quietly.

"None," he lied. *Only the trouble I brought myself. . . .*

"Go and get some sleep, then." Spring sat down in his place, her eyes sweeping the forest beyond. "I'll keep my nose out for any danger."

"*Is* there any danger?" Lucky asked.

"Not really," Spring replied. "It would be a foolish dog who tried to take us on."

"I suppose you're right," said Lucky as Spring loped off. He turned his sleep-circle on the patch of soft moss that was his bed, glancing up into the sky and hoping the Sky-Dogs were listening to him.

I am sorry for being such a dishonorable dog, but my friends need help. . . .

He lay down, shutting his eyes, but sleep refused to come. No doubt the Moon-Dog was angry. *Oh, Forest-Dog, please explain to her that I had to do it.*

It was no use. Besides, every time his eyes closed, his terrible nightmare of the Storm of Dogs rumbled distantly, threatening to return. Between the dream and the way his loyalties seemed to bite and scratch at each other, he knew he wouldn't be able to sleep now. But if he was up and wandering the camp after patrolling during the night, other dogs would ask questions. And Lucky felt like he had told enough lies recently.

This was why he had always preferred living as a Lone Dog. Who could bear being torn in so many directions? Loyalty to other dogs was a curse, he thought bitterly, because you could not be loyal to everyone at once. How in the name of the Sky-Dogs had a loner like him come to run with two Packs, and somehow not *belong* to either?

It's like the Big Growl turned the whole world upside down, he thought.

The Sun-Dog was pushing his muzzle above the horizon, a bright glow of gold that lit up the whole forest and burnished the pine bark with shining bronze. There would be no more sleep now, Lucky realized with an inward sigh.

He did not want to lie here anyway. If he did, he knew that thoughts would tumble around his head more and more. How was he going to get himself out of this mess without disappointing— or betraying—dogs that he cared about?

CHAPTER THIRTEEN

"Hold on!" barked Dart. "Everybody stay still!"

Lucky lifted his head and pricked his ears, watching Dart carefully as she sniffed the wind, her fur prickling. Her muzzle was curled back, and Lucky felt a tremor of unease in his flanks.

Sometimes, he got the feeling Dart *hoped* for there to be trouble— so she had something to snarl and fight about. She was an angry dog.

The sunup patrol had been straightforward, thank the Sky-Dogs, because Lucky knew he was too tired and confused to deal with any nasty surprises. But what could Dart have noticed in this broad, pleasant meadow, with a clear view of any possible danger from far away? All Lucky could see was rippling grass, right up to the dark line of forest beyond.

"What is it?" he howled.

"I don't know." Dart sniffed the air again, urgently. "Something strange."

Twitch was silent too, casting around for any scent of what Dart had detected. Lucky followed Twitch as he drew closer to Dart; he hoped that what Dart had found had nothing to do with Bella's Pack. He wasn't sure he trusted Bella not to do something stupid without him there to talk her out of it. What if they had strayed into Alpha's territory in their desperate search for food?

Suddenly Lucky stopped, one paw raised. He was close to Dart now and a hint of the strange scent had come to him, too. It took him only a second to identify it: crushed earth, metal, and animal-hide . . . That strong-smelling drink that a longpaw would give to a . . .

Loudcage!

It was no ordinary loudcage, though; it was one of those monstrous ones he would occasionally see in the city. They smelled different from the little loudcages—stronger and more threatening. Lucky had seen them chew up entire roads, spitting out black chunks of earth and flattening them beneath terrible crushing feet that rolled across the earth.

"Stop, Dart—I know what that is!"

Dart threw him a doubtful look, then slunk across to Lucky. "What?" she muttered.

"It's a loudcage scent, but that's a *big* one—"

Dart flinched away, a spark of terror in her eyes. "Loud-cages? Well, they have nothing to do with us. Let's go on with the patrol—avoid the thing—"

"They won't threaten us, not those ones with the great teeth," Lucky told her. "They are too big to bother with us. We should go and see what they are up to."

"No," Dart growled. "Why should we care that loudcages are nearby?"

"Because they can crush a dog," Lucky told them. "Not even the fastest dog can outrun a loudcage."

"Maybe Beta could," said Twitch, who had come to stand with them. "She's very fast."

"Not even her," Lucky whined. "We must be careful now."

"I've never seen a loudcage," Twitch said, his flanks heaving as he shivered. "I've never even heard of such a thing as a giant one."

"Of course not," snapped Dart, who seemed very much on edge. "You and Spring were born in the wild. I lived in the city when I was a pup, and I've *seen* the terrible things a loudcage can do. One of my littermates . . ." She shuddered.

Maybe Dart was right, thought Lucky. Maybe they should avoid the giant loudcage. But what was it doing out here in the wild? Were the longpaws building a new city to replace their destroyed one? If that was so, it was surely better for the dogs to know about it, so that they could move on in plenty of time.

"Just a quick look," Lucky promised. "I'm sure Alpha would want us to investigate."

That was enough to persuade the other two. Hesitantly they followed Lucky as he tracked the scent—which was not difficult when the smell of loudcage drink was so thick and overwhelming. Lucky felt quite sick with it by the time they crested a rise and saw a marshy plain stretching out below.

There it was: a colossal yellow loudcage, resting from its brutal churning of the ground. The tracks of its rolling paws were everywhere, mounds of muddy earth strewn around them. There was another beast with it, a long-snouted metal thing that was driven half into the earth as if hunting for the Earth-Dog herself. Lucky shuddered at the sight.

There were longpaws there, of course, wearing that strange shiny, yellow fur Lucky had seen before on the ones beside the poisoned river.

"Keep back," he growled to Twitch and Dart, but it was hardly necessary. They were already cowering against the fringe of trees. "Those longpaws aren't friendly. You were right, Dart—whatever they're doing, it is not good for us.'"

But this time it was Twitch who held his ground, staring out from the cover of the long grass. "Look at that giant metal tooth," he whispered. "They are *eating* the ground. Chasing the Earth-Dog. Do you think they're hurting her?"

"If Earth-Dog was hurt," said Dart, "she would let us know. She would Growl again."

"What if they've killed her?" Twitch whined.

"I don't know," snapped Dart, "but Lucky's right. We should leave now."

"No. We said we would find out more and report to Alpha. We have a duty to the Pack."

Twitch had a stubborn, determined look in his eyes. Lucky sighed, annoyed and impatient. Maybe the slower-moving dog was desperate to impress Alpha and improve his standing in the Pack. There was little chance of that, so far as Lucky could see: Speed and strength were what mattered for the higher-ranked hunting dogs, and even Mulch and Spring, who were less experienced and skilled than Fiery or Snap, had nothing to fear from Twitch. But Twitch had a point. The business with the giant loud-cage was strange behavior, even for longpaws—it might be good for the dogs to find out what they were up to.

For the time being, they did not seem to be up to much at all. The giant loudcage rested, still and silent, while the long-paws ambled around, exchanging curt sounds and inspecting the churned earth. One of them held a box in his hand that seemed very important to him, because he kept touching it, staring at it. Lucky pricked one ear.

It was all they seemed to do—stand and talk and prod the ground, and occasionally peer at the box. Just as Lucky was beginning to think there was nothing more to be learned, one of the longpaws strode up to the giant loudcage and mounted it. After a moment of silence, the loudcage roared—a terrifying sound that made the ground tremble beneath his paws.

With a whine, Lucky crouched low, seeing that Twitch and Dart were doing the same. What were the longpaws doing—trying to provoke another Big Growl? The giant loudcage's roar was constant and deafening, blotting out every other sound in the world. The smell of broken wet earth and disturbed crawling creatures obliterated every other scent. Lucky hated the fact that all his senses could detect was that loudcage and its work.

"We need to get away," he barked at the others. "We're blind and deaf here!"

"Yes!" yelped Twitch. Dart was already scuttling back, her

eyes alight with terror.

The sunlight that spilled over them vanished, as if a cloud had drifted across the Sun-Dog. His senses were so confused and blunted, Lucky thought he was imagining it—that the sudden cool dimness was in his head. Then he realized: a shadow cast by . . .

He spun around. A longpaw was behind him, and advancing!

Lucky's neck fur rose up and he barked as loudly as he could, but the longpaw did not hesitate the way he had known some city longpaws do in the face of a strange dog. Dart and Twitch were barking too, teeth bared and ears flattened like Lucky's, but there were more longpaws now. Friends of the ones with the giant loud-cage? They were dressed just the same, though they'd come from the opposite direction. Their faces were black, and seemingly without eyes, noses, or mouths. They wore those yellow, shiny furs.

Worse, each one carried a sharp metal stick.

The back of Lucky's neck prickled almost painfully with the sense of threat. His flesh and fur rippled with fear, as the dogs beside him trembled and snarled. All three dogs let loose another volley of furious barks, but there was no stopping the longpaws.

"Bite them!" shrieked Dart. "Bite!"

"No, we shouldn't do that!" barked Lucky wildly.

"But the sticks! The *sticks*!"

"They'll use the sticks on us if we bite them!" Lucky barked, trying to sound confident. *But they will probably use them anyway!*

Then another sound cut through the air, higher even than the distant roar of the loudcage. This time it was the longpaws who halted, frozen to the spot and looking up in alarm. The sound was a wild, bone-chilling howl, full of menace and death. In that instant, Lucky could smell the longpaws' fear. They reeked of it, even through their shiny yellow fur.

No wonder. Even Lucky felt horror thrill through his guts, and he knew he had nothing to fear—not from his own Alpha....

Everything around them was still; even the loudcage had fallen silent. A few leaves drifted in the breeze, touching a longpaw's eyeless face. The howl came again, echoing eerily, and the longpaws looked all around now, turning, searching desperately for the source of that threatening sound. One of them yelped in unease, but Lucky could not tell which one.

The longpaws were confused and uncertain. It was the dogs' only chance....

"Now!" barked Lucky.

The three of them bolted, skidding past the frozen longpaws and racing for the forest. Lucky heard the longpaws' barks, but he did not look back. He was certain they wouldn't chase them into the trees—not now they'd heard that dreadful menacing howl.

Slowing down once they were under the cover of the trees, with Twitch and Dart at his paws, Lucky drew breath, his heart pounding. Dart was panting with the remnants of panic, but Twitch managed to gasp, "Good for Alpha. That showed them!"

It did, thought Lucky, impressed despite himself. He glanced around, peering through the trees, but he could not see his leader. Nor could he see the longpaws—Alpha's howls had terrified them into submission, and they had not even laid eyes on him.

Delight in their escape, and admiration for his new leader, faded to something far less pleasant as the three dogs made their way carefully back through the unfamiliar patch of woodland. By the time they could smell their own camp again, there was a hot, clenching ball of dread in Lucky's belly.

Who would ever want to get on the wrong side of that lethal, ill-tempered dog-wolf? What dog in his right mind would deliberately set out to deceive and betray Alpha?

Yet, that was *exactly* what Lucky had done.

CHAPTER FOURTEEN

Lucky could feel cold tremors in his skin. Alpha's yellow eyes seemed to focus just on him as the three dogs padded into the clearing, and the tip of the dog-wolf's tail twitched slightly.

What had the dog-wolf known? Lucky wondered. Had his howl been simply a coincidence, or had he saved them deliberately?

Lucky felt the hard tug of tiredness in his bones. He would have liked nothing more than to slump down in his sleeping-place and doze until sun-high, but he knew they had to report to their leader.

"Well?" drawled Alpha, his throat rumbling. "What happened?"

Dart was still out of breath, as much from fear as from the run. "Longpaws, Alpha. And the biggest loudcage I've ever seen."

"Loudcages?" came Fiery's voice. Lucky could not tell if the muscular dog was afraid, or contemplating hunting the enemy.

"It was like a house that could run," Dart continued, and Lucky saw Twitch glance quickly at Spring, the wild-born litter-mates clearly wondering what *house* meant. "Lucky knew what it was."

Alpha turned back to Lucky. "Did he now? Oh, *I* know about loudcages, too. Dirty, dangerous brutes."

"I used to see these big loudcages in the city, Alpha," said Lucky, keeping his eyes low and his tone respectful. "They are not like ordinary loudcages—they can chew up the earth and eat it for dinner. And something else was there, too—"

"What?" Alpha's tongue lashed his jaws.

"I'm not sure. It wasn't another loudcage. It was more like a giant fang, biting into the earth."

"That's right, Alpha," confirmed Dart. "And the longpaws there were like nothing I've ever seen."

"I've seen these longpaws before," said Lucky in a low voice. "They've been around since the Big Growl, lots of them. I think they might have something to do with it."

"They had shiny yellow fur." Twitch shivered. "Black faces without eyes—or mouths! And they weren't afraid of us, as they should have been. They had big sticks, and tried to capture us."

The other dogs glanced at one another with alarm, and Omega's ears flattened with fear. Mulch backed a few steps closer to Fiery, the hair on his hackles rising as he growled low in his throat.

Dart took a step forward, giving a short, sharp whine. "But they *were* afraid of you, Alpha."

"Of course," growled the half wolf. "But you were right to flee. Never get closer to longpaws than you have to. It is good that you found out about them, but . . ." His head slowly turned to Lucky. "It was *careless* to put yourself at risk of capture. Don't do that again."

Lucky bit back a retort, his eyes briefly meeting Sweet's. She stood beside Alpha, with a similarly stern look. Lucky tried to see kindness beneath the expression, but wasn't sure it was there. He sank lower to the ground. "Yes, Alpha."

The dog-wolf gave a great wide yawn that showed every one of his white teeth. "Longpaws like these were always encroaching on wolf territory. Always trying to take over the wild, eating up the earth, and stripping the land of cover and prey. Perhaps they are up to the same tricks here. We need to stay alert."

"Yes, Alpha."

Lucky blinked at his leader. It was just the briefest of glimpses into the world of wolves, but still Alpha's words thrummed in his belly, sparking a hot curiosity. Why, he wondered, had Alpha left the wolves to run with dogs? Was it his choice? Or had he been thrown out, perhaps? He would not have been surprised if the wolves viewed a half dog as weaker, inferior.

But he did not dare ask the Pack leader. Instead he went down on his forelegs and flicked his ears forward. "I don't know how you knew we were in trouble, but your howl gave us our chance to escape. I'm grateful to you." Dart and Twitch bowed onto their forelegs as well, their eyes fixed on their leader.

Alpha did not reply for a moment, nor did he explain his insight. He gazed down coolly at Lucky, his tailtip still lightly drumming the ground.

Then he looked away disdainfully. "That? That was nothing. All I did was open my jaws. That's why I'm Alpha of this Pack, *City Dog.*" Behind Lucky, Mulch snorted a scornful half laugh.

Feeling awkward and a little humiliated, Lucky rose and stretched, then shook himself. He would have liked to snap at Alpha, but that would have been foolish. What would it have cost the dog-wolf to simply accept his thanks? He had wanted to show his gratitude, because the longpaw attack and their close escape had shaken him to his core. He'd been polite—deferential, even. Yet all Alpha had shown in return was his arrogance.

Lucky felt like a fool. He couldn't win. Alpha's arrogance gnawed at his patience, making him feel constantly on edge. Great Howl or no Great Howl, he could not live like this.

Alpha had closed his eyes again, as if entirely uninterested, and his huge body sprawled languidly across the rock. Clearly their audience with him was at an end; Twitch and Dart were already drawing an excited circle of listeners with their tale of the terrifying longpaws and their savage loudcage.

"You would not have believed how big it was!"

"And the noise." Dart shook her head violently. "Like nothing you've ever heard!"

As the dogs in the Pack discussed their new threat, their barks and yelps tumbled over one another like play-fighting puppies.

"What damage can loudcages do?"

"Is there any way we can hurt them?"

"Do they really have longpaws *inside* them?"

Lucky knew that, soon, the questions would come to him. He did not feel much like being the center of attention, so he slunk across the clearing to a warm patch of sunlight beneath a thin birch tree.

Remember this feeling, Lucky—you will not be with this Pack forever!

He would have to use his time wisely from now on. Patrolling was all very well, but he'd been in danger of relaxing too easily into his comfortable Pack role, and that was not why he was here. If he was going to find out everything he could about this Pack and its leader, he was going to have to get himself promoted to hunter.

Head on his paws, he breathed out a sigh as he watched Pack life go on around him. Twitch had stretched out on a grassy bank to catch a lucky ray of Sun-Dog's light, and Dart had trotted across to visit with Moon, sniffing affectionately at the clumsily crawling pups, whose eyes had fully opened now. The largest pup tumbled over to land on top of his sister and Moon patiently pushed him upright again.

"Squirm," Moon said. "Be careful." The female pup wobbled back upright, only to trip over Dart's paws. The brown-and-white swift-dog nosed her affectionately.

Fiery, sprawled alongside Mulch, had just growled a lazy order at Omega, who whined submissively before trotting off obediently.

For the moment Pack life was settled, ordered, stable. Each dog knew his place and accepted it. That might be good for the Pack, but it was not what Lucky needed. He had to *rise*, so that he might gain Alpha's trust, and convince him that the Leashed

Dogs were not to be feared or attacked. He did not have time to work his way quietly up the ranks, waiting for some other dog to put a paw wrong and be demoted. A small tremor rippled through his spine. *And if I stay here too long, I might get too settled. I might start thinking of this as my Pack.*

He needed to do what he came here to do. And he needed to do it soon. There was only one other way to change his status. He would have to challenge a higher-ranked dog, and then beat him in combat to take his place.

Lucky swallowed hard. Which Packmate would he challenge?

Fiery was pacing toward the nest where Moon still lay with their pups, and Lucky followed him with his eyes. The huge dog was well fed and powerful, sleek with rippling muscle. There was no way he could take on Fiery and win.

Mulch? he wondered. Lucky cocked an ear, thinking hard. He thought he could defeat Mulch . . . but the long-eared black dog's initial dislike of Lucky hadn't lessened, judging by the way he seemed keen on disagreeing with him all the time. He would take a challenge very personally, and very seriously, and would not easily let himself be beaten by a "City Dog." Lucky suspected he would fight dirty if he had to. *And the last thing I need right now is a bad wound.*

Across the clearing, the young tan-and-white Snap basked in her sleeping-place, her paws and belly turned to the thin rays of light from the Sun-Dog. She was a hunter who ranked above Mulch, Lucky remembered, but she did not have the same vicious resentment. She would not fight so bitterly, and would be less likely to hurt him badly if she defeated him.

Plus, she was smaller than he was. . . .

If I gnaw this over any longer in my head, I'll never do it. Lucky rose and stretched carefully, clawing the mossy ground, testing his muscles. There were no aches that were bothering him. Standing up straight, he shook himself, then padded determinedly to Sweet.

She sniffed at him. "What is it, Lucky?"

He dipped his head slightly in a gesture of respect. "I want to make a challenge, Beta."

Sweet sat back on her haunches. Raising an elegant hind leg she scratched long and painstakingly at her ear, then sat still again, studying his eyes. "Very well," she said crisply. "Who do you wish to fight?"

"Snap," Lucky told her.

There was a hint of an amused gleam in Sweet's soft eyes.

"Good luck," she said with a huffing laugh, and she stood on

453

all four paws and surveyed the clearing. "Packmates! Hear me!"

Surprise and curiosity showed in the dogs' faces as they hushed and turned to face her. Ears pricked and tails thumped expectantly.

"Lucky the City Dog challenges Snap the hunter," announced Sweet simply.

Snap's eyes widened as she rolled onto her front. "He does?"

Lucky padded forward from Sweet's side, and dipped his head politely toward Snap.

She gave a small, sharp bark. "You're in a hurry to challenge, new dog."

Is it that obvious? Lucky wondered, as he heard an amused whine on the other side of the camp. "The City Dog must be tired of living." It was Mulch.

Lucky ignored him and gave Snap a gruff bark. "I want to rise in this Pack. I may as well start now."

Snap's reply was a silky growl. "You won't rise too far. But every dog is free to try."

Glancing back, Lucky saw nothing in Alpha's eyes but cynical amusement. Alpha was so far above the others, Lucky realized, their petty challenges meant nothing to him—except perhaps as entertainment.

"Fight me, then." Snap rose and stood squarely before Lucky, her muscles tight as drawn-back branches, white teeth bared.

Her eyes were bright and hard and unafraid, Lucky realized, wondering if he'd bitten off more than he could gnaw. But it was too late to turn back now, and besides, it was a risk he was always going to have to take. He curled back his own muzzle as his hackles stiffened.

Sweet stepped forward, her tail high and her muzzle raised. "Before we begin, do you both understand the consequences? That if Lucky wins, he will join the hunters in Snap's place?"

Lucky said, "Yes," at the same time that Snap growled, "It will not happen!"

"May the Sky-Dogs look with blessing on your combat!" Sweet barked formally. "May your fight be fair, and may the outcome be favored by the Spirit Dogs. When the battle is done, we all remain Packmates. And we all shall protect the Pack!"

Just when Lucky thought Sweet's proclamation might go on forever, the swift-dog closed her muzzle. *Thank the Sky-Dogs there was nothing more for her to say,* he thought. *I'm nervous enough as it is!*

"On my word." Sweet sat down, studying each dog for a long moment. "Now—fight!"

They sprang, claws raking for each other's weak spots: noses, ears, eyes. Snap was a tan-and-white blur, moving quickly, her ears perked forward and her tail curling over her back. She cannoned into Lucky, slamming the breath from his body, and making them roll over and over. She was trying to beat him with shock before they even started, he thought, but that wasn't going to work. Springing back to his paws, he flung her off and circled her warily.

Snap too was upright again, but now she was more cautious. Lucky was a good bit bigger, and as his paws found a slight rise in the ground he took advantage, pouncing from above, teeth gnashing at her tail.

"Watch out for his dirty city tactics, Snap!" Mulch barked.

Snap was fast, though. She yelped and wriggled from beneath Lucky, aiming a snap of her jaws at his flank. He dodged just in time, feeling them scrape along his fur and skin. Snap rolled and leaped back, then darted swiftly under his belly for another nip. An excited yelping rose from the crowd of dogs around them. "Nicely done, Snap!" Fiery barked in approval.

Snarling, Lucky lunged, driving her off, then hopped back a couple of paces. Snap was quick, and had surprisingly strong jaws. She was a trickier opponent than he had expected her to be—but as he'd predicted, she did not have the viciousness of Mulch.

She fought not to hurt or maim her opponent. She fought only for the victory.

Still, Lucky knew she would sink her teeth into his flesh if she needed to.

He growled, slinking sideways to keep her in his sight. This time, when she shot forward for another quick strike, he had time to dodge and lunge for her, grabbing her by the scruff of her neck and shaking hard before releasing her. Snap scuttled out of reach again, panting and snarling. An excited yapping came from the pups. "So fast, Mama!" one said, and Lucky heard Moon give a low bark of agreement.

"Do you give up, City Dog?" Even as Snap caught her breath she was grinning, tongue lolling. "You might be big, but you're very naive."

"Finish him off!" Mulch again, sounding like he wished he were in the fight himself.

Lucky glared a warning at Snap as he stalked, drool dripping from his own jaws. Once again she was quick as Lightning's fire, shooting under him to bite at his hind leg. The move was one he had never seen in the city, and the pain was sharp and hot. Lucky yelped—as much in anger as in pain—and twisted to lash his jaws, catching her ear between his teeth. Snap squealed, but he did not let go, rolling her over with his sheer weight.

Lucky heard a growl of protest from Fiery. "Don't let him take you down, Snap!"

"Release!" Snap screamed as blood began flowing from her ear. "Release!"

"Release," commanded Sweet, and reluctantly Lucky loosened his jaw. It might have been a dirty trick to hang on to Snap's tender ear flesh, but he was a City Dog—as they never tired of telling him—and he would do what he needed to do to get his victory. The Earth-Dog could take their sense of honor!

The other dogs were barking their opinions at both of them, making suggestions that were almost entirely useless. "Not a fair move," Lucky heard in Fiery's deep bark. "Don't let him get hold of you like that, Snap."

"Keep her on the run, Lucky," Twitch yelped, and Lucky twitched his ear in irritation—what did the other dog *think* he was trying to do?

Some dogs were simply yelping their support for Lucky or Snap—and mostly Snap, Lucky noticed. He let his eyes sail briefly over the watching dogs. The only one not barking or yelping encouragement was Omega.

The little dog just sat on his haunches, watching everything through narrowed eyes—somehow as if he wasn't seeing the fight at all.

Lucky turned back to his opponent, feeling himself beginning to tire. He had to finish this.

As Snap bared her teeth once more, he was ready; he didn't want those sharp white fangs in his hide again, but he had to tempt her in. This time, when she leaped for him, he didn't side-step her but let her fasten on his shoulder, then whipped his head around to grab the same ear he'd wounded before. Snap howled, but Lucky gave her no time to plead with Sweet. He flung her onto her back and pinned her down with a forepaw to her throat. Her legs kicked and scrabbled, but her claws couldn't reach his belly.

Through a mouthful of ear he snarled, "Yield!"

Snap yelped with pain and fury, but he released her ear only to snatch a fold of skin at her throat. He shook her. "Yield!"

Very suddenly, Snap went limp, and her tail thudded on the ground behind him. She lifted her paws, letting them hang in the air as she sullenly growled, "I yield."

The clearing was absolutely silent, every pair of eyes fixed on them as Lucky released Snap and stepped back. The tan-and-white dog rolled onto her paws and struggled up, shaking off the indignity. Her flanks heaved, but so did his. They were both panting from the struggle.

A great gray shadow paced between the ranks of watching dogs; it was the first time Lucky had seen Alpha get off his rock for anything other than to eat or sleep, or to fight. Lucky gave him a wary glance, but the dog-wolf sat down on his haunches beside Sweet, looking from one combatant to the other.

"Impressive," he rumbled, his yellow eye sparking with fire, "for a City Dog. Snap, you are now demoted one rank. Lucky takes your place as hunter."

Lucky risked eye contact with his defeated opponent. She was expressionless, and for a horrible moment he thought she might fly at him again, or attack when he turned his back. But after one long, cool look, she lowered her ears and dipped her head.

"I will ask him to teach me some of those City Dog moves, Alpha," she remarked dryly. "Congratulations, Lucky."

A flood of relief went through him, together with a thrill at his victory. Lucky let his tongue loll, baring his teeth happily, and lowered his head to accept her lick. "I will be glad to show you a few. If you teach me to move as fast as you can."

"Done." Snap's jaw opened cheerfully too.

"Yes, you both fought well. Now you can stop stroking each other's backs," snapped Alpha. "As for the rest of the Pack: It has been clear that Lucky was needed on the patrol, in place of Moon, but he's a hunter now. Mulch?"

Startled, the black dog took a pace forward. "Yes, Alpha?"

"You are now demoted," said the dog-wolf brusquely. "You will patrol with Dart and Twitch from this no-sun."

"What?" Mulch's surprise and anger must have got the better of his good sense. "Alpha, that is not fair! Demote *Spring*; she's lower than me!"

Lucky heard a faint rumble of anger from Twitch's sister, but she kept her head bowed and her eyes low. She knew better than to stick her snout into another dog's argument with Alpha.

"Not anymore," Alpha growled. "Beta, explain to Mulch that he should not question my decisions."

Sweet bounded forward to give Mulch's nose a sharp bite that drew blood. He sat back on his haunches, shocked, his eyes dazed with pain, and she gave him a clout with her paw for good measure.

"Moon's pup Fuzz could have understood that," she told him sharply. "So I hope you can. Understand?"

"Yes, Beta," he whined.

"You have not been my best hunter," said Alpha, with more than a hint of threat in his voice, "to put it mildly. If you are so keen to climb the ranks, you should try harder, instead of whining about other dogs."

Lucky had got his breath back after the fight, but the tension in the camp was making his flanks heave nervously. *I just wanted to rise a few ranks,* he thought. *I didn't mean to cause all of this.*

"I'll see how he does on patrol," Sweet barked. "And take that look off your face, Mulch. You have had this coming since you tried to take Snap's place in the feeding. Accept it and learn—it will make you a better dog in the future."

Mulch was trembling as Alpha and Sweet stalked back to the central rock, but Lucky knew it wasn't only from fear. Sure enough, as soon as they were out of earshot, Mulch slunk to his side.

"You did this to me," he snarled in Lucky's ear. "Watch your scabby back, City Dog."

Lucky watched him creep away, all the more glad that it was not Mulch who he had challenged. *That could have gotten even nastier. . . .*

He did not have time to dwell on Mulch's animosity, because the rest of the Pack was crowding around him—even Snap— wagging their tails and giving him friendly barks and licks, congratulating him on his rise in status.

"You really deserve it," said Twitch. "That was some impressive fighting." Lucky saw Moon and Fiery exchange a skeptical glance—did they think he had used unfair moves?—but soon Dart and Spring had blocked them from his view as they eagerly added their praises.

Even as he yelped and licked them in return, Lucky could not shake the feeling that the dogs were seeking his favor to ensure that he did not pick on them in the future.

They're watching their own backs, Lucky thought. *Every wag of their tails is . . . tactical.* Unlike the Leashed Dogs, Alpha's followers were not bound together by affection, but by dependence. Personal loyalty was not as important as survival.

Lucky bit back a whine of frustration and confusion. *I'm not sure I like the struggle against one another here,* he thought. *But does this Pack have a better chance of surviving?*

CHAPTER FIFTEEN

"*Where do you think you're going,* Lucky?" Spring turned to blink at him, one ear cocked and one paw raised. "You're not sleeping in that drafty old patrol den anymore."

Once again he felt the stares of the whole Pack on him, and Lucky's skin went hot beneath his fur. Retreating from his old sleeping place, he followed Spring and Snap to a larger pile of leaves in the cozier shade of the hunting dogs' den. The snug hollow had been scraped deeper and filled with moss and rotted bark as well as leaves and soft pine branches, and it was certainly a good few paw-paces up from the beds of the patrol dogs.

As he turned his ritual circle, Lucky sent a prayer to the Forest-Dog for safety in his sneaky deception. The Sun-Dog and the Moon-Dog might not approve of what he had just done to Mulch—maybe even the Sky-Dogs would not like it—but he hoped the Forest-Dog at least would appreciate the daring that had lifted him in the ranks, the cunning and trickery that was preserving his fur so far. In the Great Howl that night, Lucky had thought he caught the quick movement of the Forest-Dog running through the undergrowth and felt for a moment a sense of approval, warm as the sun.

The recess where he settled to sleep reeked of Mulch's dark and musky scent, and he felt a flash of guilt. But he couldn't allow that to last. Lucky was not happy that he had to deceive them, but he *had* played by the Pack rules—and that was what Mulch must do too. If he wanted his place back, thought Lucky sternly, he could fight for it.

Fiery's bulk shifted beside him as the huge dog grunted and began snoring. He had been no more friendly to Lucky after the fight, but at least he had not been antagonistic either. Snap and Spring, who slept on his other side, had welcomed him into the hunting division with some warmth.

"We can use your quick moves hunting," Snap had said, as Spring wagged her agreement. "And your cleverness as well." Lucky admired Snap enormously for that. The rest of the Pack—the patrol dogs and the humble little Omega—had definitely gained respect for him, and they had treated him with deference today, though he was glad to realize his friendship with Twitch still seemed intact.

There was only one problem, he realized with a horrible suddenness. He wasn't on patrol anymore . . . so sneaking out of the camp to see Bella was going to be more difficult from now on. Lucky felt a burning tingle in his belly—he had got so caught up in rising through the ranks, he hadn't stopped to consider that he might actually be creating a problem for himself. Resting his muzzle on his forepaws, he pricked his ears and gazed up at the stars. How many nights had it been since he'd seen Bella? The Leashed Dog Pack could be in serious trouble, and he would have no idea.

They could also have found clean water of their own by now. What if Bella came out every night to meet Lucky, to tell him that it was fine to return, that he did not have to spy on the Wild Pack anymore, but Lucky could not get the message because he could not speak with his litter-sister? Would he be stuck here, in Alpha's Pack, forever?

And would that *really* be a bad thing?

He heaved a sigh. The black sky of no-sun was clear and cloudless, the stars pinpricks of glittering clear-stone. Lucky could make out all the constellations: the wily Rabbit, the Wolf and her Cub, the Great Tree, and the Running Squirrel. They seemed to spin above him, whirling and taunting, until his eyelids began to droop and sleep fuzzed his brain.

Distantly, a sound pierced his doze: the caw of a crow among the trees. In an instant Lucky was awake again. On one side of him Fiery snored mightily; on the other, heaped against each other, Snap's and Spring's flanks rose and fell with the steady rhythm of deep sleep.

He'd never known crows to be so fond of no-sun. But it reminded him he wanted to try to see Bella, to find out if he needed to go on with this deception. The Moon-Dog was climbing the sky now.

Heart pounding, Lucky eased up and slunk between the others' sleeping forms. His breath caught in his throat when Fiery's leg twitched twice, but after a moment the big dog's snores rumbled again like the Sky-Dogs' thunder. He was just dreaming.

Stepping carefully on the softest moss and moldy leaves, Lucky picked his way with painful slowness out of the hunters' den. From the position of the Great Tree and the height of the Moon-Dog, he thought it must be Dart's turn on watch; but she was looking for enemies trying to get into the camp. She would never expect an enemy trying to sneak *out*.

All he had to do was stay low, keep to the undergrowth, and be silent. So long as he did not trip over Dart as she made her rounds, he should be able to get safely away from the clearing. Then it was an easy run to the longpaw camp, and he would have plenty of time before the Moon-Dog yawned and went to sleep.

A twig cracked under his paw, and his heart almost stopped. But no dog stirred, and he placed one paw after another cautiously, scared with every step that he would make a noise that would wake one of his Pack. He had to crouch low to avoid the branches, too, and that did not make it any easier to be silent. But at last he was beyond the thickest of the undergrowth, and could stand tall again, and spring into a scamper.

It was a relief to stretch his legs and run, after the dreadful, tense creep-and-crawl out of the camp. Lucky breathed in the cool air of no-sun as he bounded through the trees and across the meadow. The stars above him, the solid ground beneath his feet, and the smell of the forest: This was perfect. This was how he was meant to be. Free and happy. No one watching him or expecting his aid. Alone!

Craaarrrk!

That no-sun crow again! Now he remembered seeing it before on his travels, and he was more certain than ever that it was a messenger of the Forest-Dog, sent to keep him in order.

He wished he could understand its messages better.

His happy heart plummeted when he caught the first scent of the longpaw camp, and he slowed to a jogging pace, then a steady plod. *Oh, Sky-Dogs, what am I doing?*

Once inside the camp he stood still beside an overturned table, sniffing the air. It was hard to tell through the old reek of charred wood and meat, but he was sure Bella was not here. A wasted journey, then.

So why did he feel this swamping sense of relief?

Lucky was tempted to pad away as fast as he could. If Bella had not made it here tonight, that was not his fault. He could put off his treachery for another journey of the Sun-Dog.

He had already begun to turn when a flash of pale fur caught his eye. Hesitating, he looked back. Two small, familiar figures were squirming out from beneath another toppled table, panting with excitement.

"Lucky!" Sunshine's yelp was quieter than usual, he was glad to hear.

"Sunshine. Daisy!" Despite his uneasiness, Lucky felt his heart stir with warmth at the sight of the two Leashed Dogs. He crouched to lick their faces as they both jumped up to greet him. Then his heartbeat skipped. "Where is Bella? Has something happened to her?"

"No, no—nothing bad has happened!" Sunshine whined happily as she nuzzled his nose. "Bella's fine. She sent us to meet you."

Daisy jumped in. "She has a special mission of her own. So she sent us in her place!" Lucky could see that the little dog was almost bursting with pride.

Lucky felt his eyes narrow. "What is she up to now?" It was not like Bella to hand over control to the most junior members of her Pack; he was sure she would have wanted to talk to him herself if she could.

"Bella has a brilliant plan," said Daisy. "We have to trust her!"

Lucky cocked his head doubtfully—*Bella's recent "brilliant plans" have brought us a lot of trouble*—but the little dogs' eyes gleamed with suppressed excitement. He could not cope with any more scheming, anyway; not right now, when he was still deep in the heart of the Wild Pack. Whatever it was, Bella could deal with it on her own this time.

"All right. I will tell you what I have seen." He licked his chops. "Will you remember it all to take back to Bella?"

"Between us we will," yelped Daisy eagerly.

It seemed he had little choice. It felt strange reporting back to these two inexperienced Leashed Dogs, especially now that he had lived with a true disciplined Pack, but he carefully recounted all that he had done and seen since he last spoke to Bella, including the terrifying encounter with the yellow-furred longpaws, his challenge to Snap, and his promotion.

"But that . . . that is so strange," said Sunshine, awed. "Do you have to fight all the time in that Pack?"

Lucky squirmed inwardly. "Not all the time, Sunshine. Just . . . when we want to rise in the Pack." Said like that, to these friendly dogs with their easygoing solidarity, it sounded silly and aggressive.

But Daisy cheered him. "Oh, Lucky! You're so brave!" She gave a happy yelp. "And so clever!"

Sunshine panted up at him, adoring, her misgivings instantly forgotten. "Now you will be able to find out even more about our enemies!"

"Yes . . ." Lucky found he didn't like that phrase. The Wild Pack did not *feel* like his enemies—most of them, anyway. And he did not want enemies any more than he wanted a Pack.

The two went together, he supposed.

"We will let Bella know," yapped Daisy. "She will be so proud of you!"

Lucky ignored this, and asked, "How is Bruno? And Martha?"

Sunshine's dark eyes veered away, as if the edge of the clearing was suddenly the most interesting thing in the world. Daisy sat back and scratched her belly.

"They are getting better, but they need more time. Martha's leg wound was really very, very bad."

"And Bruno was so unwell," put in Sunshine. "Thank the Sky-Dogs that you were there to save him, Lucky, or he might have choked!"

Lucky whined in confusion. "They should be getting better by now. Especially Martha . . ."

"Oh, there was some poison in her leg. Maybe from swimming! She is getting better, but it's taking longer than we thought it would."

Sunshine still avoided meeting his eye, and Lucky felt a tremor of sick anxiety in his belly. Poison in a wound? That might get better if Martha licked it well, but what if the poison got too deeply into her leg? And Bruno . . .

"They are going to be fine, Lucky. Don't worry."

Sunshine, usually so full of drama whether it was good or bad, sounded quite flat. Lucky could not shake the feeling that she was lying to him—but why? Could the news be worse than they were letting on? It seemed the only explanation: that they were trying to protect him from some kind of horrible truth.

Martha, Bruno. You came so far with me. Please be all right.

Did he have time to go back to Bella's Pack and see for him-self? The Moon-Dog was padding languidly across the sky, the time of no-sun coming to an end. But perhaps . . .

"Lead me to the camp," he told them. "I really should talk to Bella. And maybe I can help Martha and Bruno."

"She's not finished with her mission," Daisy yipped, her tongue lolling. "And the Sun-Dog will be up and running soon."

Lucky whined his agreement. He did have to get back to the hunters' den.

I'll just have to trust Sunshine and Daisy.

"Then I guess I should get back," he said, "before anyone wakes up and realizes I'm gone." He licked Daisy's ears affection-ately. "When I do come back, I'll have some great hunting tricks to show everybody. We will never be hungry again."

"You'll be a terrific teacher, Lucky," Daisy said. "You always are."

"It has been so good to see you, Lucky!" yipped Sunshine. She looked mournful. "We miss you a lot. Especially me and Daisy."

"That's why we offered to come in Bella's place," said Daisy with a whine of agreement.

"I miss you, too," Lucky assured them, caressing their heads fondly with his tongue. "But it will not be forever. I'll be back as soon as I can." *I hope so, anyway.*

As he licked and yipped his farewells and trotted away into the woods again, he felt sick with worry.

Earth-Dog, we already lost Alfie. Surely you can't want two more of my friends. Not now.

Lucky could barely focus on the sounds of the forest around him, on the stir of leaves and the rustle of small beasts in the undergrowth. It was only when a bigger shadow flickered through the bushes that he was finally jolted out of his unhappy thoughts.

Another longpaw? he thought, his heart thudding.

No, too small for a longpaw. All the same, Lucky stopped, ears pricked, and gave a soft growl.

A small fox, perhaps, on its nightly hunt. As long as it was alone, and had not brought friends, it was not a threat Lucky needed to worry about. . . .

But the shadow was creeping closer through the dense bracken, and from its rustling and occasional snuffling he could tell it was not nearly as cautious as a fox. Stiffening, Lucky yipped a challenge.

A squat, ugly little face shoved out through the leaves. It was not a fox, but the black eyes glinted with just as much cunning.

"Omega," breathed Lucky, shocked. "What are you doing out here?"

"I could ask *you* the same question," said Omega, his bark high-pitched and impudent. "You are not a patrol dog anymore. Are you, Lucky?"

"I . . . I . . ."

"You don't have to explain yourself to me," said Omega. "I *saw* you sneaking out of the camp."

Lucky thought his heart had actually stopped beating. Omega looked so smug, and the instinctive knowledge struck Lucky that if any member of the Pack had to find him out, Omega was the worst. "I just needed to be alone for a bit."

"Is that right?" That glint in Omega's eye was not friendly. "If you needed to be alone, why were you meeting up with the Leashed Dogs?"

Lucky instinctively glanced over his shoulder before he realized that he had just confirmed Omega's suspicions. His heart thudded in his chest as his panic rose. "But I didn't—"

"Yes, you did, you Liar Dog. Did you enjoy spending time with the little fluffy dogs? All that licking! Ugh!"

He did see me.

Omega sounded unbearably smug. "You are a spy for that

475

Pack. I have known all about it right from the start."

No! thought Lucky. *That is not possible!*

There was a horrible trickle of suspicion in his gut, though. That scent he had caught, when he and Bella had first discussed her plan . . . the half-drowned smell he could not quite place, the paw prints he could not identify. Could it have been Omega, sneaking around alone, ignored by his Pack as always?

"You spied on us!" Lucky exclaimed, and instantly knew how stupid that sounded.

"I do not spy," Omega sneered. "*I'm* better than that."

Lucky had nothing to say. There was nothing he *could* say. He did not know which was stronger: the fear, or the horrible shame.

"I was confused in the storm," the small dog went on. "The rain was so fierce that night, I thought the River-Dog was going to rise and drown the whole world. I got lost and I wanted to hide until it was over. It was your bad luck I happened to be hiding near you and your friend."

"Bad luck," echoed Lucky bleakly.

"Bad luck. Well, either that or the Sky-Dogs led me to you."

I would not be surprised, Lucky thought. *They probably never approved of what I was doing. . . .* "You're going to tell the others, I suppose?"

He wondered how fast he could get himself and Bella's Pack

away from here, and how far they would have to go to be safely beyond the fury of Alpha.

"Actually, I haven't decided yet." Omega sat down and scratched an ear in satisfaction. "A lot depends on you."

Lucky did not think his heart could sink further, but he was wrong. It plummeted like a heavy stone in still water. "What do you mean?"

"If you help me, I'll help you." Omega snickered. "Well, at least I won't get you killed. I do not like being Omega. I'm not Omega; my name is Whine."

Lucky swallowed. His spit tasted of fear, but he understood the small dog's attitude. He would not want to lose his own name, be called "Omega" in that contemptuous way by the whole Pack. It had never even occurred to him to ask the Omega what his real name was, and he felt ashamed of it now. "I wouldn't like it, either," he admitted.

"I want a proper place in the Pack." Omega padded back and forth, licking his chops. His face was so squashed and ugly, drool kept escaping and dripping from his jaws. "I have been Omega for far too long—taking orders, fetching, and carrying! And half-starving too, since nobody ever leaves enough food for me!"

"I tried to—"

"Not very hard. Not when Sweet ordered you to stop. And why would you leave food for an Omega anyway? Every Pack needs an Omega. I just want it to be a dog who is not me."

Lucky remembered the way the other Pack members treated the flat-nosed dog: as if he were barely a dog at all, sometimes. They would have given more respect to a sharpclaw.

"I want to help, but what can I do?" he said, cocking his head sympathetically. And he really did want to help. It was not just that he felt sorry for Omega; the simple fact was, he could not let this ugly, sneaky dog go back and tell Alpha his secret. He had to make some kind of a deal—it was that, or kill the little dog.

And Lucky knew there was no way he could ever do that.

And that is one more reason why I will never be fit for Pack life. I certainly could never be an Alpha. The thought did not displease him. It probably went against his dog-spirit—and no doubt it was a result of his Lone Dog life and his bond with the Leashed Dogs—but at least he knew that he would never sink so low as to kill another dog.

Lucky sighed. "It is a pity you're not with the Leashed Pack yourself," he remarked. "You would be happier there. No dog has to be Omega in their camp."

"I am no Leashed Dog." Omega's squat muzzle wrinkled even more with contempt. "But I will be of higher status than I am now, and you are going to help me get my promotion."

"I want to help you, Whine. And I suppose I don't have a choice, anyway."

"No," Whine grumbled arrogantly.

"I still don't see what you think I can do for you."

"It should be obvious—especially to a Street Dog like you." Whine licked idly at a paw. "Nothing I do is ever going to impress Alpha. I can't lie to myself about that. But if another dog behaves badly enough, or does something really stupid or dangerous . . ."

"Alpha will demote *that* dog to Omega," Lucky finished, a chill running through his fur.

"Exactly. Oh, and you shouldn't panic—I am not expecting *you* to sacrifice yourself. If I asked that, you might just kill me."

I would not, thought Lucky, *but I'm glad you have that wrong.*

"Since you are a hunter now, you will be perfectly placed. When you bring back food tomorrow, all you have to do is make it look as if another dog has stolen some before the others get to it. You know how much Alpha hates that."

"Yes . . ." agreed Lucky dismally.

"Anyone who eats before Alpha is going to go straight to the bottom of the heap."

Anyone who eats before Alpha will be fortunate if that is all that happens to them, thought Lucky. "Why can't you just do it yourself?"

"Because I have *you* to do it for me, obviously. Look, the risk is much less for you; you must see that. If you get caught in the act, you will be demoted, but you'll soon have clean paws again. You can do something clever, or keep using your charm on Beta. Dogs like you are always . . ." He gave an amused whine as he finished his sentence: " . . . *lucky.*" Sitting down, thumping his stubby tail, Whine wrinkled the corner of his mouth.

"Do not insult me," snarled Lucky, ignoring the sting of truth. "Remember, for this to work, you need me!"

"You need me even more. Or rather, you need me to be *nice* to you." Whine's eyes gleamed with arrogant triumph. "You know I'm right, Street Dog. You wouldn't be risking nearly as much as I would."

Lucky took a deep breath. He knew he could not lose his temper.

"If it happens, you will work your way back up eventually," Whine went on. "But how can Alpha demote a dog who is already at the bottom? It would be simpler for him to just kill me."

Lucky knew in the pit of his stomach that Whine was right. He had no choice. There was no way he could allow the Omega dog to reveal his secret, or it was Lucky who would probably be killed. So yet again, he was going to have to do the bidding of another dog, and if anything this job was even more dishonorable than the one that Bella had given him. Lucky felt a surge of desire to be on his own again, free of all these terrible demands that were being placed on him.

Why did I get myself into this?

In fact, he did feel sorry for Whine, despite his cunning and his dangerous threats. Maybe it was time someone else took a turn at being Omega—they would soon work their way back up the Pack once more, but at least Whine would have had a taste of higher status, and might even be encouraged to try harder in the future.

"All right," he said at last.

"I knew you would help!" For a moment Whine looked happy, his eyes bulging with excitement. His tail thumped the ground, but then he seemed to realize he was giving too much away. He stilled and closed his smiling jaws. "Thank you. I will see you back at the camp. And be quick."

With a new bounce in his step, Whine turned and trotted off into the undergrowth. Lucky sagged with relief as he watched him go, but he could not calm the churning misery inside him.

Who was he going to target? He had friends and comrades in the Pack; they trusted him.

But I have no choice!

He was more certain than ever that, as soon as he could free himself from both of these Packs, he was leaving. He was going back to being a Street Dog, a Lone Dog—a happy dog.

In the meantime, he had to go through with all his deceptions. *I am doing this for Bruno and Martha,* he told himself firmly. *It does not make me a bad dog, or an evil one. I'm just tangled up in a mess, and there are things I have to do to get out of it.*

It was all about survival for Lucky now.

The world has changed. For a skin-shivering instant, he thought the Forest-Dog himself had whispered in his ear.

Yes, the world *had* changed. And Lucky needed to do whatever it took to stay alive, to see the Sun-Dog rise and stretch again. Once he had achieved this, then . . .

Then he was going to be free of *all* of them.

CHAPTER SIXTEEN

Lucky watched as the patrols left camp the next day. He was resting in the snug hunters' den, Snap's warm back against his. Fiery was standing up and stretching in the misty morning light, his tail thumping slowly with contentment. Lucky pricked his ears, his nerves singing inside his skin as Mulch padded by. The black dog showed no open hostility, but there was a sullen look on his face as he glanced at Lucky.

Lucky found himself enjoying his new status, now that Twitch wasn't constantly dragging him out to check the boundaries or keep an alert eye on Moon and the pups. His first long, lazy day as a hunter would have been easy and trouble-free, had his neck fur not prickled every time Omega slunk into sight. Once or twice the cringing dog cast Lucky a look that was sly and knowing. *Stop it!* Lucky thought. *You don't want any of the other dogs to notice.* He wasn't sure Omega was clever enough to hide his newfound satisfaction.

The Sun-Dog was loping lazily down the sky and the shadows were lengthening by the time Fiery barked gruffly, summoning the hunters. Lucky didn't resent this command. His new role and higher status excited him; besides, his blood thrilled at the thought of a hunt. *Let's get started!* He was first to Fiery's side, and when Snap and Spring joined them they all trotted out of the camp with ears and tails held high.

The sunlight was still warm, and the Sun-Dog cast golden shadows that dappled the landscape and sprinkled the lake like glittering clear-stone. It could not have been a better evening for him to begin, Lucky thought: With any luck their prey would be drowsy and off-guard after the heat of the day. He hoped he'd make a good first impression, and prove himself worthy of his promotion.

Lucky was relieved to discover that Fiery was a good leader. He didn't waste time or effort bossing the other dogs about how to track scents or stay hidden. He trusted them to get on with their jobs. It was so different from Bella's pack, where Lucky'd had to go through the motions of beetle-catching over and over again for Sunshine's benefit. . . .

Fiery was a good hunter, too, even if he wasn't the cleverest of dogs. Watching him and Snap and Spring as they prowled was like watching three paws of a single dog. Lucky realized with pride that he was the fourth paw.

"Stop here," commanded Fiery in a low voice as they approached the edge of the forest. Lucky, Snap, and Spring halted and waited in alert silence. Fiery lifted his muzzle and sniffed the air, one paw raised and trembling slightly with anticipation. Snap and Spring watched him, patient and trusting, and Lucky was happy to go along with their instincts. Later, perhaps, he'd get a chance to prove his own individual skills—the way he could silently pad up to a prey, or snap a neck with his jaws.

At last Fiery glanced back at them all and nodded. "Twitch reported a few deer here this morning. Let's be quiet."

Lucky and Spring followed Fiery as Snap slunk quietly off to the side, soon disappearing into the undergrowth. Twitch had been right, Lucky realized as his nose prickled with the musky scent of large prey animals. He was determined not to let down the hunting group, but he was confident too. *I'm good at hunting, no matter how much they sneer at my old city life.* Deer were fast, sure enough—but so were rabbits, and a deer made a bigger target.

Spring melted away into the bushes to his left, so that Fiery and Lucky were the only dogs following the main trail. The pungent scent of deer was strong now. When Fiery nodded at him,

Lucky knew immediately what to do; it wasn't unlike the times when he'd join up with other City Dogs, just for a hungry night or two, to hunt in a group. Lucky followed the rules and tricks he'd learned then; he separated from his leader, taking a wide circle but keeping Fiery in view.

A ray of sunlight through the branches burnished a furry golden flank; leaf and branch litter rustled beneath delicate hooves. Three of them, Lucky counted, and the deer were still browsing, unaware. He went entirely still as a slender head lifted to snuff the air. Suddenly there was alarm in the buck's huge, dark eye.

But it wasn't Lucky's scent the buck had caught. It leaped with a flash of white tail, and the hinds followed, but they were fleeing from Spring at the far side of the clearing—and toward Lucky. The buck bounded, crashing through bracken and brush, the two hinds following in a panic, but one hind was slower than the other, and was dashing in a straight line between Fiery and Lucky.

Lucky's blood raced as he smelled her fear, his muscles tightening. He sprang at the same time as Fiery, and they fell on the hind together. Lucky's teeth closed on her flank as Fiery seized her throat, and the deer stumbled and went down with a high squeal of terror.

Lucky held on grimly on as she kicked and struggled, but Snap and Spring were with them now too, piling onto the struggling prey. As Fiery held the hind down, her eyes lost their terrified light and she sank down into the undergrowth, kicking feebly. Lucky couldn't help feeling a thrill of pleasure at their success. They'd hunted well.

When the fight had gone from the hind completely, and she went limp and heavy with death, Fiery drew back. He was panting with effort, but clearly pleased.

"Well done, Lucky," he said gruffly. "And you two. That was fine flushing."

"Alpha's going to be happy with this," Snap barked.

"Don't relax," growled Fiery. "He will be happy, but we can do better. Let's prove it! The gopher meadow next. Spring, you guard this prey."

Fiery was right. As Lucky had suspected, it was a particularly good evening for hunting: warm enough to draw out small animals into the open, but with a light breeze that kept the dogs' scent from their prey. They caught two rabbits and a sleepy gopher before Fiery was content, and even as they returned to Spring and the deer, Snap caught sight of a weasel that froze and bared its teeth before losing its nerve. When it scurried into a rabbit burrow Lucky thought they'd lost their prey, but Snap wormed her way after it and reemerged with an earth-spattered head and a limp stoat in her jaws.

She's surprisingly nimble, thought Lucky in admiration. *I don't know many dogs who could have followed a weasel down that hole. Or many dogs who would have dared. . . .*

Spring, still dutifully guarding the dead deer, barked a greeting as they trotted back to her with their haul. "No trouble. A fox liked the look of this deer, but I made him change his mind!"

"Good," said Fiery. "I knew I could count on you, Spring. Now let's get back to the Pack. The pups are growing fast now, and Moon will be hungry."

There was a note of fierce pride in the huge dog's voice, and Lucky felt a new affection for Fiery—and his pups—steal into his heart. Besides, he'd seen how Spring's rib cage swelled with pleasure at Fiery's compliment. The big brown dog was a fine leader in all kinds of ways.

Alpha and Sweet and Fiery each have their own methods, he mused. *Their ways are different. But all of them manage their parts of the Pack unchallenged.* Lucky stored the knowledge away. *I'm not going to be in a Pack forever, but still—there are lessons here worth learning.*

It was hard work dragging the deer back to camp together

with the rest of their prey, but Fiery was big enough to do most of the heavy work, helped by Lucky. He took hold of a hoof in his jaws and pulled it along, the hardness of the hoof clattering against his teeth. The other dogs gripped the smaller prey. Saliva pooled in Lucky's mouth at the taste of deer flank, but he knew better than to risk a bite—and he was surprised to find himself unwilling to take any share before he was with his Pack. *Strange,* he thought, *but it does feel right to wait. . . .*

The feeling intensified inside him when they reached the camp, where the other dogs bounded out to greet them with delight. They barked and whined in excitement, praising the hunters' skills and yelping with appreciation.

"Well done!" Twitch said, looking at Lucky.

"That will feed all of us—with leftovers!" Dart agreed.

"Moon will be pleased," Fiery said smugly, letting the deer fall. "Our pups are getting big and hungry."

Lucky's proudest moment, though, was when Sweet padded up to him and licked his ear. "Fiery told me how much you contributed to this catch," she murmured. "I'm glad you rose to be a hunter, Lucky."

They dumped their prey beside a pine at the edge of the camp and Lucky withdrew and lay down, panting. He was tired, but it was a good sort of exhaustion from a job well done. His feelings were mixed as he watched the rest of the Pack play and squabble and stretch aching limbs. He was still so worried about Martha and Bruno, not to mention his uncertainty about Bella's intentions, but he couldn't help this sense of contentment that stole over him. It was good to have a role here, to know his place, and to be appreciated for the skills he brought with him.

He thought back to Bella's Pack and the chaos that sometimes took over, the way the other dogs had all expected him to lead them in the early days. *Sometimes I just want to be given a job to do,* he thought. *Be part of a team. Not the dog making the decisions.* Of course, Bella was that dog now—but even so. There was part of him that still felt the heavy responsibilities of being involved in that Pack. Here, he didn't have to take charge of anything, and there was something in him that liked it that way.

The bushes rustled, and abruptly his peace was broken. Lucky didn't even have to turn to know who was sidling up to him. His hackles rose automatically, and he stiffened but lay still.

"Hello, Whine," he murmured. "What do you want?"

The little Omega snuffled and licked his chops. "Why, Lucky. I just wanted to ask if there was anything our fine hunter needs?"

"Nothing. Thank you."

"I can bring you anything, as you know. That's my job."

Lucky turned his head sharply. He mustn't anger the snub-faced dog—and that very fact made Lucky angry with himself.

"No, Whine, thank you."

"You must call me Omega," the dog said, with a submissive little whimper that sounded mocking to Lucky's ears. "For now. Until you do what you promised to do, City Dog."

Lucky turned his head, tempted to nip him whatever the consequences, but Omega had vanished into the tree shadows once more. Unhappiness roiled in Lucky's belly; his earlier haze of contentment had vanished altogether.

Omega wasn't going to forget the promise he'd forced Lucky to make, and Lucky couldn't risk Omega telling what he knew. He'd have to eat some of this prey—steal the food he'd been so proud to bring to the Pack—and make one of the other dogs suffer for his own crime.

It has to be the deer, he realized, with a hollow sense of shame. The deer was the most impressive thing the hunters had brought back in days. With that on display, its smell and size so tempting, Alpha might not even notice something like a missing gopher leg. *My crime has to be so bad that the other dogs are stunned.*

He dreaded the horrible task. *You are a liar, Lucky. A liar and a spy and a cheat.*

But he had no choice.

Who to frame, though? Whose life should I destroy? Lucky glanced around the Pack, keeping his face calm and disinterested despite the turmoil in his innards. *Who am I going to sacrifice, just to keep myself and my lies safe and hidden?*

One thing was so clear in his head it hurt: When the choice was made, he'd have to go ahead immediately. No more delays; no more excuses.

Maybe that was why he was putting off the moment of decision. But it didn't matter how often his eyes roamed the other dogs: The choice had been obvious from the start.

Mulch.

Mulch was a known food-stealer. Mulch had pawed selfishly at that rabbit, had tried to sneak an extra portion out of turn. No one would be very surprised if it was Mulch who stole a mouthful or two of deer before it was time to eat. And horribly, Lucky was already plotting the details of his deception. Mulch had long, shiny black hair, distinctive among the others of the Pack. There were already strands of it all over his new sleeping-place among the patrol dogs, but even better—or worse—there were still plenty of them in the hunter's den. The very bed Lucky now slept in was lined with Mulch's molted hairs. How hard could it be to transfer some of those long rippling strands to the deer's pale-gold hide?

How hard can it be, Lucky?

Lucky closed his eyes and shoved his nose beneath his paws, feeling sick. He tried to remember how unfriendly Mulch had been to him since he arrived, but it was no good: He still couldn't bear to think of what he was about to do to an innocent dog.

Strangely enough, what he was about to do to the Pack seemed even worse. He was going to betray their trust, to sow resentment and hatred, to lie to his Packmates. He was more like them than he'd ever known before he began this game of Bella's. He respected them, liked them, trusted them with his life each day . . .

I can't do it. I CAN'T.

But I must, a small, cowardly voice inside him whispered. *I have to do this, or I'll die.*

A great sigh escaped from the depths of his belly. He wasn't just doing this for his own survival—he was doing it to help the Leashed Dogs. He opened his eyes again to gaze around at the Pack.

They're not like me; they're NOT. I don't care. I'm a Lone Dog and I always will be. I survive. That's what I do.

It comes down to one thing. Do I want to go back to being who I really am? Or do I want to give all that up, to be a Pack Dog, to be like Fiery, or Snap, or Sweet . . .

Or Omega.

Lucky shivered. No, he couldn't be lulled into Pack life, just for the fun of a group hunt on a warm evening, or the bone-deep thrill of a Great Howl. Omega could not be allowed to tell his secret; he had to survive, to escape, to be Lucky again. Whatever he had to do must be done. That was all.

I'm never going to feel good about this, he thought, *but I'll just have to live with it—if I want to live at all. Because I'm Lucky, Lone Dog Lucky, and I'm going to survive.*

Before he could gnaw it over for another instant, Lucky stood up. He took a deep breath. Then, shaking himself, stretching lazily and clawing the ground, he padded idly over to the hunters' den and began to scrape at his own soft hollow, as if simply adjusting it to his needs.

Surreptitiously he nosed a few tangled bits of Mulch's hair into a straggly pile. With a deep breath, he licked it into his jaws. It caught on the sensitive flesh inside his mouth, tickled his throat. Lucky wanted to gag, but the horrible sensation of the hair against his teeth was as much to do with his feelings, he decided, as the taste of Mulch's fur.

It didn't matter how carefully he checked that no one was watching; as he crept through scrub toward the tree where the food lay, he felt as if every eye in the Pack was on him—two yellow ones in particular. *Don't look around. Behave naturally!* But when he cast a last glance over his shoulder, he was as sure as he could be that he hadn't been seen. Alpha lay on his favorite rock, his eyes closed and Sweet curled against him. The others were relaxing, grooming one another, exchanging the day's news, settling arguments, playing idle games, or staging mock-fights. The larger of the male pups, Squirm, was wrestling with his sister, Nose, nipping at her with his harmless milk teeth, while the smaller male, Fuzz, chased his tail determinedly, his short legs scrabbling in the dirt. Moon and Fiery watched them proudly, their attention fully focused on their pups.

It was now or never, and never was not an option. Lucky brushed his tongue against the deer's flank, trying to dislodge the hairs in his mouth. He spat and dribbled as best he could, but though some of the hairs had stuck to the deer, more of them had stuck to his teeth, caught in the gaps between them.

No! Lucky began to panic, pawing at his muzzle, clawing at his teeth, all the time trying not to look too agitated in case one of the other dogs noticed. The hairs were sticky and stubborn, clinging to his tongue and the soft skin inside his mouth till he wanted to be sick. And wouldn't that give him away, he thought, half in fear and half in a sort of excitable panic.

At last! One of his claws hooked into the tangled hair and pulled it free of his mouth, and he licked the rest of it against the deer's leg. He rubbed a last strand from his nose.

And now?

Lucky peered around the tree again, his breath in his throat, but still no one was paying any attention to him—not even Omega. *Whine's so sure of himself and his plotting,* Lucky thought with resentment.

There was no more time for guilt. Lucky tore into the deer's belly, ripping open a gash in the hide and then savaging the still-warm meat, gulping down great mouthfuls as fast as he could. He'd helped catch the creature, after all; his scent on the prey would be nothing strange.

He tore, gulped, swallowed; then did it again, and again. *Enough! Surely that's enough? One more bite. Quick, Lucky. HURRY.*

When he could bear the tension no longer, he sprang back

from the hind, his heart beating ferociously. Turning abruptly, he crept hurriedly through the trees and trotted away from the camp boundary.

I'm surprised I'm not falling over my own paws. He was furious at the way his skin and muscles trembled, and the anger helped drive out the fear, just a little.

He bounded to the lakeshore with his blood still racing. There was no time even to drink; he simply dipped his bloody muzzle into the cool water, washing away any possible last traces of Mulch's hair along with the deer blood. Then he loped silently around to the far side of the camp. He paused as long as he dared for breath, then wandered back in as coolly as he could.

If my Packmates could hear my heart, I'd be a dead dog in an instant. But it seemed none of them could. Slowly, so slowly, Lucky's heart stopped pounding, and he lay down in a new spot as if nothing had happened, as if he'd merely moved position out of restlessness.

I've gotten away with it.

Ecstatic relief was swamped almost immediately by horrible guilt, and the terror of what might have been. Noticing Omega slinking across the clearing, Lucky curled his muzzle and gave him a silent snarl that the little dog couldn't see.

He could not doze, as some of the other dogs were doing; his belly was full and his nerves and bones still throbbed with tension. They waited for Alpha's signal to eat, and Lucky felt dread growing with every instant. At last, when Lucky thought he could bear it no longer, Alpha blinked and yawned, rose and stretched, and Sweet stirred beside him.

The great dog-wolf leaped down from the rock and padded to the center of the clearing, his deep bark summoning his Pack.

"Now we eat."

It was the patrol dogs who dragged the prey into the open, and as soon as they did, Lucky saw them exchanging glances, their hackles rising and their tails stiffening. Far more nervously than usual, they dropped the food in the eating place, and hurried back from it as if they couldn't get away fast enough.

They've noticed. They've seen the damage!

They know trouble's coming. . . .

The hind's leg, stiff and straight, sank to the ground as the corpse settled, and Alpha stepped forward.

He stood stiff, foursquare, and silent, and the hush spread to the whole Pack.

The air of the clearing seemed to prickle with invisible fire as Alpha lowered his head to sniff the deer's flank. When he raised it again, his huge teeth were bared, and there was crackling fury in his eyes. Lifting his muzzle, he gave a howl of pure rage.

The silence that fell was unbroken by so much as a cracking twig. Even the birds were silent.

Alpha's growl was deadly.

"Who. Has. Done. This?"

CHAPTER SEVENTEEN

Alpha spun around, the look of violent fury on his face like nothing Lucky had ever seen.

"Who?"

The dog-wolf slammed a paw onto the ground. Jerking to one side, he spat something out. When he raised his head again, he was looking directly at Lucky.

The bolt of cold fear through his bones was so shocking, it was all Lucky could do not to cower and confess. He was desperate to scratch at his muzzle, to remove the black hair he was sure he must have left there. No . . . no, he couldn't have been so careless.

Could wolves read the minds of dogs? Did Alpha know?

Lucky wondered how fast he could run. Not fast enough . . .

The howl of confession was rising in his throat when Alpha took a pace forward. Not toward Lucky, though; his ice-cold eyes were locked on Mulch. With a great swipe of his paw, he sent a clod of earth flying into Mulch's muzzle. When the dirt settled, a hair lay balanced delicately on Mulch's nose.

The bewildered dog shook it off, making his long ears flap. "Alpha?"

Alpha didn't answer, but stalked menacingly close to him.

Mulch cowered. "Alpha, I don't know—"

"Silence!" The dog-wolf's muzzle curled. "Food-thief. Did you think it was your right to eat before Moon's pups? Before ME?"

Mulch's jaws hung open. "I didn't! I never—"

Alpha leaped for Mulch, bowling him over, clawing his face and neck, fangs sinking into his ears. Mulch gave a long howl of terror, scrabbling hopelessly to get out from under the huge beast. He was on his back now, and one of Alpha's hind legs raked cruel claws into his belly. Mulch's howl became a frantic series of agonized yelps.

Lucky wished he could put his paws over his ears. *Stop*, he wanted to bark. *It wasn't him, it was ME....*

No, Lucky. SURVIVE.

The other dogs looked on, shivering, eyes wide, tails low and tight between their legs. Sweet was stiff and trembling at his side. Lucky glanced at her, hoping desperately that she would put a stop this. Drops of Mulch's blood spattered her face as she watched, and her muzzle wrinkled into a snarl.

Now, he thought frantically. *Stop him, Sweet, before it gets worse. No one else will. . . .*

Suddenly the swift-dog leaped forward in a graceful spring, and Lucky almost gasped with relief. *She's stopping him! Oh, thank the Sky-Dogs—*

But he wasn't to get off so lightly, Lucky realized. He gaped as Sweet bared her teeth and sank them into the base of Mulch's tail, renewing his howls of pain. And then Sweet was attacking him too, her jaws snapping at those vulnerable ears as Alpha seized the folds of flesh at Mulch's neck and shook him like a rat.

Lucky couldn't stand it anymore. With a bark of protest he bounded toward the struggling Mulch, but when Sweet took her teeth from Mulch's ear to give him a warning glare, he came to a shocked halt. Her muzzle curled back from her bloodstained fangs, but that wasn't what brought him up short. He was sure he didn't imagine the softness in her dark eyes.

She doesn't want me to get hurt. She's protecting me!

Trembling, he stepped carefully back as Sweet renewed her assault, biting and scratching.

It felt like a turn of the Moon-Dog before Alpha finally

clouted Mulch one last time on the head and stepped back, snarling softly. Sweet sat down beside Alpha, tongue lolling as she gazed at Mulch with contempt.

Mulch rolled onto his belly, but when he tried to crawl away he could only flop, his flanks heaving, a terrible high-pitched whimper coming from his throat. The rest of the Pack watched him with pity, but none of them, Lucky noticed, moved to help him.

"You," growled Alpha at the cringing, wounded dog, "are now Omega."

"Which is more than you deserve," added Sweet, licking blood idly from a forepaw.

"But, Alpha . . ." Mulch's breathless whine was barely audible.

"And since you feel inclined to argue, you may not challenge another dog until a full turn of the Moon-Dog." Alpha flicked the tip of his tail. "Your hairs were on the carcass, Omega. Your hairs. How dare you try to deny it?"

Mulch laid his head on his forepaws, doing his best to raise his haunches, miserably submissive. He had clearly decided it was not worth arguing anymore.

There was a slight coughing sound from the circle of watching dogs, and the former Omega crept forward a little. His bulging eyes flickered briefly to Lucky, but they held no expression.

Don't start thanking me, thought Lucky ferociously. *Don't you dare be so stupid!*

But the little dog was now gazing pathetically up at Alpha, who watched him in scornful silence for a few moments.

"Yes. I suppose you're a patrol dog now, Omega. Or Whine, as we will call you. For now." Turning his back, Alpha padded back toward the prey-heap.

Sweet cast a last disdainful glance at Whine before following her leader. "And try to prove yourself worthy, Whine. For the Sky-Dogs' sake, and your own."

Any appetite Lucky still had after the theft of the deer was gone. He couldn't take his eyes off Mulch as the beaten dog slunk into the bushes to lick his wounds. Lucky had to force himself to join the feeding, lying down miserably next to Twitch.

"Don't feel bad for Mulch," Twitch told him airily. "I mean, Omega. He deserved that."

He didn't, thought Lucky.

When Fiery and Spring had eaten their fill, Lucky had to creep forward and force himself to eat a second full meal, though he was afraid it might choke him. Doing his best to mask his disgust, he ripped mouthful after mouthful from his share of the carcass and gulped it down his tight throat. *I have to eat. It's supposed to be the first I've eaten all day. . . .*

If he had to bring it back up later, he'd do it in secret; but Lucky couldn't let the others suspect that he'd already eaten. There was a thin covering of leaf litter beneath the tree, and he managed to push a few bitefuls beneath that, but he couldn't risk Sweet seeing him do it, so most of it he had to choke down. His body heaved with the effort and he had to concentrate on each swallow. He couldn't even show his relief when he'd eaten enough, and could crawl back from what was left of the hind.

I don't think I'll ever enjoy deer again. . . .

After Snap, Twitch, and Dart had eaten, it was Whine's turn. Lucky had never seen a dog wolf down food with such relish, and he'd had no idea such a small, pathetic dog could cram so much meat into his belly. Obviously the pudgy creature's conscience was clear about what they had done. Despite the abundance of tonight's prey, despite what had been a huge bounty when the Pack began to eat, Whine left scarcely anything for Mulch, and Lucky felt his anger at the sly little dog grow darker and deeper.

If any dog ought to have had sympathy for the new Omega, it should have been the old one. Whine knew what it felt like to go hungry, to be despised and overlooked.

Surely he could have shown a little pity! Lucky felt his muzzle curl as he watched Whine's smug, flat face, still smeared with deer blood. *No, I can't think about him; I'll only get angrier, and I can't afford to do that.*

Lucky could only hope the Great Howl would make him feel better about himself, but as the dogs gathered and the eerie sound swelled into the night sky, his gaze was drawn against his will to Mulch. The newly appointed Omega was trying to join in, but his howls were faint and brief, and he was obviously too weak from his beating to take his Pack-place in the great bonding time. No shadow-dogs bounded across Lucky's vision that night; there was no enchantment in the Great Howl for him.

Mulch—Lucky found it impossible to think of him as Omega—was the first to slink away when the sounds of the Howl had died off. Lucky waited till the rest of the Pack had dispersed to their sleeping-places before he carefully retrieved the meat he'd hidden, then padded across to the uncomfortable shallow scrape where Mulch had to make his new bed. As the branches rustled, Mulch looked up at him, startled.

"What do you want?" There was resentment in the black dog's eyes.

"I brought—" Lucky took a breath. "I brought you food. There was some left."

"That's not allowed." Mulch glared at him suspiciously.

"No one's going to know." Lucky pawed the chunks of flesh closer to Mulch. "I'm certainly not going to confess to Alpha."

Just saying those words sent a tremor of guilt through his spine, but Mulch didn't notice. "Why would I take food from you?"

Lucky couldn't blame him. "You didn't get much."

"No. That little dung-scraping Whine didn't want to leave me any."

"It didn't seem fair. When there was so much today."

"No. It wasn't fair," grunted Mulch. His nose was stretching toward the food, however reluctant he seemed. "You're not trying to trick me, are you, City Dog?"

"Of course not," protested Lucky. *Not now, anyway.*

In the end Mulch couldn't help himself. He licked a few times at the meat, then dragged it closer and began to tear into it with his teeth. Lucky could barely watch. He'd eaten a good half of it before he glanced up again.

"Thank you," he growled, a little sadly. "Though I don't know why you'd help an Omega dog. Especially when I didn't exactly welcome you to the Pack."

And that's one of the reasons I picked you as my victim. Lucky swallowed. "I just . . . felt bad about it. I'm not used to Pack rules. Especially rules about Omegas."

"Well," said Mulch gruffly, "thank you anyway." He gulped down more mouthfuls of flesh.

Leaving Mulch alone to eat the scraps of his own dinner, Lucky squeezed through the branches again and padded back to the hunters' den.

Forest-Dog, he thought unhappily, *please don't let Mulch get any smarter. Don't let him figure it out.*

Don't ever let him realize that all the trouble started when I arrived.

CHAPTER EIGHTEEN

It was too hot and close in the hunters' den, and after much squirming and circle-treading, Lucky gave up his attempts to sleep. He crept into the clearing to slump down on the cool grass. Above him, in the circle of the star-silhouetted pine tops, the Moon-Dog glowed fierce and full, spilling silver light that was bright enough to cast shadows. *Thank the Sky-Dogs that I'm not sneaking out to see Bella tonight,* thought Lucky. *I'd be seen straight away.*

Something moved at the other side of the clearing, catching his attention, and Lucky pricked his ears with curiosity. In the moonlight it was easy to see a huge shape emerge from the finest den of all, the one that was soft with long grass and sheltered by flat stone.

Alpha, thought Lucky in surprise, watching his leader pace restlessly across the clearing. The dog-wolf's eyes glowed as he gazed up at the Moon-Dog. Lucky's ears went forward in surprise as Alpha strode on and vanished between the trees.

Sweet's slender form appeared from the bushes and she stretched languidly before padding across to Lucky.

"Can't sleep?" She lay at his side, ears pricked, her eyes on the spot where Alpha had disappeared.

"No. I can't. Where has Alpha gone?"

She gave a low, perplexed growl. "He always leaves when the Moon-Dog reveals her full face—he wants to be alone with her for a time." Sweet shook her head as if she didn't really understand. "It's a habit he brought from his Wolf Pack days. They always sang to the Moon-Dog together, Alpha says. It was even more special than the Great Howl. Even more special," she repeated in disbelief.

Though he understood no more than Sweet did, Lucky felt a tingle in his backbone. He could barely imagine a sensation more thrilling than the Great Howl, but if that was true of the Moon-Dog ritual, it was no wonder Alpha wanted to recall a little of it, even though he had no Wolf Pack to share with. Once again Lucky wondered what could have driven Alpha to leave his wolf-comrades and run with a Pack of feral mutts.

Of course, one of those feral mutts had almost drawn Lucky into Pack life himself. . . .

Lucky gazed at Sweet's elegant head, raised to sniff the night air and perhaps to follow Alpha's scent trail too.

"Sweet," he said, "could you walk with me for a while?"

She turned her head and tilted an ear, studying him. "You mean, outside the camp?"

"Yes. I want to talk to you. Alone."

Sweet tapped her tail thoughtfully on the earth. "I'm not sure that's a good idea, Lucky. What would Alpha say if he knew?"

"From what you told me, he won't be back for a long time." Catching her doubtful expression, he pressed his advantage. "Do you have to do everything he says?"

Sweet tensed. "Certainly not. But he's my Alpha and I respect him."

"And he obviously respects you." *Cunning ploy, City Dog.* "And trusts you. I need to talk to you, that's all. And it's hard to do that when the Pack is all around."

Sighing, Sweet thought for a while, then gave a reluctant nod. "All right, Lucky. Just for a while, then." She stood up on her long legs. "The lakeshore, I think. It's a good place to talk."

Lucky padded at her flank as she slipped silently between the trees. They soon came to the long silver line of the lake's shore and heard the soft rush of its gentle waves on the pebbles.

The Moon-Dog blazed a brilliant path across the water, making the skyful of stars look dim in contrast.

They paused at the water's edge, letting waves tickle their forepaws. Suddenly tongue-tied, Lucky bent to lick at the wet fur between his claws, teasing out burrs with his teeth.

"What did you want to talk about?" asked Sweet, less impatiently than he expected. She cocked her ears, inclining her head to watch the rippling river of moonlight.

Lucky took a breath. "Was it really necessary? What you and Alpha did to Mulch?"

Sweet was silent for a moment; then she sighed and sat down on her haunches. "Yes. Yes, Lucky, it really was. In a Pack, things are sometimes necessary even when you don't like doing them."

"Didn't you?" He hesitated, not wanting to sound insolent, but wanting very much to know. "Like it, I mean?"

"Of course not." She was indignant now. "How could I enjoy something like that? It was my duty. I'm Alpha's partner and I have to stand by him. I have to support him in all things, especially where Pack discipline is concerned. If we weren't strong together, the Pack would fall apart."

The tide of bitter jealousy that raced through his blood receded, leaving a small seed of hope in his gut.

"Sweet. You said partner."

"Yes?"

"Partner. Not mate."

There was an expression in her dark eyes that he couldn't read at all. Lucky's fur prickled under her intense gaze.

"That's right," she said at last. "Partner."

"So it's strictly a Pack rank thing? It's your place in the hierarchy, not—"

"Exactly." She shook herself and turned back to her study of the lake.

"Sweet . . ." He paused, thumping his tail nervously. "I've wanted to ask you for a while. How did you rise so fast in the Pack?"

She sighed and splashed a paw in the shallow waves, scattering shards of light. "I don't really want to talk about it, Lucky. There was . . . well, there was another Beta before I arrived. We didn't . . . get along. She isn't around anymore."

The hair stood up on the back of Lucky's neck. To fill the awkward silence, he stood up on all four paws and lapped at the water. Presumably he could drink freely so long as he wasn't on patrol; it was deliciously cool against his tongue and throat.

"Alpha and I are a team." Sweet's voice broke the silence. "We work together, run the Pack, keep discipline, and keep it strong.

Maybe we'll become mates someday; that's what usually happens. But there's no hurry."

Lucky forced himself to keep drinking, and to focus on that one part: *There's no hurry.*

"I like my place in the Pack," she went on stubbornly. "I've never been a Beta before. I didn't know I could do it. It makes me feel . . . I don't know. Stronger. Confident. It's not easy to keep a position like this, but I've done it."

"I understand, Sweet," Lucky said slowly. "I truly do." Still, the constant striving, the shoving for power and position made his head spin. It had been bad enough taking Snap's place. How could Sweet bear the tension: always fighting to keep her status, always having to prove herself, day after day? He didn't let her see his shudder.

At least in Bella's Pack they were all equal. They might not be as efficient at survival as Sweet's Pack, but if he had to be in a Pack at all, Lucky thought Bella's way was the better one.

"I'm glad we met up again," he told Sweet awkwardly.

"So am I." She pricked an ear and watched him curiously.

Lucky scraped at the pebbles with his claws. "I think I'd like to go for a walk on my own now. Is that all right? If Alpha can do it . . ."

Sweet's eyes widened. "You can't do everything Alpha can do."

"A walk alone can't hurt the Pack."

"No." Her voice had grown harder and cooler again. "But just because you beat Snap, don't start thinking you can challenge Alpha's authority. That would be a different game altogether. Even Fiery couldn't defeat Alpha, if he was stupid enough to try."

Lucky bristled at her tone. "Fiery doesn't have enough ambition to challenge Alpha. That's all."

"Fiery's smart enough to stick to the rules. And you should be too." Standing, Sweet turned her haunches to him and began to pad back toward the camp. She paused only to glance back once more over her shoulder. "Remember what happened to Mulch."

Remember what happened to Mulch.

How could he forget?

Lucky stood staring at the space where Sweet had been for a long time after she vanished into the forest, but at last he turned back to the lake. It rippled so calmly, so peacefully, and the Moon-Dog trail still lay broad and bright on its surface. If the Moon-Dog was Alpha's special Spirit Dog, would she betray Lucky to the brutal dog-wolf? Or would Moon-Dog understand what he was about to do?

Lucky gave a high brief whimper of unhappiness into the night.

Remember what happened to Mulch. . . .

He couldn't go on like this. Sweet's last words had finally made up his mind. That she could do what she'd done to Mulch was bad enough—but to threaten Lucky with the same fate? He caught a whine gathering in the back of his throat and swallowed hard. *Stop that, Lucky!*

He was filled with a fierce longing to put as much distance as he could between himself and Alpha's Pack—between himself and his terrible guilt. For the sake of protecting his own hide, he'd done a terrible thing to Mulch, and all on the orders of that sneering little creature Whine.

After all, he'd found out everything Bella could possibly need to know. There was no reason for him to stay, none at all. Part of him knew that he had only stayed this long because he'd wanted to: because he was a hunter, a dog with status; because of the Great Howl. It was a part of himself he was afraid of. If he gave in to it, would he lose the rest of what made him Lucky?

Almost without realizing, he was already walking away. Along the edge of the waves he broke into a loping run, eager now to get far from Alpha's Pack, and as fast as he could. He would miss

Sweet, he couldn't deny that, but she was Alpha's partner, and would soon be his mate. She could not have made clearer where her loyalties lay. He would miss some of the others, too, he realized—Twitch and Snap especially. He remembered with a pang how he'd promised to teach Snap some City Dog tricks.

But I don't belong with Snap, or with Sweet, and I certainly don't belong with Alpha.

Do I?

The Moon-Dog was still high; Bella would be at the longpaw campsite. Urgency lent him speed and nimbleness, and he made his way swiftly through the darkly shadowed wood, feeling a nip of nervousness whenever the pale clear moonlight picked him out. His legs pumped beneath him. The thought of what he was doing drove him on; what if Bella left before he arrived? What if she wasn't there at all?

What if she's given up on me . . . ?

A great rush of relief hit him when he smelled the old-smoke reek that reminded him of the camp. He bounded into the clearing to see Bella there waiting for him. With a low bark of greeting, she trotted up and licked him as he stood panting.

She cocked her head, waiting patiently for him to catch his breath. "I'd almost given up on you, Yap. I was about to leave!"

He nuzzled her. "Don't give up on me, Squeak. Not yet!"

Her eyes were bright and happy, he noticed. "It's been a few no-suns since you met Daisy and Sunshine. What kept you?"

"I'm running out of excuses to slip away," he said, and sat down. Now that he could see her clearly in the pale light of the Moon-Dog, he noticed signs of tiredness in the creases around Bella's eyes. There were scratches on her nose, and a shallow gash on her left shoulder, but despite all that she seemed carefree. Almost triumphant . . . and there was something strange about her smell. Tentatively sniffing at her shoulder, he caught it distinctly: the scent of other animals, dark and musky.

A chill ran through his blood. Lucky took a step back from her. "Bella. What's going on?"

"We're all fine," Bella said brightly. "Your instructions about getting to the lake and the hunting grounds worked perfectly! I'm sure we'll be much stronger soon."

"Well . . . that's good, but it's not what I meant. You look hurt!"

Bella tossed her head dismissively. "Some Wild Dogs we had to fight off. But we managed!"

Lucky was speechless. Since when had his litter-sister happily fought battles with Wild Dogs, and won? And all while he was stuck in the Wild Pack, doing her tricky spy work. There was a rustle in the grass as a field mouse stole past—the sound only made the silence between them seem even more painful.

"What about you, Lucky?" Bella asked eventually. "What's happened since last time?"

She sounded so bright and curious, Lucky found himself telling her everything, even though he begrudged each word. He had the strongest sense, in the uneasy tingling of his fur, that she wasn't telling him the whole truth—yet she expected just that from him!

Bella was listening keenly, and gave a sharp little bark of encouragement as he paused. "And Daisy's already told me about your adventures with the giant loudcages—they sounded terrible!"

"They were. And it wasn't much of an adventure," he pointed out, miffed. "It was frightening, and if it hadn't been for Alpha—"

Bella's ears pricked sharply. She must have heard the respect in his voice when he was talking about the Pack leader. "What about him?"

"Never mind." He found he didn't want to explain his complicated feelings about Alpha—not to his litter-sister. "Anyway, that's what I've been dealing with, and those yellow-fur longpaws, too, while you've been fighting battles with Wild Dogs."

Her eyes were suddenly full of sympathy, and she nosed anxiously at his flank. "Were you hurt, Lucky?"

"No." *Thanks to Alpha.* "But, Bella, I've had enough. I want to come back, and we can move on together somewhere else. It's not just loudcages and longpaws—it's dangerous just being with that Pack. Omega—I mean Whine—could expose me at any moment. I'm not sure he's finished with me—and after the Moon-Dog's next turn, he'll be Omega again, I'm sure of it. That'll make him even more bitter and vengeful!"

"But that's a long time away!" barked Bella cheerfully. "You've kept that horrible dog happy for now. You'll be fine!"

Lucky stared at her. "That's not the point. It isn't just Whine! If those dogs ever find out I've betrayed them—well. You won't be seeing your litter-brother anymore. I'll be hunting worms with the Earth-Dog!"

Bella looked at her paws. "But you can't, Lucky. You can't come back."

His heart seemed to stop. "What do you mean?"

"Oh, Lucky, I don't mean forever. Just for now. You don't understand."

"No, I don't!" he barked angrily.

"Listen," Bella placated him. "Later, of course you can come back, Lucky. In a few days, perhaps! But Martha and Bruno are very unwell."

His gut turned over. "Still? Bella, this isn't right. They should be—"

"Oh, you mustn't worry, Lucky!" she said hurriedly. "You have enough to think about. It's a strange illness, that's all—their bellies ache all the time. I think the sickness might cling to food or water. Maybe even air! And it's creeping into other dogs' stomachs. That's all. They'll get better, but it would be silly for you to come back, and get sick. Wouldn't it?"

He stared at her for a long time. The nausea and disappointment were almost overwhelming, robbing him of his voice, and for a moment he felt his legs wobble and thought he'd have to lie down. *I still have to stay away?*

"I suppose . . . but . . ." Suddenly his disappointment turned into panic. "I put my life on the line for you and the Pack! I did everything you asked of me, I betrayed a dog, and now you're telling me I have to go back there?"

Bella quickly interrupted him. "While we're at such low strength, we still need you in the other camp. Do you see? We need you to spy for us a little longer, to keep the land safe for us to travel through, for food and water. It's best that you're . . . with them. You have to stay well, Lucky! We need you!"

She knows just where to nip me where it hurts, thought Lucky dismally. He gave a wretched whine.

"Please, Lucky? For me?"

Everything has been for you, Bella. "If I have to."

"Please, Lucky." Her eyes were dark and intent and solemn.

He shut his own, so that he wouldn't have to look at her. "Just a little longer, then. Only a little. Can I come back with you and see Martha and Bruno first? I'm worried about them."

Bella's tail drooped. "I wish you could," she said. "But I don't want you to catch this sickness."

Lucky slumped with disappointment. "You're right," he said sadly. "Tell them I'll be back as soon as I can."

"Thank you, Lucky." Bella nuzzled his ear. "Thank you."

"Bella, even going back tonight will be difficult. One of them—well, I think my absence might have been noticed." His gut twisted when he thought of how he'd left Sweet, and the things she'd said.

"Then you have to be careful, Yap." She licked him affectionately. "Don't get hurt. I don't want my litter-brother in any trouble."

Why not? It's you who got me into it! But in spite of his dread and misery, Lucky had to admit the sense in what she said. There was certainly no point in making himself ill, and it wouldn't be for much longer. Just till the sickness had worked its way out of her Pack, if it was as bad as she said it was. . . .

"Don't forget, then," he sighed. "Whine's a patrol dog now, and he's weak. And however cunning he is, he's not too competent as a Pack Dog. That's a soft spot you can exploit when you need to move around. And remember, the Wild Pack hunts late after sun-high. The meadows on this side of the forest have good hunting. If you do it in the early sunup, and avoid scent-marking, your presence should have faded enough by the time we come around."

"Yes, yes. I understand all that, Lucky." Bella seemed thoughtful and serious, but there was a hint of impatience in her tensed muscles, too. "Now you'd best be getting back, if you're worried. Be careful. And I promise you can be back with our Pack. Soon! It'll be before another turn of the Moon-Dog, I'm sure of it. Go on!" She licked his nose fondly, her tail wagging.

"Good-bye, then?"

"Good-bye, Lucky! May the Forest-Dog be with you!"

She'd dismissed him like a pup, he thought, as he loped back in the direction of the Wild Pack camp. *She wanted me gone. She couldn't wait for me to leave.* The very thought sent a chill of dread down his spine.

Don't be silly, Lucky! You're both anxious.

Still, he could feel his litter-sister watching him until he was well out of sight. The low-burning resentment in his belly was bad enough without this tingle of apprehension, too.

There was something Bella wasn't telling him.

He couldn't place his paw on it, but he knew it for sure. Something was horribly, dangerously wrong.

CHAPTER NINETEEN

The next day, Lucky sniffed carefully at each patch of grass among the gopher burrows, and even licked at tree stumps, but there was no trace of Bella or the other Leashed Dogs. Had they covered their tracks so well, and moved like ghosts as they hunted? Or had she ignored his advice and stayed away from the hunting meadows?

There was nothing about her he could be sure of anymore, he thought with a ripple of sadness and unease.

"Have you turned into a grass-eater?" Snap's cheerful bark made him jump. "Come on. There are rabbits!"

Snap was in a fine mood this afternoon, skittish and eager, and strangely enough her enthusiasm was catching. Lucky gave her a happy bark, suddenly glad to be jolted out of his misery.

"Drive a few my way and we'll see who's a grass-eater!"

Snap yelped a laugh and darted off, veering across the sun-splashed grassland until she disappeared beyond a rise in the ground.

Only moments later panicked rabbits were careening toward him, and Lucky leaped after them with a gleeful bark. The creatures were in chaos, tumbling and racing across one another's paths to reach their burrows, and some were too mindless with fear to even try to avoid him. One furry streak bolted almost between Lucky's legs, but instead of doubling back he sprang for its companion, rolling the terrified rabbit over and over until he could grab its neck in his jaws and snap it.

The others were having just as much success. Out of the corner of his eye he saw Fiery shaking the life out of a rabbit with his powerful jaws, and Spring was playing with another almost like a well-fed sharpclaw. She tossed it into the air and caught it.

"Good hunting today!" she yelped as she slapped her rabbit to the ground with a deadly paw.

Lucky barked his agreement and turned to chase another before they could all vanish underground. He was so charged with the thrill of the hunt, his blood fizzing in his ears, that he didn't hear the first sharp barks of alarm.

It was Snap's wild cry that finally made him look up, letting another rabbit scamper free and down into its hole. Snap wasn't hunting anymore; she was staring at a dog who was racing across the meadow toward them, panting with distress.

"Dart?" she barked.

Fiery and Spring had frozen now, too, staring at the brown-and-white dog as she skidded to a halt.

"The camp!" Dart barked, breathless. "Come fast! The camp's under attack!"

"What?" snarled Fiery, and then: "My pups!"

"Dart, who? Who's attacking?" Spring bounded toward her, dropping a squealing gopher that skittered away as fast as it could.

"That Leashed Pack! There are more of them! And they're attacking us!"

No! Lucky thought, his brain in turmoil. *No, Bella! What have you done?*

"That's not possible—" began Snap.

"Yes! They sneaked past that slug-brain Whine! I knew he'd be a useless guard! They must have known the hunters were gone, and they're going to kill us!" Dart turned and bolted back the way she'd come.

Without another word, the hunters raced across the meadow after Dart, Lucky at Fiery's heels. He kept up with the furious pace though his heart was a stone inside him.

Branches whipped Lucky's muzzle as they plunged into the trees, but all he could see was Fiery's brown haunches as he pounded through the flickering sun-shadows. He didn't dare think. His Packmates were a blur of speed at his sides. *Packmates.* Lucky's belly twisted with guilt.

They were out of the trees and into the clearing before he could stop his brain from spinning. Lucky scrabbled to a halt beside Fiery as the huge dog squared up to the invaders, snarling and bristling.

The scene in the camp made Lucky's stomach turn over. His Pack, the dogs he'd guided and protected and spied for, facing up against—

My other Pack, he realized with a jolt.

Bella was clearly in the lead, her tail stiff and her hackles high as she grimly faced down Alpha. Daisy and Sunshine were both trembling, but they stood firm, small teeth bared. Mickey was beside them, looking determined and fierce.

And there were two others.

Bruno. Martha.

The sturdy dog and the massive water-dog looked sleek and healthy and ready for a battle, not a sign of sickness in their eyes or their coats. Martha wasn't even limping anymore. *Bella lied to me . . .*

They all lied to me!

Lucky watched as the two Packs circled each other warily,

growling and tense, each waiting for the first sign of weakness in the other.

Every hair on Lucky's body was erect, and tremors of tension ran through his skin and muscles, but there was nothing he could do. He couldn't even move, and though his mind raced in frantic circles like a rabbit, he couldn't come up with a single useful thought. Where did he fit in this stupid, dangerous situation?

Whose side are you on, Lucky?

For a moment, his resentment and bewilderment made him dizzy. Why hadn't Bella told him this was what she was planning? Did she not trust him, or had she wanted to make him some kind of unwitting bait? And what in the name of the Sky-Dogs made her think this could work? Alpha's Pack was still bigger and fiercer than hers.

I can't stand by while my litter-sister fights for her life. . . .

Can I?

"Get *out*, longpaw pets!" Sweet barked. "We'll destroy you for this."

"We'll go where we want to," Bruno snarled.

"And that includes the lake, and the hunting meadows," growled Mickey. "If you don't like it, by all means try to fight us."

Twitch made a feinting move forward, but still none of the

dogs launched a proper attack. Alpha's eyes were cold and deadly, riveted on Bella's, and Lucky knew that if any dog was going to die that day it would be her.

But he feared there would be more than one going to the Earth-Dog, before the Sun-Dog lay down to rest. Many more . . .

Maybe I can still talk them all down from this.

No. It's hopeless. Oh, Forest-Dog, help me. I don't know what to do!

The dog-smells around him were sharp and rank: anger and hatred and fear. The air was thick with it, but there was something else, something that made him sniff the breeze. None of the others had noticed, too concerned with threatening one another. Snarling and whining filled the glade, making his ears ache, but there was nothing wrong with his nose.

I know that scent.

Frantically Lucky opened his nostrils and snuffed the air, desperate to pinpoint the elusive odor. It was familiar somehow . . . and then he knew why. He'd smelled it on Bella at their last meeting—that dark, dusky scent he couldn't place.

Bella had said it was dogs they'd fought off. Had she lied about that, too? Had she brought them as hidden reinforcements? Or had they returned to have their revenge on her; were they even now waiting beyond the trees?

A great courageous bark silenced the low growls of challenge. Bella.

"Alpha!" she cried. "We're here to demand a share of this territory. You have food, water, shelter. Share it, or we'll take it by force!"

Lucky stared at her, open-jawed. Had she lost her mind?

Alpha clearly thought so. "You're welcome to try," he told her in his silky growl. He shared an amused glance with Sweet before turning back to Bella. "If you're stupid enough to take us on. But if you're smarter than I take you for, you'll leave now. And then," he licked a huge paw idly, making the long claws gleam, "we'll say no more about it."

Lucky doubted it would be that easy, but still he barked at Bella inside his head. *Slink away now, Bella, while you have the chance!*

She didn't even blink or cower. Instead she drew herself even stiffer and higher, and said, "You're making a huge mistake, Alpha."

For the first time the dog-wolf looked genuinely surprised, his ears pricking forward in disbelief. Then he gave a great bark of laughter. "I'm not the one making a mistake, Leashed Dog. Not me!"

Bella said nothing, only wrinkling her muzzle in disdain. Then she gave a great summoning bark.

Shadows rippled through the bushes; pointed snouts lined with gleaming teeth emerged from all around. Lucky felt a roiling dread in his belly. The other dogs of the Wild Pack were glancing around nervously, showing the whites of their eyes. From all around, creatures were creeping slyly into view. . . .

Foxes!

In sheer disbelief, Lucky watched them, gray and thin and savage. One snapped its cruel teeth, its tail standing up straight.

"With you, Bella-dog," it leered. "Hello, smelly-dogs."

Lucky's head reeled and his stomach churned. So that was the reek on Bella's fur, the scent he couldn't quite identify. Not dogs at all. And not Bella's enemies—they were with her!

"Foxes!" howled Alpha in rage. "Foxes in my lair!"

The dogs around him erupted into a din of furious yelping as Lucky backed away, horrified. Foxes were creatures of the city, feral and wily and savage. Why had they come here? They belonged in the broken longpaw town, scavenging and lurking and killing by stealth. How in the name of the Sky-Dogs had Bella found them, and why?

Did she go back to the city? For these?

A great hideous shudder went through his bones. *What has she promised them?*

"I told you you were making a mistake." Bella's growl was cool and certain. "We're not weak Leashed Dogs now, Alpha, and you can't drive us from this valley."

Alpha stood stock-still in disgust, rigid and stunned.

"My friends," barked Bella. "Attack!"

CHAPTER TWENTY

"NO!"

But Lucky's howl of protest was drowned out by the deafening barks and screams of dogs colliding in battle. Bella had knocked Sweet flying, but Sweet was already on her paws again, snarling her rage as she tore at Bella's neck. Mickey and Bruno were taking on Snap and Spring, and they rolled on the crushed grass and earth, snapping and biting and scratching. Yelps of pain and fury battered Lucky's ears as he saw the foxes spring like streaks of gray mist at the Wild Pack, tearing and raking at their ears and eyes and throats.

His heart was pounding so hard it felt too big for his chest. *Oh, help me, Forest-Dog! I don't know what to do!* He didn't want to see the Leashed Dogs defeated and killed, but how could he fight against his comrades in the Wild Pack? How could he ally himself with foxes? They weren't to be trusted, ever!

His whole body was shaking with the struggle to choose, but if he didn't get involved soon, one or the other of his Packs would start to fail. His friends would be killed. He didn't want any of them to die! The foxes could go to the Earth-Dog as far as he was concerned, but not the dogs he knew, the ones he fought and hunted beside—

The foxes . . .

Lucky crouched, creeping forward, peering into the pitching, tumbling bodies as they fought and howled. All dogs, though—all dogs, killing one another. Where were the foxes?

He sprang to his paws and spun around. Six gray shapes were scuttling around the food store, grabbing any scraps they could. *Treacherous brutes!* Lucky almost felt sorry for Bella, with her trusting innocence. He'd been wrong about these animals—they weren't city foxes at all. They were too ruthless and cunning. Foxes living off scraps in the city would look slow and lazy by comparison.

He snarled and bolted after the thieves. The foxes wouldn't get even a scrap if he had anything to do with it.

As he ran, the sickening realization hit him like a longpaw's kick. The foxes had lost interest in the meager food store, and had come to circle Moon's den. They paced around it, their eyes fixed on the pups, lips curled back in snarls. They didn't want scraps, Lucky thought with a flash of pure rage. They wanted prey, live prey. Moon's pups.

Moon was crouched before the den, snarling her hate, spittle flying from her jaws as the foxes darted in one by one to bite and torment her.

"Mommy-dog, tired, all alone," Lucky heard one of them say. "Can't fight our hunger!"

Moon was weak from nursing, but she was as fierce as Alpha ever had been, clawing and snapping at her tormentors. Squirm, Fuzz, and Nose were cowering somewhere behind her, and Lucky could hear their terrified whimpering.

Lucky cannoned into the middle of the fox-pack, sending them scattering and rolling onto their backs, but his surprise attack gave Moon only a short reprieve. The foxes bounced back to their paws, flying at him.

All of Lucky's fury poured through him as he leaped and snapped and drew fox blood, flinging one away as the next came at him. This was a fight he could throw himself into without doubts or torn loyalties. Moon's eyes met his with a flash of gratitude, and she turned on the foxes with new hope and energy, fighting as hard as she could from her post at the den's mouth.

The foxes were clever fighters, taunting and nipping her, trying to draw her away from the den.

"Give us tasty pup-snacks!" one of the foxes whined.

Lucky heard the pups howling in terror. "No, Mother, don't go!"

"Don't leave us!"

Moon looked exhausted, but she battled on.

A fox sprang onto her neck, snatching a mouthful of skin and hanging on. Lucky snarled and struck his own attacker across the snout with a paw, then dashed for Moon, seizing the fox and tearing it from her. Yelping with agony, Moon rolled away. At the same time, Lucky felt sharp fangs sink into his flank, and he had to turn to crunch his jaws into the fox that had grabbed him.

Are these creatures unkillable? he thought in despair as it tumbled over in the grass, then came back at him, drool and blood flying from its muzzle.

They were so strong, so resilient—much hardier brutes than the ones he used to fight in the city, and worst of all, braver. Any of the foxes of the city would have run from him by now.

He snapped at one that was sneaking to his flank, but suddenly there were two more. They came at him from both sides, biting his neck fur and holding on hard. Lucky felt the warm flow of blood and the sting of pain, dazing him and making his head spin. They were dragging him, but he didn't know for a moment which way was up and which way was down. He was falling, rolling, over and over—

His skull cracked against a rock, and suddenly, horribly, he couldn't see. The world was a blur, swimming before his eyes as if he were underwater. Trying to stand, he found his legs wouldn't work.

Moon! She's alone!

He dug his claws into the earth and dragged himself toward the courageous Mother-Dog, but there was blood in his eyes now. He could see her still fighting, raking at the attacking foxes, but there were too many of them. Too many . . .

Something gray was slinking past Moon's back legs as she defended her shoulder. Lucky tried to bark a warning, but the sound was feeble; maybe he hadn't managed to make it at all. The next thing in his vision was that gray thing again, crawling from Moon's den with a small bundle of wriggling black-and-white in its jaws. A mewling, terrified pup . . .

Two high voices seemed to echo through his mind. "No, Fuzz, no!"

With a last surge of energy, Lucky struggled to his feet,

swaying. The world whirled around him.

What was that? Among the trees!

Oh, he was imagining things now. His head wound must have flung him into a dream. He couldn't help Moon from a dream.

Lucky blinked blood furiously from his eyes, staggering. No, there were forest-shadows. He couldn't have imagined them.

There. Big ghosts in the woods, sleek and strong ghosts: not moving, just watching. Two great black-and-tan Fierce Dogs, still as stone, eyes burning. *Dogs! Why don't they help us? Why don't they move?* One of the dogs turned its head away. The other raised a paw, as if it might finally step out of the shadows. Lucky stumbled forward, then jerked his head up again. *No. Lucky, you fool! There were no dogs; it was a dream. There were no shadows in the trees. . . .*

Get away, dream dogs. This was what was real, this turmoil of blood and struggle and fear. Moon was defending her pups to the death, and he had to get to her.

He staggered forward. Two of them, and the helpless pups. Him and Moon, and six savage foxes.

If I have to die, I'll take the Earth-Dog a gift—of foxes. Lucky opened his jaws in a howl of defiance and sprang.

CHAPTER TWENTY-ONE

As the leader fox turned on him with bared fangs, Lucky snarled his furious challenge.

"I won't go easily," he warned them. "If you try to kill me, I'll take you with . . ." But before he could finish, a blow knocked him sideways into the grass. Lucky yelped in shock, shaking his head violently.

Not a fox. A great brown shape hurtled past him, all muscle and fury and slavering jaws. Fiery!

Fiery landed among the foxes like a great falling tree, sending them yelping and flying onto their backs. Seizing a straggler, he flung it aside and lunged at another. Lucky, still woozy from the blow to his head, felt his heart swell with new courage. Struggling back to his paws, he plunged in alongside Fiery, fighting the foxes fiercely. He let loose a volley of barks, hoping it would alert some of the other dogs who still battled among themselves at the other side of the clearing, oblivious to the foxes' treachery.

Only two of them must have heard, but they came racing at once—Mulch, his black ears flying, and Daisy, a small ball of teeth and fierceness.

"Help Moon!" Lucky had time to yelp before he was attacked once more, a fox darting in to sink its sharp teeth into his hind leg.

The pain was like a scorch of flame, but it finally cleared his head. Lucky snarled and bit, tossing the fox away.

From the corner of his eye he saw another fox slash viciously at Daisy, its claw slicing a line of blood across her muzzle. But she rallied, her eyes flashing; she sank her sharp little teeth deep into its throat, hanging on fiercely until it stopped moving.

Lucky dodged as another fox threw itself at him, then pounced on it, clamping its leg between his jaws.

"Out of the way, stink-dog!" one of the foxes shrieked. Lucky looked up and saw three foxes pouncing on Mulch. The black dog vanished under a pile of scratching, gnawing fury. Lucky saw Mulch kick helplessly at his attackers, blood drops scattering.

"Mulch! Hang on!" Fiery barked, a single swipe of his massive paw scattering the two foxes that were trying to take him down.

Panting, free of attackers just for a few moments, Lucky stood stiff-legged and barked, high and desperate.

"Alpha! Sweet! Bella! Help!"

At last, at last, his cries were heard. Across the clearing, dogs stumbled apart, shaking themselves, momentarily stunned. They all seemed to realize in the same moment what had happened. Alpha gave a high howl of fury, and plunged forward; behind him, like a single Pack, the rest of the dogs hurtled across toward Moon's den.

Lucky was too busy tearing the three foxes from Mulch's prone body to see the end of the struggle. He was only dimly aware of the onrush of the dogs, the yelps of the retreating foxes. One by one Mulch's attackers fell away, scrambling off him and dashing to defend themselves, but Alpha and Sweet were moving among them now like Lightning, slashing and springing with deadly efficiency. Tails between their legs, the foxes fell over one another in their frantic bids to escape.

"Run time!" they called to one another. "Out, out, out!"

Silence, when it came, seemed very sudden. Lucky stood with his head hanging down, tongue lolling and flanks heaving. Three thin, gray fox-shapes were racing away into the undergrowth; the other three lay broken and battered on the churned, bloody earth.

The leader-fox's voice cried shrilly into the eerily still air. "Be back! We come back, filthy dogs. For your other pup-prey!"

Then he was gone, and only the breeze stirred the bushes.

Grimly, Alpha lifted a limp fox-corpse into the air with his jaws and tossed it away from him. It thudded to the ground close to where Mulch lay.

As if their leader had broken some awful spell, Fiery let out a great baying howl of distress, and Moon lay down, whining with grief and shock. As two small bodies wriggled fearfully from the den behind her, she and Fiery curled protectively around their surviving pups, and Moon licked feverishly at their tiny heads.

Lucky couldn't bear to watch them. "Daisy!" he barked gruffly. "Are you all right?"

The little dog shook herself, rubbing her muzzle against a patch of soft grass. "I'm fine, Lucky. It's a scratch. Quick, it's the black dog you should look after." Daisy turned her nose unhappily toward Mulch. "He's much worse."

Together with the others of the Wild Pack, Lucky limped across to Mulch, who lay in a pool of thickening blood.

Pain jolted through his wounded leg, but that wasn't what made him stop after a few paces. There was no need to go to Mulch. Flies were already settling on his wounded side, and the scent drifting from him was bitterly familiar.

Like Alfie . . .

"He's gone to the Earth-Dog," came Alpha's growl. "Leave him."

"No," murmured Lucky, feeling despair take over.

"Leave him, I said! Mulch fought bravely, but he's gone."

The sound of Mulch's proper name coming from Alpha's jaws stunned Lucky, and he sat down heavily on his haunches. The leader hadn't called him Omega. In death, Mulch had regained his status and his dignity.

The things Lucky had taken from him.

The black wave of misery that swept over him was worse than anything Lucky had felt before, in all his deceptions and double-dealing. Guilt and shame coiled around his heart and guts like a snake, crushing his innards. The pain was wrenching, so much worse than the gash in his leg.

I brought it on myself. And I brought this all upon the Pack.

He couldn't contain the feeling inside him; it wasn't possible. Lifting his head, Lucky let out a great echoing howl of grief and agony.

Snap turned to him, shocked, but she sat down and raised her muzzle to howl with him. Then Twitch was howling too, and Dart, and suddenly Martha and Bruno and Daisy were joining in. In moments all the dogs were howling to the sky, united in mourning.

No Spirit Dogs bounded across Lucky's vision now. *They've deserted me,* he thought, *and so they should.* His voice broke, his howl faltered, and Snap stopped too, to lick his ear comfortingly.

"It wasn't your fault," she said.

"No," added Spring, at his flank. "You did all you could, Lucky."

"You fought for Moon's pups," added Dart. "Mulch came to help you, and he died bravely."

As the three of them resumed their mournful cries, Lucky found himself voiceless. He sat among the grieving dogs, their howls tearing through his heart. Whine was watching him very intently, but he found he didn't care about that sly little brute anymore.

I did all I could, he thought bitterly. *I betrayed my friends, and brought Bella and the foxes here, and destroyed Mulch. And Fuzz.*

If the Earth-Dog opened her jaws to swallow him now, Lucky thought savagely, he'd go willingly. Without so much as a whimper.

CHAPTER TWENTY-TWO

The Packs were subdued as they cleared the camp of bodies. They dragged the three foxes out to the hunting meadow for the crows. Martha used her giant, webbed feet to push their bodies across the ground while Daisy did her best to help, despite the injury on her muzzle. *She fought well,* Lucky thought, watching her.

Over them all lay a sense of dread; Lucky could feel it like a wet slab of mud-slip. This wasn't finished; there were things still to be done and said that were only waiting out of respect for the dead. Lucky didn't dare look at Alpha, or even at Sweet; and he couldn't bring himself to glance at his litter-sister. He had betrayed the Wild Pack for Bella, and she had given him nothing but lies.

For all the vicious fighting, no one had won, and they all knew it. The sense of doom and despair weighed in his belly like a great stone, and he knew he couldn't bear the guilt he carried for long.

The Wild Pack turned to their own dead, gently moving Mulch's and Fuzz's bodies down under a brightly flowering bush just outside the camp.

Sweet turned and pressed her muzzle to Moon's neck. "There's no time for a long good-bye right now. I promise we'll mourn them properly."

The realization that he didn't know how the Wild Pack honored their dead stung Lucky like a fox bite. He would fight to the end for these dogs, but he still wasn't one of them—not really. Not yet.

Fiery and Moon crouched together beside the bush for a second, with Squirm and Nose trembling between them. Then they got up and walked away.

"Now let us settle this," barked Alpha from his rock. "Both Packs, to me." Lucky was almost relieved. At last his fate would be clear.

Some of the dogs trotted eagerly to the circle, keen to see matters resolved between the Packs; others, like Lucky and Bella, limped there, whether hurt or filled with dread. Alpha waited till all the dogs had gathered, then gazed around them with his cold, unsettling eyes. Sweet, at his side, looked almost as fierce and unforgiving as he did.

"You," growled Alpha, turning to Bella. "Leashed fool."

Despite everything, Lucky couldn't help but admire his litter-sister's staunchly defiant stance. As she stepped forward she looked Alpha full in his yellow eyes, her head proud.

"You brought foxes into my camp," growled the dog-wolf, "and death to my Pack. If you want to speak before you die, do it now."

The other dogs stirred uneasily, the Leashed Dogs whining and barking in protest, and Lucky's fur prickled. Sunshine whimpered softly and Bruno's brow creased in deep folds of anxiety. Lucky had been afraid of this; only Bella could save herself now.

"You denied us hunting and fresh water," she told Alpha fearlessly. "We had no choice. If you'd listened to reason from the start, none of this would have happened. And you killed one of us!"

Alpha gave a belly-deep bark of anger. "You've had your vengeance for that, haven't you? I wonder if it will be worth it." The light in his yellow eyes was as dangerous as fire. "You Leashed Dogs invaded my territory. You had no right under the Law of Dogs—none. Unless you were willing to fight for it, and you couldn't even do that until you'd made allies of those . . . vermin."

Bella dropped her eyes. "The foxes lied to me," she said softly. "I was wrong to bring them here, and I'm sorry."

"You'll be even more sorry." Alpha curled his muzzle. "I'll kill you myself."

"No!" barked Sunshine, and Alpha turned to her, crushing her with his fierce glare. "Please don't," she whimpered more humbly. "Please. Bella's a good dog."

"A good leader," put in Bruno. He threw Lucky a glance as if to say: *Tell them!*

But Lucky didn't have the chance. The Alpha shook his head. "A good leader would have thought ahead. She put you in as much peril as she put my Pack, and it's only our bad luck that none of you died. It's time to rectify that. Bella of the Leashed Pack, come here."

"Alpha, wait." Moon paced forward, leaving her two remaining pups between Fiery's protective paws. "May I say something?"

Every dog in the circle looked at her in surprise, but none more than Alpha. He licked his chops thoughtfully. "You of all dogs here have a right to speak, Moon. What is it?"

Moon turned, studying each dog in the circle very carefully. At last she tilted her head directly at Alpha, her gaze forthright.

"I lost a pup today because of these Leashed Dogs and their foolish leader," she began.

Lucky's heart fell. If Moon spoke against her, Bella truly was doomed.

"I have as much reason to hate them as you do, Alpha. More." Moon's ear twitched, and she shivered a little, then recovered, her voice strengthening. "But Bella told the truth. It's obvious the foxes duped her; she never intended this to happen the way it did. That's stupidity, Alpha, not wickedness."

Alpha nodded. "That may be, but she may still deserve to die. I think you have more to say, Moon. Tell us."

"We've all done foolish things. We've all made mistakes. And we'll make many more in the days to come. Look how the world has changed!" Moon scraped the earth with her paw. "Who's to say who will make the next deadly error? We need to stick together, live together. It's hard enough for dogs to survive in the world of the Big Growl without turning on one another."

Alpha gave a reluctant nod, but his voice remained stern and hard. "They also have to act properly. Respect the Law of Dogs."

"I haven't finished." Moon closed her eyes. "They brought the foxes here; it's true. But when they knew they'd made a mistake, they did their best to make it right. Three of my pups would have died today if not for Lucky and poor Mulch . . . and for this Leashed Dog."

Moon turned her head to gaze at Daisy. The little dog's eyes were wide and awestruck, and she trembled a little, but didn't move.

"This Daisy came to my pups' aid when Lucky called her, and fought like a warrior for their sake." Lucky listened even harder as Moon continued. "And when they heard, so did the rest of her Pack. That means, in my eyes, they are forgiven. I still have two pups I might not have had."

Moon lay down, her paws in front of her, as if she was too weary to say more. But Fiery licked Squirm's and Nose's little heads, settling them where they were, and lumbered forward to her side.

"I agree with Moon," he growled. "It was our pup who died, but it was our other two pups who were saved. The Leashed Dogs were wrong to do what they did, but they did the right thing in the end. That shows courage and honor, Alpha, and I respect it."

Fiery's tail lashed slowly as he bent down to nuzzle Moon's head. The other dogs stood in hushed silence, watching Alpha as he scowled down at the two mates. There was fondness in his frown, though, and Lucky found his hopes rising just a little.

"Beta. Do your job." Alpha sighed and glanced at his elegant partner. "Advise me."

Sweet scratched thoughtfully at her ear, then placed her paw gracefully back on the rock. "It's true that they fought well," she murmured. "Whether against us or for us."

"And which of those carries most weight?" asked Alpha.

Sweet made a rumbling sound in her throat. "They would be worthy allies, and bad enemies. I suggest we put aside our differences with the Leashed Pack, Alpha. There's more that draws us together than divides us. As Moon said, we are all dogs, and we're living in a changed world. When I came here after the first Big Growl, I thought this Pack was safe from its effects, but I nearly died in the second Growl, and who knows what else is to come?"

"And their leader?" Alpha's baleful gaze rested on Bella once more.

"Hmph." Sweet gave her a cutting look. "I'm willing to do what Moon and Fiery want. It seems to me they have the right to decide."

Alpha licked his jaws again thoughtfully, his pointed white teeth gleaming.

"Very well," he said at last. "Beta talks sense yet again, and she also talks me out of my instincts. Again. How shall we arrange this new order?"

Sweet sat down, eyeing the members of Bella's Pack. "I suggest we invite their Pack to join with ours. But every one of them will have to accept a low place in the hierarchy. They must be loyal only to you. If they're willing to do that, it'll prove we can work together for the good of all."

Alpha nodded as Bella's Pack exchanged nervous but hopeful glances. Lucky stared at the ground, torn. Could Bella's Pack really fit in with these true Wild Dogs? He shuddered to imagine Sunshine in the hierarchy, trying to find a place for herself that was survivable. How did he feel about the Packs uniting?

Bad, was the answer. And good. And everything in between. Lucky shut his eyes in despair.

He blinked them open when Alpha scraped his claws against the rock, a screeching sound against the stillness of the clearing.

"Very well. We'll organize the Pack roles as best we can, if the Leashed Dogs agree to join us. Which they will, if they have any sense. We still won't tolerate outsiders trespassing on our land, so they will join us or run far away."

"And their leader?" prompted Sweet.

"She will be Omega," growled Alpha. "Do you know what that means, pet dogs? She will fetch and carry for the Pack, take *all* orders without complaining, and if she has any time to sleep she'll be in the Omega den, drafty and damp. That can be justice for Mulch. When a full turn of the Moon-Dog has passed, she can challenge if she likes. If she survives that long."

Bella stood up, her hackles raising. Lucky's fur shivered. Was she deciding whether to fight after all? Around her, her Pack muttered and whined.

"Don't do anything you're not comfortable with," said Martha.

Bruno growled: "Show them you can survive!"

Lucky longed suddenly to be one of them, to be able to guide and advise them like he used to. Becoming Omega for a turn of the Moon-Dog was Bella's best hope, he knew. Surely she did, too? But he couldn't interfere. He didn't dare.

I'm not one of them. Not openly. Not if I want to live. . . .

This whole battle, everything that had happened, was his fault. He'd agreed to Bella's suggestion of becoming a spy, not thinking for a moment that she would deceive him. Worse, he'd told Bella about Whine and what a poor patrol dog he'd be; he'd given her the information about when the hunters would be away from the camp. All his spying hadn't helped Bella and her Pack; all it had done was harm all the dogs, and in the most horrible way. When Bella and her friends made their choice, what would he do?

Will I remain with a larger Pack? Or if they stay separate, will I stick with Bella, or find a new place here with the Wild Pack?

Or will I do what I always meant to do, and strike off alone again?

Bella and Alpha were still staring each other down, but Bella was licking her chops nervously now. At any moment she'd make her choice.

"Well?" sneered Alpha. "The decision's yours, Bella the Leashed Dog."

"Wait," barked a new voice.

Lucky took a breath, startled. As all the dogs turned, the pudgy dog who'd gotten Lucky into this mess trotted forward, head and tail high, an expression of cocky vindictiveness on his snub-nosed face.

"Don't decide anything yet, Alpha." Whine sat down, tilting his head at Lucky.

Sweet snapped her teeth at him. "Who are you to interfere, Whine? If Bella rejects our offer you'll be back to Omega, and don't you forget it."

"Oh, but I have something interesting to tell you." Whine's tongue lolled as his mouth stretched in a wide grin. "Alpha needs to know this, before he takes any new dogs into our Pack. You see that City Dog?"

Alpha glanced at Lucky, irritated, and back at Whine. "What about him?"

Lucky's heart was frozen in his chest. Nowhere to run,

555

nowhere to hide. Whine was watching him closely, licking his teeth. Lucky felt himself shrink, his forequarters ready to bow, ready to beg uselessly for mercy.

"He's one of them. One of the Leashed Pack." Whine gave a bark of angry excitement. "He's been spying for them all along!"

Silence. Lucky's tongue felt thick and unwieldy in his jaws, and his coat prickled all over with icy fear. Bella's friends watched him with horror, giving him away just by their aghast expressions. The Wild Pack were all turning to him, one by one, their shock and disbelief plain.

Sweet bounded an abrupt pace forward, swinging a paw across Whine's face. He squealed, but didn't back off.

"That isn't true!" she barked angrily. "You'll take a beating for that lie, Omega."

"Stop!" barked Lucky, lunging forward between Sweet and Whine. His jaws opened as he panted for breath. Terror filled him, but he couldn't let yet another dog suffer for his misdeeds. Not even Whine.

"Lucky?" Sweet sounded bewildered.

"It's true." Lucky lowered his head, then jerked it up again to look her in the eyes. He owed her that, while he told her the truth. "He isn't lying, Sweet. What he says is true."

Sweet's eyes were wide and hurt, disbelieving. "No!"

"Yes. Sweet, I'm so sorry. I never meant for it to go this far. I . . . I wanted to belong here too."

She stared at him in silence for moments that seemed like days. Behind her, Alpha was ominously still.

Sweet's throat sounded tight. "You couldn't . . . You *wouldn't* . . ."

"Yes, Sweet. I did. I'm sorry."

"But you're one of us now," Sweet barked suddenly. "Even if it is true, you're . . ." She broke off and slammed her jaws shut.

Lucky opened his jaws. There was so much in her eyes: anger, hurt, fear, betrayal. A plea for him to say what she wanted him to say.

Lucky swung around to look at Alpha, and then at Bella. Glancing at the other dogs in the circle, he caught sight of Whine's smug scowl, and Snap's bewilderment, and Fiery's gruff challenge. Daisy and Sunshine were trembling. He could smell the tension in the air, sense the raising of hairs and the racing of blood.

Time to choose, Lucky. Time to choose where your loyalties lie.

Then the great dog-wolf paced forward toward him, and Lucky stood to meet him, shaking.

Perhaps there was no choice for him to make at all.

Perhaps it was only time to die.

ERIN HUNTER

is inspired by a fascination with the ferocity of the natural world. As well as having great respect for nature in all its forms, Erin enjoys creating rich, mythical explanations for animal behavior. She is also the author of the bestselling Warriors and Seekers series.

Visit her online at
www.survivorsdogs.com.

For exclusive information on your favorite authors and artists, visit www.authortracker.com.

Lucky froze, his legs trembling. Silence fell over the circle of dogs.

Alpha's broad, wolfish face was unreadable. He drew himself up on his rock, towering over the two Packs. By his side on the grass was Sweet, the beautiful swift-dog, staring at Lucky. Lucky could scarcely look at her.

Little snub-nosed Whine's tongue lolled and his jaws gaped. "You see, I was right! The City Dog was spying for the Leashed Dogs. He met with that one, the one who looks like him!" Whine turned to Bella, who glared until he cringed and cowered. "I saw them. . . ." The little dog's words trailed off.

Lucky fought to keep his tail high. He could not let it droop in submission. That would show weakness—it would be the end of him in the eyes of this fierce Wild Pack.

They were all waiting for an explanation, but what could he say? He had spied on them, just as Whine had said. He had never imagined, though, that Bella would use the information he'd provided to attack the Wild Pack's camp.

Lucky searched the faces of the dogs in the circle.

What do I do now? If I show loyalty to the Leashed Pack, the others will kill me. But how can I turn my back on the Leashed Dogs? Bella's my litter-sister. . . .

He had been through so much with the Leashed Dogs. But the Wild Pack had accepted him as one of their own. He had shared the Great Howl with them, where Spirit Dogs ran before his eyes. He had felt the power of their bond, even as he balked at Alpha's strict hierarchy.

Then there was Sweet. . . . He stole a glance in her direction and she met his eye. He saw pain and confusion there, but also hope.

She raised her muzzle. "Lucky fought bravely to defend the pups from the foxes. Whatever he may have done before . . . he's no *Leashed* Dog. He's one of our Pack now." Her velvety ears twitched and she looked away. Her voice was uncertain, despite her words.

It's as though she wants to believe it, thought Lucky. *She* wants *to believe that I'm who she thought I was....*

Lucky barked gratefully, even though he wasn't sure *where* he belonged.

He looked at his litter-sister. Bella stared hard at him, head slightly cocked.

She knows it's true. A part of me has grown loyal to the Wild Pack.

For a moment he felt guilty. Then he reminded himself that it was because of Bella that he had joined the Wild Dogs in the first place! And it was she who had brought the foxes into their home! She must have been crazy to trust those wily creatures. They'd betrayed her as soon as she'd led them to the camp, attacking Moon and threatening to eat her pups. He remembered how dogs from both Packs had broken off their battle to defend the pups when the foxes attacked them—first Daisy and Mulch, then the others. They had come together, repelling the vicious foxes. They had worked as a single, powerful Pack....

Lucky noticed Moon and Fiery standing a few paces behind the others, their pups Squirm and Nose—the ones who had survived—nuzzled between them. Lucky's chest tightened with sorrow when he remembered the terror and turmoil, the frenzied barking, and the dogs who hadn't made it: little, helpless Fuzz, and poor Mulch.

Alpha growled low in his throat. "Lucky may have served our Pack for a time, but that does not excuse his treachery. What do you have to say for yourself, *City* Dog?"

Lucky licked his leg where the fox had mauled it, playing for time. His quick thinking rarely let him down, but this time he couldn't find anything to say in his own defense.

It was so much easier when I was a Lone Dog. A Lone Dog answers to nobody. But what if I'm not meant to be a Lone Dog at all?

Lucky swallowed, his throat dry. "It is true that I have been helping both Packs," he began. A growl rose from the lean brown-and-white hunt-dog, Dart, and was quickly echoed by the long-eared littermates, Twitch and Spring. They had been his Packmates, but now they were glaring at him fiercely, their hackles raised. Lucky struggled not to turn and run into the forest. If he did that he could never, ever come back. He had to keep his courage.

"I have gotten to know you all," he said. "And I've been thinking . . . what if my original mission to join the Wild Pack was *meant to be?* The Earth-Dog growled; the River-Dog revealed the path of fresh water; the Forest-Dog protected me on the way to this camp. At each turn I met friends . . . Sweet in the Trap House. My litter-sister Bella . . . even the Sky and Moon Dogs seem to have led me to this point."

Dart still growled, but the others grew quiet. Lucky could tell that he had their attention.

"See how the Packs joined to fight the foxes?" he went on. "Everyone had a role—not just big dogs like Fiery and Martha, but smaller fighters like Snap and Daisy. Dogs from different backgrounds, wild and leashed . . ." He paused, his eyes trailing over the assembled dogs. "You don't even know one another, yet you all fought fearlessly for a single purpose. Maybe the Spirit Dogs brought me here so that both Packs could unite?"

Alpha's face contorted in a menacing snarl but Snap, the Wild Pack's white-and-tan hunter, had a thoughtful look on her face. A few paces away, Moon and Fiery were still standing by their remaining pups. They exchanged glances and Moon stepped forward.

"Without the Leashed Dogs' help, we would have lost all three of our pups, not just little Fuzz."

Alpha watched her a moment and turned back to Lucky. The dog-wolf's yellow eyes bore into him. "That does not change the fact that he deceived us," he snarled. "Lucky brought danger and death into our camp." He turned his fierce gaze on the Leashed Dogs. "My Pack had to save this band of weaklings many times during the battle with the foxes. We cannot be expected to protect

565

grown dogs who are feeble as pups."

Daisy bristled at this insult and Mickey scratched the grass next to his longpaw's glove with a forepaw.

But it was Bella who stepped forward.

Lucky's heart tightened in his chest. If his litter-sister challenged Alpha, she'd only make matters worse. He might destroy Lucky and throw out the Leashed Dogs just to teach her a lesson. But Bella dipped her head, addressing Alpha respectfully without looking up.

"I am sorry that I brought the foxes to your camp. It was unwise, and it was *stupid* of me." Her tail fell limp behind her. "I was duped into believing that foxes would act honorably. It was a mistake I will never make again. Truthfully, we wanted only to *share* in what you have here. We didn't intend to harm your Pack."

Alpha growled at this, his ears erect and his upper lip peeling back to reveal his fangs.

Lucky watched in astonishment as Bella lowered herself onto the ground submissively. With a whine she rolled to expose her belly. "I make you a solemn promise, Alpha, on behalf of my Pack. If you let us stay, the Leashed Dogs will serve you faithfully. We will obey your commands and fight alongside you, making your Pack even more formidable. We are better hunters than we look and we are keen to help with the tasks of the Pack. All we ask is to share in your food and water, and that you spare Lucky. He meant you no harm. He didn't know our plans; I swear it. And he did his very best to defend the pups when the foxes attacked; the Mother-Dog said so." Bella looked briefly at Moon, then lowered her muzzle.

Moon whined her agreement. Guarding the two remaining pups, Fiery licked their heads as they leaned against his forelegs.

Lucky's heart swelled in his ribs, his anger draining away. He knew what it had cost Bella to surrender to Alpha in front of both Packs. He was sure that the last thing she wanted was to serve the ruthless half wolf. She was doing it to provide for her Pack—and to save Lucky's skin.

She hasn't deserted me.

He remembered her as a puppy, when she was still known as Squeak, bright, bossy, curious, and loyal—she had always been loyal.

Alpha shook his shaggy gray fur and scratched a large, pointed ear with a ragged claw. He was looking around at his Pack, gauging their reaction to Bella's submissive speech. Dart's hackles were still raised, but Twitch and Spring seemed more relaxed, and Snap's tongue was lolling from her jaws in a grin. Whine turned away while Moon and Fiery stood tall and gazed back at their leader.

Lucky held his breath, waiting for Alpha's verdict.

"I am willing to let you join us," the dog-wolf said at last, "but you will take low positions. You will be trained as Patrol Dogs and given the most tiring routines. If you believe you are capable of joining the more prestigious hunting group, you will have to *earn* that right through hard work and honorable combat. Those are the rules of my Pack."

Martha, Bruno, and Daisy turned instinctively to Lucky, used to following his advice. Lucky licked his chops. What choice did they have? Without Alpha's permission, they would not have access to food or clean water, which was in the Wild Pack's territory.

Before he could say anything, Alpha spoke again. "Foolish Leashed Dogs, looking to him. Don't you know that he's the lowest-ranking member of your new Pack? The *Omega*."

Alpha glared at the Leashed Dogs, challenging them to respond, but none of them dared. Lucky saw Whine smirk, his ugly face a crisscross of wrinkles. Lucky lowered his head, biting back a snarl. He remembered all too well the humiliations that Whine had faced as the lowliest Pack member.

But Alpha wasn't finished yet. "And the new Omega will be given a permanent reminder of his treachery: a scar on his flank so that none can forget what he has done."

Lucky yelped. He thought of Mulch, who'd been blamed for eating out of turn . . . framed by Lucky and Whine, to get him demoted to Omega. Alpha had sprung at Mulch, scraping and gouging. Sweet had backed him up, adding savage bites to Mulch's wounds.

"Oh, Alpha," whined Martha, the huge Leashed Dog with webbed paws. "Be merciful!"

By her side, little Daisy yipped: "Please. Lucky will do everything you say; we promise. You don't have to do this."

Lucky whined softly with gratitude as Twitch and Spring joined the chorus of protests. "We agree," barked Twitch. "Becoming Omega is enough punishment."

Fiery cocked his head questioningly and even Sweet seemed unsure, though she stayed silent.

Alpha howled to be heard, his wolfish cry cutting through the whines and yaps. "The Pack will need stricter rules if it's to survive with all these extra dogs! That will be the price of Lucky's treachery and deceit."

Lucky couldn't imagine any stricter rules—Alpha's Pack was

already so organized, the hunting and eating rights clearly regimented. A dog's rank even dictated where he slept!

Lucky had risked his life to battle the foxes, and yet the Wild Pack's leader was determined to hurt and humiliate him. His leg throbbed and his head felt thick and heavy, a grim reminder of that furious tussle.

The dogs were growling, barking, arguing with one another—divided over Lucky's fate.

"Wait!" snapped Mickey, the Farm Dog. He stood over his longpaw's glove, his ears flat but his head held high. "We're wasting time fighting with one another. We should be devoting our energies to surviving in this strange world, not arguing about who is higher in the Pack." Mickey tapped the glove absently with his paw. "Bella and Daisy are good hunters. The Pack would benefit from their skills. Why *wait* to use them?"

"Because we must have order," said Snap, the white-and-tan mongrel from the Wild Pack. "It's not about whether you *like* it—a Pack can't work without order. That's how it's always been." She spoke reasonably, without anger or malice.

Mickey's ears pricked up. "The Big Growl changed all the rules. Leashed Dogs are joining Packs, and Pack Dogs need to change too. Hierarchy doesn't seem necessary—not anymore. It just makes things complicated."

Lucky had rarely heard Mickey say so much.

Snap watched the Farm Dog, as though considering his words. But before she could speak again, Alpha sprang toward Mickey. Standing over the cowering black-and-white dog, he snarled: "The Big Growl is an even greater reason to *stick* to order and tradition. The world is more dangerous than ever. What we need is discipline, not some lazy group of ill-trained house-pets." He lifted his muzzle, his yellow eyes cold.

Most of the dogs lowered their heads, careful not to challenge the half wolf. None of them spoke.

Alpha looked from each dog to the next, then glared at Lucky. "It's time for the marking ceremony. Hold him down."

Panic surged through Lucky's body, his legs trembling and his paw pads growing damp with sweat. His eyes shot across the dogs, wondering who would launch the attack. Several of the Leashed Dogs whimpered, but they didn't dare speak up for him anymore. Even Bella, who had risen to her paws, said nothing.

Sweet broke forward. Lucky yelped in dismay as she pounced at his back, hugging his shoulders with her paws and bringing him down. His shoulder smacked the earth and a twinge shot through his injured leg. His body crackled with fear and panic.

Sweet was stronger than she had been when they had escaped the Trap House. Snap leaped forward to assist Sweet, slamming into Lucky and helping to keep him pinned down. Lucky whimpered as Sweet's teeth sank into his neck.

"Relax," she whined as he kicked and twisted beneath her. "It will be easier for you if you don't struggle."

Lucky's heart thumped faster in his chest but for a moment he froze, seized by panic and confusion. Out of the corner of his eye, he saw the Leashed Dogs cringe. Sunshine started barking in her shrill yap. Martha looked away with an unhappy whine.

Bella found her voice again. "Please let him go; this isn't fair! What is the point of injuring him so badly that he can't hunt or shield us from attack? What good will that do any dog?"

Alpha growled impatiently. "None of an Omega's duties are so honorable. I won't cause him any serious injury." His lip curled as he approached Lucky, who started to thrash again, fighting against Sweet and Snap. "Just a good bite. Something he will never forget."

The surrounding dogs were barking wildly, scared and excited, as Alpha stepped forward. He loomed over Lucky.

Alpha snarled. "Be brave, traitor. It's time to take what's coming to you." His yellow eyes glittered and he licked his chops.

No! I won't let you do it! thought Lucky with a surge of anger. *You will not touch me!*

He shook and scrambled against Sweet until she loosened her hold on his neck; then he growled as he threw his forepaws against her. Sweet fell back, stunned, and Lucky spun his whole body around, forcing Snap off his back. He scrambled to his paws and pushed through the circle of dogs.

He threw a breathless look over his shoulder. The dog-wolf wasn't prepared for this. Alpha barked in fury as Lucky passed Bella and Daisy, who made no move to stop him. Sweet looked surprised, even upset.

I'm sorry, Sweet. I just can't stay here!

Lucky hesitated long enough for Snap to launch a second attack. He was about to throw her off when a great weight fell on top of him. Thick brown fur with black patches obscured his vision for a moment, and then he looked up into the pointed face of Bruno. His heavy, powerful body pressed Lucky to the ground and Lucky yelped, more from shock than pain.

Bruno! But he's a Leashed Dog!

Lucky could hardly believe it. A moment later Sweet had joined him, her forepaws digging into Lucky's neck. With three dogs holding him down, there was no way he could flee.

The dogs surrounding Lucky were barking feverishly. Sunshine, the white long-haired dog, hopped and spun in panicked circles while Mickey retreated a few paces, his longpaw glove held protectively between his teeth.

Alpha's shadow fell over Lucky as he drew closer, baring his gleaming fangs.

"A traitor walks among us," Alpha began. "According to tradition, he must be marked so that all may know what he has done. As Alpha, it is my duty to make this mark."

Lucky closed his eyes. He promised himself that, however badly it hurt, he would never let them know it. He would not whine, yelp, or howl as Alpha's teeth sank into his flank—he would not give Alpha the satisfaction.

Alpha brought his face to Lucky's ear and snarled softly. "You can forget your life of freedom now. You will be known as a traitor for as long as you live. No Pack will ever make the mistake of trusting you again."

The half wolf dipped his head, about to bury his fangs into Lucky's fur and flesh.

There was a high-pitched sound like shattering clear-stone. The air felt cold.

Alpha froze. The sound grew in volume, almost unbearably

sharp. It clawed into Lucky's mind and chilled his blood. Pressed against him, he could feel Sweet's heart pounding and hear Snap whimpering with fear. Even Bruno gave a yelp of confusion.

Lucky's eyes rolled up to the sky. Squinting, he saw only the pale blue of sunup. Then another sound roared through the air. It was coming from the direction of the city, sounding like thunder—but longer, lower, and more menacing. Waves of anxious yaps ripped through the group of dogs.

"A storm!" barked Sweet, her heart racing as she pressed closer to Lucky.

More high-pitched shattering sent tremors through Lucky's whiskers. It sounded as though the sky were about to fall right on top of them! A moment later the air howled so shrill and loud, it drowned out even the wildest barks.

Lucky was dizzy with terror, his stomach clenching and his flanks heaving. The sky was sick, whining desperately like a dog in pain. This was no ordinary storm.

The howling air had *nothing* to do with the Sky-Dogs.

ENTER THE WORLD OF
WARRIORS

Warriors: Dawn of the Clans
Discover how the warrior Clans came to be.

Warriors
Sinister perils threaten the four warrior Clans. Into the midst of this turmoil comes Rusty, an ordinary housecat, who may just be the bravest of them all.

Download the
free Warriors app at
www.warriorcats.com

HARPER
An Imprint of HarperCollinsPublishers

Warriors: The New Prophecy

Follow the next generation of heroic cats as they set off
on a quest to save the Clans from destruction.

Warriors: Power of Three

Firestar's grandchildren begin their training as warrior cats.
Prophecy foretells that they will hold more power than any cats before them.

Includes
WARRIORS

Warriors: Omen of the Stars

Which ThunderClan apprentice will complete the prophecy that
foretells that three Clanmates hold the future of the Clans in their paws?

Warriors Stories

Download the separate ebook novellas or read the first three in the paperback bind-up!

Don't Miss the Stand-Alone Adventures

Delve Deeper into the Clans

HARPER
An Imprint of HarperCollinsPublishers

Warrior Cats Come to Life in Manga!